WHERE THE SEA LAVENDER GROWS

Summer Harbor, Maine ~ Book 1

Jenny Worster

ISBN-13: 978-1-7356776-1-3

Cover design by: Jenny Worster
Photography by: Cookie Studio and Jenny Worster
Printed in the United States of America

To my Lord and Savior, Jesus Christ, without whom I can do nothing

To my husband, Ken, who believes in me even when I don't believe in myself

To my 'oldest', Jared, who sparked the idea for Noah and answered my endless questions

CONTENTS

CHAPTER ONE

L ily Emerson held the long blue envelope at arm's length and swallowed back the lump in her throat. They always meant the same thing. Summoned. Again. She had grown weary of being summoned. Her uncle kept stacks of blue paper and blue envelopes on his desk. He wanted the permanence of a paper summons. No phone calls, texts, or emails. He liked a handwritten date and time and he liked it to stand out in the mail. The hotel tycoon's summons could mean anything from walking his dog to overseeing the months' long construction of a new hotel, from a promotion to being fired.

Lily gritted her teeth and ripped the envelope open.

My office
Monday, June 8th
10AM

Only a week to worry about it this time. She tucked a stray strand of honey-colored hair back into her perfect French twist and rubbed her temples. A tension headache was beginning to build up the back of her neck and the blue envelope hadn't eased it one bit. She checked the time. Well past six. Time to call it a day.

With the renovation proposal and estimates she'd spent the afternoon pouring over tucked into her briefcase, she uncurled her legs from beneath her and slid her feet back into her Jimmy Choos. Her diminutive stature benefitted a great deal from the heels, but her feet screamed if she wore them all day. At least no one could see her bare feet behind her desk.

She slipped her blazer on over her silk shirt and paused to

take in the view from her corner office window. Far below she could see Quincy Market, busy with tourists and locals alike. Street performers drew crowds for their dance routines, acrobatics, and music. She imagined she could smell the wonderful, eclectic odors wafting from the myriad eateries within the elegant stone building. She had a fleeting thought of grabbing dinner on her way home. The noise and chaos that pushing through the crowd would entail quenched the idea. She wanted nothing that would feed the headache throbbing behind her eyes.

After locking her office door, she stopped at her assistant's desk.

"Better put this in the calendar," Lily said as she handed over the blue envelope.

"I'll take care of that right away Miss Emerson," the older woman said, but her delightful dark-chocolate face betrayed her true thoughts on Herbert Emerson and his blue envelopes. In her fifties and married to the job, Deidra arrived before Lily in the morning and always left after her in the evening. She was the gem who made Lily's life bearable under the stress that her uncle piled on.

"Don't stay too late," Lily admonished as she headed down the hall toward the elevator.

Deidra had already turned back to her computer. "Of course not," she threw over her shoulder as she tucked a pencil back into the riot of black braids piled on the top of her head. There was little doubt in Lily's mind that the woman would stay too late. Lily wondered, not for the first time, if Deidra might be able to do Lily's job.

They shared the floor with a smattering of other employees. Few remained at this time of day. Those, like Lily, who were loyal to the company, and those too scared of Herbert to risk leaving at five, were all that lingered. She raised her hand to wave to a junior executive who was on the phone. His hair stood in clumps from being pulled in frustration and his brow was creased. He didn't return the gesture, and Lily knew he hadn't even seen her. She turned around and retraced her steps until she was in his line of sight. Once he focused on her she mouthed 'everything alright?'. He gave her a tired smile and nodded his head. She plucked a post-it off of a nearby desk and scribbled 'go home' on it. He gave her a thumbs up when she leaned over and stuck it on his monitor, but resumed his conversation before she'd even walked away. Lily sighed. She'd tried.

At the elevator, she pressed the button and waited. The dark offices on either side of the bank of gleaming silver doors caught her eye. She was surprised that the one on the right was dark. Alistair Amias, Herbert's business partner, seldom beat her out the door. The left-most office, on the other hand, didn't surprise Lily at all. Her sister, Olivia, fresh out of college, graced the building with her presence on the rare occasion that she was bored. Maybe she should call and check on her.

Olivia picked up on the fifth ring. She sounded breathless and loud music droned in the background. "Lil! What's up?"

"Hi, Liv," Lily strained to hear her sister. "Where are you?"

"Oh, I'm at this great club! It's new. You should come!" Olivia spoke again, but it was muffled and Lily doubted it was meant for her anyway. Then, "I'm not sure where it is, but I can find out."

"No, thanks."

"You need to live a little."

Leave it to Olivia to equate living with partying. The pain creeping in behind Lily's eyes ratcheted up a notch. "Isn't it a little... early... to go clubbing?"

Olivia let out a squeal of laughter. "I don't even know what time it is!"

Lily put a hand over her eyes. Why had she called again? "I noticed you haven't been into the office in a while."

"Lil, why do I need to come in? They've got you, they don't need me."

"That's not true." But it was. What could Olivia do at Emerson Hotels International? Yes, she had a business degree, but Lily suspected she'd majored in partying and only minored in business. "I need to go."

"Suit yourself! Love you, Lil."

"Love you, too, Liv," she replied, but her sister had already disconnected.

The elevator chimed and Lily stepped into the empty car. She rested her pounding temple against the cool metal wall. The frigid surface felt refreshing against her cheek and she closed her eyes as she descended to the lobby of EHI's corporate offices. How was it that her sister was immune to their uncle and the way he wielded his power? The hold he had over Lily, Alistair, and every last employee, from junior executives to housekeeping, skimmed over Olivia like magic.

Lily would give anything to be out from under that control.

The elevator chimed and she stepped off into a glass and granite lobby gilded in the glow of late afternoon sunshine.

"Have a great night," she nodded to the doorman, Javier. "Say 'hi' to Sarah and the twins."

"Yes, ma'am!" He tipped his hat, a broad smile lighting his face. "You have a real nice night, too, Miss Emerson." He stood a little straighter as she passed him. Unlike her uncle, Lily understood the importance of treating employees well. It resulted in better work. She smiled back and stepped through the door he held open and out into the hot, humid early June evening.

Tonight the air hummed and the city seemed to have taken on a life of its own. She smiled at her uncle's driver, patient as always, waiting by the shiny black town car that would carry the man three blocks to his condo. Her eyes flicked up the street, amazed, as always, that she could see the portico of his building from where she stood, but he insisted on the car.

"The Yankees must be in town," she said to the driver.

He grinned and tapped his ear, showing her an earbud.

"Already in the second inning, Sox up 1-0." Baseball was king in Boston.

Her favorite part of the day was this walk. Golden sunlight splashed onto the sidewalk from where it slipped between buildings and turned the glass and steel and stone into shimmering fire. Boisterous laughter spilled out of the corner pub, followed by shouts. She slowed and watched a giant television screen through the window. The runner rounded first and pulled up for an easy double, cheers and high fives evidence that it was a Boston player. She tamped down a twinge of envy at those gathered around tables to watch the game with friends.

Just past the pub was a newsstand and beyond that the riotous colors of her favorite flower peddler.

"Good evening, Seamus," she said as she stopped to admire the few bunches of flowers that he hadn't sold that day. "Anything special I could take home?"

"They're all pretty, Miss Lily, just like you," the old man said as he swiped the cap from his bald head. She knew he charmed all the ladies and she didn't care.

"I'll take these." She fingered the petals on a bunch of deep yellow daffodils. Her favorite color.

He grinned as she handed him the flowers. She didn't always buy flowers on her way home, but when it appeared business had been dismal she would pick up a cheerful bouquet to help him out. He reached behind his stool and pulled out a few bunches of greenery, a little baby's breath, and a few extra flowers. Like magic, he turned a simple handful of daffodils into a stunning bouquet and took care to wrap them in yesterday's newspaper.

"You never disappoint," she said as she paid for her flowers.

Seamus returned her smile and pocketed the change she waved off.

"See you tomorrow," she called as she continued down the sidewalk, heels clicking. Her heart strummed as she neared the realtor two blocks from her condo. It was her favorite spot on the five-block walk. The variety of properties for sale in the greater Boston area was vast and varied. On her way home in the evening, Lily allowed herself a few moments to dream. Her dream. A hotel or inn that she could call her own. A new life away from EHI and away from her uncle.

She could picture each building in the window turned into a small hotel. The brownstone in Cambridge? A quaint little B&B

catering to parents in town to drop their kids off at college. The weathered cape in Provincetown? A quiet inn with local artists' paintings gracing the walls. The warehouse near Fenway Park? A sports-themed hotel perfect for the out-of-town baseball fan. None had grabbed at her heart yet, but it was fun to dream.

She saw the new posting long before she reached the realtor's window. A sprawling victorian with gingerbread trim and a vast wrap-around porch. Lily's breath caught in her throat. It was the one. Her dream. Buttery yellow with white trim, soft green lawn dotted with rose bushes and daffodils. She read through the tiny blurb of information on the posting three times. A blush bloomed across her cheeks as she realized her nose was pressed to the glass, but she didn't care. She read the listing a fourth time.

Quaint turn-of-the-century inn located in Summer Harbor, Maine. The main building boasts ten bedrooms, each with a private bath, two suites, a vintage kitchen, dining room, library, parlor, and a generous front porch. The 6-acre property also contains a cottage converted from a carriage house, a boathouse, and private access to Butterfly Cove Beach. The property has been run as an inn for over a hundred years. A perfect turnkey business.

Lily pulled the realtor's number up on her phone.

"Patriot Realty, John Markam speaking."

"Good evening Mr. Markam. I'm sorry to bother you after hours."

"Not at all! Realtors are always on the clock!" he said with a laugh. "What can I do for you?"

"I'm interested in a property you posted in your office window today. The inn in Summer Harbor?"

"Of course, of course! Ms...?"

Lily paused. Under normal circumstances, she had no problem giving her name, but she didn't want this to get back to her uncle. After all, an Emerson asking about an inn for sale was akin to a Hilton calling about an available hotel or a Kerzner interested in a resort. She should have thought this through before she placed the call, or maybe had her lawyer do it instead. Too late now.

"Hayes," she said, giving her mother's maiden name, her middle name.

"I would be delighted to show it to you, Ms. Hayes. Let me check my schedule…" There was a long pause. The rustling of pages was the only indication that John Markam was still on the phone. "Oh, this is unfortunate! I won't be able to meet you in Summer Harbor until Monday next week."

The tension headache drummed a loathsome beat on her temples. She rubbed the back of her neck. "Do you have another day? I have a prior commitment on Monday."

"Does a week from Friday work for you?" He asked.

Lily's heart sank. "Yes, fine." A weariness born of discouragement settled into her bones. The property was too perfect. There was no way it would still be on the market in a week and a half. Someone would make an offer sight unseen. Lily wasn't that daring.

Others, like her uncle, might be able to take a risk like that. In fact, she'd seen him do it. That, however, was with company funds. Her bank account wasn't flush enough to allow for liabilities like that. She had managed to save enough for a sizable down payment, but she knew better than to buy sight unseen. She'd at least learned that much from her father before he'd passed away. She was an Emerson and people assumed that came with a certain amount of wealth. Breaking it to bankers, realtors… boyfriends… that she wasn't wealthy aside from the company was a bitter pill. She'd gotten rather good at skirting the issue.

As she walked she gave the realtor her contact information and confirmed the arrangements to see the inn. She put her key in the door to her condo just as she finished the call. Her headache, which had evaporated with the discovery of the posting in the window, throbbed anew, and her heart was heavy. She shed her shoes by the door and tossed her blazer over the back of a chair as she walked past her hall desk. Before she reached her bedroom she had pulled out the bobby pins holding her hair and pulled her blouse from the trim waist of her pencil skirt. *Tylenol, take out, bed* became a mantra.

She flicked on a light in the modern loft space she called home. Lots of brick and glass and steel made it trendy, or so her realtor had told her the year before when she'd needed a place closer to the office. She supposed it was nice enough, but it didn't feel like home. Maybe if she had someone to share it with. A familiar pang squeezed her heart. Once upon a time, she thought she would share this crazy, busy life with someone, but he had shown his true colors and crushed her heart.

Maybe she didn't need dinner after all.

Despite the exhaustion pressing on her like a heavy blanket, Lily lay awake thinking about the inn. She could picture it, down to the last nook and cranny, just the way she wanted it; a fresh coat of paint, a renovated kitchen, a pastry chef trained at a top culinary school, and updated bathroom fixtures and bed linens. She couldn't help it. Hotels were in her blood.

In the wee hours of the morning, after a night spent half planning/half dreaming about the property, an idea dawned on Lily. Who said she couldn't go see the inn by herself? She didn't need to meet a realtor there, she just needed to see it.

Grabbing her cell phone off the nightstand she found the inn's website. Since it was past Memorial Day and still weeks away from the Fourth of July there was a room available all week.

"As long as I'm back by Monday morning I'm good."

Now too excited to sleep, Lily started packing. What did one wear in Summer Harbor, Maine? She was used to fine restaurants, going to the symphony, and executive office wear of expensive suits and killer heels. Would that work in Summer Harbor, too? She doubted it but packed them anyway along with a bit of every other type of clothes she owned. Ridiculous. She didn't need four suitcases for a few days in Vacationland. She dumped out all four suitcases and started over.

When she was satisfied that her suitcase now contained an appropriate variety of clothes, Lily sat down at her desk and flipped open her laptop. She needed to email Deidra to let her know she'd be out of town and to have her forward all her calls to her cell. No need to explain, Deidra wouldn't even question it.

While she had the laptop open she did a little research on Summer Harbor. The town was nestled on the northwest corner of a large island off the coast. There was one bridge onto the island and a couple of ferries. By all appearances, Summer Harbor was a popular tourist destination. Tens of thousands of visitors flocked to the town each year to eat lobster, wade in the cold Atlantic water, and hike the rocky trails of the National Park.

It looked idyllic. Pictures showed a blue-green harbor with a smattering of boats, busy streets, and people enjoying bike rides and rock climbing.

"Climbing!" She grinned and abandoned the laptop to gather her gear. She had taken up rock climbing in college to help her focus, to be alone with her thoughts, to pray, to work off the freshman fifteen. It had stuck. She loved being outside and loved the challenge of a new place to climb. She unpacked the bag and checked each piece of gear for wear or damage then placed it into one of two smaller duffles. When it came to rock climbing you could never be too careful.

In the parking garage under her condo, Lily loaded her suitcase, climbing gear, and briefcase into the trunk of her jet black convertible. The sun wasn't even up yet, but Lily couldn't wait to get on the road. She wanted to avoid rush hour and be well on her way to Maine before the city woke on Tuesday morning. She slipped behind the wheel and reached for the ignition, but paused.

God, if this inn isn't a good idea, isn't Your best for me, please make it obvious. Direct my steps, give me wisdom. I want everything I do to honor You!

Lily was well past the Tobin Bridge by the time the sun came up. When she stopped for coffee, she put the top down and cranked up the music. The miles evaporated as high-rises and narrow streets yielded to strip malls and traffic lights. Those soon gave way to pine trees and by early afternoon she had crossed the bridge onto the island. The feeling of coming home was instantaneous. It was the most picturesque place she'd ever been to. For miles, nothing but salt marshes stretched out on either side of the main road. Small villages appeared, with their clusters of gray-shingled buildings. Artist studios, motels, a few local residents, and even one small shack with a handwritten sign offering clams, steamers, cherrystones, and quahogs, lined the sides of the road.

"What on earth is a quahog?" She laughed as she passed it. There was so much to learn. It was a different world from Boston for sure.

The road wound past picturesque coves and seaside hamlets before it narrowed to streets filled with people. The warm sun and salt air made an intoxicating mix. No wonder so many people chose Summer Harbor as their vacation destination. Lily drank in the sights and sounds. The gulls called to each other. A harbor buoy clanged. There were shops selling overpriced souvenirs, art galleries, restaurants, a cupcake shop, a candy store, and so much more. The smell of the sea air was mixed with steam from a lobster pound's giant pots.

At the town pier, Lily found a parking space and got out to walk. She stood for a long time leaning on the railing, watching the gulls and cormorants fishing. The murky green water lapped the pilings under the pier, and the seaweed swayed in time to the waves. She breathed in a deep breath and felt her shoulders relax.

Below, on the rocky shore, a couple of terns ran in and out of the water looking for little morsels to eat. Many of the rocks were covered with seaweed and shimmering mussel shells. Dotted among the rocks, a hardy plant had taken root. It added a deep green to the unique color pallet that was the shore of Maine. Pink granite, blue mussels, the brilliant azure of the sky, and the water that turned from green near the shore to a deep turquoise in its rolling depths. It was a feast for the eyes.

She stood and watched, soaking it all in. People picked up shells and skipped rocks. Little kids chased seagulls and ran into the freezing surf, only to squeal and run back out again. A group of kayakers lined up on the shore, ready to head out into the bay. A tall man in jeans and a t-shirt ran behind the boats checking life jackets and helping them into the water. He grinned and stopped to laugh along with one of the participants. It drifted up to where Lily stood at the pier and she decided it was the perfect sound for the moment. Pure joy.

I want to be rational, God, but I feel like I love this place already. Help me to listen for Your still, small voice. Help me not to jump in because I'm desperate for this kind of peace and that kind of joy.

Shadows were beginning to stretch across the road before Lily turned onto the private lane leading to The Butterfly Cove Inn. The drive curved past the carriage house with its stone walls and copper weathervane. She came around a towering oak tree and stopped short. It was even more beautiful in person.

Rows of crabapple trees and lilacs in full bloom lined the driveway. Beyond them, the lawn rolled, soft and lush, up to the magnificent porch. The yard beyond was rimmed with spruce, pine, and forsythia bushes that must be impressive when in bloom. For a moment she couldn't decide if she wanted to stay on the crushed shell drive and drink it all in or continue up to the inn. The place took her breath away.

The walkway from the gravel parking area wound around a beautiful flower garden and up to the porch steps. Lily took her time meandering up the walk to the front door. The building appeared to be well cared for and the grounds were immaculate. Clusters of wicker furniture, rocking chairs, and a swing invited her to wile away the hours on the porch with a good book. The merry ring of a small bell greeted Lily when she opened the large red front door and stepped into the foyer.

"Welcome, Dea-ah." The woman who greeted her hobbled out to the front desk, leaning over her cane with stooped shoulders. "Checking in?"

"Yes, I have a reservation. Lily Hayes." It was impossible not to be charmed by the woman. Her blue eyes sparkled when she smiled, and her laugh lines were deep and plentiful. She had a carefree mop of gray hair piled on top of her head in a sort of bun that swayed when she shuffled.

"Oh, yes, yes, yes. My son handles all the reservations from that... that... interweb thingy. He called me just this morning and said you'd made a reservation. Now let me see..." She plucked a pair of half-round reading glasses out of her hair and peered at an index card on the desk. "Here you are! Lily? What a pretty name! I do love my June lilies. They just might be my favorite flowers. It isn't going to be hard to remember your name. No sir. Now... Hayes... Hmmm. Are you one of the Rockland Hayes? I only knew Jimmy Hayes and, gosh, that was sixty years ago. Not the most reputable fella," she added in a hushed tone as if he might be listening.

"I don't think he's any relation," Lily grinned. "And you are?"

"Oh, goodness me, where are my manners?" the old woman fussed. "Ava Allen. I own the inn."

"Nice to meet you." Lily took the gnarled, outstretched hand with care.

"My husband, Byron, God rest his soul, ran it with me for years. Since he passed away I've been on my own. Oh, well not on my own of course. My son helps out with the reservations and the two girls who come in to do the cleaning, and I have the most wonderful handyman." While she talked, Ava filled out a form she'd pulled from a drawer in the desk. Now she spun the form around toward Lily. "If you would just fill out this top part, initial here that you won't have any pets stay with you, and," she said as she flipped the form over, "sign here, I can give you your key and show you around."

Lily jotted down her personal information and signed the form. "You must know this place inside and out."

"Oh, yes, yes, yes. I know it like the back of my hand! It's been in our family for four generations. Now, come on this way and I'll show you to your room." Ava shuffled out from behind the counter and put both hands on her cane. Peering over her glasses at Lily she squinted at her for a few seconds. "I think you should stay in the yellow room."

"That sounds perfect."

Ava led the way to the beautiful curved staircase just off the foyer. Between her slow gait and the fact that she stopped often to tell Lily an interesting fact or story about the inn, it took a while for them to reach the second floor.

"This staircase was built by my granddaddy when my great-granddaddy built the inn. My grandaddy was away on a ship for most of the construction of the place. When he came home he wanted to contribute to the building. I think he did a fine job, if I do say so myself." She leaned in, an endearing glint of mischief in her clear eyes. "I will admit I slid down it a number of times back in the day."

Lily hid a laugh in as she ran her hand over the polished wood and pictured a much younger Ava flying down the stairs.

"These here," Ava paused on a step and tapped an old sepia-tone photograph with a gnarled finger, "are my great-grandparents. They built the inn and it has been in the family ever since."

"Did I understand correctly that the inn is now for sale?" Lily asked.

"Well, my goodness, word travels fast! My son said it was just listed yesterday! He doesn't have any interest in it and, well..." Ava let her words trail off and sadness settled over her. "My son says I'm too old to run this place on my own. My health isn't too good these days and he says it's time to face the fact that I can't do this anymore. I hate to think I'm the last one in the family to own it."

The sadness lingered the rest of the way up the stairs, but

evaporated as, with a flourish, Ava pulled a key out of the deep pocket of her cardigan. She unlocked a door down the hall from the landing and swung it open.

"Here we are, the yellow room."

The sunshine that flooded the room was muted by gauzy white curtains in the windows. The four-poster bed was covered with a thick handmade quilt and yellow shams. Two white and sunflower-yellow striped easy chairs by the window beckoned Lily to sit and savor the view of the cove and the salt air blowing through the open window.

"Oh, Mrs. Allen, it's perfect."

Ava beamed. "Let's go find Walter and he can help you with your bags," she said as she handed Lily the keys. "This one is for the front door and this one is for your room."

They headed back to the lobby and out onto the porch. "Walter!" she called.

A gentleman in a bright red t-shirt, worn overalls, and a tattered cap materialized from around the side of the house. When he saw Lily he pulled his cap off. He clutched and twisted it in his hands after trying to smooth the wisps of gray hair that had blown free.

"Afternoon, ma'am," he said, his head bobbing up and down. The childish manners of the man didn't fit with his aged face. He had to be in his late fifties. He was a big man with broad shoulders, shy and quiet. The eyes he turned on Ava when she spoke were full of absolute devotion. Again, childlike.

"Walter, Dea-ah, would you please help Miss Lily with her bags?" Ava spoke to him as though he were a child as well.

"Yes, Miss Ava."

"Now, you get yourself settled and then you come see me. I'll tell you the best place in town to get steamers for dinner," Ava said to Lily, her eyes twinkling again. With that, she turned and shuffled back through the front door.

"There isn't much," Lily said as she led the way to her car. "Do you do all the grounds work?"

"Yes, ma'am. I like it to look right pretty for Miss Ava."

"It's beautiful. You do a wonderful job." Walter flushed at the compliment. His pride in his work was obvious. She stopped to admire a bed full of plants she didn't recognize. "These are interesting."

"Those there are all plants native to Maine. I collected most of them, but some, like that one there," he pointed out a breathtaking pink lady slipper. "I had to special order. You can't just dig up anything you want. There are laws."

"It's lovely."

"This one here, it's called jack-in-the-pulpit. It looks plain right now, but later on, it has a right pretty flower. That there's a wild rose that grows all over the island. Did you know you can make jam from its rose hips? Miss Ava makes the best."

He was charming and his love of plants was infectious. Lily didn't want the horticulture lesson to end. The more he told her the more she liked the idea of including native plants at the inn. Could the breakfasts be designed to showcase native Maine ingredients? She made a mental note to check out endemic plants.

"Those ones there are blue flag iris, and this one here's one I snuck off the beach. Probably shouldn't have. You won't tell, will you?"

"No, of course not." She bit back a smile.

"It puts out the prettiest little purple flowers in August and it always smells like the ocean."

"This garden is wonderful Walter. It all is. You should be proud."

He blushed again and bobbed his head as he moved down the path toward her car. She popped the trunk and he reached in for her bags.

"Land sakes these are heavy," he exclaimed as he hefted her duffles.

"It's rock-climbing gear. I plan to do a little climbing while I'm here. At least I hope I'll have time." He made a face that said he didn't see the appeal. She laughed. "It's fun, I swear. You can leave those in the car though. I doubt I'll get to it for a few days anyway. Business, then play."

Walter bobbed his head and beamed his shy smile again as he placed them back in the trunk.

Before leading her up the path he paused. "Traffic in town can be right tiresome, so if you ever need to be dropped off or picked up so you don't have to find a parking space or walk you just let me know. I'd be more than happy to drive you wherever you need to go. Any time."

Could the concierge at any Emerson Hotel make a guest feel as welcome and taken care of? She doubted it. They catered to the more affluent guests, hoping for a larger tip. They also carried themselves with an air of importance, and disdain for the 'lesser' employees. She had trouble picturing Walter belittling anyone, or treating one guest with more care than another. He was a gem for sure. Did he plan to stay on after the inn sold? She wanted to ask but didn't want to give away her interest in the place.

With her suitcase on the chest at the end of her bed, and her briefcase stowed securely in her closet Lily felt settled and content. She wandered downstairs and peaked in various rooms until she found Ava in the kitchen.

"All settled in? Everything to your liking?"

"Yes, thank you. I did have one small problem. I tried to check my voicemail, but couldn't seem to get a cell signal."

"Oh, no, Dea-ah, those new-fangled cellular devices don't work too well here on the island. You are welcome to use the phone in your room any time though, and you can use the interweb thingy at the library if you need to."

No cell service and no internet. Was this for real?

Ava, done with the discussion of the internet, or lack thereof, went to the fridge and filled two tall glasses with ice and tea. Handing one to Lily, the older woman scooted herself up onto a stool at the counter and breathed out a tired sigh.

Lily took a sip. "Yum!"

"It's called sun tea."

"Sun tea?"

"Yes, I put the tea in the water and then set it in the sun to steep."

Lily sipped the sweet, spicy tea again. "Oh, this is wonderful!"

Ava beamed with pride. "I make it myself."

"That's amazing! It has a unique flavor. I recognize it, but..."

"That's the nutmeg. I make the tea from wild plants I harvest myself, except for the nutmeg. That I just add because I love the flavor." She tapped the counter with her cane. "I've made many a batch of tea and cooked many a meal in here, but I suppose it's time for new counters and such. My Byron had the whole kitchen renovated, but that was many years ago now. As you can see it gets wonderful sun in the afternoon. That's nice on a day like today, but in the middle of the summer it gets so hot in here you'll be glad you can walk into town for dinner. Now, let's see. Let me show you around a bit. This way is the dining room." Ava led the way into a large room with tall east-facing windows. Small wooden tables with white chairs filled the room. Each table had a vase of fresh flowers and two or three linen napkins. The wallpaper was a little dated, but the hardwood floors more than made up for it.

"Breakfast is served between seven-thirty and nine. There was a time we served three meals a day, but with all the restaurants in town now we don't need to."

"Do you have a lot of guests?" Lily asked.

"Oh, fourteen to sixteen a day during the busiest part of the summer. Ten to twelve this time of year and in the fall. We also stay open until New Year's, unlike a lot of the hotels on the island. The town has an annual Christmas party and we stay open for a few of the out-of-town guests. I guess the new owner might do things differently." A wistfulness came over Ava as she spoke.

It seemed odd fishing for details about the inn from Ava. It wasn't just a business, it was her whole life. Lily tried to be subtle, not wanting to give away the fact that she was interested in buying the place, but there were so many questions she wanted answered!

"I think I'll just walk down to the beach before dinner. Thank you for the tea."

"Oh, yes, yes, yes. Please do. You have any questions, any at all, you just ask me. Or Walter. He knows everything there is to know about this place. He's been here for nigh on fifty years himself. I must admit, he knows the grounds better than I do at this point."

Lily left Ava straightening the flowers in a vase on the buffet table. She headed back toward the kitchen and out the back door. On the far side of the yard, a gazebo stood silhouetted against the backdrop of sky-blue and sea-green. The sea. She'd waited all day to walk the beach and had to restrain herself so as not to run across the lawn like a child. Instead, she meandered down a path to the pebble beach and strolled along the edge of the water. It lapped against the rocks and now and then it would rush toward her feet making her dance away to avoid soaking her tennis shoes.

She stopped a short way from the inn and turned back to consider it with a critical eye. Windblown pines and firs hid part of it from view. The property sat up above the beach on a cliff, protected from the worst of the winter storms. As she wandered back, she spied a cave the surf had cut into the base of the rugged cliffs. It wasn't much more than a hole where the rock face met sand littered with rocks and plants. Along the top edge of the cliff, a bald eagle had built a nest in a rumpled pine. It lifted off from a branch and swooped to snatch a fish from the swell of a wave. Breathtaking.

Everything about the property was what Lily had waited for, plus so much more. The town, the sounds and smells of the ocean, the screech of the gulls, and the salty wind and wet sand. Those were all things Lily hadn't known she wanted until she had stepped out of her car that afternoon. Now, just an hour later, she knew any other location would pale in comparison. This was her dream.

She climbed back up the path to the yard and studied the structure with a critical eye. Straight rooflines under a metal roof, fresh paint, and clean chimneys. She would need to replace the windows with more energy-efficient ones down the road, but that wasn't a deal-breaker.

OK, God, I asked for a clear 'no' and all I've seen since I arrived is a very clear yes. If I'm missing a red flag, please show me!

As she walked back into the kitchen her stomach growled and she realized she'd been in such a hurry to get to Summer Harbor and see the inn that she had never stopped for lunch. Ava was right, the kitchen would need a complete renovation. If she were to offer more than a simple continental breakfast each day she would need to employ a chef and that would mean a state-of-the-art place to cook. She stood for a moment picturing the new kitchen. Her stomach growled again. It was time to sample the local flavors.

"Mrs. Allen, you told me you had recommendations for dinner?" Lily asked as she passed Ava in the foyer.

"Oh, yes, yes, yes. And please, call me Miss Ava. Everyone else does. Now, if you're hankerin' for fish and chips, you'll want to head on down to The Captain's Cabin on the corner by the pier."

"Oh, fish and chips sounds amazing."

"They use the most delicious cod at The Captain's Cabin. You won't be disappointed. Now, if you want steamed clams, we just call 'em steamers, I'd go to The Lobster's Tail across the road."

"Oh, steamers sound good, too."

"If it's lobster you're craving William's Lobster Pound right on the pier has the best."

"I think I'll save the lobster for another night. I don't want to have to work for my meal this evening."

"Oh, well, if you'd prefer a place that's a bit fancier I highly recommend The Hungry Whale over on Cottage Street. They make the best Reuben sandwiches."

"Too many good choices, Miss Ava," Lily said with a smile. She thanked the older woman for the recommendations and stepped out the front door. Abandoning the car in favor of walking, Lily headed down the drive. She'd changed into white capris and a thin sweater. The sun had started to sink toward the sea, and the breeze was cool and refreshing. She took her time, trying to take it all in.

Could she do this? Could she buy an inn and move to Summer Harbor? Could she stand on her own two feet, outside the shadow of her uncle? The thought made her heart pound. Fear wound its way around her chest and constricted her breathing. What if she failed? Uncle would never let her back into EHI once she left. And yet... And yet she was utterly enchanted by the town and the inn. Besides, once she left EHI would she ever want to go back?

God, Since I know that fear is not from You, I'm giving You my fear of failure and trusting You. I can do this with Your strength and Your wisdom.

After walking back to the inn later that evening, Lily picked up the phone in her room and dialed the number for John Markham, the realtor in Boston.

"Patriot Realty," he answered.

"Good evening Mr. Markam. This is Lily Hayes. We spoke last night about the inn in Summer Harbor. I want to make an offer."

CHAPTER TWO

A warm sea breeze blew in through the open window the next morning, waking Lily. It smelled of salt and lilac blossoms and contentment. She smiled and stretched. The giddy feeling of the day before seeped into her. If things went well this would be her inn before too long. She got goosebumps just thinking about it. Her inn. Hers alone. No answering to anyone. No one else setting the limits of what she could and couldn't do. It was a glorious, freeing feeling. The only thought that dampened the feeling was that she had no one to share it with. For a fleeting second, she thought she might call Olivia, but dismissed that idea almost as soon as she'd thought of it. If Olivia thought she worked too much as an executive what would her sister say to owning and operating her own inn?

Thank you, Lord, for this opportunity. Thank you for hearing the cry of my heart. I pray that everything I do here will honor You. I don't want to get lost in the excitement and lose sight of why You have given me this opportunity. Your Word says that whatever I do I should do with all my heart, as though I were doing it for You. That is my desire. Please help me.

While exploring the day before, Lily had found a little second-story balcony at the end of the hall. It overlooked the backyard and the beach beyond. This morning she took her Bible and padded barefoot to the quiet veranda. With a contented sigh, she slid into one of the two Adirondack chairs facing the ocean. She sat for a long time drinking in the solitude. She imagined herself coming to this spot early in the morning, watching the sun lighten the sky and reading her Bible before guests started arriving in the dining room.

She opened the worn cover and fingered the dog-eared pages covered in highlighter and penciled notes. It was a cherished possession. She had received it the day she was saved and had written notes in it ever since. Returning to familiar passages and rereading them, along with her notes, had gotten her through hard times. A few verses had dates scribbled next to them, like the day she was baptized and the minister had read Galatians 3:27. *For as many of you as have been baptized into Christ have put on Christ.*

Today's reading was in Isaiah. After reading chapter 26 Lily highlighted verse 3. *Thou wilt keep him in perfect peace, whose mind is stayed on thee.* In the margin, she wrote *Help me to always keep my mind on You!* She bowed her head and poured her heart out to God - her joys and her frustrations, her dreams and her fears. A dear friend had once told her that if God loved the dream in her heart He would bring it to pass. She prayed in earnest that God would love the dream of her owning The Butterfly Cove Inn.

Realizing that she had taken far more time than she had intended on the balcony, Lily scrambled back to her room and dressed in her favorite navy blue pencil skirt with yellow pinstripes, white blouse, and the highest of high heels. She grabbed her blazer and hurried down the stairs.

The Bible reading was, as usual, perfect for the day. She hadn't felt this kind of peace in a long time, maybe ever. It was splendid. There was no place in the busy city to experience this kind of quiet. It had lulled Lily into feeling like she was the only person at the inn, to the point that she was surprised when she stepped into the dining room for breakfast and discovered that there were many more guests.

Ava made the rounds of the tables, chatting with each person as if he or she was the only one in the room, refilling coffee cups, and laughing. Lily smiled. That's how she wanted to treat her guests, too. Ava made it seem so easy. Years of practice, Lily thought.

She selected a piece of fresh fruit and a popover from the

small breakfast buffet and found a table by the window. It wasn't long before Ava stopped to fill her coffee cup, cane in one hand, carafe in the other.

"Did you sleep well, Dea-ah?"

"Oh, yes. It's so tranquil here. I love it."

"It is a delightful spot. Now, what's on the plans for today? A little sightseeing? I can give you a bunch of ideas if you're searching for a way to spend the day."

"Business first."

"Well, as long as it isn't all work and no play," Ava said with a wink and turned to move onto another table.

"Miss Ava," Lily said, catching the older woman before she walked away. "I was wondering if Walter might be able to drive me into town? I have an appointment and it's doubtful I could find a parking space in time. I enjoyed the view from the balcony so much that I lost track of time," she admitted with a sheepish look.

"Oh, yes, yes, yes. Let me just get him." Ava shuffled out of the dining room toward the back of the inn. She returned a couple of minutes later. "He's just bringing the car around to the front."

Lily had just stepped out the door onto the porch when a dated black sedan pulled up to the front walk and Walter climbed out from behind the wheel. He seemed out of place in his new job of chauffeur. He was still dressed in overalls, and today sported a bright orange t-shirt. He had, however, replaced his worn Red Sox cap with a smart black one more befitting his current role.

"Well, my goodness, Miss Lily, you look right pretty," Walter blushed as though he hadn't meant to say the words aloud.

"Thank you, Walter," Lily smiled.

"Where to?" he asked as he held the back door open for her.

"Colonial Bank, please."

Other than a simple "yes ma'am" to her destination, Walter was quiet on the drive into town. Lily used the few minutes to put her thoughts in order, rehearsing what she planned to say to the banker. She had enough in savings to make a large down payment on the inn, but she would need a loan to cover the rest, plus much of the updating she planned on doing. She had a number in mind but needed to talk face to face with the gentleman at the bank to put all the numbers in order. She'd helped with enough of EHI's acquisitions that she knew the drill. It felt decidedly different when it was for her own place.

Walter pulled up in front of the bank and hurried around the car to open Lily's door.

"Would it be too much to ask you to pick me up back here in two hours?" she asked as she took his offered hand and slid out of the car.

"No, no. Of course not. Happy to." He bobbed his head and smiled his endearing, boyish smile.

"Thank you, Walter." His manners were sweet. What a charming gentleman the big man was. She hoped he would be able to stay on once she owned the inn.

Lily waited until Walter had pulled away from the curb before she took a deep breath, smoothed her skirt, and swallowed her jitters. Why was she so nervous? She was an Emerson after all! Resolved to ignore the anxiety, Lily squared her shoulders and took a determined step toward the entrance. She reached for the door just as it flew open.

A large, familiar figure loomed in the open doorway.

"Uncle?" she asked in disbelief.

His face clouded into a menacing mask. "What are you doing here Lilianna?" he asked in the gruff, unkind voice he used for the hired help. "I told you Monday morning, not today."

"Yes, I was just..." Lily's voice trailed off as she searched for words. "I took a few days off."

"Days off?" Herbert Emerson scoffed. Even though his empire was built on people traveling and vacationing and taking time off, he himself didn't believe in it. Vacation days were merely a way for employees to get less work done. "Just as well you're here. I made an offer on a property and I'll need you to handle the acquisition of it. Great little spot on the water. Perfect for the next Emerson. A little place with a private beach.

Nothing much now, but as an Emerson..." Greed gleamed in his eyes for a split second before he turned, expecting Lily to follow.

How could this be happening? Lily's heart was in her stomach. If "little place" was The Butterfly Cove Inn, Lily's dream was gone. There was no way she could compete with Uncle. He always got what he wanted. But why on earth would he want the inn? Emerson's were all mega-hotels. Not a single one of EHI's seventy-two properties was as small as hers. Lily huffed out a dejected breath. She might as well stop referring to it as hers, even in her mind. Tears of disappointment pricked her eyes.

"Come along, Lilianna," he ordered from where he stood beside a car so expensive it screamed status symbol. The driver, in his black suit and tie, held Herbert's door and didn't even acknowledge Lily. He knew where his paycheck would come from. She walked around to the far side of the car and opened her own door to get in. As a rule, she didn't bother using a driver, but right that minute she missed Walter with his heartfelt smile and worn overalls.

"Back to the hotel," Herbert snapped at the driver.

To Lily's disbelief, the hotel was less than two blocks from the bank. She rolled her eyes as they pulled in the entrance and up under the portico. Herbert waited for the driver to open his door before heaving himself out of the car. Without so much as acknowledging the man, let alone a 'thank you', her uncle marched into the hotel with the expectation that Lily was right behind him. The car pulled away. No doubt waiting close by for Herbert's next summons.

Lily had to force herself to walk into the hotel. She gritted her teeth and followed him to his suite. Employees shrank away when they saw him coming. He had made his usual impression. His disgust at having to stay at such an inferior establishment was obvious.

As they neared his room Lily could hear yipping from the other side of the door. Princess, Herbert's pride and joy, had accompanied him to Summer Harbor.

Herbert threw the door open, not caring if it hit the wall. He tossed his room key on a side table and marched to the window, snapping the curtains closed before he released the dog from her kennel.

"Take Princess for a walk," he ordered as he turned up the AC.

"Excuse me?"

"I haven't contacted the kennel to hire a dog walker yet and she needs to go out. Take her for a walk." He waved his hand to dismiss her.

Lily couldn't even process this morning's chain of events. It felt like she was trying to think through cotton. She stood at the door as though she'd been struck dumb. What was happening? The dream from the day before had turned into a nightmare. She had now missed her appointment at the bank, but what did it matter? In light of the fact that Herbert Emerson planned on obtaining the inn, which still made no sense, Lily would not need that appointment anyway.

"What about—"

"Now," Herbert barked.

"Yes, Uncle." She gathered Princess and her leash and headed back out the door. Dog walker. She was a dog walker. Twenty-eight-year-old niece of Herbert Emerson and part-owner of Emerson Hotels International, now relegated to walking Princess Penelope's Shadow, Herbert's prize-winning purebred Shih Tzu. Lily sighed. She was a long way from the happy, carefree girl who had woken up that morning thinking she was free of this wretched man.

The door closed with a snap that echoed in the overpriced hotel room. Ghastly place, he thought. Brown. The floors, the walls, the furniture, the blankets, the curtains, even the smell, were all brown. His head throbbed, from behind his left eye and down the back on his neck. He dimmed the lights before pouring himself a drink from the glass decanter he'd placed on the table by the window. At least the otherwise useless staff had left ice. He swirled the amber liquid and held the glass to his forehead. The condensation cooled his brow and calmed his headache, and the slow burn of the first sip helped him ignore it.

In hindsight, he shouldn't have been so short with Lilianna. She was, after all, her father's daughter. Competent, efficient, complacent. Did what needed to be done, never complained. Good at her job, no matter what it was. She'd do well at the helm one day. Not today, but eventually. The vacation thing was an issue. He'd speak to her about that on Monday at their meeting. Make sure she understood you couldn't run the tight ship this business demanded if you flitted your time away on holidays.

Before shrugging out of his suit coat he slipped an envelope from the inside pocket and crammed it into the bottom of his briefcase. He winced at the crack of the lid slamming closed and rubbed his beefy palm into his eye socket. If he'd known Lilianna was in Summer Harbor he could have stayed in Boston. She could have handled business here. If only she'd told him. The bitter taste of guile settled in his mouth.

His reflection in the mirror over the desk caught his eye, even in the dim light. Disgust burned like acid in his stomach and he turned away. Once upon a time, he could look at himself, but those times were long gone. It wasn't so much that he'd let himself go. Whatever. He knocked back what was left in the glass. So he'd put on a bit of weight. Big deal. What ate him alive was who he had become on the inside, not the outside.

When had he stopped being able to look himself in the eye? While working deals to salvage the business after Prescott had worked himself to death? Maybe. No. Farther back. The first time he'd swindled a friend for profit's sake? No, if he was honest it was before that. Margo. Anger smoldered, then ignited. It had been twenty years. Why did every thought have to drag him back to her? Why couldn't he be free? The glass hit the top of the table with a loud thwack. For the barest hint of a second, he worried that he'd broken it. But what did it matter if he had? What did anything matter anymore?

He shoved his hand through his hair and tried to will his temper under control. Why was he angry this time? Because he couldn't face himself. He wanted to blame Margo, but in reality, it was a shame of his own making that kept his eyes from meeting in the mirror.

The phone beside the bed chimed. He sneered as he reached for it. The backward little town didn't even have decent cell service. Maybe the hotel wasn't a dump, maybe it was just the town as a whole. He answered with his typical gruff greeting and listened. Sweat beaded along his upper lip as the throbbing in his head threatened to deafen him. Anger contorted his features as he listened.

"Are you sure?" He listened, his mood growing darker. A vile word hissed from between his teeth.

He slammed the receiver down, ignored his pulse echoing in his ears, and snatched his coat from the arm of the sofa where it had landed.

"My car," he bellowed as he passed the young lady manning the front desk. She recoiled and seized the phone. Good, he thought, at least one of the employees knew their place.

He stepped into the bright sunlight and his headache neared migraine levels. He was dizzy and puffed out a sigh of relief when his car pulled up as though it had been waiting in the wings. If the man knew what was good for him that's exactly what he'd been doing.

"Find my niece," he ordered the man at the wheel.

"The young lady from earlier?"

"Yes, of course, the young lady from earlier," he thundered. Idiot.

As the car pulled onto the street he opened a bottle of water and shook a pill into his hand. Closing his eyes against the searing sunlight he panted, waiting for the pill to work.

Noah Kingsley straightened the straps on another life jacket and tossed it to Harley, who checked the size and placed it on the correct shelf. They made a good team.

"Last one, man," Noah said, tossing him the remaining jacket. "Hand me those towels."

Harley caught the jacket, then handed back half a stack of bright yellow microfiber towels and they started wiping down dry bags.

Since opening Acadian Adventures, Noah had worked hard to hire an assistant manager who was easy to work with. Harley was a terrific fit. Noah had concluded that they worked so well together because they were so different - Noah's rangy height to Harley's stocky frame, Noah's easy smile to Harley's brooding intensity, Noah's beach-bum-esque sun-streaked hair and hazel eyes to Harley's black-haired brown-eyed biker demeanor, Noah's carefree go-with-the-flow mentality to Harley's meticulous planning.

"I wasn't sure we'd ever get on the water this morning."

"Truth," Noah groaned.

Harley dragged his brilliantly-inked hand down his face and smoothed his jet-black beard. "I wish people realized that when we say 'sunrise tour' we don't mean that it leaves at sunrise."

A wry laugh was Noah's only response. This morning's tour had been delayed multiple times as people wandered in five, ten, twenty minutes late. In the end, they had left with three people signed up who still hadn't shown. He knew Harley would try to fit them into another tour if they ever did show up. It was what he did.

"Maybe we should start telling them to be here half an hour earlier?"

"At that rate, we'll need to have them here the night before. No, we just roll with it. Besides, it's good for some laughs latah on," Noah grinned, his Maine accent peeking through.

"I don't know how you don't lose your cool," Harley said.

"Practice."

They finished the dry bags and turned their attention to the master schedule. A huge whiteboard on the wall in the storage room kept track of all the tours. It listed the tour leader, who their backup was, how many people were signed up, how many of each kayak they needed, and when the tour was leaving. They planned tours months ahead of time, but this master schedule only covered a week at a time. Harley was in charge of it and no one, not even Noah, touched it.

"I have the noon one," Noah pointed to the space on the schedule, "plus I'm taking the sunset. You scheduled Owen with me for both tours, but your backup space is blank for your tours this morning and later this afternoon. Who are you taking with you?"

Harley thought for a second before answering. He picked up the pen and started to add a name to the schedule. "I'm going to take one of the new guys, Gage I think, get him broken in before the schedule gets crazy."

"Good. Can you let me know how long it takes to get everyone from the meet time at the shop to on the watah? Last summah we were pretty efficient by the end of the season, but we need to be that efficient from the get-go this year."

"Sure thing, boss."

"Is driving the kayaks to the sandbar ahead of time and having the tour meet here at the shop and walk down working?"

"So far. We're saving a ton of time not driving each tour back to Gull's Cove. I still think we could open a second shop over there or even on the mainland and run tours on both sides of the harbor." Noah knew Harley was aware of his opinion concerning a second shop, but it didn't stop him from suggesting it.

Noah ran a hand behind his neck and tried to ease the stress tightening his muscles to iron rods. How could Harley talk about opening a second location when Noah couldn't seem to keep the first one out of the red? Determination set his mouth in a grim line. He had worked too long and too hard to watch Acadian Adventures go under just because he wasn't savvy in the business department.

Sensing his darkening mood Harley squeezed his shoulder. Noah knew he got it. He'd started out as a loud-mouthed newbie three summers before, but had matured into Noah's right-hand man. He covered shifts when needed, kept the schedule from getting chaotic, handled payroll, helped with hiring, and keeping the books. He'd seen the numbers.

"I think we need to add a couple more tours," Noah said. "Maybe a couple more evening tours. The sunset ones are already full into next month."

Harley gave him a pointed look. "I'll add them to the newbies' schedules, not yours. You are already putting in too many hours most days. You're the boss. You hire these guys so you don't have to work every tour."

"I don't work every tour."

"How many did you work yesterday?"

"Four."

"Four tours at three and a half hours per tour…"

"OK, OK. I won't take the additional tours. We do need to add them though. Can the new guys handle it?"

"Sure. I've almost got them broken in." Harley let out an amused snort. "I think I scared Jeremiah half to death yesterday. I told him we had sixteen on the tour, then later on had him do a headcount. We only had fifteen. He thought we'd lost someone. Scared the livin' daylights out of him! We had a good talk when we got back to the shop about keeping track of people from beginning to end and not relying on other people's information."

"You are a cruel man, Harley."

"It gets the job done."

Noah shook his head. He almost felt sorry for the new hires. Almost. He knew Harley was tough on them for their own good. By the end of the summer, they would love Harley like a big brother.

Stepping away from the schedule Noah wandered to the double barn door leading from the back of the shop. His Jeep was parked on the scant piece of driveway that wound around from the alley. He stopped and rested his hip against the side of the door frame. Sun washed over him as he stood there, arms crossed over his chest. He took a deep breath and let the heat of the sun drain the stress away. "Man, it doesn't get much better than this."

Harley joined him in the doorway, arms crossed as well, but with his feet planted wide and his weight rocked back on the heels of his work boots. Noah was the consummate kayak guide. Tall and lanky with tanned arms under a faded t-shirt. His sun-streaked blonde hair was in desperate need of a trim. He was sure his mother would point it out when he visited next. Maybe he'd get it cut before then, he thought as he ran his hand through it.

Harley, on the other hand, seemed out of place in his role as a kayak guide. His stocky frame and full sleeve tattoo on his left arm would fit better in a bar than in a kayak. When he wasn't on the water he was garbed in black jeans, black wife-beater, and black work boots. If Noah didn't know his story, and know why he was in Summer Harbor, he might wonder if the guy had picked the wrong profession.

They stood in companionable silence as the sun beat down on them. Moments like this Noah could almost forget his troubles.

"Days like today, with the sky that blue, and the sun so perfect, and the breeze smelling like the sea I almost wonder if my dad was right. That there might be, I don't know, something or someone out there," Harley murmured.

Noah glanced at him out of the corner of his eye. "Seriously?"

"Yeah, I mean I doubt it, but it just makes you wonder, you know?"

"No, not really. I mean Parker dragged me to Sunday School when I was a kid, but it just seemed… far-fetched I guess. Fairy Tales. I believe in what I can see and touch."

"Yeah, you're right." Harley didn't sound convinced, but if he wanted to get all spiritual he'd have to go talk to Parker. Noah wasn't going there.

Before either of them could continue, or change the subject, a high-pitched, frantic scream interrupted them.

"What the—" Noah didn't get all the words out before he heard it again. Without a second thought, he turned from the door and ran down the short alley between his business and the restaurant next door. His long legs ate up the ground and he burst out onto the sidewalk. Hurtling toward him was a black and white ball of fluff. About the size of a cat, it was remarkably fast. The dog gained speed despite trailing the evidence of its escape, a bright pink leash. Noah chuckled in spite of himself. The little dog was quite pleased with herself and her newfound freedom.

The petite blonde trying to run after the dog, not so much. She was hysterical with panic, screaming at the dog to stop, but the pup gained ground at an impressive rate.

"No! Come back!" she shrieked.

Taking one more step onto the sidewalk, he positioned himself to intercept. As the black and white bullet flew past he brought his foot down on the leash, bringing the escapee to an abrupt, and rather spectacular, halt. Unfazed by the severe stop, the small dog sat down, panting, and scratched its ear, its tongue lolling to one side in a delirious grin.

"You little rascal!" Noah scolded as he leaned down to ruffle the pup's fur.

Out of the corner of his eye, he saw a blur and managed to brace himself in the nick of time. The tiny woman's ridiculously high heels were no match for the uneven sidewalk or her fast rate of speed. She lost her footing and all but launched herself into Noah's arms. He managed to keep her from sprawling on the ground while also keeping the leash held fast under his flip-flop. No easy feat. She had stopped her plummet toward the pavement and lay in his arms as if dipped in a waltz. Noah's right arm had taken most of her weight and held her shoulders while his other arm was looped around her waist to keep her from falling.

"Oh, my word! Oh, my word! Oh, my word!" the woman sputtered. "I'm so sorry! I can't even... I just..." A becoming blush crept up her neck and her long lashes fluttered down in embarrassment. He was mesmerized. The smell of lilacs clung to her, making Noah work to engage his brain. He stood holding her and staring. She resembled a star of the silver screen. Perfect porcelain skin, rosy lips, honey-blonde hair, diamond earrings, and manicured nails. Nails that had a firm grip on the front of his shirt. Despite her flight down Carriage Street, nothing was out of place. When she opened her eyes he thought he caught a glimpse of unshed tears before she blinked them away and cleared her throat.

Noah realized he still held her dipped back on his arm. He also realized, to his own embarrassment, that he was staring at her. Heaven help him, he didn't want to let her go.

"Are you alright?" He asked as he righted her, keeping his hands on her waist until he was sure she was back on her feet. How could anyone walk in heels that high? Let alone run. It was a miracle she hadn't broken an ankle.

"Yes, quite," she replied in a refined accent that spoke of money. "Thank you for catching Princess Penelope for me."

At the mention of the dog's name Noah shared a meaningful look with the pup. She seemed to agree with him that the name was as ridiculous as it sounded. He winked and was answered with a cheerful yip.

Quite capable of maneuvering in four-inch heels when she wasn't in hot pursuit of her dog, the woman crouched down and scooped up the end of the leash from near Noah's foot. He stepped back to release his captive only when he was sure she had a good hold. He watched her loop the leash around her wrist to secure it. Smart. He had a feeling the dog would try to bolt again at the first chance she got.

"Thank you, again."

"It was my pleasure."

The lashes fluttered down again before she squared her shoulders and changed before his very eyes. Gone was the flustered damsel in distress, and in her place was a poised woman. "You are my hero. I honestly don't know what I would have told Uncle if I had lost his precious Princess. I do believe he would be more upset than if I were to leave and not come back." She said it with a laugh in her voice, but Noah got the impression there was too much truth in her words.

"You mean Princess isn't yours?"

"Oh, heavens no!" She laughed. "I've never had a dog, but I imagine I'd be more of a mixed-breed-mongrel-from-the-shelter kind of girl. Of course, Uncle would not approve." Her tone changed and under her breath she added, "Then again I do not approve of his choices either." With that, she gave Princess a pointed look, and Noah would have sworn the pup rolled its eyes before her interest was caught by a beetle scurrying by. "Anyway, thank you again."

The realization that she might walk away and disappear into the crowds of tourists already clogging the sidewalks had Noah scrambling for anything to keep the conversation going.

"Are you enjoying your vacation?" he asked. Unlike many of the folks who worked in Summer Harbor over the warmer months, he wasn't a seasonal resident of the island. As a registered Maine Guide he loved the hot, sunny days running his business, but he also loved the quiet, winter months. He delighted in showing tourists the many things he loved about the island, but he also relished the quiet winter hours he picked up at Finnley's, a hardware store/handyman company up the street. As a result of being a year-round resident, he knew just about everyone on the island. She didn't live here. If you didn't live on the island you either worked there for the summer or came there on vacation. She wasn't summer help.

She opened her mouth, but nothing came out and she snapped it closed again. Her eyelids fluttered and she turned away. Was she trying not to cry? When she turned back there was a grim set to her mouth. "Not a vacation. Sort of... business... I guess." Sadness clouded her face and seeped into her voice. Noah felt like a heel for having even asked.

When she turned to continue heading toward Main Street Noah fell into step beside her. He towered over her five feet five inches, including the heels, and had to make an effort to slow his pace to keep from walking ahead of her. He hunched his shoulders a bit and shoved his hands into the pockets of his jeans. "I hope you find time to enjoy the island. I mean, don't make your trip all work and no play."

The woman stopped short and checked her watch. She gave a furtive look up and down the street.

"Everything OK?"

"Yes. It's just…" She kept straining to see. "I think my driver might be around to collect me."

Towering over her Noah had a clear view of the street. "Is that him?" he asked, pointing to where, a few doors up, a sleek black sedan had pulled to the curb.

Lily felt her face blanch. She tried to step away from the gallant surfer who had saved both Princess and her knees, but her feet had turned to cement. Ahead, Herbert Emerson was trying to heave himself out of the backseat of the car. When he emerged his face was stained with rage. As he advanced the man beside her moved forward as if to protect her. Herbert didn't appear to even see him.

"Lilianna Hayes Emerson, I demand an explanation!" He bellowed.

"I…" An explanation of what? Had he somehow learned that she'd let Princess escape? How was that even possible? Lily's hands started to tremble. She hated that he wielded this kind of power over her. Intimidation was a tactic he used on a regular basis to keep her under his thumb.

"I have just been informed that I am not the only one who has made an offer on the inn," Herbert snapped, so angry that bits of spittle flew from his mouth. His doughy cheeks had reddened and his blue eyes narrowed to slits. "I am told that two other parties have as well. One of them being you!"

For a brief moment, Lily wondered how he had obtained that information. If she didn't know better she would think he was omniscient. She stepped around the man standing his ground in front of her. This wasn't his fight. Besides, she'd dealt with her uncle for years. "If you are talking about The Butterfly Cove Inn, then yes, I made an offer last night."

"How dare you!"

"I made a fair offer, but nothing you can't outdo. The inn is worth what they're asking, if not more."

"I don't want it for what they're asking! I want it for a song! I want it for what the land is worth, not the decrepit old building." His anger built like a thunderhead and Lily cast a nervous peek at passersby, afraid they would hear. At this rate, they would soon become a spectacle.

Keep me calm, Lord! I want peace, but I don't feel very peaceful right now! Give me patience and help me imitate Christ.

"I don't understand," she hissed as she tried in vain to quiet her uncle's outburst.

Herbert leveled his steel gaze at her. "Withdraw your offer, now."

"I didn't think EHI would want a historic property like the inn," Lily said, perplexed.

"I don't! I want to tear down that puny motel and build the next Emerson in its place. I can't do that when you've made an offer on it. What do you even think you're doing?"

"I want it."

"No, you don't. You're an Emerson. You don't even associate with insignificant little places like that. If you feel the need to be here," Herbert waved his chubby hands dismissively at the surrounding area, "I suppose I could let you oversee the construction of the hotel."

"No." Lily had no idea where the boldness came from. "I don't want to oversee another hotel construction. I want my own place. I want to run my own hotel. I've worked hard for EHI and—"

"And you are well compensated! Really Lilianna," he said in a condescending tone that grated on her nerves. "It's cute that you think you can run your own place. But no, you will withdraw your offer so that I can have the place for pennies on the dollar. Otherwise, you'll be forfeiting your father's shares."

Herbert had a habit of dangling those shares like a carrot. When that didn't get him what he wanted he would use rage, and threats, and anything else he could leverage to gain him what he wanted. If she quit her job she would lose the shares. She couldn't sell them or even give them away, but she could abandon them. For years Lily hadn't even considered leaving Emerson Hotels International. Abandoning her shares would mean letting go of what her father had worked so hard for. Now, she wasn't sure she even wanted them anymore.

"No."

Herbert's eyes darkened. His fists clenched at his sides. Other pedestrians were now giving them a wide berth, a couple even crossed the street to avoid the confrontation.

"Hey man, calm down." This from the man trying to step in front of her again. His broad shoulders blocked part of her view. Herbert blinked as if seeing the man for the first time. Fury flashed across his face and he uttered a foul string of words telling the man in precise detail what he could go do. Lily cringed. He'd said it in a growl, but she was sure people had heard. The broad shoulders didn't even flinch. Herbert made a dismissive gesture to the man and brought his attention back to Lily.

"Lilianna, you will do as I say."

For the second time, she stepped around the man to face Herbert head-on. She'd never stood up to him, Not once. Not when he had absorbed her shares into the company. Not when he'd sent her on months-long trips without even a day's notice. Not when he told her to fire competent staff. Not even when he ordered her to walk Princess earlier that day. But this time she couldn't bring herself to cower and give in. She had to fight for the inn. She stepped closer to her uncle and spoke through her teeth. "I don't want the inn torn down! I like it the way it is and I want to buy it. I will not withdraw my offer."

"You most certainly will, Lilianna! If you try to get in my way on this you will be sorry. You think you know what I'm capable of, but you have no idea," Herbert hissed through clenched teeth. With that, he wrenched Princess's leash from Lily's hand, spun on his heel, and stalked toward the waiting car. The driver already had the door open.

As he walked away Lily sagged back against a warm, solid wall. Startled, she swiveled around and discovered her guardian, stone-faced, and watching Herbert depart. He rested his hands on her shoulders and gave them a reassuring squeeze.

"You're right," he said. "That inn shouldn't be torn down."

"It's no use," she groaned in defeat. Her shoulders slumped under his warm hands. "He always wins."

"Did you say you put in an offer on Ava's place?" He asked. His hands slipped away as she turned around to face him.

"Yes, I did." Her eyes followed the car disappearing around the corner. "Not that it will do any good."

"There are an awful lot of people in town who wouldn't want that place torn down. You aren't the only one who'd be getting in his way."

"I'm not in his way. Not really. He'll just make another offer. I can't compete with Uncle." Lily felt tears of frustration burn the back of her throat. She swallowed them away. "He said there was a third offer on the table. Chances are I wouldn't have been the one to purchase it anyway."

Movement on the street caught Lily's eye. Walter waved. He stood by the open driver's door of the black sedan, hat in hand.

"Thank you, again, for stopping Princess and for saving me from skinned knees earlier." He took the hand she offered. His was large and engulfed hers. He waved Walter off and opened the back door of the car himself.

"Happy to help. And happy to catch you again if need be." He winked and his eyes twinkled.

Lily smiled, too, but it failed to reach her eyes.

"Hey, Walter, say 'hi' to Miss Ava," he said over the roof of the car.

"Sure thing, Noah, sure thing."

Walter climbed behind the wheel and shut the door before catching Lily's eye in the rearview mirror. Concern etched hard lines in his brow. He didn't say anything for a long moment. Lily's eyes pleaded with him not to mention the argument. Finally, he spoke. "I see you met our Noah?"

"Hmm? Oh, is that his name? Yes, I met him just now."

"He's a right nice young man. Right nice. He helps me out every winter with projects too big for me to do myself."

Relief that Walter wasn't going to question her about the argument washed over her. How much had he heard? She couldn't imagine Ava hearing that her beloved inn would be torn down. Lily's stomach soured at the thought and she wrapped her arms around herself. Desperate for the distraction she latched onto Walter's conversation. "He's a handyman?"

"Oh, not this time of year. He runs that there adventure business over the summer." Walter nodded to the quaint two-story building before easing the car into the traffic that crawled past. The weathered gray shingles were trimmed in deep aqua and the windows sported sunny yellow mullions. She wondered if the inside of the shop smelled like him. Would it have the same distinctive mix of citrus and sea? She was so lost in thought that she almost missed the rest of what Walter said. "But in the winter he does all sorts of jobs."

He moved along with the slow trickle of cars turning onto Main Street. Lily didn't feel much like talking. Instead, she watched the picturesque little town flicker past her window and let him ramble on.

"My boy Noah has been dreaming of owning that there sea kayaking business since he was in high school. Took him a good many summers of working odd jobs and long hours to save enough to get started. That shop is where the tours gather. The store downstairs sells t-shirts and postcards and what-not. They live upstairs."

The word 'they' wasn't lost on Lily. "He and his wife?" It figures that he'd be married. She shook her head. Not that she cared! What was wrong with her? She didn't date. She wouldn't date. Why was her brain even taking her there? She scowled and tightened her arms around her waist.

"Nah, Noah ain't married. I meant his employees."

She felt foolish, for asking in the first place and for the relief when Walter said the man wasn't married. "Oh, I see."

She shifted away from him in her seat and lost herself in thought. In one day she'd gone from the high of having found the exact place she wanted and the knowledge that it would soon be hers, to the crushing heartache of watching it slip away. Lily tried reminding herself that God worked all things out for the good of those who love Him. Easy to say, harder to see.

Back at the inn Walter, always the gentleman, opened her door, bobbed his head when she got out, and then drove off leaving her alone on the front walk. She didn't want to talk to anyone and was thankful that the porch was empty. As was the foyer when she slipped in the front door. She managed to make it to her room without running into anyone. Dejected, she flopped onto the bed and kicked her cursed heels onto the floor. Her cheeks flamed remembering how she had fallen into the muscular arms of a complete stranger. Well, almost a stranger. A smile tugged at her lips remembering the glimpse she'd caught of him the day before. Down on the beach, laughing. Her heart thumped hard against her chest. Mortified, Lily groaned and pulled her pillow over her head.

Who did she think she was? She couldn't leave. Not after everything he'd done. The feeling of betrayal was an acrid taste in his mouth. Or was that the stale booze he'd poured himself as soon as he was back in the car? He couldn't quite tell. He nursed both, the betrayal into a hot ember and the Macallan whiskey until the glass was empty. He wouldn't put it past the other one to leave him. Olivia. She was worthless. It was his own fault, but he'd never seen anything valuable in her, so it was easy to dismiss her. If he was honest he wasn't even sure where she was at this point. He should know. It rankled him that he didn't. No doubt wherever it was she was getting into mischief.

Lilianna, on the other hand, had what it took.

He'd seen to it that she learned all aspects of the business from the best of the best. How did she thank him? By learning it all and then skipping out on all he and her father had spent a lifetime building? An expletive hissed from his lips. His brother deserved better than this treachery. She couldn't do this to Prescott. Or to him. He wouldn't let her.

It might have been him alone these last twelve years, but in the end, it was always Prescott. Prescott's ideas. Prescott's dreams. Prescott had always been Emerson Hotels International. He wouldn't let it go under on his watch and he wouldn't let Prescott's sellout daughter get away with abandoning EHI either.

His headache which had, for a moment, been dulled with the drugs his doctor kept prescribing, was back with a vengeance. He rubbed his pudgy fingers into his temples and tried to stop thinking. It didn't work.

In his mind's eye, he saw another face. Taking on a partner who wasn't Prescott had almost pushed him over the edge. If it hadn't been for the threat of losing the business... The only outcome worse than replacing Prescott would have been to lose everything his brother had worked for, died working for. The fact that, to this day, he couldn't look the interloper in the eye only seemed to fuel his contempt. He knew it wasn't the man's fault. It was no one's fault but his own. And yet... He needed Prescott back! Needed life to make sense again. He needed the man gone. Had even, perhaps, found a way.

His hands had started to shake and Princess crawled over to him, laid her head on his lap, and licked his wrist. He flexed his fingers trying to regain control. He had a fleeting thought that he should be careful of his blood pressure. It wouldn't do any good to have a stroke in this backwater town. Did they even have a hospital? His zeal for building the next Emerson in Summer Harbor had waned. If he backed down now, though, Lilianna would be gone, slipped from his grasp just like Margo. Just like Prescott. Gone.

Alone.

The word rattled around in his head and settled in his chest. He hadn't always been alone. When he and Prescott had first hatched the idea of Emerson Hotels International it had been the two of them against the world. Prescott had been out of college for a year and hadn't yet found his niche. He'd talked his little brother, still with one year of a business degree to go, into what he had thought at the time was an unattainable dream. He would have followed his big brother to the moon if that's what Prescott wanted.

Against all odds, two years later they opened their first hotel. Over the years, with Prescott calling the shots, the chain had exploded onto the world market. International grand openings, champagne and caviar, fast cars, and beautiful women. No, not women. A woman.

Margo.

It was the first time he could remember wishing he was the older, more handsome, better brother. Margo had blown into Prescott's life like a breath of fresh air. His brother had fallen hard and fast. But his brother wasn't the only one who'd fallen in love with her. No, he hadn't always been alone. First Prescott. Then Prescott and Margo. Then Prescott, Margo, and the girls. They had included him in everything from Sunday dinner to Christmas morning.

His car slowed and he focused again on the present. Back at the hotel. Back to his room. No, he hadn't always been alone. Just now. No Margo. No Prescott. No Olivia. And if she got her way, no Lilianna. He couldn't let that happen. Wouldn't. As long as he held a few of the cards he was still in the game.

CHAPTER THREE

Noah watched Walter's car as it wound down the street and turned the corner. Harley gave a low whistle from where he stood leaning on the railing by the front door of the shop. A small porch topped the steps leading to the corner door with its wooden paddle door handle.

"You catch all that?" Noah asked as he joined him.

"Yeah. Not good."

"I don't know who that guy thinks he is, but you don't speak to a woman like that." Noah thumped his fist on the railing, irritation simmering as he replayed the scene in his mind.

Harley shook his head in agreement. "The man's a bully. Nice save on the dog by the way."

The creature sure had been pleased with itself. A smile tugged one side of Noah's lips up, but it was fleeting. His instinct had been to gather the woman into his arms as her uncle drove off. He hadn't missed the tears swimming in her eyes or the way she rubbed her wrist where the dog leash had chaffed her skin when her uncle snatched it away. He sort of wished he had. He could imagine how she'd feel in his arms. Soft and delicate.

He started when Harley clapped him on the shoulder before heading into the shop. Noah stayed, forearms leaning on the railing. He knew he shouldn't let the other man get under his skin. He shouldn't let a pretty face get to him either, and yet here he was. What had the man called her? Lilianna? It suited her. He liked her spunk, standing up to the man. He'd had a hard time not reacting to the crude suggestion the man had thrown at him and then out of nowhere the pint-sized firecracker had stormed forward like she needed to protect him.

He realized he was smiling and swept it away. Not good, Noah. Not good. He needed to let it go. He had work to do and besides, he had a strict 'no summer girls' policy for a reason.

The next tour had assembled in the back room of the shop by the time he got there. Harley had handed out life jackets and dry bags, getting everyone outfitted before walking down to the shore. Noah propped his hip on the edge of his cluttered desk and gave his customary spiel about safety and rules. He smiled and joked with the participants, and yet he felt like he was on autopilot. How had the tiny woman with beautiful gray eyes inserted herself into his thoughts? He tried to shake her off, but each time he let his mind wander it went straight back to her. His blood boiled when he recalled how she had been spoken to. Not kosher. At all. He needed to get his mind back where it belonged, on the group.

"Harley, you make sure everyone's all set with jackets and paddles, I'm going to grab the camera."

"Got it, boss."

He tried not to play favorites, but it seemed like every tour someone stood out. Without fail, there would be a man, woman, or child who needed a little extra TLC, a little extra direction. They ended up being favorites because the joy, or awe, or courage was always a bit more with that one. Today it was a middle-aged father with a balding head and a resigned expression.

Noah jogged up the two flights of stairs to his attic apartment and grabbed his camera. He snagged an extra SD card and a spare battery and attached a decent telephoto lens. He didn't always take a camera, but today felt like a good day for it. Back downstairs he slid it all into a dry bag and hurried to catch up.

As he came up to the group, the man he'd noticed at the start of the tour and his wife were bringing up the rear. Their sullen teenage daughter kept her distance near the front of the group.

"Perfect day to be on the water," Noah said as he joined them.

The wife flashed him a tense smile, while the father simply nodded, focusing straight ahead. Noah had his work cut out for himself. He trotted up to the front and leaned in close to Harley. "Put the grumpy teenager in the orange Scaredy Cat t-shirt in a double with her mother and the dad in a single."

Harley gave him a quick thumbs up. "She's been my shadow since we left the shop. Asked me three times if we'd see a seal."

"Better make sure we loop through the deep water off Paddle Beach," Noah said with a conspiratorial wink.

They arrived at the sandbar where the kayaks were laid out in a neat row by the water's edge. One of this summer's new hires, Owen, sat in the cab of the truck and another newbie, Gage, waited, his hip braced on the trailer, for the 'all clear' to head back to the shop.

"All set boss?" he asked.

"Ayuh," Noah replied. He wasn't below ramping up his Maine accent for the tourists.

Gage grinned and hopped in the cab with Owen.

All the tourists donned their life vests and stood waiting for boat assignments. Almost all. Spinning in a circle on his socks and sandals, the father he'd pegged as needing a little special care tried to grab the other side of his life vest. The wind lifted the man's gray fringe off the sides of his head as he spun. Noah felt a pang of pity when he saw how the man's turquoise and royal blue Hawaiian shirt clashed with the orange life jacket.

"Can I give you a hand with that?"

The man sighed and gave up trying to find the other end of the strap. "I don't know why I'm even bothering," he mumbled in a baritone that struck Noah as mighty deep for such a slight man. Noah fished the missing piece out of the back of the jacket and clicked the clasp into place.

"Why you're bothering... with the life jacket?"

"No, with this whole..." he waved his arm toward his daughter. "Never mind."

Noah watched as Harley loaded up the man's wife and daughter into a two-person kayak, handed them their paddles, and pushed them into the surf. He hung back, making sure each boat got into the water, counting heads, assessing skill levels. It wasn't a full tour and they'd been quick getting underway. They could afford a little extra time on the water this morning.

As they meandered their way around Bar Island Noah pulled up next to the father and matched his speed.

"Is this your first trip to Summer Harbor?"

The man sighed, watching his wife and daughter up ahead. He took a long time to answer. "We thought…"

Noah waited. There had been times in his life when he had carried the same bleak disposition. Different reasons, but not all that different a feeling. He had craved a listening ear. Now he could recognize that dismal frame of mind. So he listened. And waited. When he had planned his business he hadn't thought about helping people on an inner level. He'd wanted nothing more than to share his love of the water. After years of watching and listening he was amazed at the burdens folks carried with them on vacation.

"It's… it's been a rough year. We… I… thought if we could just get away for a little while, as a family, things might get better. I didn't think it was possible, but I believe they've gotten worse." The man was silent for so long Noah wasn't sure the man would continue. Then "She hates me."

No need to ask who. The daughter wore rebellion like a badge of honor. "How old is she?"

"Sixteen."

"Ah, I remember sixteen. I think I hated the whole world."

"That about sums it up."

"I hear it's just a phase."

"Do you have kids?" The man's question caught Noah off guard. An unfamiliar pang settled in his chest. He'd pictured himself married with a family by now. A couple of little blonde boys learning to paddle, or a little girl with dark curls like his mom. He knew his parents would make the best grandparents in the world. There was one problem. He was as single as they got. He'd had a few semi-serious girlfriends, but the community didn't lend itself to long-term relationships. The locals were more like family, and the girls who came to the island during tourist season didn't hold any interest for him. At least not since... "No, I don't."

"One minute they think you can do anything and the next they think nothing you do is right. We used to be so close. I remember when she thought I could do magic." Failure edged the man's voice. "I hoped this vacation would bring us back together, but she doesn't even want to be here. She thinks all the activities we have planned are 'lame'."

"You know, as hard as I pushed in my teen years I just wanted my folks to see me, you know?"

"She's not the only one. I just wish she'd look at me and see the man she used to see."

"You want her to see who she used to see, and she wants you to see who she's becoming."

The man considered Noah with a thoughtful expression. "I hadn't thought of it like that."

"I've got an idea," Noah said as he spun his kayak around and paddled backward. He edged closer and explained his plan.

The man raised a skeptical eyebrow.

Noah winked and grinned. He pulled behind the man and paddled away. Hard stokes pulled him well out to the side of the group. Stopping, he rested his paddle on the gunwales and watched the group. Camera in hand, he waited. At first, he wasn't sure the man would take him up on the idea, but then he watched the other kayak work its way forward until the man was even with his daughter. Noah couldn't hear the conversation, but through the telephoto lens he could see it. Dad talking, daughter sulking, more talking, an eye roll, more talking.

"C'mon," Noah whispered.

At last, he saw the father say 'Let me call a seal for you.' Then the man closed his eyes, raised his hands high above the water, arms widespread. Noah couldn't tell what he said, but he brought his hands down, pointed at the water, and opened his eyes. A moment later a seal broke the surface a foot from Scaredy Cat's boat, right where her dad had pointed. She turned the largest eyes Noah had ever seen on her father. He watched her father laugh and point frantically at the seal. 'Look at the seal!' he yelled. The seal eyed them with curiosity for a couple of minutes before returning to the deep water of the bay.

An excited squeal reached Noah's ears as they hauled the last of the kayaks up onto the shore.

"Daddy! How did you do that?"

He turned to see the teenager run over to her father and throw her arms around him. The man caught Noah's eye above his daughter's head. *Thank you*, he mouthed. Noah nodded, a smile on his lips. And that's how he ended up with favorites.

"That trick never disappoints," Harley murmured as he helped Noah load a kayak onto the trailer.

"Never. And, I got the whole thing," he added, tapping the dry bag containing the camera.

"Nice. She's not a bad kid. She was sort of glued to me. I think she was trying to tick her dad off." Harley flexed his tats and gave Noah a wry smile. "Anyway, I told her to cut the guy some slack. There are those of us who would give everything we have for one more conversation with our dad."

As they walked back to the shop, the man sidled up to Noah. "I don't know how to thank you."

"No thanks needed. It was my pleasure."

"Norm Kessler," the man said, extending his hand.

"Noah Kingsley."

"I can't believe it, but I just heard the words 'best vacation' come from my daughter's mouth." He shook his head in disbelief and grinned at Noah. "How did you do that?"

"The seal? They always come visit the kayaks when we come around that point. Thankfully, one cooperated today."

Norm laughed and squeezed Noah's shoulder. "You are a good, good man Noah Kingsley."

The praise made Noah feel awkward, but he smiled and gripped the man's shoulder in return. "Don't let this feeling go. Feed it. Have a fun dinner down by the pier, maybe take a nature cruise or go whale watching. Get her in on the planning so she doesn't think it's 'lame'. And trust me, the teen years will pass -

like a kidney stone, but they *will* pass."

Norm was still grinning as he jogged ahead to catch up to his wife and daughter. With an arm around each of them, he laughed at something his daughter said and then kissed his wife's cheek. Yup, this was how Noah ended up with favorites.

He'd fallen asleep on the too-hard mattress, in the too-cold room, on top of the too-brown blanket. The migraine had pulled him under until sweet oblivion washed over him. The gentle hum of the AC did its best to drown out the sounds of passing cars and neighbors and foot traffic.

He'd done what he could to seize the scant tranquility that an unfamiliar room had to offer, but still, his sleep was fitful. The migraine drugs left him both groggy and jittery. Dreams slipped in, teased, and slipped away again. At last, deeper sleep claimed him and dragged him into dreams that lingered.

Margo!

He woke with a start, unsure if he had said her name aloud. She'd smiled at him the way she had once upon a time. She'd touched his hand. She'd whispered his name. Dream Margo had used the breathy tone he'd only heard once. Had she laughed? The dream was already fading and he couldn't remember. He did remember that she'd waved goodbye, fading, and he had bellowed her name. He blinked his eyes to clear the sleep but was torn between dragging himself awake and burrowing back into the dream.

The more he thought about the dream though, the more he realized it hadn't been Margo at the end after all. The woman waving goodbye in his dream had the same pale golden hair, the same large, silver eyes, the same heart-shaped face.

Lilianna.

She resembled her mother so much that it hurt to look at her. Not Olivia. She had more of the Emerson look in her. Her grandmother's violet eyes and, like him, her grandfather's button nose. But Lilianna was all Hayes. He wondered if Prescott had seen it. Was that why he'd sent her away after Margo died? On the horrible day they'd lost Margo, he'd lost Prescott and Lilianna, too. Today on the sidewalk, with her eyes flashing, he thought Margo had come back from the grave. If only that were true.

With a great deal of effort, he hauled himself to a sitting position on the side of the bed and hung his reeling head. The migraine had faded some, but in its place his mind whirled again toward rage. He let it. After all, it was a familiar place. One where he spent more and more time. It felt better than the other places his mind took him, so he hunkered down and let the bitterness envelop him.

The phone rang and he pawed at the nightstand for his watch. He'd slept the entire afternoon away and it was now well past dark. Cursed painkillers. He should have worked through the headache. He was getting weak. The phone rang again and he lifted the receiver.

"Emerson."

He listened as the other person spoke. His eyes narrowed and his mouth took on a grim line. He hated being out of town for myriad reasons, but worst of all was that he had to handle his own calls. It couldn't be helped though. And in this case it was prudent that he handle it alone.

"Yes, I agree. We need to talk."

Another pause.

"Are you serious?"

His face darkened as his temper simmered.

"Fine. Wherever. I just want this done." He slammed the receiver into its dock.

No, he couldn't let Lilianna leave EHI. Leave him. He would do whatever it took to keep her. This wouldn't be the first time a deal had been made under the cover of night. He doubted it would be the last. This business had taught him that only those willing to seize what they wanted won. Even if that meant seizing it out of someone else's grasp.

In one hand he still held the tattered letter he'd been clutching when he fell asleep. He didn't need to read it, knew each line by heart. Still, he lingered over every word again. He couldn't explain it, but holding it, reading it, snuffed a little of the enmity between him and the world. He smoothed the dogeared edge and refolded it before slipping it back into its envelope, and back into its home beside the others.

He wasn't in a hurry, just edgy. He blamed it on the painkillers. Even, almost, believed himself. He took his time shrugging back into his suit coat and running a hand over a shock of uncooperative white hair. He poured a glass from the decanter and knocked it back with one flick of the wrist. Another? He had time. No, he needed a clear head. Or as clear as it got these days. He checked his watch again and left the room.

The lobby was empty, as was the street. Music from a distant side street hinted that there were still people up, but the sidewalk in front of the hotel was his alone. Rancid yellow light puddled under the street lights, but shadows crept in along the edges. He ignored them. Shadows crept in along the edges of everything in his world.

The moon slipped along the edge of thick clouds, making the night even darker. The ocean crashed against the pilings to his left, far below street level. He rounded the last building on the street, a lobster pound, and the empty pier stretched out before him. Why here? His irritation simmered.

The lobster pound was dark and quiet, but the distinctive aroma of boiled lobsters, crabs, and clams still hung in the air. The souvenir shops, public bathrooms, and ice cream counter all faded into the fog. The murky air that rolled off the water blurred the end of the pier, but he thought he saw a shadow just outside the glow of the last street light.

"Let's get this over with," he growled as he approached.

The painkillers and whiskey must have dulled his reflexes. He saw the movement as if in slow motion, but he was incapable of reacting. Pain exploded across his cheekbone and into his eye socket. His vision blurred, the edges getting fuzzy and dark. He never saw the second strike coming, just felt the sickening pop of his skull shattering above his temple. He had a momentary sensation of flying before the darkness claimed him.

The knocking penetrated the haze of deep sleep. Lily opened her eyes and tried to get her bearings. Not her room. Not in Boston. At the inn. Summer Harbor. Weird light. What time was it? She sat up and blinked again. The knocking began again in earnest.

"Coming," she called.

Throwing on a long sweater over her pajamas she opened the door to find a distraught Ava on the other side.

"I'm so sorry Lily, but the chief of police is here. He wants to speak with you."

Lily rubbed her eyes. The sleeping pill she'd taken the night before dragged at her, making it difficult to wake up.

"What?"

"The chief of police wants to speak with you."

"Me? Why me?"

"I don't know. He just asked me to come get you."

"What time is it?"

"A little before 6AM."

"Oh." Four hours of sleep. No wonder she struggled to shake off the drowsiness. She tried to corral her mussed hair into a ponytail and pulled her sweater closer around herself as she closed her door. Ava led the way back downstairs.

"Here she is," the older woman said to the barrel-chested policeman standing at the check-in counter, hat in hand.

"Good morning, Ms. Emerson, Chief Briggs," he said, extending his hand. "I wish we could have met under better circumstances. I'm afraid I have bad news." He turned his hat over a few times in his hands and shuffled his feet. It was obvious that he did not relish his current task.

"What seems to be the problem, Chief Briggs?" Her mind

raced with a thousand what-ifs. Dread crept in and planted itself in her stomach. Had Olivia been in an accident? The girl was careening toward trouble like a freight train. Wouldn't she have gotten a call though? Why send a policeman? Unless it was the worst case and they needed to notify... *Oh, God, no!*

"Ma'am, are you—" he paused and flipped open his notebook. "Lilianna Emerson?"

"Yes."

"Is Herbert Emerson your uncle?"

"Yes, he is. What's this about?"

"I'm sorry to inform you that your uncle was found dead this morning."

Lily's field of vision narrowed and she felt the words like a punch to the chest. She reached for the counter to steady herself at the same moment Chief Briggs reached for her elbow.

"Here you go," Ava said as she eased Lily down onto a chair in the foyer. She placed a comforting hand on Lily's shoulder. "I'm so sorry for your loss, Dea-ah."

"Yes, I'm sorry for your loss as well," Chief Briggs chimed in as he took an awkward perch on the edge of the other chair.

"How? I mean, I just saw him yesterday. How can he be dead?" she asked.

Ava shuffled toward the kitchen, her cane clicking on the polished wooden floor. It drummed a steady rhythm before fading behind the closed door. Lily turned back to the man and wondered if he wanted to flee as much as Ava had. She wouldn't blame him.

"It appears he fell off the town pier late last night. A tourist discovered him while jogging on the beach around four-thirty this morning."

All at once, Lily couldn't get enough air. Her thoughts tumbled one over another and she struggled to grasp what the man had just told her. Uncle couldn't be dead. She put her head in her hands. He had been wretched, but he had still been family. Her only family other than Olivia. How could he be gone?

"He fell off the pier?"

"Yes, ma'am," Chief Briggs nodded. "I spoke with a couple of employees at the hotel where he was staying. He was seen leaving the hotel lobby on foot after midnight. We asked a few of the business owners around the pier, but no one was there at that time. We assume he went for a walk and fell. Most unfortunate."

"Where..." How did one ask where a person's body was? "Where... is he?"

"I took the liberty of calling the local funeral home. Is there another family member I should contact? A wife perhaps?"

"No, no one."

"We called his office in Boston once we determined who he was. I reached his assistant who directed me to you."

"Yes, I would be his next of kin. What do I need to do?"

"The funeral home will take care of... him... as soon as the medical examiner has completed his examination. Here's their number," he said, handing her his business card with a phone number scribbled on the back. "You can call them and make the necessary arrangements."

"Of course." In shock, Lily took his card. "Thank you."

"Please feel free to call me if you need anything."

Lily sat, numb, staring at the closed front door.

Lord, You said that You have given me Your peace. Not like the world gives peace, but peace that allows my heart to not be troubled or afraid. I trust You to give me that peace now.

A gentle hand on her shoulder made her start.

"I've brought you a cup of tea, Dea-ah," Ava said.

"Thank you."

"That must be quite a shock," Ava whispered with the voice of a person well acquainted with loss. "Were you close?"

"No, we weren't," Lily said. She was still trying to grasp the reality of the policeman's words. "He was... a hard man."

Ava sat across from Lily, resting both hands on her cane. "Hard or not he was still family and that makes it tough."

"Yes," Lily agreed. She sipped her tea and appreciated Ava's ability to sit in silence. How was she supposed to feel? Was she supposed to feel anything? Yes, she should. But she couldn't. It was like she'd gone blank. After a while, the sleeping pill began to give up its hold. Confusion was the first emotion to find the surface. How could this have happened? There was no way it was as simple as the Chief of Police had made it sound.

After confusion, fear made an appearance. What would happen now? As much as she had wanted out from under her uncle's thumb the reality of it terrified her. Who was she without him? What if the truth was she couldn't stand on her own?

The realization that she and Olivia were all that remained of their family hit like an icy wave. They were it. They were on their own. Deep down she had known this day would come, but it hadn't been a reality, just an idea. Now that it was real she felt stunned.

"Thank you for the tea. I need to make a phone call."

"Yes, yes, yes, of course. If you need anything at all you just let me or Walter know."

"Thank you." She patted Ava's gnarled hands in thanks as she walked past.

She wasn't sure where to even begin. Back in her room, sitting in an overstuffed chair facing the windows, she picked up the phone. She pulled both feet up under her and ran her thumb back and forth over the handset. She had new sympathy for Chief Briggs. Delivering bad news was hard.

Sucking in a calming breath Lily dialed her sister's number, staring at the sea as she waited for Olivia to pick up.

"Hey, Sis," Olivia answered in a sleepy sing-song voice.

"Hey."

"What's wrong?" Her voice lost the slur of slumber and showed instant concern.

Lily swallowed the lump in her throat. "It's Uncle. He's dead."

"What?"

"Uncle Herbert passed away late last night or early this morning." After their mother's death, Herbert had faded from their lives as well. He had been consumed with EHI. Years later, after their father passed away he had hardened even more into the miserable man they knew so well. Since college, his presence in Lily's life had been day-in and day-out. Olivia, however, had managed to avoid his encroaching on her life. How? Lily wasn't sure. His death would affect Lily's world much more so than Olivia's.

"Did he... die at home?"

"No, in Summer Harbor, Maine."

"How did you find out so soon?" Olivia asked.

"I'm in Summer Harbor, too."

There was a long stretch of silence. Then Olivia huffed out a breath. "I'm so confused."

"Let me back up," Lily said. "The day before yesterday I came to Summer Harbor. There's this inn that's for sale—"

"Your dream!"

"Yes. Oh, Liv, it is. It's perfection." A thought struck Lily. Now that Uncle was gone she might have a chance at owning the inn after all. With his offer out of the way she only had one other to compete with. A thrill ran through her. It was short-lived as the realization settled in that she couldn't leave Boston now. Not with EHI in the precarious state it was sure to be in without Herbert Emerson at the helm. "Anyway, I made an offer on it, and then yesterday Uncle showed up."

"He showed up in Maine? Why?"

"He made an offer on the place, too."

"What on earth did Uncle want with an old inn?"

Lily tried not to take offense at Olivia's tone. Her sister was smart, but seldom put that knowledge to good use. At one time Lily had envisioned them working side by side at EHI. Olivia's party-over-office-hours and clubs-over-boardrooms philosophy had squelched that dream. "That's what I wanted to know, too. Turns out he wanted to tear it down."

"Oh, Sis," Olivia whispered.

"This morning a jogger found him on the beach. The chief of police said he fell off the pier."

"Fell off the pier? Uncle?" complete disbelief shading Olivia's voice.

"That was my reaction, too! Uncle? Uncle would never have taken a walk on the pier. I keep going over it and I can't think of a single reason he would have been on the pier late at night. Uncle hated going outside, and walking, and nature. And people. He took a hired car two blocks to confront me yesterday, for goodness sake!" Lily sucked in a sudden breath.

"What?"

"Oh, Liv, could he have been pushed off the pier?"

"Well, Uncle did have more enemies than friends. Scratch that. Uncle only had enemies."

"I know, but none of them are here. Maybe it was just an accident. I doubt even Uncle could manage to make an enemy capable of killing him in just a few hours."

Olivia was silent for a moment. "What now?"

"I have no idea. I was pretty young when Daddy passed. Uncle handled all the details. I don't know what to do next."

"I'll call his lawyer and we'll come up with a plan," Olivia offered.

Lily pulled the phone away from her ear. Had her sister just offered to do something as adult as calling Uncle's lawyer? "Ummm... Thanks, Liv. I'll call Alistair and have him get in touch with the lawyer, too."

"Love you, Lil."

"I love you, too, Liv."

"It'll be OK."

"I know."

Lily sat gathering her thoughts before calling Herbert's business partner. Alistair had come along when EHI had been desperate for an influx of funds. Lily had been charmed by the man from day one. Her uncle, not so much. Quiet and unassuming, Alistair was the antithesis of Herbert. On more than one occasion he had expressed to Lily how much he would like to be a part of running EHI, but her uncle had kept him on the periphery. Always just outside looking in. Yet Alistair handled it all with class and decorum. Now he picked up on the fourth ring.

"Hello, Alistair Amias speaking."

"Hello, Alistair, this is Lily."

"Good morning, Lilianna." No one called her by her full name except Herbert and Alistair. It grated on her nerves when her uncle used it, but Alistair's cultured, rich voice made it sound like a soothing balm.

"It's early, even for you. Is something wrong?"

"I'm afraid I have… news." She took a steadying breath, but the words stuck in her throat.

"Yes?"

"Uncle Herbert has passed away."

"What?"

"It happened late last night or early this morning. He was found on the beach in Summer Harbor, Maine."

"Summer Harbor?" Shock shrilled his voice.

"Yes. I didn't know he had plans to come here. Did you?"

"No, no, I had no idea that he would be out of the office at all, let alone that he went to Summer Harbor! This is all so… I don't even know what to say." There was a long pause before Alistair continued. "Here? Meaning you are in Summer Harbor as well?"

"Yes. I came to check out a property that's for sale and was quite surprised when Uncle showed up as well."

"Yes, I imagine you were. What do you need me to do?"

"To be honest, I don't know yet. I suppose either you or I should get in touch with the lawyer."

"I can do that as soon as I get off the phone."

"Can you hold down the fort until I get back?"

"Absolutely."

"Thank you, Alistair."

"When are you going back to Boston?"

"I don't know yet. Soon. Uncle is still… here, so I feel like I should wait until that is sorted. Maybe Monday?"

"Lilianna, I'm so sorry for your loss. I know you were not close, but it must still be a shock."

"It doesn't feel real. I'm sure it will, but right this second it feels like a wretched April Fools' joke."

"We'll get through this Lilianna, I promise."

"I know we will, Alistair. I know we will."

She twined her arms around her knees and rested her chin on them. Her mind alternated between racing and stuttering to a vacant standstill. It was unsettling. Her racing thoughts were too haphazard to be useful, and the vacant moments were too numbing to be helpful.

An hour later the shrilling of the phone roused Lily from where she sat staring, unseeing, out the window.

"Hello?"

"Hello, Ms. Emerson?"

"Yes?"

"Thelma, down at Chief Briggs' office. I'm sorry to bother you, but the hotel called. Did your uncle by chance own a dog?"

"Oh, my goodness, Princess!"

"They said she'd been barking for hours. I'm going to the hotel and collect her, but I need you to come get her as soon as possible."

"I'll be right there."

"Thank you, Ms. Emerson."

Lily gathered her keys and hurried out to her car. Traffic was slow and it took her a while to find a parking space behind the police station. Picturing Chief Briggs, annoyed with dog-sitting duty, she rushed into the lobby, breathless. She needn't have worried. Princess was sprawled on the lap of the receptionist. When Lily came through the door the pup's ears perked up and her tail thumped, but she didn't even try to get up. Instead, she was content to stay flopped on the woman's lap.

"Good morning, I'm Lily Emerson. I think you called me about picking up Herbert Emerson's dog." Lily indicated the pup with a nod of her head.

"Yes, indeed. Thelma," the woman said, offering Lily a hand. Sympathy radiated from the firm grip. Lily liked her at once. "This little sweetie and I were just getting acquainted." She scratched Princess behind the ear and the pup turned adoring eyes on her new best friend. "Funny little thing. What is she?"

"Shih Tzu."

"It appears she might have a bit of a mischievous streak."

"Oh boy, does she ever!"

"That must be why we get along so well," the woman said, addressing the dog. "We're kindred spirits, you and I." Thelma gave Princess one last scratch behind the ear and slid her onto the floor. "I brought her over with her leash, but nothing else. My guess would be you might be able to get her things from the hotel."

"Thanks. I'll give them a call," Lily said, taking the leash. The whole situation was surreal. She felt like she was in an odd movie where she was the main character, but she didn't know the script.

Thelma placed a comforting hand on Lily's shoulder and gave it a gentle squeeze. "I'm wicked sorry for your loss. If you need anything you just let us know, OK?"

Not trusting her voice, Lily acknowledged the kind words with a nod. She tugged Princess toward the door, and they stepped out into the warm sunshine and fresh air. Lily cast about feeling disoriented. She was in Summer Harbor, Maine. She had Uncle Herbert's dog because he was dead. In the office in Boston, she was the problem solver. Nothing phased her. Co-workers would seek *her* advice when they needed a solution to a particular situation or tricky problem. Yet here, out of her element, she felt small and confused. The need for another set of shoulders to help her carry the burdens she'd been handed was acute. She'd called the only two people she had in the world, and while she knew they would do what they could, it was still going to fall to her to deal with the rest. To be the strong one. To come up with the answers. She needed to figure out the answers, but at that particular moment, her brain refused to cooperate.

All around her people went about their normal, everyday lives. They walked along chatting and laughing, or stood perusing maps and taking pictures.

How, God? How can everyone else go about their lives as if everything is fine?

Lily wanted to stamp her feet and scream. She longed for a

familiar face. Someone who understood that nothing felt normal or fine at that particular moment.

Princess tugged on the leash, sniffing all along the edge of the sidewalk, circling the planters full of early summer flowers, and around the side of the police station. Lily followed, pulled along by the little dog.

They walked back to Lily's car with Princess strutting ahead at the end of her leash. Tail held high, nose up in the air. They reached the car and Lily stood wondering what to do. She couldn't take the dog back to the inn, they had a no pet policy. She scanned the immediate area for inspiration. What did you do with a dog you were unexpectedly responsible for? A dog that you didn't want. A dog that wasn't yours? Of all the things she had tried to figure out that morning, the future of Princess hadn't even made the list.

Lily fished her cell phone out of her purse and held it up. No signal and no data. Frustrated, and still trying to formulate a plan, Lily started walking toward the end of the parking lot. There had to be an easy solution, but her brain refused to come up with a single viable idea. The parking lot exited onto Carriage Street. Lily let Princess lead the way and followed along, trying to engage her brain. The pup, nose in the air, led the way toward Main Street. Recognition dawned as Lily realized this was the same place she'd lost her hold on Princess's leash the day before. Without thinking she tightened her grip and grabbed the leash in both hands.

As they neared Acadian Adventures, Lily had an idea. Face flushed from memories of her spectacular fall into a pair of oh-so-strong arms the day before, she tied the dog leash off on the steps and walked into the shop.

"Is the owner available?" she asked the young redhead behind the counter. She couldn't be out of high school yet. Trendy haircut, Acadian Adventures t-shirt, and way too much eye makeup. She snapped her gum with a cheery smile.

"I think so. Let me just check," she said and disappeared through a door behind the counter.

Lily browsed the t-shirts and water bottles with the Acadian Adventures logo while she waited. The shop was paneled in rustic pine and had a clean feel that was pleasing to the eye. It smelled of the sea air blowing in the open windows and the balsam fir pillows and bayberry soap displayed by the register. Lily was fingering a plush sweatshirt when the man from the day before bounded in through the back door.

"Good morning," he grinned. "What's up?"

"Oh... Ummm..." she said, at a loss for where to begin. Her face clouded.

"Hey, what's wrong?" he asked. Concern wiped the smile from his face and he reached out to touch her elbow.

She drew in a shaky breath. "Long story, but I need to find a place to board my uncle's dog and I don't even know where to begin."

"Sounds like you need a kennel. My friend Micah's place is great. I can give you directions." He paused as if rethinking that idea. "Better yet, I can take you."

Relief washed over her. "Thank you."

He turned to lead the way but stopped short. "Wait. Was Herbert Emerson your uncle?"

"Yes," she said, surprised. "How did you know that?"

"The whole town's talking about it. I'm so, so sorry."

"Thank you. We weren't close." At the look on his face, she added, "I'm sure you already guessed that after yesterday." Anyone walking past would have figured that out with little trouble. He studied her for a second, and she thought he might comment. Instead, he turned and guided her toward the door with his hand on her back.

"Come on, I'll take you over to Micah's."

CHAPTER FOUR

Noah knew there was a lifetime worth of story there, but this was neither the time nor the place. Taking care of small things like the dog would help the most right now. As they walked out the door he caught a whiff of lilacs, like he had the day before, and he had to resist the urge to lean into her as they walked.

He stepped away to unhook the dog's leash. The sudden loss of contact bothered him more than he would like to admit. He didn't let summer girls get close, let alone tourists, so why was he letting this little slip of a woman with huge gray eyes wedge her way in? He was baffled, and yet he felt powerless to stop it.

"I'm Noah, by the way. I don't think we ever introduced ourselves yesterday. And you're Lilianna?"

"Lily." She took his hand. "Nice to meet you, Noah."

Her hand was cool and silky smooth. He expected a light touch but was quite surprised at her firm grasp. All too soon she'd pulled her hand from his. They meandered away from the noise of Main Street. The crowds thinned out and sounds changed from chatter and car engines to gull calls and rustling leaves. Towering oaks and maples lined the street casting it all in cool shadow. He heard Lily take a long, deep breath of fresh air, and watched her try to force her shoulders to relax.

"Thank you again," she said.

"No problem. It isn't far away and I like the walk." He paused. "I really am sorry about your uncle."

"It's so... I don't even know what to call it. Shocking? Overwhelming? There are phone calls to place and arrangements to make and papers to go through and lawyers to meet with..." she trailed off, her voice catching, as she looked away. With stiff shoulders, she hugged her arms around herself.

What was it about this woman that made him want to shed his self-imposed rules and take her in his arms? He placed a comforting arm around her shoulders for a fleeting moment. He'd do that for any friend, right? Except that if he put his arm around Harley's shoulders, his heart didn't slam into his ribs and his palms didn't start sweating.

"I'm fine, honest," Lily assured him as she stepped away.

They turned left and walked away from the shore for a few blocks. The street was populated with old captains' houses, an antique shop, and a few inns. The clamber and crush of the sidewalk near the shop had faded and Noah breathed in the peace-filled air. He sensed that Lily would appreciate quiet and he was willing to just let the quiet be. When she tipped her face up at him and smiled, it was sad and he could see the stress around her eyes. Even sad, it was a beautiful smile. His heart thumped hard in his chest again. What would he have to do to see that smile reach her eyes?

"I appreciate this, Noah. I was at my wits' end. At home, I'm the problem-solver, but today... here..."

"No worries. I'm happy to help. Micah's place is right up there past the library."

They crossed the street and turned, passing a few historical buildings, another inn, a church, and a museum before reaching the library. Just beyond the old red brick building was a subtle black sign with gold lettering. *Creature Comforts, Boarding and Grooming.* The house was as subtle as the sign. A nondescript one-and-a-half-story craftsman style with green shingles and a wide front porch, it sat off the street and was shaded by a huge ash tree. Noah, still with a tight hold on Princess, walked up the porch steps and through the front door without knocking. A bell above them gave a pleasant jingle and a man came to the front desk at once.

"Mornin', Micah," Noah said.

Both men broke into broad smiles and clapped their hands

together in a part handshake, part high-five, part hug that spoke of camaraderie. It had been too long since he'd seen Micah. He needed to do a better job of keeping up with his friends. If he didn't have to spend so much time working his business, he'd be able to shake free long enough to meet up for a little pick-up basketball. Soon. He'd have it sorted soon.

"Noah, man, what have you got there?" His friend laughed and pointed at Princess.

"Micah, this is Lily Emerson. She's in a bit of a bind with Princess here and I was hoping you could help her out."

"Sure, sure. What's the problem?" True concern had sobered his face.

She took a deep breath. "I'm sure you've heard that a gentleman died down by the pier last night?" Micah nodded. "Well, he was my uncle, and this is his dog. I need to find a place to board her while I handle things."

Micah's eyes had turned deep with compassion. "I am certain I can help you out. Let me just check..." Micah slipped on a pair of rimless reading glasses and started clicking through screens on his computer. "Here we go. I've had two cancelations, so no problem finding a place for her. She can have the smaller run near the back porch for now and then I'll move her to a little bit bigger one tomorrow after Samson leaves. Come this way and see if that's to your liking."

Micah led the way down a hall to the back door which opened onto a small porch. The massive fenced-in backyard was divided into sections. The sections were divided again into runs of various widths. Most of the runs were occupied and each pup had toys, bones, and a comfortable bed under the roof at the far end.

"This is the only one I have open for today," Micah gestured to a smaller run that started by the back steps and ran along the porch and under an oak tree on the far side of the yard. It was more than big enough for Princess. Micah kept walking, speaking to dogs as he passed each run, reaching in to pat heads and scratch ears.

"Here's the one I can move her into after Samson leaves to-morrow morning." Micah stopped at a larger run. A tiny chihua-hua came bounding out of the dog house at the far end, yipping, its tail wagging so fast it made a fan behind it.

"Samson? Is a chihuahua?" Noah asked, laughter in his voice.

"Hey man, I don't name 'em." Micah turned to Lily. "Will this be alright for Princess?"

"Yes. More than alright. I'm not sure how long I'll have to be in town. How long can she stay?"

"As long as you need," Micah said, compassion softening his voice.

Noah tamped down the sudden, ridiculous spurt of jeal-ousy at seeing his friend charming Lily. What was the deal? He reached out and put his hand on Lily's shoulder. He hoped Micah got the message. At the same time, he hoped it didn't appear as possessive as it felt. He was being absurd and he knew it.

"Thank you," she said to Micah, then turned to Noah, her smile for him mirrored her words.

"We have a couple of dog walkers who will take Princess out multiple times a day. If she's good with other dogs we have playtimes here in the back yard as well. Let's go back in and fill out the paperwork." Micah took Princess from Noah and let her into the run. She pranced around the edge, sniffing and yipping at her next-door neighbor. Noah and Micah chatted as the three of them headed back inside. At the counter, Micah pulled out a packet of papers for Lily to fill out. A few minutes later she wore a dazed expression on her face.

"What does Princess eat? I have no idea. I don't know how old she is or if she's up to date on shots or who her vet is…" Tears clogged her voice.

Noah reached over and squeezed her hand. He turned to Micah and caught his eye. His friend understood. "No problem. We can figure it out as we go," he said, pulling the paperwork back from Lily. He flipped to the last page and handed it back. "Just fill out this part here with your contact information."

Lily jotted down her cell number, not that it would do any

good, and the number at the inn. She handed the paperwork back and took the card Micah handed her.

"Any time you want to check in on Princess or have any questions, just give us a call, OK?"

"Thank you, Mr..."

"Micah. Just Micah. And no problem at all. Happy to help out any friend of Noah's."

"Thanks, man," Noah said, clapping his friend on the shoulder and clasping his hand in a firm shake. "Catch ya later."

"Where are you headed?" Noah asked when they were back to the sidewalk.

"The parking lot behind the police station, but..." She peered down the street. "I'm not sure where we are."

"No worries. This way." Noah started down the hill past the library. "The police station is just on the other side of The Green."

They strolled back past the church and down the street toward the road to the inn.

"I would have been forever trying to retrace my steps," Lily admitted. "I'm glad I wasn't on my own."

"No worries," Noah assured her. She seemed a little less lost, but his protective nature drove him to fix things for her. "Is there anything else I can do?"

She didn't answer right away. Instead, she focused on a point in the distance and rubbed her upper arms. He doubted she was cold. He itched to wrap his arm around her as they walked and offer the comfort she was craving, but he shook it off. No summer girls, even beautiful ones in need of a hug.

"If I had any idea what I need to do I could answer that, but I am at a complete loss. Thank you, though. I... I appreciate the offer."

They had reached her car and Noah opened her door. She paused to smile at him. "Thank you, again."

"If you need anything, call. I know just about everyone on the island."

"I'd believe that."

"I mean it. Call. OK?"

She laughed. "OK."

"Just do the next thing."

"The next thing?"

"Ayuh." He leaned over her door and met her eyes. "You said you didn't know what to do. Just do the next thing."

Do the next thing. What was the next thing? Lily sat watching Noah as he crossed the parking lot. He hunched his shoulders a little, hands in the pockets of his loose jeans. At the curb, he glanced back and she averted her eyes so he wouldn't catch her staring. Pretending she hadn't been admiring the view, she backed up and disappeared into the gridlock that was Summer Harbor during tourist season.

As she let herself back into her room at the inn a sudden thought struck Lily. What had been done with Uncle's personal belongings? Had the police only collected the dog? Or did they also have his briefcase? She imagined it full of sensitive documents from EHI.

Do the next thing.

The next thing would be to get her uncle's things. But how? She wasn't sure, but knew who could help, and called EHI's lawyer in Boston. She breathed a sigh of relief. Olivia had, as promised, called the firm earlier and they were able to put Lily right through to the person she needed to speak to. A much too chipper paralegal named Kean.

"I need to get Herbert Emerson's things and make sure there's nothing sensitive. I know I can't just walk into the police station and take them."

"Ms. Emerson, I have been working on this all morning. I can fax the necessary paperwork to the police, but it boils down to this. Mr. Emerson left you, your sister Olivia, and Alistair Amias his shares in EHI. It places you as the controlling partner," Kean said, in a tone that came across as a bit too happy for the situation.

"Excuse me?" Lily asked. Stunned.

"It's interesting because last week Mr. Emerson was in and asked us to go over his contract with Mr. Amias. We faxed our findings to him at his hotel yesterday. Now that you are the controlling partner that information would apply to you. If the fax is not in his personal belongings, I can forward you a copy."

Lily thanked the young man for his help and ended the call. She sat staring at nothing and trying to process what she had just learned. She, Lilianna Hayes Emerson, was the controlling partner of Emerson Hotels International. Controlling partner. She felt like she couldn't breathe. Placing a hand on her chest Lily ordered herself to get it together.

Do the next thing.

Herbert's briefcase. Anything that had to be dealt with today or tomorrow would be in there. Lily closed her eyes.

Lord, I need You right now. Your guidance. If returning to Boston and running EHI is Your plan for me, I know I can do it with Your help. I know I can't do it on my own, but maybe that's why You allow some things? Things we can't handle so that we have to lean on You? Whatever I do, Lord, I want it to honor You.

She sat for a few more minutes, breathing in deep, calming breaths, before going back to the police station for the second time that day.

"Hello, Thelma. May I speak to Chief Briggs?" she asked the receptionist.

"Of course, Ms. Emerson." The older woman smiled and disappeared into the office behind her for a minute. "You can go right in."

"Ms. Emerson," Chief Briggs said as he half stood from the chair behind his massive desk. His size alone must be intimidating to would-be criminals. Maybe that was how he kept law and order in his town. She imagined that in his younger days he must have had the girls swooning over his broad shoulders and deep dimples, but now his graying hair and saggy jowls gave him a well-worn, tired quality. He took her offered hand in his large, blunt one and gestured to a chair near his desk.

"Chief. Thank you for seeing me."

"Of course. What can I do for you?"

"I'm concerned that there might be time-sensitive papers in my uncle's briefcase. I would like to have it. I spoke to the hotel's lawyer and he is happy to fax over whatever paperwork you need."

"Well, our policy would be to give his personal belongings to next of kin."

"I am next of kin."

"Right. You mentioned that this morning."

"My father was his only sibling. It's just me and my sister now, and she's quite a bit younger. You can check with his lawyer if you need to."

The man nodded and took the number Lily handed him. "With accidental deaths like this, we don't need to hold onto any of his effects."

"Are you sure it was an accident?" She asked, voicing the question drumming in her mind.

"Is there any reason to think it was anything else?"

"I just— Well, I just can't imagine him out walking on the pier," Lily said. "He hated being out of doors."

Chief Briggs picked up his spiral-bound notebook from his desk and flipped it open. "Like I said earlier, the night desk clerk at the hotel says he saw Mr. Emerson leave the hotel. That was a little after midnight. He was alone and did not speak to anyone in the hotel. The clerk said he was pretty sure Mr. Emerson turned toward the pier. Am I correct that your uncle didn't know anyone in town?"

"No one that I know of. I believe this is his first trip to Maine and he had only been here about a day."

"Foul play seems… well… unlikely. I had a guy from the state medical examiner's office here this morning." The man paused as if he wasn't sure she would want to hear the rest and his oversized office chair squeaked as he squirmed.

"What did he have to say?"

"Well, without a doubt, Mr. Emerson drowned. The coroner believes he hit his head on rocks when he fell."

Lily flinched at the thought.

"Were you aware that your uncle had a brain tumor?" Her face must have registered her shock because the police chief hurried on, reading from his notebook again. "I'm not going to pronounce this correctly, but he had cranio...pharyngi...oma. The medical examiner said if the deceased hadn't drowned he would have died from the head trauma. But even if nothing had happened here, your uncle was on borrowed time."

Lily sat in stunned silence. Had he known? If he'd known, wouldn't he have gotten treatment? Or had he ignored symptoms, too consumed by work for self-care? A million questions flooded her mind.

"Did the coroner say anything more about the brain tumor?"

"He mentioned a few symptoms here," Chief Briggs answered and checked his notebook. "Headaches, vision changes, weight gain, and personality changes. He also said that if it had been treated, your uncle would have recovered, but since it had been left untreated..." He trailed off. "Unless you have more information I have no reason to continue investigating."

"No, I don't have any information. It just doesn't... feel right."

"I understand Ms. Emerson." He had taken on a tolerant tone that she found irritating. "These things can be hard to accept. It's human nature to want some explanation. Some reason. That's just how we're wired. Sad as it is, there are times things are... well... just illogical."

Lily couldn't shake the feeling that something wasn't right, but she also couldn't argue with the police chief. He wasn't wrong. What other explanation could there be?

"I was planning on sending a deputy over to the hotel this afternoon to collect all of Mr. Emerson's things. I'll get them to you as soon as I can."

"Thank you, Chief Briggs." Lily stood and extended her hand.

"If you think of anything, be sure to let me know," he said, shaking her hand. She got the distinct impression that he didn't want her letting him know what came to her mind. He came around his desk to show her to the door. "I'll get those things over to you at the inn just as soon as possible."

Satisfied that she would have Uncle's briefcase soon, Lily headed for the inn. It was afternoon by the time Lily, tired and sluggish, climbed the stairs to her room and slumped against the closed door. Her mind wanted to wander to a thousand different places but refused to focus on anything long enough to think about it. Her knees wobbled and she considered sliding to the floor where she stood.

A gentle knock startled her and she dragged herself away from the door so she could open it. Ava waited on the other side with a plate of food in one hand and her cane in the other. The plate was piled with fruit, cold cuts, fresh bread, and cheese, and was accompanied by a tall glass of Ava's spicy sun tea. Lily's stomach let out a tremendous growl in response to the sight. It occurred to her that she hadn't eaten anything all day.

"I thought you might need a little lunch," Ava said.

"Oh, thank you. I just realized I haven't had anything but that cup of tea you gave me this morning."

"I thought as much," Ava said, handing her the plate. She patted Lily's hand before shuffling back to the stairs.

Lily sat at the small table by the window and watched the fog rolling in over the ocean. As emotional and chaotic and downright crazy as the day had been, she had so much to be thankful for and she bowed her head before she ate.

Dear Heavenly Father, thank You for sending people like Noah and Ava to help me today. Thank You for holding me together when I thought I would fall apart. I know that there will be so much to do going forward. Please keep me grounded and give me wisdom.

The quiet peace that settled over her was a welcome change to the turmoil of the day. As she sat and watched the air thicken until she could no longer see the shore, Lily let her mind wander back over memories of Herbert. She struggled to find ones that were even the least bit happy.

He'd been different before her mother died, and Lily focused on those memories. She wondered if Herbert would have stayed the jovial, mischievous, fun uncle had her mother lived? Or was the slip into greed already beginning even then?

The sun sank low on the horizon as hot tears filled her eyes and scalded her cheeks. Tears for the parents she'd lost so many years ago, tears for who Herbert could have been, and tears for the uncertainty of the future. But more than anything, tears for a lost soul. Lily had tried so many times to talk to Herbert about God and His love for her uncle and His desire for all men to be saved. It had always come to naught. Herbert had scoffed that she was weak, she was gullible, she had been deceived. Best case, he had laughed at her, but a few times he had threatened to cut her off from the business. And now he was out of chances.

Lily crawled onto her bed and sobbed.

Frigid fingers and a wet pillow woke Lily the next morning. She had fallen asleep on top of her quilt and last night's warm breeze from the window now felt icy cold. She stretched her stiff limbs and wondered what time it was. From the dull gray light, she guessed it was right around dawn. She wasn't sure how she'd slept. As tired as she was the night before, she had still doubted that rest would come. Each time she had started to drift off a new memory or worry would wash over her and bring her back awake. But during the dark hours of the night, she must have succumbed.

She'd been right about the hour. As she closed the window she could see that the first rays of sunshine had yet to kiss the tops of the trees. Too restless to stay in her room, she peeled off yesterday's clothes and pulled on a thick cashmere sweater and a pair of skinny jeans. They felt warm and familiar. She slipped on her tennis shoes and headed for the backyard. Not enough energy for a run, but maybe a walk would help to clear her head.

The fog from the night before had thinned and now muted

the colors without blocking the view. The yard and the beach beyond were somber. Even the bright flowers in Walter's garden by the back door had taken on lackluster dullness in the gray minutes just before dawn. Did the day know that she needed the calmness? She wrapped her arms around herself as she crossed the dew dampened grass to the gazebo.

Sitting on one of the benches she watched the sunlight work its way down a towering pine near the edge of the yard. She could use a cup of Ava's unique tea to warm her fingers. She would have to learn Ava's secrets, including how she made the tea, before making the inn hers.

Reality hit like a wrecking ball. How could she still be thinking of buying the inn? Her life was now hitched to EHI whether she liked it or not. Her responsibilities were in Boston and to the company. And yet the glimmer of her dream held on like the red glow of a spark rising from a campfire, refusing to die even when battered and blown.

Lord, I want to pray. I need to pray. I need You. But the words won't come. Please hear my heart!

She brushed away the moisture on her cheeks and strained to bring God's word to mind.

From the end of the earth I will cry to You, When my heart is overwhelmed; Lead me to the rock that is higher than I.

Yes, Lord! My heart is overwhelmed! Please lead me to the rock. Please lead me ever closer to You.

The sound of lapping waves and screeching gulls beckoned Lily toward the beach. She picked her way down the path to the water, careful of the loose gravel. High tide had come and gone, but only just. She wandered along the line left by the receding water where bits of seaweed and small shells littered the pebbles.

Tucked along the edges of rocks and the base of the cliff a broad-leafed plant had, despite the harsh environment, not only taken root but flourished. How did it fight against the currents that hammered it day in and day out? How strong must its roots be to hold it fast in the sandy soil? She rubbed her arms, more for comfort than warmth, and turned to gaze out at the sea. She felt numb.

In the distance, lobster boats headed out to their various trap lines. A couple of private yachts were moored offshore and she thought she could make out the vague outline of a massive cruise ship far out to sea. She turned toward town and picked up tiny shells and bits of sea glass as she walked. The sun was up now and the fog was beginning to burn off. She had a clear view of the town pier, boats, and pilings supporting buildings that perched out over the water. She slowed as she realized she was headed for the place where they had found Herbert's body. She stopped, not wanting to continue.

Instead, she turned back toward the cliffs below the inn. The tide was still going out and the rocks were slick with the salty water. Seaweed clung to many of them and lay in thick green-brown mats on the sand. A crab skittered under a thatch of it as she walked past making her jump. City girl. If she decided to live here she couldn't go jumping at tiny crabs on the beach. If she lived here. If...

God, I don't know how to do this new life. I know You are with me and I know You have my best in mind. I wish that Olivia was able to shoulder some of this. I don't see how I can go through this alone. I can't. Only with Your help. I trust You to send help when I need it and give me strength for what I have to face alone.

Happy chatter offshore caught her attention and she turned back to the ocean. A long row of red kayaks, both singles and doubles, was headed toward the beach. The single one in the lead landed well ahead of the others. A stocky man with black hair, a full beard and arms thick with muscle and covered in tattoos, sprang out and pulled his kayak up on the shore.

"Mornin'," he said with a tip of his head and a smile in her direction. He turned back as the next kayak came ashore. With little effort, he pulled it onto the sand so the passenger could get out. One by one they were each pulled in and unloaded. The passengers removed their life jackets and retrieved their dry bags from the storage compartments. They laughed and chatted about birds they'd seen, a funny harbor seal who swam with them for a ways, the beautiful sunrise over the ocean, and the wonderful guides. As the last kayak neared the shore Lily recognized the blonde beard and easy smile.

Noah had seen Lily on the beach long before the tour had come to shore. He couldn't help grinning when he saw her. She waited on the sand where the first kayak had pulled up, her hands in the back pockets of her jeans. Was she waiting for him? He skimmed his kayak along a wave with little effort and hopped out as soon as it came to a stop.

"Hey," he said as he pulled his kayak up to join the first. "How are you doing?" It was a dumb question even to his own ears and he winced. Her eyes were red-rimmed from crying and dark circles marred the perfect skin under them. Her hair was sleep mussed, but he found it adorable. She was more beautiful now, in jeans and a sweater, with no make-up than she had been the first time he met her. He doubted she'd agree.

"I'm alright, I guess." Lily rubbed her arms. "Is this one of your groups?"

"Ayuh, sunrise tour. This morning was perfect. The water was about as still as it gets and the sunrise was beautiful."

"I'm sure it was." Lily cast a longing glance at the kayaks. He knew that look. To be able to paddle out to sea and leave all the worry behind was a call he'd answered many times. He'd felt that call a lot in the last month, but had found little time to answer. Taking a tour out was great, but solitude would be brilliant.

"Would you like to go?"

Lily swung her eyes back to Noah's. "No, I couldn't poss—"

"Sure you could," he smiled, his eyes crinkling. He held her gaze as he called to the man with all the tattoos. "Harley, you all set getting this crew back to the shop?"

"No problem," the bearded man called from the other end of

the line of kayaks.

He held her gaze. It was fun watching her expression change. Hesitant, thoughtful, shy, unsure, interested, excited. Indecision had her biting her lip. After searching his face one last time she nodded. He hadn't realized he was holding his breath. He grinned at her and was amused to see her cheeks pink.

"Folks!" Noah called. "It was an absolute pleasure taking you all out this morning. I'm going to leave you in Harley's very capable hands. Thank you so much for choosing Acadian Adventures." He smiled and shook a few hands. Then spent another few minutes talking to Harley before he scooped up two life jackets and headed in Lily's direction.

"Are you sure?" she asked.

"Oh yeah, I'm sure. The conditions are perfect this morning and I nevah feel like the tours are long enough. Any excuse to get more time on the watah." He winked at her. "You're going to want to take off your shoes and roll up your jeans, otherwise you will get soaked," he said, holding a dry bag out to her for her shoes.

Lily did as instructed and handed Noah back the dry bag before taking the life jacket he handed her. She snapped it into place, but it was still way too big.

"Let me help you get that on," he said and tightened the straps.

"How... Ummm..." She squirmed, her unease at climbing into the boat obvious. "How tippy is it?"

"Not much. Once you get a feel for it you won't tip much at all." He studied her for a second before turning to Harley. "Hey, man, can we borrow your shades?" Without a word, the other man pulled his mirrored aviators off and tossed them to Noah who wiped them on his t-shirt and placed them on her nose. "Trust me, you'll want these."

"Thanks."

She was adorable. He had to shake himself to get back on track. "OK, safety. I do not think you will fall in or tip over, but on the crazy off-chance that you do, I will help you get back into the kayak, OK?" She shuddered and he reached out and tipped her chin up until her eyes met his. "You're not going in the drink, I just have to make sure you know what to do."

"OK."

He walked her through the rest of the procedure for getting her back into the boat if she fell out, how the kayaks maneuver, and safety guidelines. Then he pushed her kayak partway into the surf and steadied it with one hand while offering her the other so she could get in. She smiled and Noah's mouth went dry. He had no problem being everyone's friend, but he didn't let anyone get closer than that. What was it about this girl that made it so hard to remember his rules?

She took his offered hand with a light touch, but when the kayak lurched under her weight it became a vice on his fingers. She dropped into the seat with a panicky yelp.

"It's a lot more stable once you're settled, I promise," he assured her as he held her hand and steadied the boat.

Once she was seated, calm, and smiling again, he pushed her all the way into the water. He watched her awkward attempts to not get pushed back onto the sand. After a few blunders, she started to get a feel for the kayak and pulled herself away from the shore enough to not get washed in with every wave.

"Good job," he called, giving her a thumbs up.

He climbed into his kayak in one fluid motion that had him seated and pushed away from the shore at the same time. Like he'd done a thousand times.

"Ready?" he asked. His smile was sincere and Lily returned it, even if hers was a little forced.

"Ready."

"Let's head southeast along the edge of the island," he suggested as he pulled up alongside her.

"You know best."

They headed out into deeper water. Noah turned his kayak with almost no effort at all. Lily tried but kept ending up pointed in another direction. Noah pulled up alongside her. He could tell she was frustrated, but he had trouble feeling bad.

She had her face scrunched up in a charming frown with her lip caught between two teeth.

"Try holding the paddle out farther away from you." He demonstrated. "After you take a stroke, use the paddle like the rudder on a boat to turn yourself. Once you're moving it will get easier to maneuver."

Lily tried again. This time she went forward and the delight that glowed on her face touched him. He'd wondered the day they met what it would take to see her face light up, see her smile. It was as charming as he had imagined.

The sun was hot and bright, but the wind was cold out on the water and he hoped she was warm enough. He looked over and discovered she had turned her face toward the sunshine. He watched her for a breath of time and then turned his face to the sun as well, allowing the peace of the moment to wash over him.

"Amazing, isn't it?" Noah asked as he drifted next to her.

"Yes," she sighed, opening her eyes.

"The water is where I come when I need to be alone, or think, or just... be."

He pulled himself well ahead of her and spun his kayak around so that he was facing Lily and paddling backward. He grinned and gained speed, pulling away. She pulled harder on her paddle trying to keep up.

"Push with one hand while you pull with the other!" Noah yelled.

Lily adjusted her grip on the paddle. He watched as she concentrated on pushing and pulling. It was like she was trying to pat her head and rub her stomach at the same time. The paddle came up out of the water and splashed back down. She snuck a quick peek at Noah, embarrassment written all over her face. Did she expect to find him laughing at her? OK, yes, he found her amateurish attempts amusing, but he was charmed by her tenaciousness. He waited several yards ahead, not in any hurry to get off the water. Determination bloomed on her face. She worked hard at establishing a rhythm with the paddle. Push, pull, push, pull. Little by little she gained on him until she slid alongside him. He reached out and steadied her kayak, holding it close to his own while they bobbed on the rolling water. She was panting but grinning. She flexed her arms and rubbed her shoulders. He cringed.

"Lookin' good," he winked. "But I'm guessing you can already feel where it's going to be sore tomorrow."

"I don't even care. Your office sure beats mine,"

"Yeah? I think this would beat any office. I can't imagine not being out on the water all the time."

"Rock climbing is my escape."

"For real?" He had a hard time reconciling the prim and proper woman in heels that he had first met with one crawling up the side of a cliff. No doubt she climbed a harmless wall at a gym. "I've been known to go climbing on occasion, too. Don't get me wrong! I love it, but not the way I love the water." He let go of her kayak and pulled his back around to face forward again. "Let's go out around those rocks," he said, pointing to the left away from the shore.

They adjusted their direction and came around the backside of two huge slabs of granite. Waves broke along the edges in frothy plumes. Perched on the top, gulls and cormorants watched them with disinterest. Now and then one would push off the rock and soar up into the sky or dive down into the water after a fish.

"Do the birds live on these rocks?" She asked as she watched them.

"Nah, these rocks are too small for the birds to live on. They stop here to rest or eat, but they nest farther out. There's an island about a mile out that has tons of puffins nesting on it."

"I've enjoyed watching the birds on the beach. I love all the songbirds at the inn, too. There are so many different ones in the gardens and around the house."

"Ava feeds them."

"That doesn't surprise me."

"Are you still thinking of buying the inn?" he asked as they continued around the rocks.

"Honestly? It's hard to think at all right now," she sighed. "I love the inn, but I don't know what tomorrow will bring, let alone next week or next year."

"I suppose you'll need to head home soon."

"I should."

And there it was. The reason he didn't date girls who were only there for the summer. They always left. The few who stuck around year after year, Hope who owned a hotel, Zoe the chocolatier, Belle who made the most amazing cupcakes, were like the sisters he never had. They'd been friends in high school. At one time he'd thought... But he shook the thought from his head. That was in the past and Lily was here now. Would it be so bad to date someone you knew wouldn't be in town for long? Just for the fun of it? If he knew ahead of time that she would leave, he could keep his heart from becoming involved. Right? A whisper of unease rippled through him, but he tamped it down.

"I also have to deal with things here," she continued. "I need to gather Uncle's briefcase and go through the papers in it. I need to make arrangements for his funeral. I've put a lot of the specifics back home on my sister and my uncle's business partner. The lawyers are taking care of their part, too. I guess I'll head back as soon as I have things wrapped up here."

Noah hated how disappointed that made him.

Just be, he'd said. She didn't have many opportunities to *just be*. It felt good. The sun was above the trees now and the fog was gone. The air was warm, but the occasional spray from a paddle splashing or a wave cresting felt frigid.

"There's a beach up ahead that can only be reached by boat. Let's pull in there for a rest," Noah suggested. He pulled ahead and led the way past craggy cliffs and seaweed covered rocks. They came around a steep cliff of red granite and nestled at the base was a stretch of sandy beach. It was surrounded on three sides by cliffs, making ocean access the only way in. Dried seaweed, shells, and driftwood littered the sand alongside broken lobster traps, lost buoys, and bits of rope and nets.

They pulled ashore and Noah helped her out of her kayak. She squished her toes in the warming sand. Did people live like this? Free to kayak to a deserted beach on a Friday morning just because they felt like it? It didn't seem possible. And yet here she was. She tried to push her hair out of her face. Not happening. This was beyond a bad hair day. Had she even brushed it this morning? The wind wasn't helping. Lily pulled an elastic from her jeans' pocket and tugged the whole windblown jumble out of her face and up into a messy bun.

"I'm amazed at the quiet here," she said as she sat down on the sand.

He plopped down next to her, pulled one knee up, and draped his arms around it, relaxed and at ease. She absentmindedly fingered the leathery leaves of a plant growing out of the rocks. She'd seen it before on the beach near the inn. "What is this?"

He leaned forward in order to see around her. "The plant? It's called sea lavender. Why?"

"No reason, just... it grows where it doesn't seem like it should be able to. It's tough."

"That it is. They don't look tough on the surface, but then they surprise you."

She closed her eyes and willed herself to relax. "There is no place back home that is quiet. Even in my condo, there is constant noise. This is..." She trailed off, lost for words.

"Peaceful."

"Yes! And perfect. I'm in awe that God would make a place this wonderful and then share it with me. Even for just a couple of days." She took a deep breath and closed her eyes. When Noah didn't respond she added, without opening her eyes, "I take it by your silence that you don't quite agree with me." There was no malice, or even disappointment, in her words. Just a simple statement.

"No, can't say as I do. So," he asked, changing the subject. "Where is this noisy place you're from?"

"Boston."

He raised his eyebrows in surprise. "You don't sound like most of the folks I know from Bawston."

"Ah, that's what boarding school can do for you. No accents allowed. But I still pahk my cah in the yahd."

He laughed at her thick Boston drawl. "Boarding school, huh? I always thought that sounded... sad. To be away from family I mean."

"It wasn't so bad." Longing edged her voice and she swallowed it before he could hear it. "I lived at home and went to a private school in Boston until my mother passed away. After that boarding school was easier. My father traveled a lot for business and it just ...made sense." She didn't meet his eyes. Didn't want to see sadness, or worse, pity in them.

"What does your father do?"

"He and Uncle were partners."

"Were?"

"Yes. Father passed away while I was still in high school." Noah reached out and squeezed her hand. "He and Uncle started Emerson Hotels over forty years ago. By the time my sister and I came along, it was already a popular luxury hotel chain. Now, Uncle— I mean..." Lily stopped. Uncle wasn't there to run the business anymore. "He was such a hard man. He wasn't kind to anyone, and greed had seeped into every part of his life. But, as vile as he was, he was still family." A tear ran down her cheek. "The medical examiner found a brain tumor. He said they can cause personality changes. I have to wonder how long he had it. I tried so hard to be a light to him. To show him that he didn't have to be that way, live that way. I wanted him to know how much God loved him, but..."

Noah put his arm around her shoulders and drew her to him. Lily rested her head on his shoulder and tried not to cry. Noah was a sweet guy, but she didn't know him. Why was she spilling her life story to a complete stranger? But she knew why. Because she had no one else. Once upon a time, she thought she might have that person. That one you could pour your heart out to. But it had been an illusion. Now she sat on a beach with a handsome stranger's arm around her and tried not to embarrass herself by crying all over him. She admitted, if only to herself, that it felt good to have a shoulder to lean on. At home she was the one people leaned on. She was the strong one. For once she wanted to be the one doing the leaning.

"Sometimes it's grieving what could have been rather than what was," he whispered.

His words mirrored her thoughts from the night before. With them, the tears came uncontrolled. She turned her face into his shoulder and wept. Noah rested his chin on her hair and smoothed his hand up and down her arm. He let her cry. Quiet and strong, he sat on the sand and held her.

As her tears dwindled Lily pulled away. She turned to give him a teary smile and discovered that she had soaked the front of his shirt. Mortified, she covered her eyes. "Your shirt...I'm so sorry."

"No worries." He reassured her with a squeeze of her shoulder before pulling his knees up in front of him and wrapping his arms around them. "Please don't apologize. It'll dry." He was so at home on the beach that Lily couldn't picture him anywhere else. She tried wiping her face but knew it was a lost cause. She stretched her legs out in front of her with her ankles crossed and leaned back on her hands. Out of Noah's peripheral vision, she took the opportunity to take a good, long look at her companion.

His wind-tousled hair was either in need of a trim or an elastic. It curled over the collar of his faded t-shirt and flew out from where he'd tucked it behind his ears. She guessed he liked it that way. So did she. His broad shoulders tensed and relaxed as he shifted his position. He sat staring out to sea and Lily marveled at the fact that they could be there together in silence and yet she didn't feel the least bit awkward or uncomfortable. She didn't feel the need to grasp at conversation just to fill the time.

The silence stretched on, punctuated by gull calls and breaking surf, before Noah turned toward her. Lily feigned interest in the sand on her foot, unwilling for him to catch her watching him.

"Where did you grow up?" she asked.

"Right here in Summer Harbor," he said. "My dad's a lobster-man and my mom's a chef. They moved onto the mainland a few years back." He pointed out across the bay. "Now they live right about... there."

"But you stayed," she said.

"I can't imagine living anywhere else. I think I might have saltwater in my veins."

Lily smiled. She could imagine not wanting to leave. She'd only been here a few days and the place was already feeling like home.

"It's expensive to live on the island though, so I don't blame them for deciding to live elsewhere," he added.

"It must have been amazing growing up in such a beautiful place," she said, wistful longing in her voice.

"Yes. And no. I love it here, but it isn't perfect. During tourist season it gets so busy that it's hard to move around. Good for business, but tough if you're a local needing to live your life. Then the offseason arrives and it's the exact opposite. Nothing's open and three-quarters of the town leaves."

Lily hadn't thought about that. "I can see how that could be hard."

"It can be. There are four groups of people who live on the island. Summer residents who are rich enough to live where they please. Summer residents who come to the island to earn enough over the summer to live a simple life elsewhere in the winter. Year-round residents who can find good work in both summer and winter. And year-round residents who struggle to make the summer earnings last through the long winter. My folks used to be the latter. I make-do easy enough though. Nobody wants work done on their mansions or inns or businesses during the summer so in winter there's a lot of maintenance, repair, remodel-type work. When I can't be on the water, I don't mind that kind of work."

"Walter told me that you work for a local company."

"Yup. Finnley's. Been working winters for them since high school."

If the inn needed work done, call Finnley's, she thought. Got it. Then she gave herself a mental slap. She *had* to stop thinking in terms of owning the inn. It was hard enough to think about leaving as it was. She had responsibilities now that far outweighed staying in Summer Harbor. She needed to wrap her head around that. The realization sobered her.

"I think I should head back," she mumbled.

Unfazed, Noah hopped up from the sand and dusted off his jeans. He offered her a hand up and she found that his fingers were strong and warm and work-roughened, and felt like safety and calm. She didn't want to let go and felt it to her toes when he did.

CHAPTER FIVE

Saturday morning dawned dreary with heavy rain clouds sagging from the sky. The scenery was all still beautiful but far less inviting. Lily lingered in the dining room well after breakfast. Unable to sleep the night before, she had gotten up and started a to-do list. It now lay in front of her on the table. She sat by the window and sipped her coffee, trying to think what else would have to be taken care of right off.

Do the next thing. She smiled, hearing Noah's voice in her head.

Chief Briggs had caught up with her the day before and given her Herbert's wallet, briefcase, suitcase, dog bed, dog food, pet carrier, and medications. Too overwhelmed to deal with most of it, Lily had taken Princess's things to the kennel and left the rest in the trunk of her car. Going through at least his papers was high on her to-do list.

Ava came to the table and sat down in the opposite chair with a heavy sigh. "How are you doing, Dea-ah?"

Lily gave her a weak smile that she hoped came across as sincere. "I'm fine, thank you."

"Have you been able to make all the... arrangements you needed to?"

"Yes. Everyone's been so kind. The funeral home is arranging to have Uncle transported back to Boston. My sister and I decided to skip a grand funeral. The thought of a bunch of people showing false grief was not how we want to say goodbye. My sister is taking care of the details in Boston."

"I suppose you will head home soon?" Ava asked.

"I should, I guess. But... Oh, Ava, I don't know. I feel so... at home here. I don't want to leave."

"Oh, Dea-ah, I know that feeling," Ava reached over and patted Lily's hand. "I never have wanted to leave this place."

"I'm only booked through tomorrow morning. Do you have room if I wanted to extend my stay?"

"Yes, yes, yes. I certainly do," Ava assured her.

"Today, with it being the weekend, I can't do much anyway. The lawyer's office and the bank are closed. I started making myself a list of what needs to be taken care of, but…" she trailed off. "I need to tell you, Ava. I came here to look at this place." Lily gestured with her hand, encompassing the dining room and the grounds out the window. "To buy it."

"Well, land-sakes child! Why didn't you say so in the first place?"

"I don't know. I just wanted to see it before I made an offer on it. Which I did by the way. And then everything happened… so fast. I don't even know if I'll leave my offer on the table."

"I knew that the gentleman who drowned had made an offer on this place. I didn't realize there was more than one."

"Not one, three."

"Three? Well, for heaven's sake!"

"You won't have any trouble selling this place, whether I keep my offer on the table or not," Lily assured the older woman. She hated the thought of causing her worry by mentioning that she might withdraw her offer.

"I never imagined there'd be that much interest in this old place."

"Oh, Ava, this place is exquisite. I'm having a hard time convincing myself not to buy it."

"Is that so?"

"Up here," she tapped her head with her pen, "I know I should go back to Boston. That's the logical thing to do. But our hearts don't follow logic very well, do they?"

"I can't say they do, Dea-ah."

"So here I sit, trying to talk myself into leaving and failing miserably. Did you know that EHI has seventy-two hotels worldwide?" Ava's eyes grew into wide circles and her mouth formed a silent "o". "Yup, seventy-two. I should be happy with seventy-two, but it turns out I want just one. This one."

"And here I thought all the Emerson hotels were in Boston."

"No. Our corporate offices have been in Boston from the beginning. We still own four hotels there, but most are elsewhere."

"How did your uncle get into the hotel business?"

"He and my father started EHI when they were both fresh out of college. They were eager to make a name for themselves. The first place they bought was an old, but elegant, hotel in one of Boston's classier neighborhoods."

"Old, but elegant you say?" Ava gave a wry smile and wriggled her eyebrows as she ran her hand along the windowsill.

Lily chuckled. She liked Ava's pluck and wit. She reached out and ran her own hand along the time-polished wood. For the first time ever she had a glimpse of how her father must have felt with that first hotel. Walking through it, seeing the potential, feeling the history seep into him. She could see him running his hand along a windowsill the same as she was doing.

A memory flitted through Lily's mind. Her father holding her in his arms as they walked through the lobby of a hotel EHI had just acquired in Boston. Was it the one right on the harbor? No. More likely it was the small brick one off of Franklin Street downtown. He'd grinned as he pointed out what would stay and what would go. She'd had her arm around his neck, grinning with him, his excitement contagious.

"I think I fell in love with hotels when my father showed me how to see the potential in them."

"And now you have seventy-two of them."

That she did.

"I'll just keep you in your room until you're ready to head home," Ava said as she got up. "Don't you worry your pretty little head about that."

"Thank you, Miss Ava. You know, you make it almost impossible to want to leave."

❧

The inevitable had been put off long enough. Lily braced herself for the task ahead and retrieved Herbert's briefcase from her trunk. It was heavier than she thought it would be. What did Uncle carry around with him? She took it to her room and cleared the table by the window. She could at least enjoy the view while she sorted through his papers. The combination lock on the case worried her for a moment, but on her second try the lock popped and the top sprang free. A creature of habit, Herbert had used his apartment security code for his briefcase lock as well. Maybe all the times she'd been sent to walk Princess had paid off.

Lily groaned at the stack of papers inside. *Do the next thing.* Noah's voice echoed in her head again.

OK, Lord, help me deal with this.

The first sheaf of papers Lily removed from the case was topped with the bill from Herbert's hotel stay in Summer Harbor. Lily was appalled at the amount he would have spent on a few nights' stay. It was ten times what she would end up spending on her perfect room at the inn. She'd been in his room, albeit briefly, so she knew for a fact it was duller than the one she was sitting in. Darkened by the drapes at the window, it had seemed cold and impersonal. Was that what Herbert thought of as luxury? She shook her head.

On her list, Lily made a note to pay his bill. It wasn't the hotel's fault that he had passed away. Besides, if she ended up buying the inn she wanted to cultivate as much goodwill with her neighbors as possible. Buy the inn. Lily let the words seep into her. The thought brought such peace that she smiled. It would be lovely to stay here. Lovely to stay in Summer Harbor and lovely to stay where Noah was.

Her hands stilled. Where had that thought come from? She whipped her focus back to the papers in her hand. She had no time for getting involved, no matter how handsome or sweet he might be. If she stayed in Summer Harbor, it wouldn't be for a man. It would be to run her business. Besides, her past experience had taught her that she wasn't the type of woman that men wanted for who she was on the inside. Just for who she was on paper.

She shook her head and brought her full attention back to her uncle's belongings. In addition to the bill for the hotel, there was a bill for Herbert's driver, his return airline ticket to Boston with a departure time that had already come and gone, and a memo from Herbert's personal assistant. Lily set the bills in one pile and amended her list to say 'pay bills'.

Pulling a chair over to the table, she brought one bare foot up and sat on the cushy seat while she read the memo.

Mr. Emerson, As you requested I have located Stella Tucker. She is living in Summer Harbor, a small town on the coast of Maine, where she owns an inn. Please find below her address and phone number.

Who was Stella Tucker? Lily reread the memo trying to make sense of it. Nothing. Had Herbert known someone in town after all? She bit her lip in confusion. Setting the memo aside, she scooped up another small stack of papers. A thick stock summary from Herbert's financial planner, charts and graphs of projected earnings and expenses from the accounting department, and the fax from the lawyer's office that the paralegal had spoken of the day before.

Lily made a new stack of business-related documents. Important, but not time-sensitive. The fax, however... She slipped set it on the table and pressed it flat. It contained whole paragraphs of legalese that made little sense to her. Skipping to the end of the third page she found what she was searching for. A summary she could understand.

In conclusion, we are confident that you could move ahead with breach of contract actions against Alistair Amias. His blatant involvement in a rival hotel is a clear violation of section d, sub-section 3, paragraph 7. Please advise how you wish us to proceed.

Breach of contract? Alistair? The man was as by-the-book as they came. In all the years she'd known him she had never even seen him litter. Could the meticulous man who triple-checked reports and verified everything that crossed his desk have breached a contract worth millions? Lily wasn't privy to the terms of their transaction, but it seemed so out of character she didn't believe it could be true. Dumbfounded she reached for the phone and dialed his cell without a second thought.

"Good morning, Alistair Amias."

"Good morning Alistair, it's Lily." What now? She should have thought this through before she called. She chewed her bottom lip as she tried to come up with an appropriate way to ask what on earth was going on. Hey there, are you swindling EHI? Yeah, that's a great way to get a straight answer.

"Lilianna?"

"I've started to sort through Uncle's briefcase..." she trailed off. "Is there any chance that you... that you... might have...?"

"Lilianna, what is it?"

"Is there a possibility that you breached your contract with EHI?"

Silence on the other end had Lily clutching the phone tighter, waiting for an explanation. Her heart pounded. If he had breached his contract she would be expected to deal with it. Alistair was like a father to her. Could she remove him from the company? Oh, please don't be true. Please!

"Not... the way he thought."

"Are you saying the report is accurate?"

"I have been... helping a friend. Herbert accused me of help-ing a rival hotel. It wasn't... there isn't an Emerson anywhere near it. I didn't breach our contract because it isn't a conflict of interest."

"Uncle had a letter from his lawyer in his briefcase. It says he could take action."

"That doesn't surprise me." Alistair's voice had turned hard. "He never wanted me to be a part of EHI, Lilianna. I imagine he had been waiting for a situation like this to come along. I assure you, I am committed to our hotels. I wouldn't work against the company. I always just wanted a chance to be a part of the business."

"I know." Lily closed her eyes. "I know."

"Lilianna?"

"Hmm?"

"You and I, we're not like him."

Tears pricked her eyes. She didn't want to be anything like her uncle. "No, we aren't. I'll be in touch if I find anything else."

She hung up the phone and returned to the open briefcase. The edge of a blue envelope sticking out of the back-most pocket of the lid caught her eye. It was another of her uncle's infamous summons' envelopes, but this one seemed worn. She reached into the pocket and extracted three envelopes. Two blue ones and a white one. The top envelope, the one she'd first seen, was sealed and unaddressed. She tucked it behind the other two and studied the next envelope. The white one. It was dog-eared and discolored from handling. Lily fingered the edge where the envelope had torn, feeling like a voyeur. She turned the envelope over and felt the world stop spinning. It was postmarked twenty years before and addressed to her uncle... in her mother's beautiful cursive handwriting.

CHAPTER SIX

ily's fingers trembled as she withdrew the slip of stationary from the envelope. It had the feel of having been read
over and over. The creases had begun to tear where they
had been unfolded and refolded again and again. The faint smell
of age clung to the paper.

Back in Boston, on the top shelf of her closet, was a wooden
box holding the entire sum of things she had of her mother's.
A pair of diamond earrings, two birthday cards, a handful of
family photographs, small trinkets and mementos, and a letter
her mother had written her the summer she turned eight and
could go to sleep-away camp for the first time. That letter had
the same tattered edges and torn creases. And had them for the
same reason. Read, reread, memorized.

With great care, Lily unfolded the letter and, taking a shud-
dering breath, began to read.

*Herbie, Sweetheart, I'm so worried about you. The fact that we
haven't seen you since Christmas has us both very anxious. I know
that Prescott keeps both of your feet on solid ground. He does the
same for me. I need it as much as you do. I guess you and I both need
Prescott. But Herbie, I also need you. I shouldn't, but I need someone
who sees me even when I feel invisible. That has always been you. I
can't imagine that after three years you'd stay away because of my
foolishness. You don't know how many times I wished we could have
everything back to the way it was before. But you've always been in-
credible at making things right again, so it must be something else.
What's going on? You won't return our calls. Whatever it is, we'll get
it sorted. I promise! You have to know we both love you ever so much.*

I'm coming to your place on Saturday. I need to see with my own eyes that you're OK. Love you Bub!

Lily pressed a hand to her lips. She picked up the envelope and took a closer look at the postmark. February 22. The car crash that had taken her fun, vivacious mother had happened on Saturday, February 28th. Her mother had been driving to visit Herbert.

Tears soaked her cheeks. Her father had never spoken of the events surrounding his wife's death. Had he known she'd been on her way to visit his brother? Had Uncle known she died on the way to see him? He must have if he'd kept the letter.

Lily reached for the third letter. It was tucked in a familiar blue envelope, but it had been opened. Not as dog-eared as the one from her mother, but worn on the edges as if it had been read numerous times as well. It was addressed to her mother in her uncle's harsh script, but it had no stamp or postmark. She slipped the letter out and opened it next to the one from her mother.

February 28th
Margo,

I've been waiting hours for your promised visit. I don't know why, in the end, you decided not to come, but it's just as well. I'm afraid I've made quite a mess of things. I don't want to look you in the eye and tell you what I've done. My foolishness, as you put it, was only the beginning. And now, I couldn't bear to see you disappointed in me, even though I deserve it. Oh, how I deserve it. I long to be the man you used to see when you looked at me. You still make me want to be better, do better. Without that, without you, I have no hope.

Bub

Lily fingered the letter. It was as if it had been written by a stranger. Her mother's letter had sounded like her. She could see her mother's smile as she wrote it, and the concern in her voice. Not Herbert's. Had she ever known the man who wrote it? He sounded... contrite. No. She did not know that man. The last line drew her eyes again. *Without you, I have no hope.*

"Oh, Uncle," she whispered as fresh tears filled her eyes.

She slipped the letters back into their envelopes and returned them to the briefcase. The second, unaddressed, blue envelope lay on the table and Lily turned it over. It was thicker than the others and sealed tight. She debated returning it to the briefcase with the others, but curiosity was a strong pull.

The pencil drawer in the corner writing desk produced a letter opener. She slipped it into the corner of the envelope, but tears blurred her vision. With trembling fingers, she set both down on the table. She couldn't do this. Not yet. Desperate for air, she grabbed her sweater and bolted from the inn. She wiped her damp cheeks as she escaped down the drive.

The smell of lilac blossoms drifted on the breeze. The shells covering the driveway crunched under her feet. A long way out to sea a foghorn bellowed. It was all lost on her. With the singular focus of finding a distraction, she headed for the commotion of Main Street. Her mind spun out of control. More questions than answers flooded her, one after another.

The gray-flannel fog that had wrapped the town earlier that morning had lifted to a fine mist rolling in off the harbor. The sun trying to break through had driven hopeful tourists to the streets. The sidewalk was packed. Within minutes Lily had lost herself in the crush of people. They moved in and out of stores, congregated outside art galleries and ice cream shops, and jostled their way in and out of eateries. Despite the throng of people Lily had never felt more alone.

"Lily!"

She must have heard him because she stopped and turned, searching the crowd. Noah jogged up the edge of the street, deftly avoiding parked cars, dogs on leashes, and oblivious pedestrians. His heart slammed in his chest. The woman was gorgeous. Her delicate smile sparkled in her gray eyes, her hair blew where the wind had freed it from her ponytail, and her cropped pants hugged her curves. She met his eyes and her smile deepened.

"Hi," she greeted as he came alongside her.

She'd been crying again and it made his heart hurt. "Mind if I join you?"

"Sure. I'm just... I don't even know. I just needed to get out of my room for a few minutes."

The sun beat down on them, warm and pleasant. They strolled, chatting about the weather, the tourists, and the tides. Nothing that mattered at all. Noah had called Lily's name without even thinking when he saw her on the street. He felt like a lovesick teenager, excited to see his crush. He didn't even care. The sight of her had drained him of logical thought. He was, in fact, headed in the opposite direction. It didn't matter. He'd walk all the way around the island if it meant breathing in the smell of her. Like fresh, line-dried sheets on a warm spring night with his mother's lilacs blooming outside his open window. Her expressive eyes gazed up at him and he glimpsed blue and lavender flecks in them. They made eyes that color?

He took her elbow to steer her through the crowd and couldn't bring himself to let go. As she slowed to admire a piece of art in the Whippoorwill Gallery's front window, his fingers slid down her arm to lace with hers. She stilled but didn't pull away. His eyes traveled down to where their hands joined. He hesitated and then took a firmer hold.

She was silent as they continued walking and he started second-guessing himself. Had he just made things awkward? But she dragged her thumb across the back of his hand and in that one motion drained all thought from his head. Had she just asked him a question?

"Hmmm?" he mumbled as he attempted to refocus his brain.

"I asked if we were supposed to turn there?"

Carriage Street. His Street. Work. Tour. He tried to put his thoughts back in order while soaking in the feel of her delicate palm against his calloused one. "Nah, the tour doesn't leave for a few hours. I've got time."

She smiled and his heart thumped hard in his chest. Much more of that and he was a total goner.

"Tell me more about growing up in Summer Harbor," she asked as they continued toward the water.

"My favorite times of year here have always been May and October. In May the weather is warm enough to get on the water, but most of the tourists haven't shown up yet."

She turned, taking in the press of tourists. When she faced him again there was a questioning look in her eye.

"This? This isn't busy. You wait until the middle of July. They have to close the park because there are too many people. Every inn, hotel, motel, and bed and breakfast is booked solid. It gets crazy. But by the first of October, most of the tourists have gone home and, while it is cold at night, the days are still hot and sunny."

"Walter mentioned you live at Acadian Adventures?"

"Sure do. I live in the attic above the shop. The guys who work for me live on the second floor. Quick commute," he added with a wink.

"How many people work for you?"

"Well, let's see. Harley, who you met yesterday, Jeremiah, Owen, Sam, and Gage. So five employees. Oh, and Gemma, our cashier slash everyone's kid sister." He said the last bit with undeniable affection.

"And you all live above the shop?"

"Well, not Gemma, she and her mom live out near the park. And Harley—"

"Black beard, lots of tats?"

"That's the one. He has a place out past the kennel, but it's a fixer-upper and I doubt he'll be in it any time soon. So yeah, me and five others for now. But it's cool. We're kind of a big family, all watching out for each other."

"That sounds... nice," she said. Her voice had turned wistful and Noah wondered what he'd said to change the mood.

"I grew up rock climbing, hiking, biking, stuff like that. I'd like to expand the shop to offer those types of tours, too." Saying it out loud made it sound so doable. Yet it was a dream that seemed to hover just outside his grasp. What was it going to take? He swallowed the worry that had snuck up on him. He was walking beside a beautiful woman, holding her hand, and worrying. Get it together, Kingsley!

They'd reached the end of Main Street, but instead of turning right toward the pier, Noah tugged her across the street and out onto one of the long wooden moorings where small sailboats and dinghies were tied up. He leaned back against the railing and turned her to face him. The wind blew more of Lily's hair free and Noah reached out to tuck it behind her ear. He let his hand linger on her cheek.

"How are you doing?" he asked.

"Oh, I'm fine," she said, not meeting his eyes.

"No, how are you doing for real?"

Her silvery eyes met his hazel ones. Emotions swam in them that he couldn't read and she couldn't hide.

"I'm overwhelmed," she admitted and her voice caught.

He pulled her into his arms and rested his chin on her hair. He felt her melt into him. She was soft and warm against the cold ocean breeze. She let him hold her and just for a minute he let all the reasons he shouldn't be holding her fade away.

"Remember, just do the next thing," he whispered into her hair.

She giggled and he leaned her back far enough to see her face.

"What?"

"I hear your voice when I start to stress about what to do. *Do the next thing*," she mimicked.

"Is that how I sound?"

"No, just in my head." She grinned up at him as she leaned back in his arms. Wow, it did feel good to see a bona fide smile on her lips, and it felt even better knowing he put it there.

Lily disentangled herself from his arms and stepped away. He felt a chill where she'd been pressed against him. She rubbed her arms, so he was sure she felt it too. He hoped anyway.

Noah checked his watch and sighed. "I kind of need to head back. Tour and all."

"No worries. I should get back to sorting through papers anyway." She sounded as disappointed as he felt.

"Are you?... do you?... do you think?..." Get a grip! When had he turned into a tongue-tied buffoon? He knew when. The moment she'd grinned at him. He tried again. "Will you be doing that all evening? Or... could we grab dinner?"

She considered him for a second before answering. "I do have to eat," she teased.

His grin was infectious. "Sweet! My sunset tour doesn't get back until eight. Meet me at the Hungry Whale around eight-thirty?"

"That sounds wonderful."

They cut back across the street and Noah led her through a maze of side streets, alleyways, back yards, and driveways, emerging onto Carriage Street right across from the shop. They crossed the street and Noah paused long enough to turn her toward him and run his hands up her arms to her elbows.

"See you in a few hours," he murmured.

For a split second she had thought Noah would kiss her. Her face must have given away her unease, because instead he flashed her his knee-weakening grin, winked and then loped out of sight between his building and The Hungry Whale.

She picked up a sandwich and a latte from the corner coffee shop on her way back to her room. The breeze that moved the gauzy curtains had lost its damp quality as the sun had won out. She spread her little picnic on the table and grabbed the phone.

"Hello?" Olivia answered in a polite, business-like tone that Lily didn't recognize.

"Liv? It's Lil."

"Oh, Sis!" Olivia's voice changed in an instant. Businesswoman Olivia Emerson was gone, replaced instead with spunky little sister Liv. "How are you? What's going on there? I hate that I can't get you on your cell. That place must be down-right primitive. Please tell me they have electricity."

"Yes Liv, they have electricity," Lily chuckled. "It's not so bad. You know, I haven't even missed it."

"OK, now I know you aren't my sister. What have you done with her? Do I need to come there and rescue her?"

Lily let out a full-on laugh.

"But seriously. How are you?"

"I'm..." Noah's face flashed in her mind's eye and she couldn't stop the smile that spread through her entire body.

"Ooooooooo!" Olivia squealed. "Tell all! Who is he?"

"Gosh, how do you do that?"

"I'm your sister. I know you."

"Alright, alright. I give up." Lily got comfortable in her chair and pulled her sandwich over. "There's a gentleman who owns a business here in town and... well... we're going to dinner to-night."

"Eeeeeeeeep! Tell me ev. er. ry. thing!"

Lily laughed. "There isn't a whole lot to tell. He's been ever so sweet since Uncle passed away, and he suggested we grab din-ner tonight after he gets off work."

Olivia puffed out an exasperated sigh. "Sis, it's awful hard to live vicariously through you with scant details like that."

Lily rolled her eyes. Like Olivia had to live vicariously through anyone. The girl must have guys lined up down the street. If anything it was the other way around. Lily sighed around a bite of her sandwich. "He's not a Christian, so that's a serious sticking point. Plus, you know me. You know I don't date and you know why. I'm just enjoying having a friend while I muddle through all of this."

Olivia was quiet for a beat. "I do know. But Lil... Would it be so bad? Fall in love, fund the guy's dream, live happily ever after?"

"That's just it Liv. It goes more like he pretends to love me, I fund his dream, he leaves, no happily ever after for me."

"I can't believe that's every guy."

"I'm sure it isn't *every guy*, but how do I know which one is and which isn't? How do I know who's just after what I can provide, or at least what they think I can provide, and who's for-real interested in me? I can't. What I can do is enjoy spending the evening with Noah and not read anything into it."

"And him? Is he reading anything into it?"

"I don't know." Lily puffed out a sigh. "I'll just have to make sure he gets it. That he understands I don't date."

"Sounds like a *fun* evening."

"A simple 'have fun' without the biting sarcasm would be nice."

"Not a chance. I mean, where would I be without my biting sarcasm? Now, on to more important things. What are you going to wear?"

Lily rolled her eyes. "Would you accept 'I have no idea'?"

"Not on your life!"

"Alright…" Lily swallowed her bite of lunch and padded to her closet. "My choices are Navy slacks and blazer, white sundress covered in dark red sweet pea blossoms, black pencil skirt and yellow sweater, or jeans."

"The skirt and sweater."

"You think so?" Lily asked as she pulled it from the closet.

"Positive. The slacks scream business lunch, the jeans… just… no… and the sundress is more… second-date worthy," Olivia added with a mischievous smile evident even through the phone.

"Liv, it isn't even a first date! Just friends having dinner."

"If you say so."

"I say so!"

"Whatever. OK, now, how about shoes?"

"I have to wear heels. He's so tall and I'm, well… not."

"Maybe he likes petite girls?"

"You mean, still being able to shop in the kids' department is attractive? Huh. Who knew?" Lily scowled. "No, I'm wearing my yellow Jimmy Choos'."

"Have it your way. You know it doesn't matter, right? I'm sure this guy is half in love with you already."

"Olivia!"

"Just sayin'!"

Lily rolled her eyes as she held up the skirt and sweater in front of the mirror. She studied her reflection for a second before setting them on the bed and going back for the pants and blazer. She didn't want Noah to get the wrong idea. This wasn't a date.

"Don't you dare switch to the suit."

Lily snatched her hand back from the closet. "How did you…? Can you *see* me?"

"No, I can't see you. I *know* you!"

"Fine."

There was a weighty pause in their conversation, and then "Lil?"

"Yes, Liv?"

"How are you, for reals?"

Lily sank onto the edge of the bed and squeezed her eyes shut. "Fine, I guess. I feel like there are a million things to do and I can't focus on any of them long enough to complete them. I know I have to come home and take on the daunting responsibilities at EHI. And then I look around here and this *feels* like home. More than Boston has since… well, since mom."

Olivia exhaled a shaky breath. "I get that."

Lily put her hand over her eyes. How could Olivia 'Party Girl' Emerson "get it"? She floated through life on a cloud of irresponsibility and only touched down in the real world for fun little discussions like the one they'd just had. Clothes and shoes and cute guys. No business meetings or office hours for Liv. Lily tried not to be jealous of her sister's ability to shirk her obligations in favor of what she wanted. Lily let out a heavy sigh. Maybe she should take a page from her sister's book for once.

"Lil, I gotta run. Have a great time on your not-date. Call me tomorrow. I want *all* the details! Love you."

"Love you, too, Liv," Lily replied, but the line was already dead.

Warm light from The Hungry Whale poured out through the floor-to-ceiling windows facing the sidewalk. Street lights twinkled, laughter, and noise spilled out of open doorways up and down the street.

Lily fidgeted as she stood outside the restaurant waiting for Noah. She felt nervous, but that was ridiculous because this was just two new friends having dinner. She smoothed her slim skirt for the umpteenth time and adjusted her sweater. Was she overdressed? Olivia had nixed the jeans, but Noah was bound to show up in his daily uniform of loose jeans and sun-faded t-shirt straight off the water. She glanced at her watch to see if she had time to go back to her room and change. 8:32. Nope.

"Hungry?"

His deep voice coming from the dark shadows in the alley at the side of the restaurant made her jump, while the black dress shirt and slacks, silver tie, and hair combed back and secured with an elastic were enough to set an entire kaleidoscope of butterflies loose in her stomach. Then he flashed his charming smile and her knees wobbled.

"Woah," he said as he caught her elbow to steady her. She hoped upon hope he thought she'd tripped and not gone all weak-kneed at his smile. It seemed plausible, given their track record. Right?

Noah skirted the line waiting for tables and caught the eye of a distinguished-looking gentleman at the back of the room. Mr. Tall-Dark-and-Handsome nodded toward a small table tucked into a corner. "I, for one, am starving," Noah said as he pulled out a chair for her.

Completely charmed and not a little impressed, Lily smiled up at him. Not a date. Not a date. Not a date. It wasn't working. This felt like a date. She was so nervous she wasn't sure she could eat.

The gentleman from the back materialized at their table with menus.

"Welcome."

Noah rose to his feet and they performed the part hug, part handshake, part chest bump that Lily had come to recognize as a masculine greeting here. It was so different from the way men in her sphere greeted each other. She had to hide a chuckle behind her menu as she imagined two executives from EHI greeting each other with hugs and shoulder slaps. A firm, but not too firm, handshake. A nod of the head. A comment on the weather or the latest Celtics' score. But no hugs. The authenticity of the camaraderie that Noah shared with the men in his life warmed her heart. He was a man's man. A friend. There was nothing forced or fake in him.

"Lily, this is my friend Parker. Parker, Lily Emerson."

"A pleasure to meet you." The man said in a deep, easy-going voice. She took his offered hand. It was large and warm and enveloped hers. He flashed her a toothy smile that she was sure made all the female tourists swoon.

"Likewise."

"Parker owns this place. He and I have been best friends since grade school."

"It's lovely," she said. And it was. All glossy wood and mirrors to make it appear more substantial than it was. Small and large tables mixed throughout the room, each topped with candles, a vase of flowers, and black napkins. The place had a pub vibe, with chunky chairs and wood floors. However, where the bar should have been there was a lunch counter and where the liqueur would have graced the back wall, there was bold art dominated by sea glass.

"Thank you." Parker nodded to Noah as he retreated.

Lily opened her menu but stole a peek at her dinner companion over the top. Her heartbeat hammered in her chest. It had never felt this way... before. In the past, polite dinner conversation, shared business interests, and similar five-year-plans had been adequate. He'd been good-looking and she knew they'd looked good together, even if she was fifteen years his junior. She had been comfortable around him. He had been pleasant and well-mannered. But for the life of her, she couldn't remember ever blushing at the mere sight of... No, she wasn't going there. Not tonight. Tonight she was going to enjoy the evening with Noah. Just friends having dinner. Not a date.

"How was—?"

"How was—?" they both began. They laughed and Noah reached for Lily's hand across the table. Her skin tingled where his fingers touched hers. An instant of panic danced across her chest. He did think this was a date! Olivia had been right. She had to make him understand, but before she could explain, he began tracing her fingers with the pad of his thumb.

"How was the rest of your afternoon?"

Little electric shocks running up her arm made it hard to concentrate on his words. Her cheeks pinked. Whether from the blundered conversation or his touch on her skin she wasn't sure. "It was... long." Concern flared in his eyes, so she hurried on. "A lot to do and it was hard waiting for dinner." Great. Now she was flirting. Nice way to make sure he knows this isn't a date, she groaned inwardly.

"I may or may not have hurried that last tour along." He winked and released her hand to pick up his menu.

Parker returned to fill their water goblets and take their order. Broiled fish-of-the-day with wild mushroom risotto and candied carrots with rosemary for Noah, and pan-seared sea scallops in a bed of spinach and creamy paprika sauce for Lily.

With the menus gone Noah reached for her hand again and rubbed his thumb along her knuckles. "You're beautiful to-night."

She could feel a blush bloom across her cheeks at the atten-tion. "You clean up pretty good, too. I have a confession. I had no idea what I should wear and almost came in jeans and a t-shirt."

"You would have been beautiful in that, too." Her eyes rolled and he laughed. "It's true."

"You are good for a girl's ego," she chuckled.

❦

Their food hadn't even arrived yet and he already wished the evening didn't have to end. "Do you have plans for tomorrow?"

"I should finish going through Uncle's briefcase."

"Is there a lot to deal with?"

"So much." He saw her shoulders slump with the load of it and wished, not for the first time, there was a way he could carry some of it for her. "I still can't believe he fell off the pier."

"It can be hard to wrap your head around it when a loved one is gone," he soothed.

"Yes, but I meant I literally can't believe that he fell off the pier. Uncle hated being outdoors and walking and fresh air and wind and... Why would he go to the pier, on foot, in the middle of the night? It just... it wasn't in character for him to be there. However, I talked to Chief Briggs yesterday and he assured me that there was no evidence of foul play."

"Do you have any? Evidence?"

"No," she sighed. "He didn't know anyone in town, so how could there be?"

He was about to speak when their food arrived. He watched as she bowed her head, and braced for the uncomfortable feeling he was sure would hit him. But it never came. It seemed so natural for her to pray. The same as when she'd spoken of God on the beach. Not preachy or rehearsed, not done for show, but more like it was just a part of who she was. For the first time he could ever remember, he was interested in knowing more.

"Oh, my word," she breathed after taking a dainty bite of her scallops.

He chuckled. "Parker never disappoints."

"You can say that again!"

"He owns the place, but he's also a chef and comes up with all the recipes himself. When it gets crazy over the summer he spends as much time in the kitchen as he does out here."

"Well, this is amazing."

He took a couple of bites of his fish, studying her across the table. "The next thing is the briefcase?"

"Before I try to tackle that I need to be fed."

"I know a great breakfast place."

She laughed. "Sorry, I meant spiritually. I want to go to church in the morning."

"Ah. Well... I don't have much experience there, but Parker goes to that white one up near the kennel. I'll admit to him dragging me along quite a few times as a kid." He paused, not believing the words that formed on his tongue, and even more surprised when they tumbled from his lips. "Tell me more about Lily Emerson the Christian."

She almost choked on her dinner. The disbelief on her face made him wince. Yeah, he was just as surprised the words had left his mouth as she appeared to be. What was he thinking? Perhaps he wasn't.

She studied him with an odd expression of confusion and tenderness. He tried to think of a way to change the subject, but his mouth had gone dry and he couldn't think of anything to say.

She dabbed the corner of her mouth with her napkin before continuing. "Well," she paused again and studied him before continuing. "My mother used to take me to Sunday school and things like that. I don't remember too much of it. She died when I was pretty young."

Noah made a noise of sympathy deep in his throat. He couldn't even fathom not having his mom growing up.

She shrugged. "After Mom passed away, Dad threw himself into work and wasn't home very often. Enter boarding school. I was a broken girl desperate to fill a gaping hole in my heart. I just didn't know how. The school had this wonderful chaplain. He had a green thumb and I would go sit with him in the gardens around the chapel while he worked and he just let me be... me."

Noah was silent, picturing a young, broken Lily sitting on the grass talking to the chaplain. She'd have been the kind of girl he would have dragged home from school for a little of his mom's 'kitchen therapy'. His mother had helped a number of his friends in middle and high school mend broken bits over cooking lessons and enormous slices of chocolate cake.

"He would weed and plant and dig, and I would talk and talk and talk. One day I told him that I hated the hole inside me left by my mom's death and my dad's obsession with his business. He told me that the hole wasn't caused by my parents, but was there because I hadn't let God fill it up. He told me how much God loved me and desperately wanted to fill that hole. Once I let God fill up the hole and mend the broken edges, I was a new person."

His hand still rested on hers and he felt her fingers tremble. He tightened his hold on her hand and ran his thumb across the back of it. She brought her eyes up to meet his again. The question of whether or not she'd scared him off yet was written on her face. Not a chance.

"Anyway, that's me. Peculiar Christian girl," she said with a nervous laugh.

"Normal's boring, I'm becoming partial to peculiar."

She rolled her eyes again. "Enough about me, who is Noah Kingsley?"

"Gee. Who am I?" He thought for a minute. How did he put who he was into words? She seemed so put together, so sure of who she was. He felt like he was a bunch of jumbled parts waiting for the final piece to make them all fit. He looked into the distance, not seeing, thinking. "I am a kayaker. I am a business owner. I am a son. I am a friend." He wanted to say more but stopped there.

"A kayaker, huh? I would NOT have guessed that," she teased.

A hearty chuckle erupted from deep in his chest and he leaned back in his chair. Her laughter had put him at ease again. "Ayuh, the summer I turned fifteen I got a job bussing tables at the restaurant where my mom worked. At fifteen I could only work six hours a week. I saved every penny and by the end of the summer I had enough to buy my first sea kayak. I was hooked from the first moment on the water."

"When did you get the idea for Acadian Adventures?"

"About seven seconds after I got into the kayak for the first time." He laughed at the memory. "I started planning over the winter and by the following summer I had a basic business plan. It took me ten years to put the plan into action, with a lot of changes from that fifteen-year-old's version. Would you believe it if I told you my original plan included a submarine?"

She chuckled and nodded. Yes, she could picture fifteen-year-old Noah thinking a submarine was a good idea. An awareness that Noah was not like other men she knew washed over her like a cold wave. It startled her to realize that he was a simple man, hardworking, focused. Her heart squeezed. The men in her world were ladder climbers. With that came a certain amount of disregard for others. That wasn't Noah.

"I had a good time tonight," he murmured, his voice warming her. "Lily... I... Well, I'd like to see you again."

"Noah..." She slipped her fingers from his grip. *Lord, give me the words.* She'd never had trouble turning down an interested suitor. Not since... But it didn't matter if it hurt, or how much she wanted to pretend she didn't have rules. She had to. For her survival, her sanity. "I don't really... date. I..." She began to worry the edge of her napkin. How could she explain? She didn't let relationships get even this far and the reality of having to distance herself now stung.

At her hesitation, he continued. "I'd like the chance to get to know you. I'm OK with whatever that looks like. I'll still be your friend. I'll still be here. No pressure."

She lifted her eyes from her napkin and met his. Was he being sincere? She couldn't tell, but she hoped so. What she wouldn't give to have a friend right now. Could she protect her heart while still accepting his friendship? She could if she could make him understand. She took a steadying breath. "Who I am does not lend to romantic relationships." That sounded vague, but he didn't push, just waited like he had all the time in the world.

Curious, but patient. She tried again. "What I mean is that men aren't interested in the real me and I have learned to keep my distance." Now he seemed confused.

This was getting worse by the word. *Lord, please! I'm not saying what I need to say! Help me!* She cast her eyes around the room in dismay. When she looked back at Noah he was still listening, waiting for her to continue. She took a breath that caught in an embarrassing hiccup.

"Hey, it's OK," he soothed.

This time the words flowed. "Who I am is a Boston businesswoman. A sister. A hotel heiress. And a Christian."

Noah's expression had taken on a contemplative edge. "The Boston part is a little bothersome, but not a deal-breaker."

She laughed. "That's what you took away as the biggest challenge from that list?"

He grinned and brushed the back of her hand with his fingertips again. "OK, so help me understand who you are and why you don't date."

Well, he'd asked for it. "I am Lily Emerson, a businesswoman who, before coming to Summer Harbor on Tuesday, spent long hours in a top-floor, corner office, or flying from hotel location to hotel location taking care of everything from construction oversight, to staffing, to guest relations, to whatever Uncle needs— needed... me to do."

"And is that still who Lily Emerson is?"

"What? Of course. Maybe even more so now that Uncle..." She trailed off.

"I'm just saying, two days ago you made an offer on a place here in Summer Harbor."

"Point taken." Now she was the confused one. Was she still that corner office, top-floor, businesswoman? She rolled the term 'inn owner' around her mind instead. She liked it. It gave her a feeling of rightness and contentment. She blinked away the thought. "I don't know. Let's leave that one for now. It's a ways down the list anyway."

The busboy had cleared their plates and Parker arrived with

coffee. She paused until he had walked away. Noah gave her an expectant smile. He seemed to be honest in his interest in what she had to say. That was new. In business, men listened to her because of who she was. In her personal life, however, she had little experience with a man wanting to hear what she had to say. Before... before it had been all about him. What he thought and what he wanted. This listening ear was new. And empowering. She liked it.

"I am a sister. My younger sister Olivia graduated from college a year ago. It's been just the two of us for so long... I feel responsible for her. She likes to party and is a magnet for trouble. I know I need to focus on her more."

"Interesting." That was it? He winked at her. "I learned to share in kindergarten."

Of course he did. She narrowed her eyes at him but had to laugh. He was good at lightening the mood. Alright, she might let him talk her out of the first two reasons she'd given, but the last two were the clinchers. They were the reasons she had rules, and the reasons she was alone. He might not be easy to intimidate, but the next one sent men in one of two directions. Either for the hills or for her pocketbook.

"I am the heir to Emerson Hotels International, a multi-million-dollar corporation. And if that wasn't intimidating enough, my uncle just passed away, so..."

"So?"

His calm unnerved her. "So... I don't date because guys don't see me, they see what they think I am."

"Which is?"

"They think I'm a funding source."

"I don't see that when I look at you." Hurt that she would even think that danced across his face. Maybe Olivia was right. Maybe not all guys saw dollar signs when they looked at her. She didn't want to judge Noah by the actions of others, but the past had taught her well to keep her distance, build walls, hold people at arm's length. She had to protect herself.

"Even if guys can get past the first two and I find a way to get

past the third, the last reason seals the deal. I am a Christian."
She waited for his reaction. Noah, however, just sat waiting for
her to continue. "What I mean is, I won't... can't date a man who
doesn't share my faith."

His eyes took on a pensive expression as he held her gaze.

CHAPTER SEVEN

She was selling herself short if she thought heiress, businesswoman, and sister was all she was. He wasn't sure about the Christian part, that was new territory. He had friends who were Christians, but even though he wasn't, they still hung out with him, so he didn't see the problem. That being said, he understood having reasons not to date. He wished he could put into words how monumental it was for him to even ask her out in the first place. No summer girls meant no broken pieces when they left. After... last time... he wouldn't risk that again. Yet here he was, out on a date with a pretty girl who, in all likelihood, wasn't sticking around. Maybe she had the right idea.

Or maybe he just needed to be patient. "May I walk you back to the inn?"

"Yes, please."

Her relief was obvious, but whether from him changing the subject or from not walking home alone he couldn't tell. Did it matter? He stood and pulled out her chair as she stood. With his hand on the small of her back, he guided her toward the door, slowing to wave goodnight to Parker and thank the young man bussing tables. He remembered those days and slipped the boy a generous tip.

The night had quieted. Stores had closed, tourists had headed to bed. Noise still poured from the doorways open to restaurants and bars. Street lights cast the sidewalk in a warm glow. The breeze off the ocean chilled the air enough that Lily shivered despite her sweater. Noah took the opportunity to drape a nonchalant arm over her shoulders. She moved closer to him and his heart squeezed at the feel of her under his arm. She fit as if she'd been made to go there.

"I understand you aren't interested in dating right now, but I hope we can continue to be friends."

"Of course," she smiled up at him.

The coffee shop was dark as they turned the corner toward the inn. The street lights were few and far between. Lily shuddered.

"You OK?" he asked.

"I'm glad you offered to walk me home. I'm... a little afraid of the dark. Walking back alone would have been brutal. Note to self, take the car next time." she turned teasing eyes on him. "Or keep you around."

"I think you need me. I mean, who will catch you when you trip and keep the boogeyman away if I'm not here?"

They had reached the front steps of the inn and Noah stopped. He turned Lily to face him and had a momentary thought that he should lean in and kiss her. She would taste like the after-dinner mints they'd had with their coffee. Sweet and tangy. It was hard to just smile instead. "I hope you sleep well, Lilianna Emerson." Then he did lean in, but only to brush his lips along her cheek.

"Good night," she whispered as he walked away.

He whistled as he moseyed down the drive back toward town. He had never felt quite the way he felt around Lily. She made his heart lighter and the day brighter. He wanted to protect her and carry her worries for her. He wanted to make her laugh just because he loved the sound.

He had been a little perplexed when she had started making excuses for why they couldn't see each other. He got pieces of it, but other parts he would need to figure out. Hard to date when you're rich, he could understand that. Hard to date when you're busy, totally. Hard to date when you have responsibilities, oh yeah. But hard to date because of your religion? That one he had a hard time wrapping his head around.

As he neared the shop he saw Parker in the back of the

now-empty restaurant, hunched over paperwork. He waited as a couple of tourists wandered by. They stopped at the entrance to The Hungry Whale, maybe considering a late dessert, but moved on. He detoured into the restaurant. Parker lifted his eyes from the papers in front of him.

"Hey man. Forget something?"

Noah spun a chair around at the table, sitting on it backward with his arms braced across the top. "No. I need... to talk."

Parker nodded and slid the papers aside, giving his friend his full attention. Noah greatly admired that in the man. The ability to stop and be present when a friend needed him.

"What's up?"

"It's Lily..."

"Ahh, girl trouble." Parker wiggled his eyebrows.

"No, she's just a friend."

"Noah, you don't clean up this good when your grandma comes to town. This girl isn't 'just a friend'!"

"OK, maybe I want it to be more. Or at least I'd like the chance to see if it could be more."

"So what's the problem?" Parker unbuttoned the cuffs of his dress shirt and pushed up the sleeves, settling in for a long talk.

"She has all these reasons she can't date."

"As do you."

"Touché."

"OK, what are her reasons?"

"She's too rich." Noah rolled his eyes. "You know me. You know that's just not a thing. Anyway, she's too busy, has too many responsibilities. I get that, but we're all there, you know?"

Parker rubbed a hand over his tired face. "Oh, I know. Trust me. I know."

"Then she drops this one on me. She can't date me because she's a Christian and I'm not."

Parker sat up straighter, his face taking on a different expression. He didn't speak, but his silence encouraged Noah to keep talking.

"I respect her choice to follow a religion, but I just don't get why that would mean we couldn't date. You're a Christian and we still hang out."

Resting his elbows on the table, Parker looked Noah straight in the eye. "You want the truth?"

"Of course."

"As a Christian, Lily needs a partner who will draw her closer to God. Who will share her faith."

"Someone like you?" Noah didn't mean it to sound testy and was glad when his friend let it slide.

Parker fixed him with a pointed look. "No, someone like you, but with God in his life. You and I are friends, good friends, but I don't depend on you to help me grow my relationship with Jesus. *That's* how we can be friends."

Noah pondered that for a moment. "I hear ya. I mean, I guess I could do the church thing. Sunday mornings in a pew. I could handle that."

"Aww man, it's so much more than that! Don't make a fake show of it just to impress Lily. She'll see right through you. She wants the real deal."

"Why couldn't we just agree to disagree and let it go?"

"Nah, the Bible is pretty clear about not doing that."

Noah didn't like that answer. He pushed both hands through his hair and blew out a frustrated sigh.

"I'm gonna be real with you. You need to be careful. Very careful. Don't push her toward a relationship with you while you still haven't made peace with God. You'd get what you want, but she wouldn't. In the end, she'd resent you for it. If you genuinely care about her, you'll respect her on this."

That one stung a little. He'd get what he wanted, but she wouldn't? Right at that moment what Noah wanted most was for Lily to have everything she'd always wanted. It hurt to realize he wasn't part of that.

"Alright, I get that, but it's not like I'm asking her to marry me, just to go out and have fun. She isn't going to stick around anyway."

"But what if all the fun leads to marriage? Trust me. Don't

put her in that position. You see, the Bible likens a Christian's relationship with God to a marriage. A Christian lets God lead and a Christian woman needs a Christian husband to lead her. Not because she's weak, but because he loves her and wants God's best for her."

"I think you're getting a bit too theological for my brain tonight, Reverend Donovan."

"It happens."

"Thanks though. I can't say I'm happy about your advice, but I can at least see where she's coming from now."

Parker reached over and grasped Noah's shoulder. "Maybe you have to pursue *Him*, in order to pursue *her*."

"Deep man."

"I can manage deep on occasion."

Noah resisted the urge to roll his eyes. He chuckled, appreciating that Parker had eased the tension. He clapped his friend on the arm and headed for the door. "Thanks."

"Noah." He turned. "I'll be praying for you."

Noah nodded and slipped into the night. Parker, always a straight shooter, had shared about his faith many times over the years they had known each other. Noah knew he was the real deal. Maybe there was more to Lily's faith than the fairy tales Noah had always thought it to be.

He should be exhausted, but he knew sleep would be elusive. His brain seemed to be on overload. Instead of climbing the stairs to his attic apartment above the shop, Noah turned toward the ocean and walked down to the water. The tide was on its way out and patches of the sand bar had started to dry in the moonlight. He found a bare rock and sat. Pulling his knees up he stared unseeing across the darkened water.

Words from a Sunday School class Parker had dragged him to as a kid surfaced in his mind. He thought it might have been a Bible verse, but he wasn't sure. It went something like 'Seek Me and find Me, Call to Me and I will answer'. It had been a long time and he was sure he was remembering it wrong. Nevertheless, he turned his face up toward the star-studded night sky.

"OK God, if You're out there I want to know it. Not like 'show me a sign', but… If You're real, help me understand it."

He wasn't sure what he expected. Fireworks? A shooting star? A deep voice from the sky? What he didn't expect was a simmer of irritation. Why should Lily and Parker think he should change? Was he not enough? He was a good guy, hard-working, loyal, kind. He was enough all on his own, thank you very much. He was 'that guy'. That guy who showed up. That guy who played by the rules. That guy who shouldered other people's stuff. But if he was enough, why did it always feel like he fell a tiny bit short, a bit off the mark?

Noah rubbed the heel of his hand across his chest. There'd been a dull ache there as long as he could remember. An emptiness. Lily's story tonight flitted back through his mind. *I hated the hole inside me,* she'd said. Yeah, he could relate. He hated the hole, too.

Harley had taken the sunrise tour out with Noah and they had stayed out a bit longer than usual, just soaking in the beauty of the sun-dappled waves. All but one in the group had been couples who wanted the romance of watching the sun crest over the eastern horizon. Noah had been happy to oblige. He'd woken up feeling restless and had relished the extra time on the water to clear his head and calm his spirit.

The two men chatted as they unloaded gear from the trailer. Life jackets, dry bags, water bottles, a single shoe. Harley shook his head.

"How does someone not miss one shoe?" Noah asked.

"I don't know, man. I do not know." Harley tossed the shoe in lost and found and went back to the gear. Sort, dry, put away. He paused and turned to Noah. "You know just about everyone in town, right?"

"Ayuh, just about. Why?"

"What about Edwin Hurst?"

"The real estate guy? I know who he is. I wouldn't say I *know* him. Why?"

"Nothing really. Just that, last week I'd gone into city hall to register my bike and he was there trying to sweet talk Gwen, the clerk. He kept saying that he'd have the money soon because this guy from Boston owed him. I remember it because Gwen was getting nervous. That night I was walking back up from the pier and he came bursting out of The Alehouse spittin' nails. He was swearin' and yellin' about getting what he was owed. He was drunk as a skunk and most of us just ignored him. But last night it dawned on me... a big shot from Boston ended up dead this week. Just struck me as a bit of a coincidence and I just got to thinking it might be the same guy. I doubt it was." Harley shrugged and went back to sorting life jackets. "Never mind. Forget I said anything."

Forgetting he said anything was all well and good, except that Lily had said last night that Emerson hadn't known anyone in town. Maybe that wasn't the case. Not that Noah was willing to point the finger at Edwin. Yeah, the guy was a worm with his eyes on the mayor's office, but that didn't mean he'd pushed a guy off the pier. It was just that maybe Emerson did know people in town. Maybe Lily's assumption wasn't quite accurate. If Emerson knew Hurst he might have known other people as well.

The clock in the back room told him that Lily would still be at church. If he met her afterward he could still be back for his late morning tour. He stood in front of the schedule, feet apart, hand on his hip. He ran his fingers through his hair, still sticky with salt from the morning. He'd only have about an hour.

"You OK, man?"

"Just trying to figure if I had time to catch up with Lily before the next tour."

Harley stood next to him and crossed his arms, making his muscles bulge and his tats ripple. He was quiet for a long minute and then he walked up to the board with the yellow towel he'd used on the dry bags. He wiped Noah's name off the schedule and added his own. Stepping back he resumed his pose and shook his head.

"Yeah, looks like it."

"Dude. Are you sure?"

"Sure about what? I don't see your name anywhere on today's schedule."

As Noah clapped his friend on the shoulder he heard the sweet peal of church bells in the distance. If he hurried he could catch Lily on her way back to the inn.

"Thanks, man," he said, squeezing Harley's shoulder before heading out.

Lily stepped through the tall red doors of the old clap-board church into the dappled shade of the churchyard. She had enjoyed Pastor James' challenging sermon more than she expected. The man didn't sugarcoat the truth and she admired him for it. The congregation in the sanctuary this morning was made up of a mix of locals and out-of-towners. Lily loved how at home she felt. She'd been welcomed at the door by an enthu-siastic older gentleman who helped her find a seat. At least four of the women in the congregation had stopped to welcome her. Even Pastor James had sought her out after the service to thank her for coming. She was pretty sure that no one at the church she attended in Boston even knew her name.

Pastor James now stood on the walkway at the bottom of the stairs talking to a member of the congregation. They turned and smiled as a pregnant woman and a couple of teen-agers joined the group. From the adoring way that the minister beamed at the woman Lily knew it must be his wife. He con-firmed it by a quick kiss on the forehead and a protective hand on her extended belly.

Lily skirted the group as she headed for the sidewalk, but Mrs. James caught her eye. She slowed as the woman stepped away from her husband and extended her hand.

"Good morning. I'm Maggie. I'm glad you could join us this morning." Her smile was heartfelt and reached her eyes, lighting them. She was only a little older than Lily, but she appeared wise beyond her years.

"Thank you. I'm Lily. Congratulations," she added, nodding to the glowing woman's stomach.

Maggie slid her hand over the mound. "Thanks. We're very excited." She turned toward the street and walked along with Lily toward the sidewalk and away from the chatter. "Excuse me if I'm overstepping, but am I right that it was your uncle who passed away this week?" At Lily's startled face, Maggie grimaced. "Sorry, this place doesn't seem like a small town with all the tourists, but it really is. Word travels fast." She nodded down the sidewalk and Lily saw the retreating form of Walter Ashe.

Ahhh... "Yes, Herbert Emerson was my uncle."

"I'm so, so sorry for your loss," Maggie said and reached out to squeeze Lily's hand.

"Thank you." She couldn't bring herself to explain yet again that they hadn't been close.

"If there's anything, anything at all, Aidan or I can do, please just let us know." They had reached the sidewalk and Maggie pulled her in for a quick, but hard embrace. Lily had a sudden thought that they could be great friends.

"Thank you," she said, accepting the hug and relishing, even for a brief second, the support of a friend.

As Maggie headed back to her husband, Lily turned toward the inn. She was surprised to find Noah leaning against the huge trunk of a tree shading the sidewalk. He pushed away and came to join her.

"Hey."

"Hello." She smiled and tried not to analyze the quickening of her pulse just at the sight of him.

"My day cleared up and I thought we could grab coffee. If you want."

"That sounds divine."

They snagged their coffee, hers a latte, his black, and headed up the long drive toward the inn. The skirt of her sundress ended just above her knees and her strappy white sandals made her feel like her legs were long and graceful. Noah slowed. Peeking over her shoulder she caught him drinking in the sight of her and blushed at the appreciative glint in his eye. He grinned and winked, as he caught up. Yup, definitely good for a girl's ego.

They sat together on the swing at the end of the porch. Noah set his coffee aside and regarded Lily for a second. "I need to ask you something about your uncle."

"Sure."

"How sure are you that he didn't know anyone in town?"

Lily stopped with her latte almost to her mouth. "Fairly sure, I think. Maybe. Why?"

Noah puffed out a breath. "This morning Harley told me about hearing this real estate guy, Edwin Hurst, mouthing off about a guy from Boston owing him a bunch of money. I got to thinking, if it was your uncle and he knew Hurst, the cops should know that. Not that I think Hurst... did anything. Just that the assumption your uncle didn't know anyone might be inaccurate."

"I don't know why I think that I know who he did and didn't know. I'm beginning to think I didn't know him at all." She took another sip of her coffee. "Uncle did what he pleased. I shouldn't have assumed."

"You could talk to Chief Briggs and let him sort it out."

"I guess. I'll go talk to him tomorrow."

"Nah, Jim's always on duty." He rose and offered her his hand. "He lives and breathes this town. He's got a couple of deputies during the busy season, but all we ever see around here are a few drunk and disorderlies, a little shoplifting, maybe a speeding ticket. I don't think he owns any clothes besides his uniform," Noah said, tongue in cheek, as they headed back down the driveway.

Chief Briggs was buffing the SHPD symbol on the side of his cruiser when they reached the police station. He tucked the rag in his back pocket when he saw them. His dimpled cheeks creased when he smiled.

"Noah, my boy," he said, reaching for Noah's outstretched hand. "Keeping out of trouble?"

"Always."

"Your folks? They good? Haven't seen them since... Oh, good heavens, must be the Christmas party."

"They're good. Mom's right out straight at the restaurant. You know her, busy to the point of exhaustion most days. Dad, too. If he isn't on his boat, he's tinkering on the tractor, or tending his bees, or driving Mom crazy."

Lily watched the two men. Small town. She could see it now. Maggie had been right. Strip away all the tourists and summer help and the reality was it was a small town where everyone knew everybody's business.

"Chief, we found out today that Herbert Emerson may have known someone in town after all."

Chief Briggs' attention shifted to Lily and she thought she read a hint of annoyance around his mouth. "What's that now?" he asked Noah.

"I heard scuttlebutt that he might have known Edwin Hurst."

"Edwin, huh?" The cop sighed and squinted at traffic, or maybe nothing, down the street for a moment. "Not surprising that Emerson would know that weasel, Hurst. Anyone interested in property here would have to cross paths with him at some point. The guy's got his fingers in everything. But knowing someone in town doesn't make his unfortunate death anything but a tragic accident. Miss Emerson, as I told you a couple of days ago, there is just no evidence of a crime."

Noah stuffed his hands in his pockets and hunched his shoulders. "We just thought you should know."

"Of course. Thank you for passing the information along." Chief Briggs pulled his rag back out and went to polishing the front bumper, ending the conversation.

❧

"Sorry," Noah murmured as they walked away.

"Sorry? For what? He's right."

Noah took her hand as they walked back through The Green, a quiet park that lay between the police station and the coffee shop on the corner. The lush grass, shaded under towering oak trees, invited picnics and games of frisbee, while a large bandstand at one end spoke of summer concerts. Lily laced her fingers more tightly with Noah's and breathed in the delicious scent of dew-moistened earth and sun-warmed leaves.

"You know, Hurst's place is just around the corner if you want to talk to him. At least find out if he knew your uncle."

"That would be good. I suppose if I'm taking over the business, I should know the extent of the business Uncle was in."

They walked down a block and turned away from Main Street. It was a quiet part of town full of older buildings. Noah led the way to a red clapboard house with a shingle above the door that read 'Edwin Hurst, Real Estate'. He rapped hard on the door and waited. It was long seconds before it swung open.

"Noah."

"Edwin."

"What can I do for you on a Sunday morning?" His tone left no question of his annoyance at being bothered.

"Edwin, this is Lily Emerson."

Lily extended her hand and the cool hand that took it made her shiver.

"Ms. Emerson." His speech was the tiniest bit slurred. He was slim with broad shoulders. Mediterranean ancestry, once upon a time, graced him with thick black hair and flawless olive skin. He wore his hair slicked back and a white dress shirt with the sleeves rolled up to the elbows.

Noah stepped closer and placed a protective hand on the small of Lily's back. "Lily was wondering if you might have known her uncle, Herbert Emerson?"

Hurst let go of her hand and held the door open for them before leading the way to his office.

"Why? Is she going to pay me now?"

An empty scotch glass on his desk explained the slurred speech.

"I can't comment on that at this time, Mr. Hurst," Lily said as she took a seat. "Can you tell me about the nature of your business with my uncle?"

"Of course you can't comment. Shocking," Hurst grumbled as he sat down. "Your uncle hired me to help him obtain... a certain piece of property here in Summer Harbor."

"The inn?"

"Yes, the inn," he sneered.

"If you were handling things for him here in Summer Harbor what was he doing here?"

"My contract wasn't his only piece of unfinished business in town."

"Meaning?"

"Why don't you ask Stella Tucker?"

Lily was silent as she held his gaze.

Hurst steepled his hands and raised one eyebrow. "I see the name doesn't surprise you." His gaze raked her from head to toe making her skin crawl. His eyes met hers again and narrowed. "I doubt that you and I will be doing business. You don't have the... fortitude... needed for this game."

Lily felt her cheeks pink. It was the only sign that his words had found their mark, and she hoped he didn't notice. Beside her, Noah stiffened like a spring ready to uncoil. She reached out and laid a calming hand on his arm.

"I agree with you, Mr. Hurst. I doubt that we will do business in the future." She rose from her chair and offered him a polite handshake.

He held her hand longer than necessary as he added, "I do still expect to be paid. Your uncle and I had a contract."

Lily pulled her hand back and, holding her head high and her shoulders square, strode to the door. Once outside she let out a shaky breath.

"Man that guy's a piece of work," Noah muttered as he closed the door.

"Chief Briggs was right. Weasel."

Noah draped his arm over her shoulders and turned her toward the inn.

"You didn't seem too surprised when he mentioned Stella."

"You know her?"

"Sure, she owns The Sandpiper, a bed and breakfast down near the sandbar. Do you?"

"No, but I'm beginning to think Uncle did."

"And you have no idea what the connection is?"

"No. I'd never heard her name before reading it in a memo I found in Uncle's briefcase." Her lips pressed into a thin line. She was glad she had spoken to Hurst. More than that though, she was thankful Noah had been along. Not that she couldn't have confronted the creep alone, but it was nice that someone had her back for once.

CHAPTER EIGHT

N oah had watched, a bit in awe, as Lily the business-woman had emerged in Hurst's office. Her back had straightened and she'd perched on the edge of her chair, hands clasped in her lap, ankles together, knees tipped to the side. Her emotions vanished in a mask of civility. She'd been the consummate professional. Noah felt sorry for anyone who had to meet her across the table in a boardroom. She would be downright intimidating.

Her face had given nothing away. He'd been on the edge of losing his cool from the moment Hurst had answered the door half drunk. Lily, on the other hand, had stayed level-headed. His admiration ratcheted up another notch.

She was now walking beside him with stiff shoulders and a grim set to her face. He missed the smile she'd graced him with earlier when she'd seen him outside the church waiting for her. How could he get that back? He searched the street for inspiration. Up ahead he saw a sandwich board on the sidewalk and he had an idea. He laced his fingers with hers and flashed her a bright smile.

They walked in silence for a minute before Noah tugged her into a delicious smelling shop called A Box of Chocolates. "I think you need cheering up and I know just the thing."

He skipped case after case of hand-dipped chocolates, bark, brittle, truffles, and fudge, and stopped in front of a cooler packed with bins and bins of luscious ice cream. The girl behind the counter grabbed two cones and Noah ordered a large chocolate caramel concoction that looked divine.

"I'll have the same," Lily ordered. "But small."

As they waited for their cones, Lily took in the shop, eyes wide.

"Isn't this place great?" Noah asked. "The smell alone can raise your blood sugar."

"I'm glad you already knew what to get. I'd never have been able to choose." She laughed as she took the cone the girl handed her.

Noah paid and then led her the rest of the way to the back of the shop. Customers packed the place and it took skilled maneuvering. He was just about to lead her up a flight of stairs to the second-story when he heard his name. A tall brunette waved to him from where she stood at a stainless steel counter rolling truffles by hand. Her riot of chocolate-colored curls were corralled under a bright yellow bandana. She flashed Noah an adorable lopsided smile.

"Hey, Zoe." Noah grinned and waved, but kept moving up the stairs to a room cluttered with little tables topped with red and white checkerboard cloths. The end of the room had a set of french doors that opened onto a second-story deck, also crammed with tables. Noah wove through the maze and found an empty table near the railing, overlooking Main Street.

Lily took a lick of her ice cream and groaned. "This is *amazing!*"

"Right? It's the real cream. Zoe makes it herself. She makes all her own candy and sells online as well as here in the shop. The online sales keep her going through the winter."

"Well, she makes amazing ice cream. I should get a box of chocolates for Olivia before I head back."

"Do you have a plan for that?" he asked between licks of his ice cream. He wasn't sure he wanted to hear the answer.

"No." She didn't sound happy as she turned away. At least she was trying to enjoy her ice cream. It appeared the visit with Hurst had left her drained and he hoped his double chocolate salted caramel therapy was working. "Right now I'm just... doing the next thing."

He grinned at her over the top of his ice cream. "Hmmm,

sounds like good advice."

"That it is."

"And what is the next thing?" He'd leaned his elbows on the table, still attacking the mountain of ice cream atop his cone.

"Ahh, and there's the question." For a moment she was lost in thought and he didn't want to interrupt. Instead, he watched her, willing her tense shoulders to relax. A little sugar wouldn't make that happen, though. She needed help to bear some of the weight of the millstone of responsibility that was dragging her down. Didn't she have anyone? Anyone who could help her? He was about to ask about her sister when she spoke again. "To be honest, I don't know what the next thing is. It's a Sunday, so I can't take care of any business. What I should do is spend the rest of the afternoon going through Uncle's briefcase."

She looked like she wanted to add more, but instead let her gaze wander back over the street. Noah didn't push, but his heart ached for her. Before their meeting with Hurst, he wouldn't have guessed she could handle all the pressure life had thrown at her. Now he was sure she could. It was just, he didn't want her to have to carry it all on her delicate shoulders.

Across the street a car door slammed, drawing Lily's attention. Noah followed her gaze. The driver stood in the street holding his cell phone aloft trying to get a signal. Noah laughed. "Not happening, buddy."

"Right? What's up with that?"

"No cell service? Well, the National Park owns just about every hill on the island. They would never dream of putting a cell tower in, for obvious reasons. There are a few privately-owned places that could accommodate a tower, but the land-owners don't want them. The city talks every year about instal-ling 'invisible' towers. You know, the ones that look like trees and stuff? But it never happens."

"It's so different here."

"In a good way, I hope."

She winked at him over what was left of her cone. Man, he liked seeing her smile. She blushed when she caught him studying her and looked away. As her eyes drifted to the street again she stilled. Her face drained of color and Noah turned in his seat to follow her gaze.

"Something wrong?"

"He just looks like... a man I used to know."

"The tall guy in the suit?" The man pocketed his phone as he crossed the street.

"Yes."

Noah lost sight of him as the man faded into the crowd. "Who is he?"

"No one. I just thought—" She searched the street again. "Never mind. I'm sure it wasn't."

She didn't seem too sure, but Noah didn't press.

Lily's brain raced as they walked back to the inn after their ice cream. Her eyes must have played a nasty trick on her. Sitting there eating her ice cream, enjoying the conversation with Noah, and her brain convinced her that she'd seen Carmen on the street. But that was crazy. There was no reason for him to be here. No, it had to be her imagination. Too little sleep, too much stress.

Desperate for distraction she turned back to Noah. "So, Stella. There's only one way to find out what her connection to Uncle is." Lily pulled her car keys from her purse and jingled them. "Want to join me, Hardy Boy?"

"Need you ask?" he grinned.

Back at the inn Lily ran to her room and changed into a pair of flattering jeans and a light-weight sweater set. She kept the high-heeled sandals. She stood for a moment in front of the mirror. Once upon a time, she'd picked up the pieces of her heart, crammed them back into her chest, and sworn she would never let anyone near it ever again. Seeing the man in town had reminded her of her resolve. She'd almost let Noah get too close. Arms' length. Just friends. She sighed and left her room.

The Sandpiper was a sprawling two-story bed and breakfast overlooking the pebble beach that led to the sandbar connecting Summer Harbor to Bar Island. It was shingled in dark, sea-green cedar shakes and was shaded by giant maple, oak, and spruce. Lily parked along the street. The foyer they stepped into was light and airy and smelled of coffee and cinnamon.

At the jingle of the bell above the door, a middle-aged woman emerged from an office to the side. She had a pile of dark red waves pinned atop her head. Wispy bangs shaded her large hazel eyes. She was curvy and pretty and Lily had the slightest glimmer of recognition.

"Can I help you?"

"I hope so. My name is Lily Emerson. My uncle was Herbert Emerson. I was wondering if you might have known him?"

Stella recoiled at the mention of Herbert's name.

"I can't help you."

Noah and Lily exchanged a curious and concerned glance.

"Please, Ms. Tucker. Uncle had a memo in his briefcase with your name on it. I'm just trying to sort out... well... everything."

Stella regarded them with narrowed eyes. She drummed her fingers on the desk a couple of times, straightened the already neat stacks of brochures, and swiped imaginary crumbs onto the floor. Without warning, her shoulders slumped as if the load they bore had become too much. "I heard he... passed away. Frankly, I was shocked to hear that he was even here in town."

"You knew him, then?"

The laugh that bubbled out of Stella wasn't pretty or happy. "Knew him? Yeah, I knew him." There was a long pause as she regarded Lily. All at once, her eyes softened. "You've grown up so pretty. I hope you aren't following in his footsteps."

"Forgive me, but... do I know you?"

"No, I don't suppose you do. You were about eight when Herbie and I..." She didn't meet Lily's eyes as if embarrassed to confess the truth. "Herbie and I were... involved."

Herbie? "You and Uncle?"

The brittle laugh again. "I know, hard to picture, right? He was... different then. It took me too long to see who he was."

"I remember Uncle being different when I was a child." Lily covered Stella's hand with her own, trying to make a connection. "And I know what he became."

The empathy and understanding in Lily's eyes must have been enough to encourage Stella to continue. "I met Herbie right after my father passed away. I was grieving and he was so kind and helpful."

"I don't remember Uncle that way, except for little snippets from before my mother passed away."

"I was so naive. I thought we had— I don't know... a real relationship. That he cared about me. He even took me to meet his family. That's when I met you." Stella smiled at the memory. "You were adorable and Herbie doted on you girls, especially your sister. It was around Christmas time. He took me to your parents' house for dinner. I left that night with stars in my eyes, but I think he only had dollar signs in his." She wiped at moisture under her eyes.

Lily and Stella drifted to a small table near a window and Lily held a chair out for the older woman. She dropped into the seat and put her hand over her eyes.

"My father had owned a beautiful little hotel in Boston," she continued after regaining her composure. "When he passed away it became mine. I was devastated at the loss, but also excited to be following in my father's footsteps. It wasn't long before I realized I had no idea what I was doing."

Lily felt that truth in her core. It had been passed to her, but she had no idea what she was doing. The enormity of the job ahead threatened to crush her. At least she would have Alistair to help her with it all. Without him, she feared she wouldn't be able to cope.

"Herbie was helping me more and more with dad's hotel and there kept being things that would be 'easier' if he had permission to do this or that. Before I even realized what was happening, I had signed almost the entire hotel over to him. I was thinking forever while he was plotting to walk away from me with another Emerson in hand."

It shouldn't have come as a surprise to Lily. After all, she knew her uncle. Yet hearing it from Stella made it sound horrible. "I'm so sorry, Stella."

"Honestly, I've moved on. I threatened to sue Herbie and he paid me not to. I used the money to buy this place. It isn't the same as the hotel in Boston, but it feels like home now," she said as she swiped at her eyes again and gave a weak smile. "It took me years to get here, but now I go weeks and weeks without thinking of that hotel or Herbie. Then, hearing that he was in town, hearing that he had died. It just brought it all back to the surface."

"Did he come to see you?"

"Oh, no. If asked, I would have said he didn't even know I was here, except you said he did."

"Yes, I found a memo from his secretary saying she'd located you."

"I'm glad he didn't come. I don't ever want to see that man again!" She sucked in a sudden breath. "I didn't mean that the way it sounded. I just... He was wretched, you know? But of course you know that. Please don't turn into him, Lily. Your mother wouldn't have wanted it."

"I know."

"I still remember the way your mother thought you hung the moon. I left that night hoping Herbie and I would have a little girl like you." Her voice hitched and she turned to stare unseeing out the window. She didn't speak to Lily again.

At a loss for words, Lily pressed her hand to the older woman's shoulder before she and Noah left. They reached the car, but Lily handed Noah the keys and slumped into the passenger's seat. The weight of who her uncle had been at his core was never as heavy as when Stella, broken and tired, had admitted to dreaming of having a child like Lily. A cousin. She felt ill grieving the loss of someone who never even existed.

What would it have been like to have a little cousin growing up? She'd be what? Eighteen or nineteen now? Just a few years younger than Olivia. Would she have had Stella's red hair? Uncle's blue eyes? The cousins would have grown up as friends, she was sure.

The letter from Uncle to her mother flashed in her mind. *I don't want to look you in the eye and tell you what I've done.* Could he have been referring to Stella? The timing fit, but she couldn't be sure. She was lost in thought as Noah started her car and pulled out onto the road.

🌱

"Where are we going?" Lily asked. She had been staring, unseeing, out the window and Noah had wondered how long it would take her to realize he hadn't turned back toward the inn.

"Well… It's getting late in the afternoon and I have dinner plans, so… I thought I'd take you along with me." He cringed a little and flicked a glance at her out of the corner of his eye trying to judge her reaction. He hoped she thought it more of a sweet gesture and less kidnapping. "We can go back if you'd rather."

It took her a long time to answer. "I could eat."

"It's a great place. The food is amazing."

"Better than The Hungry Whale?" She asked, her voice rich with skepticism.

He chuckled. "Oh, hands down." It was his favorite place to eat, but he wasn't sure Lily would appreciate it the same way he did.

"I find that hard to believe."

He grinned. "Parker's is pretty hard to beat. But this place… does it without any effort at all."

She had settled back in her seat and was quiet for a few miles. "I wasn't expecting that from Stella."

"I wondered about that." Lily had looked shell-shocked when they left.

"The more I dig into Uncle's life, the more I don't think I

knew him at all. He was a horrible person. Mean. Spiteful. But then yesterday I found these letters in his briefcase."

"Letters?"

"Yes. A letter from my mother, of all people, and a letter that he wrote to her the day she died, but never mailed." She flexed her fingers as if trying to loosen the tension in them. His hand itched to take hers. "I think she wrote the letter the week before she died and I think she was on her way to see Uncle when she crashed her car."

Noah let out a low whistle, but let her continue.

"The way she spoke to him... I have to believe he was different then. And his letter to her. I didn't know that man. I still have one envelope I haven't opened. I want to. I just couldn't bring myself to read it yesterday."

"Do you know who the other letter is from?"

"I think it's from Uncle, but there's no address on it."

"More mystery."

"I tried opening it yesterday afternoon, but I was so drained from the first two, I just needed to step away. That's when I met you in town."

"And I'm very glad you did." He couldn't resist any longer and reached for her hand. "We'll do the next thing, which is dinner, and then maybe you can tackle that last letter."

"Mmmm, that sounds magnificent." She leaned back in her seat and watched the small villages on the west shore blur past. She didn't let go of his hand and he twined his fingers with hers as he drove.

"You know, this morning you thought your uncle hadn't known anyone in town. By this afternoon we found two. What are the chances that there are more?"

"I suppose there could be."

"What about that guy you saw while we were at Zoe's today? Did he know your uncle?"

She took a long time to answer. He rubbed his thumb along her fingers where they were linked with his and waited. He had a feeling the answer wasn't a simple yes or no.

"I'm not one-hundred percent sure it was who I thought it was. If it was... Yes, Uncle knew Carmen. We... we were together for a while."

"Was it... serious?"

"I thought it was. We enjoyed each other's company and we had similar plans for the future. He was much older than me. Too much older. Even so, it seemed to make sense to be together."

He was quiet. Two people being together because it made sense, made no sense. But it wouldn't do any good to say so. Besides, he had his own pitiful love story, why shouldn't she have hers?

"In the end, he was much more interested in getting into EHI than being with me. I'm sure you don't want to hear about it."

"You're not the only one with past heartache." He puffed out a sigh. "Veronica Moore. I was completely smitten. I had our whole future planned out. Then she dumped me for a much older third grader. I was crushed."

She smacked him on the arm. "I was being serious!"

"So was I! Roni did me in. I was inconsolable for hours." He laughed and was delighted to hear her giggle as well. "No, in all seriousness, I've had my fair share of hurt. The summer I started Acadian Adventures I hired a girl to run the store. Tansy Jobe. By the end of August I was head over heels. I planned on asking her to marry me as soon as the busy season was over. In September she gave her two weeks' notice. She'd planned all along on moving to the next sunny port and the next guy. She wasn't cruel about it, she just wanted a summer fling and I didn't catch a clue in time to save myself. Lesson learned. No more summer girls for me."

She regarded him for a minute before picking up her story. "Carmen and I had talked about getting married. I was so excited to be a part of a family that I overlooked pretty significant red flags. Like how he wanted joint bank accounts before we were even engaged. Or how he never did take me home to meet his family. In hindsight, I can see that he wasn't even interested in me. At the time I was blind."

"Love does that."

"I never loved him. Not really. I just...longed for what I thought he had."

"If it was Carmen in town this morning, is there any reason to think he had a beef with your uncle?"

"Oh, my goodness, yes. They were at war from day one. It was like they started out loathing each other. I kept them compartmentalized as much as was humanly possible. I don't think Uncle ever knew how close I came to marrying Carmen." She turned her attention back to the road and was surprised by how far they'd driven. "Where is this place you're taking me, anyway?"

"Over the bridge."

"On the mainland?" she said, surprised.

"It will be worth the drive, I promise."

The scenery glided by, as did the miles. It wasn't long before they turned off the main road. The house lots had gotten bigger and the houses farther apart. Sprawling lawns, or winding driveways through stands of pine broke up the miles of forest. Shingled capes and log cabins interspersed with elegant mansions and old farmhouses. Here and there, where the road curved back toward the ocean, she could see the sapphire water through the trees or stretching out from the rocky shore.

Noah took a winding driveway that climbed away from the water and emerged into a clearing covered in low brush and rocks. Lily wore a baffled expression as they wound through the thicket.

"Blueberries," Noah said as he nodded at the reddish-leafed bushes.

"I guess I never thought about how, or where, they grew." She gazed at the acres and acres of bushes stretching out on either side of the drive.

"Ayuh, wild Maine blueberries grow all over the place down here."

They reached the other side of the clearing and Noah pulled

to a stop next to an old pickup truck.

"Noah?"

"Hmmm?"

"This isn't a restaurant."

"I never said it was a restaurant. I just said I had dinner plans."

She gave him a pained look.

"Come on. You'll love it, I promise."

With palpable reluctance, she slipped from the front seat and waited for him. He caught her hand and led her up the walk to a small one-and-a-half-story cape with pale gray shingles and white trim. Two dormers overlooked the blueberry barren, as did the front porch.

"Whose house is this?" she asked in a whisper as they approached the dark red front door.

He wiggled his eyebrows at her and threw open the front door. "Mom! Dad! I'm home!"

CHAPTER NINE

N oah! I'm not eating dinner at your parents' house," she hissed.

"Suit yourself," he said as he stepped into the foyer. "Do you want me to bring leftovers to the car later?" His eyes twinkled to show he was teasing, and he jangled her keys dramatically as he shoved them in his pocket.

She rolled her eyes. She knew all she had to do was ask for her keys and drive away, but she was too curious about his parents to leave. How much of Noah would she see in them? She knew she looked like her mother, but she often wondered if there were other characteristics that she could attribute to Margo Emerson. Was her love of laughter from her mother? What about her fear of the dark? Did the woman have the same love-hate relationship with heels that she did?

They stood in a small room with a coat rack and stairs to the second floor. He sniffed the air and groaned at the delicious yeasty smell of baking bread. Exasperated, she followed him through a doorway into the dining room.

She was about to launch into a lengthy list of all the reasons why he shouldn't have brought her to his parents' when a petite woman with dark salt and pepper curls and a brilliant smile hustled into the room from the kitchen beyond.

"Noah!" She didn't even reach his shoulder, but she threw her arms around his neck and squeezed him tight. He wrapped his arms around her and lifted her off the floor. Her giggle sounded young and vibrant.

"Hey, Mom." The affection in his voice did crazy things to Lily's heart. He set her back down and turned to Lily. "Mom, this is Lily Emerson."

"Well. Hello, Lily. It's nice to meet you." The older woman pulled Lily in for a quick, unexpected embrace. She smelled of oranges and cloves.

"It's a pleasure to meet you, too, Mrs. Kingsley. I'm sorry to come uninvited." With that, she shot Noah another glare. Unfazed, he grinned at her.

"Nonsense! We're always happy to have company." She turned to head back to the kitchen and spoke to Noah over her shoulder. "Your father's in the living room. Please go help him yell at the coach. I don't think they quite heard him all the way down in Boston."

Noah took Lily's hand to tug her back through the foyer and into the living room. It was a room designed for comfort and Lily felt more welcome than any other place she had ever been. She could imagine rainy days spent tucked into a big, cushy chair reading a book chosen from the many shelves that lined the walls. A soft rug covered most of the floor and large throw pillows dotted the couch. A man sat in a recliner, his eyes intent on the game playing on a sizable television on the opposite wall.

"Hey, Dad," Noah said from the doorway.

The man who popped out of the chair was no doubt Noah's father. They had the same wide shoulders, the same square jaw, and the same hair in need of a trim. Years spent in the sun had weathered the older man's features so that deep laugh lines appeared when he grinned.

"Noah, my boy!" he boomed and caught his son in a fierce hug.

"Dad, I'd like you to meet Lily Emerson," Noah said after returning the back thumping bear-hug. "Lily, my father Garvin Kingsley."

"Nice to meet ya, Darlin'."

"Nice to meet you as well," Lily replied, shaking his offered hand. He was a charmer, just like his son.

Within minutes, the two men were caught up in the baseball

game. Yelling at the coaches, cheering for a player who managed to steal second base, and holding their breath as a fly ball glided toward the Green Monster for a home run. Her mind drifted back to the week before and watching the game through the window of the pub. In that moment, standing on the outside looking in, she'd longed for friends to join in cheering on their team. Her heart swelled as she nestled in next to Noah on the couch. He stretched his arm behind her and every now and then would rub his thumb along her shoulder as he and his father dissected plays and lamented calls by the umpire. It was more enjoyable than she had even imagined, being a part of the group.

As the seventh inning dragged on, Lily left the men to the game and instead meandered along the bookcases. She ran her finger down an eclectic mix of classics, gardening books, art, current bestsellers, dime store paperbacks, and thick reference volumes. At the end of the last case, she slipped out of the room and wandered toward the kitchen. She stood in the door for a minute taking it in. Noah's mom stood at the stove, towel over her shoulder, stirring a large pot that bubbled with the most amazing smell. Bread cooled on the counter, and a cutting board held onions waiting to be sliced. She must have made a sound because the older woman turned to her with a welcoming smile.

"Come on in, Lily."

"Are you sure? I don't want to get in your way."

"Oh, fiddlesticks. Of course come in! Those boys will be engrossed in that game until I tempt them away with food." She laughed and her eyes danced. Much the same way her son's did when he smiled. Lily wondered if her eyes lit up like her mother's, too.

"Mrs. Kingsley, may I help with anything?" Lily asked as she slid just inside the door. "I mean, I can't cook, but I'd be happy to… do… something."

"Pish posh, anyone can cook. Not everyone has learned how yet." She winked at Lily and moved to the refrigerator. "How about working on a salad while I finish up the stew?"

"I think I can handle salad."

"And please, call me Ana," the older woman said as she placed a cutting board and knife, bowl, and vegetables on the island. "When you're finished with the salad, I'll teach you how to make blueberry tarts."

Lily washed her hands at the big farmhouse sink and then perched herself on a barstool to start on the salad. Ana hummed while she stirred the fragrant stew bubbling on the stove.

"That smells marvelous," Lily said. "What kind of stew is it?"

"Quahog."

"And what..." She didn't want to sound ignorant, but she had to know. "What... um... is a quahog?"

Ana chuckled. "Crazy name for a kind of clam we dig here in Maine. This recipe started out as clam chowder years ago, but over time I've changed it so much, I can't rightly call it that anymore. Quahog stew fits better."

"Well, it smells divine."

"The boys love it. I try to make it when Noah's coming for dinner."

Polite conversation with her boyfriend's parents was new terrain. She almost laughed out loud as the thought skipped through her mind. Boyfriend? Hardly. And yet this still felt like stepping into new territory. She hadn't dated at all in high school and only a little in college. None of those men had ever taken her to meet their family. Her only serious boyfriend since college had regaled her with stories of his idyllic life and made numerous promises to take her home. None of them ever panned out. In the end, she wondered if it was all just stories, built to tempt the orphan who was so desperate for family that she would cling to any hope of belonging. Her vision blurred with tears and she set the knife down to wipe them away.

"Lily, are you OK?" Ana asked. Her voice was soft and quiet. It reminded Lily of music and it made her want to pour out all her troubles. She pulled a stool up next to Lily's and sliced into a tomato with her own knife.

"Yes—" She stopped and took a breath. "Yes, I'm fine. Sorry.

It's been... a week."

Ana rested her hand on Lily's and met her gaze. There was compassion written all over the older woman's face.

"It's a long story. Too long, and too complicated. But... I'm fine, really."

Ana's expression said she didn't believe Lily for a minute, but she let it go. She squeezed Lily's hand and then moved back to the tomato. "You're just about done here, how about those tarts?"

"Oh, I don't think so. I wasn't kidding when I said I can't cook."

"And I wasn't kidding when I said you just hadn't learned yet. Come on, I'll show you." She motioned Lily over to the counter and tied an apron around her waist. "OK, now the first step is to make the crust."

When Noah wandered into the kitchen an hour later, Lily stood at the counter surveying her creations. Not perfect by any stretch of the imagination, but they looked... almost... good!

"I figured this is where I'd find you."

She spun around with a delighted grin on her face. "I made tarts!"

"I've brought many friends home for Mom's kitchen therapy." He ambled into the room and stepped up to her. He reached out a hand and brushed a dusting of flour from her cheek with the pad of his thumb. "I'm glad I brought you with me. You look... happy."

And just like that Lily felt herself fall, head over heels, for Noah Kingsley.

"Noah, would you get your father, please? Dinner's ready."

"Sure, Mom." He kissed his mother's cheek on the way back out of the room. "Dad!"

"What does he mean, 'kitchen therapy'?"

"Oh, that's just what Noah calls it when he brings one of his friends around for a little extra TLC. I have been teaching Noah's friends to cook for as long as he's been able to drag them home. And listening to them. And feeding them. There are times in life when that's all you need. A good meal, a listening ear, and the confidence born from the joy of creating amazing food." She was still talking as she carried the stew out of the kitchen and placed it on the dining room table.

Was that what she was? A project? Wreckage Noah thought needed fixing? After the week she'd had she couldn't blame him. Needy much? Yeah, she probably did need 'kitchen therapy'. Only, she'd begun to hope it was more. She wanted to be special. Why? She had already decided they couldn't be together on multiple levels. So why was she wishing? She swallowed back the bitterness that rose in her throat. No. She refused to allow it to ruin the evening. The stew smelled luscious and she couldn't wait to share the tarts Ana had taught her to make.

Dinner around the Kingsley's dining room table was a joyous affair. A little loud, full of laughter and love. Belonging. At first, Lily had just sat on the periphery, drinking it all in. Soon, however, Garvin had included her in his teasing. Ana, which Lily had learned was short for Analise Jessamine, had praised her scant culinary skills. Lily couldn't remember the last time she'd sat around a table with family for a meal. Had she been eight?

"Let's walk the blueberries," Garvin suggested to Noah after they had all sampled Lily's blueberry tarts and savored cups of tangy, sweet tea. "I want you to take a look at the bees with me."

Ana rolled her eyes at him. "And I suppose the dishes will do themselves?"

"I can help with the dishes," Lily volunteered.

Ana smiled at her and then turned laughing eyes on Garvin. "You men go ahead. Lily and I will do up the dishes and meet you." She shooed them out the door and then began gathering plates and bowls from the table. "Those two... If we don't hurry, they'll have a piece of equipment out of the shed by the time we get out there and you'll never get back to town!"

"This tea was delicious," Lily commented as she gathered the cups.

"It's a blend a lady in town taught me to make years ago. Mine isn't quite the same though. I swear magic is one of her ingredients."

"That wouldn't happen to be Ava Allen, would it?"

"Yes, do you know her?"

"I'm staying at her inn."

"I just love her teas, but I'm not as big a fan of the nutmeg as she is."

Lily laughed. "Yes, it's a little strong."

"This one we had tonight is my wood sorrel blend. I'll give you a pouch to take back with you."

After finishing the dishes they headed toward the front door. Ana held out a pair of ballet flats to Lily. "You'll kill yourself in those heels walking through the blueberries."

Lily flushed remembering Noah's arms around her after she tripped over her heels. "Thank you."

They made their way down the front drive to join the men, who had stopped partway down the hill to inspect a couple of beehives. Ana looped her arm through Lily's and slowed her steps.

"Your tarts were great, Lily. I'm not kidding. I wrote the recipe down for you so you could make them again."

"Ana, thank you for this evening. It has been… wonderful."

"While you washed up for dinner, Noah told me about your uncle. I'm dreadfully sorry." She tightened her arm on Lily's as she spoke.

"Like I said. It's been quite a week."

"I'm glad Noah brought you tonight."

"Does Noah get home often?"

Ana's smile dimmed a little. "Well, this place isn't really 'home'. Not to Noah anyway. Garvin and I like it alright and it's what we can afford. I do miss the island though." She let out a wistful sigh. "No, he doesn't visit as much as my momma's heart would like, but I know he's busy, even more so with the trouble he's had with his business. It's alright. I take what I can get."

"Trouble?"

"Oh, I don't understand it all. But I guess he's trying to find an investor so he can get the business back on its feet."

"An investor?" The beautiful meal started to sour in Lily's stomach.

"He's had this dream since high school, but he's not a businessman. I think he's hoping to find a partner with more business sense to help him with the place. In the meantime, he works crazy hours to keep it afloat."

They walked down the driveway through the blueberries. It should have been a beautiful evening stroll, but Lily was having trouble enjoying it. She pasted on a smile when they joined Garvin and Noah by the beehives. Garvin seemed to be concerned with having enough bees to pollinate the blueberries. Noah stood up from where he was crouched with his dad and grinned at her. Garvin stood and grinned at Ana. Two peas in a pod. She tried to recapture the joy of dinner, but it was no use.

"Let's walk down to the shore," Ana suggested. The boys hung back at the bees for a few minutes, talking options for more hives, while Lily and Ana continued on. Ana still had her arm looped through Lily's. They had crossed the road and were nearing the rocky shore before Ana spoke again. "I miss the island, but I love it here, too. I guess it's all about thriving where you're planted."

"I'm not sure I know where I'm planted right now."

"You'll figure it out." She stopped and breathed in the salty air. Letting go of Lily's arm she crouched down to finger the leathery leave of a sea lavender plant. "Take this plant for instance. The seeds get tossed around on the waves, never knowing where they're going to end up. Then one day they wash ashore and sprout and find that they are in the perfect place to flourish. You'll find your roots taking hold and you'll let them dig in deep and then you'll flourish, too. You'll see."

Garvin came alongside Ana and took her hand. They moved ahead and walked along like they had been fitted together. She slipped under his arm and he leaned in to kiss her hair. Their love for each other was obvious. A pang of envy stabbed Lily.

"Life goals right there," Noah said as he came up next to her. She wrapped her arms around herself to stave off the dejection she was feeling. He reached out to pull her against him, but she pretended not to notice and focused instead on collecting little shells and bits of sea glass. He stopped now and then to pick up small flat stones and skip them out onto the water. They had walked a ways up the beach before Noah spoke again.

"Everything OK?"

"Umm-hmm," she mumbled. She couldn't decide if she wanted to be furious or if she wanted to burst into tears. She shouldn't care. This was why she had rules. She'd broken her own rule and now she had to pay the price.

As the sun sank behind the trees and the shore was cast in long shadows they headed back. It was almost dark by the time Noah hugged his folks, promising to visit more often, and Lily had embraced Ana, thanking her for a wonderful dinner and cooking lessons.

The ride back to Summer Harbor was excruciating. Noah kept shooting her worried glances, but she couldn't even meet his eyes. She bit her lip to keep the tears at bay and focused straight ahead into the darkening night.

"Are you sure you're OK?"

"Fine." Her answer flat.

"Lily—"

"Just leave it, Noah."

He puffed out a breath and tightened his hands on the steering wheel. How could she have been so gullible that she fell for the same old trick again? Was she that easy to manipulate? Tempt the orphan girl with the promise of family and she'll do whatever you want. The humiliation hurt almost as much as realizing it hadn't been real. None of it. From the first moment, or at least since he'd realized who she was, he'd played her.

After driving for what seemed an eternity they reached the inn. Noah parked her car and withdrew the keys from the ignition. Lily barely waited for him to hand them to her before she bolted.

"Lily!" he called after her, but she'd already reached the front door. Only years of etiquette classes kept her from slamming it.

❧

Lily hadn't managed an early morning run since she'd arrived in Summer Harbor, and while all the walking into town was great, it wasn't going to keep up with all of the treats. Rich lattes and gooey ice cream and quahog stew had to be worked off somehow. After a sleepless night, the fog-shrouded beach called to her. She found her running shorts at the bottom of her suitcase, evidence of her lack of exercise, laced up her sneakers, and grabbed her phone and earbuds.

The fog was thick and the beach was empty. Lily stretched as she watched a few lobster boats heading out for the day, then took off down the beach heading away from town. She ran as far as she could, pushing herself hard. When she reached the rocky cliffs she stood with her hands on her knees, breathing hard. That short run hadn't been enough. She turned and headed back, picking up speed until her lungs burned. The sand was hard-packed from the recent high tide and she followed the ambling line of seaweed and driftwood all the way to the town pier. She jogged up the stone stairs that led to the parking area to find a water fountain. She took a long drink before splashing water on her face and drying it with the sleeve of her sweatshirt.

The sun was up above the trees and burning off the haze as she headed back to the beach. The fog dissipated revealing a brilliant blue sky. As she walked back toward the inn Lily saw Noah's tour pulling out a few hundred yards ahead. Why hadn't she gone the other way? By the time she reached them, all the kayaks were beached. She tried to skirt the group, but Noah, at his familiar unhurried lope, jogged over to her.

"Mornin'," he grinned.

"Good morning," she said in a cool, polite voice as she attempted to skirt around him.

"Perfect morning for a run."

She ignored him and kept walking. He caught up and grabbed her elbow, bringing her to a stop.

"Lily, what's the matter?"

She shrugged off his hand on her arm. "I just don't like to get played."

"What are you talking about?"

"Honestly? How naive do you think I am?"

"You want honesty? OK. I honestly have no idea what you're talking about." On the outside he was calm, but his eyes flashed as they bore into hers. "What happened between dessert and leaving my folks?"

She sighed, too wrung out to put up any more resistance.

"I know you just want me to invest in your business, Noah, you can stop pretending you care about me."

"What on earth are you talking about?"

"Your mother told me last night. You're looking for an investor. Then I showed up and you tried to play the knight-in-shining-armor. Well, I'm sorry. I'm not that easy to con." She stepped around him and prayed the tears would wait until she was back in the safety of her room packing to return to Boston.

"Lily!" He caught her again. "Lily—"

"Don't even try to deny it."

"That I'm looking for an investor? No, I won't deny it because it's true. But I'm not looking at you and seeing dollar signs. Did it cross my mind to ask you for help? Of course. But because you're crazy smart, not because I want to swindle you." Frustration saturated his voice. "And in case you didn't notice, I never did ask for anything. You've got enough on your plate without me adding to it. And yeah, I did want to be your knight-in-shining-armor, or at least jeans-and-flip-flops. Again, not because I wanted anything from you. Just because I wanted to help. You needed a friend, I could be that friend. I stepped up."

The tears that had threatened since the night before now overflowed. She pushed her sweatshirt sleeve across her eyes and tried not to sob.

"Hey, hey, Sweetheart, it's OK." He pulled her into his arms.

"I'm sorry," she mumbled into his shirt.

"Already forgotten." He pushed her away enough to meet her

eyes. "Please believe me, Lily, I don't have any ulterior motives."

Oh, she wanted to believe him. How she wanted to! He hadn't once asked her for anything but friendship and she had assumed the worst in him. She felt like a fool. Looking up through her lashes she gave him a shy smile. "Would you accept two scoops of double chocolate salted caramel swirl as a peace offering?"

He grinned at that and reached out to catch a strand of hair that the wind had blown free of her ponytail. He tucked it behind her ear and let his fingers linger a moment. "I'll call you later this morning, OK."

The butterflies were back as she watched him turn back to his small group of tourists. If they planned to indulge in Zoe's mouthwatering ice cream later she had to run about twenty more miles. Lily turned back toward town and took off. As she neared the stairs leading up from the beach, she slowed. It was time. Time to walk past the place where Uncle had been found.

She braced herself and walked toward the water. Sturdy pilings supported the end of the pier. Against them was a jumble of rocks towering over her head and spilling out onto the shore. Squeezed in amongst the rocks were the stalwart sea lavender plants, wind-blown and sea-battered, yet holding their own against the elements. Lily picked up her pace. She couldn't deal with it after all. She pushed hard and was panting by the time she reached the public boat access by the sand bar. Her thoughts jumbled, her emotions frayed, she turned toward town and left the shore behind.

Lily had pushed herself hard and it was well into the morning before she neared the inn's parking area after her run. She slowed and took a closer look at her car. It looked odd, as if it was tipped to one side. To her frustration, Lily discovered that the two tires on the passenger side were flat. She blew out an annoyed breath and tried to decide what to do. Upon closer inspection, she found a puncture in the sidewall of each tire about the size of a quarter. Had it been done on purpose? She peeked under her car as if the perpetrator might be lurking there in the shadows. How absurd. What she needed to do was find Walter and ask him who she should call to take care of it.

She walked around the side of the house hoping to find him tending the flowers or tinkering on a project. Nothing. She checked the cottage and the backyard before she caught sight of him near the utility shed on the far side of the house. He appeared to be talking to someone. As Lily got closer to the shed, Edwin Hurst stepped into her line of sight. His face was a bit ruddier than the day before and his eyes were dark. He started when he saw her and turned on his heel. By the time Lily reached Walter, Hurst was stalking down the driveway at a brisk pace.

"Miss Lily," Walter exclaimed, not a little surprised.

"Hi, Walter. I seem to have a bit of a problem with my car. I was hoping you could help me."

"Sure thing, Miss Lily."

"Two of the tires have been popped."

"What? Oh, that's terrible. Let's go have a look-see."

They went back to her car and Walter crouched down next to the tires. He held his old cap in his hands, worrying the brim with his thumbs.

"That's terrible Miss Lily. I don't know how it could have happened. Do you want me to get them fixed for ya?"

"Would you mind?"

"Not at all, not at all. I'm right sorry this happened. Under my nose and all."

"Oh, goodness, Walter. It wasn't your fault." She placed a hand on his shoulder and he smiled up at her. His boyishness was endearing.

"I'll get these off and over to the garage straight away."

"The jack's in the trunk," she told him as she fished her keys out of her pocket and handed them to him. "Thank you for taking care of them."

Inside, Ava met her at the front desk. Her papery cheeks crinkled in an easy smile, but it faded at the look on Lily's face.

"Oh, Dea-ah, whatever is the matter?"

"I just discovered a couple of flat tires on my car. Not one mind you, two."

"That's too bad. Did you fetch Walter? He's a whiz at things like that. He'll get them fixed for you."

"Yes, Walter's on it. What a gem."

"Come along, Dea-ah, you need a cup of tea." Ava bustled toward the kitchen with Lily following close behind. "I find a good cup of tea helps just about anything the world throws at us." With the kettle on to heat, Ava began readying two cups with tea infusers and setting out honey and lemon. "You're right, you know. Walter is a gem."

"At first I thought he was your son."

"He might as well be." Ava gave a wry grin. "There are days I believe he may be more of a son than my boy. Walter broke into this house when he was about fifteen years old. He'd hitched all the way from Texas looking for a place where his old man couldn't knock him around. Got to the end of the line here in Summer Harbor. He was hungry and scared. He broke in here looking for food. I caught him and, well, never let him go."

The kettle started to whistle and Ava poured water over the fragrant tea.

"He's been here ever since?"

"Walter's the sweetest man, but he's... he's... a little..." a pained look came into Ava's eyes. She dropped her voice as if he might hear her. "He's a little slow. He learns things like gardening and fixing things real quick, but he couldn't live completely on his own. I'm glad he stayed. It's a lot less lonely here with him around. Now that my boy has this place on the market though, I don't know what will happen to him."

"Could he stay on?"

"No, I believe he would have to leave when my boy gets this place sold." The older woman sighed. Lily wanted to assure her that Walter would be welcome to stay, but she couldn't promise something she couldn't deliver. Before she could think of something to say, Ava changed the subject. "Now, tell me what you think of our little town?"

The conversation ebbed and flowed. Ava told Lily about living in Summer Harbor back when the only way onto the island was a ferry from the train station on the mainland. Lily told her about the hustle and bustle of Boston.

"Miss Ava, I do believe you are correct. A bit of tea helps whatever comes along." Lily took the cups to the sink and washed them. "Thank you for the tea and for the conversation. If I do end up purchasing the inn, I hope you will share all your wonderful stories with me to share with the guests."

Back in her room, Lily paced the floor. The tires had been slashed. The holes were uniform and high on the wall of the tire. Nothing she drove over could have done that. But why? The phone rang shortly after noon and she snatched it up.

"Hey." Noah sounded tired, but she could hear the smile in his voice just the same. She let out a shaky breath. "Lily, what's wrong?"

"It's probably nothing, but when I got back to the inn this morning I discovered that two of the tires on my car had been punctured."

"What!?"

"I've tried to figure out who and why." Maybe there was no reason. Maybe it was a random act of vandalism. Did that happen here? It did in Boston. Kids, bored with life and intent on mischief. Or drunken fans after a sporting event didn't go their way. But this seemed out of place, and it felt personal.

"Any conclusions?"

"No, not really. Edwin Hurst was here when I saw the tires, but why would he do that?"

"Why was he there?" Noah asked.

"I have no idea. He was talking to Walter and left when he saw me."

"So it could have been him."

"For what purpose, though? What could he gain from me having to get new tires? It doesn't make sense."

"Who else could it be? Teenage prank doesn't seem likely."

"No, I thought that as well," she agreed. "The only other people I've had contact with are Chief Briggs and Stella Tucker. Both seem implausible."

"What about the guy you saw yesterday in town?"

"Carmen?" What possible reason could he have for popping her tires?

"It was just a thought."

"Oh, Noah, I'm so overwhelmed." She tried to drag her emotions back into line. She felt ridiculous.

"Shhh. Hey, it's OK. I can come over right now and take care of the tires."

"No, Walter's already on it."

"I'll still come over, Sweetheart. Meet you at the coffee shop in, say... half an hour?"

She hung up the phone and fell back onto the bed. Sweetheart. The simple term of endearment probably didn't mean anything, but she felt it all the way to her toes. One word shouldn't have the ability to turn her brain to mush and set her heart to fluttering.

Oh, Lord, help me guard my heart because I am at serious risk of falling in love with Noah.

An hour later, showered and dressed in capris and a flattering faux wrap t-shirt, Lily waited outside the coffee shop sipping a small latte and holding a massive black coffee. She recognized Noah's walk, hands shoved in his pockets, shoulders hunched, long before she could see his face. She met him with a smile and handed him the coffee.

"You, Sweetheart, are an angel," he said before savoring a sip and taking her hand.

She wasn't sure which set off the butterflies again. The endearment, the compliment, or the feeling of his large, strong hand holding hers, or all three.

"I'm thinking we should talk to what's-his-name. At least find out what he's doing here."

She took a long sip of coffee. "I'm not even sure it was Carmen that I saw. And even if it was, I just can't believe that he would have any reason to puncture the tires on my car, no matter how we left things years ago. How would he even know I'm here?"

"You're right... But... if you want to talk to him, I asked around and he's staying right there at The Bellamy Hotel." He pointed across the street to a large, mansard-roofed building.

"It was him? And so close? That's... convenient." She tried to picture Carmen Franco sneaking up to her car at the inn and knifing the tires. She couldn't make the image solidify. It just felt... wrong. Yes, she loathed the man, but petty vandalism didn't seem to be his style. She chewed her bottom lip. "Even though I doubt he had anything to do with the tires, I am curious about why he's here. It just seems too coincidental that Uncle and Carmen would show up at the same time in the same town where neither of them had a hotel. Saying they didn't care for each other is a monumental understatement."

"Then let's go, Nancy Drew."

Curiosity propelled her along next to Noah. She did want to know what the man was up to. They reached The Bellamy Hotel and Noah held the front door for her. She had noticed the place when she first arrived in Summer Harbor. It filled the entire corner lot, towering above the street. Creamy tan clapboards stretched two stories and were topped with a handsome slate roof. Round topped dormers spoke of a third story in the roof.

"Good morning," Noah flashed his knee-weakening smile at the young woman behind the desk.

"Noah Kingsley, what on earth?" The attractive brunette came around and gave Noah a tight squeeze. He returned it one-armed, not letting go of Lily's hand.

"Good to see you, Hope."

She held him at arm's length. "How's your mom?"

"She's good. She and Dad are busy, as always."

"Man, I miss her cooking." She let go of Noah's arms and smiled at Lily.

"Hope, this is my friend Lily. We need to speak to one of your guests."

"Sure, who can I ring for you?" Hope asked, stepping back behind the desk to the computer.

"Carmen Franco," Lily said.

A couple clicks on the computer and then Hope picked up the phone and dialed a number. She waited quite a while and then hung up with a shrug.

"Sorry, but he doesn't appear to be in his room. Do you want to leave a message for him?"

She didn't want to speak to Carmen. She would be quite happy to go through the rest of her life not speaking to him ever again. This was a bad idea.

"I'll leave him my number," Noah answered. Hope slid a note pad and a pen across the desk and he jotted down his contact information, thanked Hope, and handed her back the pad.

Outside Lily turned to Noah with a curious smile. "Do you seriously know everyone in town?"

"Pretty much," he laughed. "The year-round population of Summer Harbor is only about four thousand and I've lived here my whole life. Of course, that population quadruples over the summer, not including tourists, but the folks that stick around from year to year become pretty tight. I went to high school with Hope. She practically lived in our kitchen there for a while. Long story," he added at her quizzical look. "Rough time at home and Mom's kitchen ended up being a safe place for her to land. What's on the docket for today?" he asked, not even trying to hide the obvious change of subject.

There was history there. Lily hated the twinge of envy she felt. How ridiculous. He had the right idea, change of subject. "What should be on the docket is getting things sorted so I can go back to Boston. It's been almost a week. I need to step up and deal with things." She slipped her hand into his as they walked. "There's so much I need to do, and yet every day I'm finding reasons not to return to Boston. It's ludicrous for me to think of buying the inn at this point. I need to run the seventy-two we already have. But then... the sun comes up in the morning and I smell the sea on the air and I just put off the inevitable one more day. I know, I know," she said on a sigh. "The next thing, right?"

Noah draped his arm over her shoulders. "Sounds like you need to clear your head."

"Well, at home that means finding a cliff and going rock climbing. Any suggestions for good places to go?"

His eyebrows shot up. "I can't picture..."

She rolled her eyes. "I took up rock climbing in college as a way to focus, think, talk to God. It's amazing how loud the world can be. Anyway, I loved it and just kept going. It's still my escape."

He was still wearing a perplexed expression. "There's a great top-rope route in the park for experienced climbers. Or are you daring enough to climb ground-up?"

"Oh, there's a ground-up route? Yes, please!"

He gaped at her. "Seriously? Ground-up?"

She grinned in response.

"Do you need gear?"

"No, I have my own."

He shook his head looking a little dazed. He slipped his hands in his pockets, silent for a few moments as they walked. "Do you need someone to belay you?"

She couldn't quite read his expression. "No, I can go solo."

"I mean," he cleared his throat. "Do you want company?"

Bashfulness! That's what it was! Her heart skittered. How adorable. She flashed him a bright smile. "I would love company. Let me change and grab my gear."

Within minutes she was in clothes appropriate for scaling the side of a mountain and they were on their way again. Her bag was slung over his shoulder, and her hand back in his. At the shop, Noah left her by his Jeep while he went to gather his own gear. Lily hunkered down by her bag and started pulling gear out, organizing it on the ground behind the vehicle.

"Lily?"

She whirled around at the sound of her name.

"Carmen?"

CHAPTER TEN

Wwhat are you doing here?" The way he said it wasn't unkind, but there was annoyance in the lines around his dark blue eyes. He hadn't changed much in the years since she'd seen him. More salt than pepper in the hair around his temples, a few more creases around his eyes than she remembered. He wore a white dress shirt with the sleeves pushed up to his elbows showing lean forearms, pale from a life in a suit.

"I beg your pardon?"

"I had a message when I got back to the hotel to call a... Noah Kingsley," he frowned. His black brows drew down in a frown. "My cell is useless here, so..."

"Yes, that takes a bit of getting used to." She willed her voice to remain emotionless.

"I guess I should say I'm sorry to hear about your uncle."

The fact that he didn't say he *was* sorry was not lost on her. She opened her mouth to reply but was spared by Noah emerging from the shop loaded with ropes and a bag of gear. He slowed when he saw that Lily wasn't alone.

"Noah," Lily said, the relief evident in her tone. "This is Carmen Franco."

"Ahh, so you're Noah. I had a message to call you." He tapped the cell phone in his pocket in way of explanation and didn't bother to offer his hand.

"Ayuh, well, Lily is trying to tidy things up here before she heads back to Boston and she's had... trouble... We wondered if you might be able to help straighten a few things out."

Carmen thrust his hands in his pockets. "I don't see how."

"Were you aware that Uncle was here in Summer Harbor?" Lily asked.

Carmen looked away. "Yes, I knew he was here. He was here to buy another piece of property. Build another Emerson."

"Did you know I was here?"

"Not until just now."

"Did you have any business dealings with Emerson?" Noah asked.

"No. Once upon a time, but not now." Carmen's eyes had gone from intense to weary. "Look, is there a point to this?"

"I don't suppose you saw Uncle the day he died?" Even Lily was a little shocked by her boldness and took a step back. Noah stepped up behind her, her guardian, and waited for Franco's answer.

"No. Why? You think I had something to do with it?"

"No, I..." But she'd thought exactly that and it must have shown on her face.

Carmen's shoulders slumped. "You want to know the truth? I just wanted to get back at him. Years ago, before you and I got together, I'd discovered a hotel that was going for pennies on the dollar. It would have been my first hotel. Herbert found out what I had bid on it, I have no idea how, and outbid me by $100. $100! I have waited years for the opportunity to square things. I saw him at the airport in Boston on Wednesday morning and overheard him talking to his assistant about the place here in Summer Harbor. I thought 'this is my chance'. I changed my plans and flew here instead. I put in an offer on the place and hung around hoping I'd get a chance to see the look on his face when he didn't get what he wanted."

"Was that why you... why you... pursued... me? To get back at Uncle?" She thought she might be sick. The humiliation was staggering. She liked it better when she thought he had pursued her for profit or to get ahead. Revenge was that much worse.

His eyes revealed the truth before he spoke. "Lily—"

"You're the third offer on The Butterfly Cove Inn, aren't you?"

"Yes, but... I don't want it. I just wanted Herbert to watch a property slip from his grasp. It sounds childish to say it out loud." His eyes searched hers, the regret in them palpable. "I never meant to hurt you."

"I got over you a long time ago Carmen."

He looked as if he wanted to say more but thought better of it. He looked from Lily to Noah and back again. "If you believe Herbert had... help... falling into the water there's a much more likely person than me. He didn't make friends."

"I know," Lily murmured.

The silence stretched on, awkward and uncomfortable. Noah began gathering their climbing gear and organizing it piece by piece in the back of the Jeep. Carmen leaned over and picked up a coil of rope, fingering it as he stood with his forearms leaning on the hood.

"If you feel the need to poke around I would start looking a little closer to home. It was only a matter of time before Herbert found a way to get Alistair out of the picture."

Lily didn't even react, just met Carmen's eyes and nodded.

"You're not surprised. I thought as much." He tossed the rope into the back of the Jeep and dusted his hands together. "I'm leaving tomorrow morning and I don't plan on ever thinking of Herbert Emerson again."

"And The Butterfly Cove Inn?" Lily asked.

"I already withdrew my offer. As I said, I never wanted it." Carmen pushed away from the Jeep and rubbed his hand over his face. He met her eyes again. "For what it's worth, Lily, I'm sorry. You look good. Happy. Don't lose that." His fist thumped the hood before he turned to walk away.

"You OK?" Noah murmured.

"Yes, fine. I just..." She turned and watched Carmen leave. Noah tugged her into his arms and held her while she collected herself. With a shuttering sigh, she stepped away and finished organizing her gear in silence. She'd gotten over Carmen many moons ago, but the truth still stung.

Her mind drifted back over the conversation. "What he

said... Alistair is— was Uncle's business partner. Uncle hated having a partner. I found a memo from Uncle's lawyer telling him that they had found that Alistair was in breach of contract."

"Do you think he could be involved?"

"No, no of course not. He wouldn't. Besides, he isn't here. I called him in Boston just as soon as I heard about Uncle. No, I think Chief Briggs is right. As implausible as I think it is that Uncle was on the pier alone... that must be what happened. A tragic accident."

Noah watched her face for a few moments before pulling her into his arms again. "Do you still want to climb?"

"More than you can imagine," she mumbled into his shirt.

The granite cliff soared high above them. Jagged edges clawed across the face and ribbons of harder stone crisscrossed the crag. A few scrubby firs had found a footing on the larger ledges. Towering white pines shaded the base of the cliff, but Lily could tell it wouldn't take much effort to get above the tops of them.

Noah watched Lily out of the corner of his eye while he readied his gear. She plucked her bag out of the back of the Jeep, set it on the ground, and pulled her climbing shoes out and onto her feet. She shimmied into her harness, triple-checking every clip and carabiner. Then she attached her chalk bag and clipped on a handful of quickdraws. Satisfied that her equipment was in order she reached back into the Jeep for her rope and tied off the end in a figure-eight knot. Taking a quickdraw off her harness, she clipped the rope to his Jeep and began threading it into the top of her pack. She was quiet while she worked, intent on stopping to tie a slipknot every twenty feet or so.

He paused, admiring her for a minute before hauling out his own rope and repeating the procedure with deft movements. She wasn't kidding. She knew what she was doing.

She was about halfway done feeding her rope into her pack

when she stopped short.

"What the…?" She stood holding her rope and staring at it in horror.

Noah stepped closer to see over her shoulder. In her hand lay the rope, frayed over halfway through.

"I checked this rope before coming to Summer Harbor last week. It was fine. How…" She scrunched up her nose in frustration and tossed the rope into the back seat. "I liked that rope, too. Light and smooth."

"Do you have another with you? I have a spare if you need one."

"No, I'm good." She pulled another coil from the back of the Jeep. This one was a little older and a little heavier. She began again and this time found no problems.

"Ready?" he asked, handing her helmet to her.

"Ready!" she replied, clicking it into place.

"If we climb over there we can anchor our ropes about ten feet apart from each other and there are plenty of bolts on the way up."

"Sounds good."

She tied off her rope and was about to start climbing when Noah walked over. He double-checked her belay device, her anchor, and stayed on the ground watching as she tightened up the rope and secured it to the second bolt, tying a slipknot for redundant safety. Good girl.

"You don't have to spot me, Mr. Guide Man, I know what I'm doing," she called down.

"Force of habit," he called back with a grin.

He had chosen the more complicated route and had to work hard to keep up. She cleared the tops of the trees and stopped to attach her rope to another bolt. He watched as she gave the rope a sharp snap to untie the slipknot at the last bolt and tied a new one to keep tension on the lower part of the rope.

"Nice. I use rubber bands," Noah said, catching up. He didn't want to admit that he was a little out of breath. His long arms and legs should have made it easier, but she appeared to be scurrying up the side of the cliff.

"It's not a race you know," she smirked.

"Says the woman beating me up the cliff."

She chuckled but didn't waste any time dipping her hands into her chalk bag and searching for another handhold.

Noah took his time getting his rope attached and watching her climb above him. She had good technique. Reach, test, pull, swing, grab. Her strength was a surprise. She was small and delicate, but when she climbed he could see the muscles in her arms and back straining to hold her in place.

He pulled himself along a crack in the rock and lost sight of her. A few yards up he cleared the crack and was back out in the open. He stopped to anchor again and get eyes on Lily. She was at least twenty feet ahead of him. Sheesh, she could move. His eyes followed her rope down and he was a little surprised at the distance between her anchors. He liked to clip on whenever he came to one. She, on the other hand, had climbed around or over a few bolts along the way.

She stopped at the next bolt and Noah sighed with relief. He tried to convince himself that it was just the climbing guide in him worrying about safety. Yeah, that was it. Not the fact that he'd started to care for Lily. Scratch that. He didn't even believe himself.

Pulling himself over an outcropping he came to an easier piece of rock and made up part the distance between them. "Are you part mountain goat?" he puffed.

"Maybe," she laughed. "I have to be content with climbing walls in Boston, but whenever I get the chance to climb outdoors..." Her voice trailed off and she gazed out at the ocean, the sun on her face. She looked happy. Not overwhelmed or worried or stressed. He understood why climbing today had been necessary. Focus, think... knowing her, pray.

They reached the top of the cliff and Noah pulled himself up next to her. She'd fished her water bottle off her harness and sat with her legs dangling over the edge. Sweat slicked her brow and she wiped at it with the back of her hand. He grabbed his own water and enjoyed just being there with her in the quiet. It was easy to see she'd needed this.

"It's impossible not to love it here."

He watched her awhile before speaking. "Lily?" He waited until she turned to him. "Stay. Don't go back to Boston. Stay here and buy the inn and be happy. Nothing you've described in Boston sounds like you."

She didn't answer right away, but instead, turned away toward the ocean. When she did turn back her expression was hard to read. "One minute I want to stay and the next I want to go back. I've asked God for wisdom. Now I just have to listen."

He raised a skeptical eyebrow. "Do you... umm... do you... hear God speak?"

"I know you don't believe in Him, but that doesn't make Him less real." Her voice was calm and there was a knowing in it as if she spoke from experience. "No, I don't hear His voice booming out of the clouds or anything like that. There's this passage I love in the Bible. It says that there was a strong wind that tore through the mountains and broke apart the stones, but the Lord wasn't in the wind. After the wind, there was an earthquake, but the Lord wasn't in the earthquake. After the earthquake, there was a fire. But the Lord wasn't in the fire. After the fire a still, small voice. That's how God speaks to me. A still, small voice whispered to my heart, or shown in a verse, or answered by a friend. The Bible also says that God will give wisdom to anyone who asks for it. I have to believe that He will give me wisdom when I need it."

Noah considered her for a minute. "Wisdom from a quiet voice, huh? That would be nice."

"I'm guessing He has already spoken to you, you just didn't recognize His voice. You may have trouble hearing Him, but He always hears you," she added as she stood and dusted off the leaves and pine needles.

They each rechecked their harnesses, reattached their water bottles, and tightened their shoes. Lily lay on her stomach and snaked her legs over the edge searching for a foothold. Noah waited until she was secure with a tight finger hold before he moved away and wriggled over the edge near his rope.

Noah watched Lily as she searched for a solid toe hold. She had unhooked her quickdraw from the bolt and was clipping it to her belt while she held on with one hand. She'd found a decent foothold with the tips of her toes and was balancing on one foot, but the other scraped along the stone face, searching.

Get ahead of her!

Noah blinked and looked around. No other climbers were close to them or paying attention. Had he heard someone say that? He turned back to Lily and watched her dip first one hand and then the other into her chalk bag.

Now!

He'd reached the area that had been a quick climb less than an hour before. His heart hammered in his chest as he descended, careful not to lose his grip or let a foot slip. He had widened the gap between them to about twelve feet when he heard Lily scream. His eyes snapped upward and he watched in dismay as a handhold crumbled and fell away, missing him by mere inches. She tried to hold on, scrabbling at the rock with her now free hand, but she had lost her footing and dangled. He could see her fingers slipping.

"Lily!"

Without thinking he yanked his rope slack and scrambled sideways. Her fingers slipped and she fell toward him, fast. He found a solid foothold, clamped his right hand onto the rock, and caught her. Their helmets cracked together and his arm muscles screamed with the effort of stopping her fall, but he had her. She hadn't fallen. She was safe.

He was breathing hard, from anxiety or exertion he wasn't sure. She clung tight to his shirt and he could feel her hands trembling. After a few deep breaths, she uncurled the fingers of one hand and reached out for the cliff, testing the solidity of her hold before letting go with her other hand and finding a stable jut for her foot. Noah was reluctant to let go. The desire to keep her safe seeped into the very fibers of his being. What if he hadn't listened to... To what? Was that the voice she'd talked about? Had a cosmic being told him to get ahead of Lily so he could catch her? He didn't buy it, and yet...

She turned and smiled at him. "I'm OK. Thank you for catching me. Falling farther wouldn't have been any fun."

He looked down to where her rope was anchored another eight feet below. She would have fallen about forty feet before her belay device cinched up and stopped her fall. His heart almost stopped picturing her rope fetching up, jerking her body to a stop and driving it against the rock. She would have survived, but it would have hurt. A lot. For the briefest instant, he thought he might be sick.

"I know, but..."

Her eyes followed his and her face paled. "I didn't realize I had that much space between anchors. I usually clip onto more bolts than that." She swallowed and let out a shaky breath. "Why were you descending so fast, anyway?"

"I don't know, I just... It was like I knew I needed to be ahead of you." He'd go with that. No higher power telling him what to do.

The rest of the descent was uneventful. Noah stayed as close to Lily as was safe, and always ahead of her. They unhooked their harnesses and flopped onto the ground, propping their backs against a couple of trees.

"Maybe we should stick to top-rope climbing next time," she said around the mouth of her water bottle.

"Maybe." How absurd was it to feel like dancing at the phrase 'next time'?

They gathered up gear, rewound rope, and packed it all away in the Jeep. Lily retrieved the frayed rope from the back seat and held it, staring at it. Noah finished tucking the last of his gear away and glanced up to find that Lily's hand had started to shake. He took the rope from her and dropped it to the ground before he turned her to face him.

"You're fine. That's why we check. And check again. And then check again for good measure. It's why we touch every inch of rope before we climb."

"But what if I hadn't seen it? What if I'd been distracted and it had slipped through? What if I'd fallen with this fray in the rope?" Her whole body shuddered.

"But you did see it and you didn't use it to climb. I caught you. You're safe. No harm done."

She took a fortifying breath. "You're right."

"That's my girl," he said and kissed her forehead.

He let go of her arms and stepped away, hoping she would think a casual kiss on the forehead was nothing. It wasn't. His heart hammered in his chest as he scooped up her rope from the ground and turned to drop it back into the Jeep. As he started to let go his hand stilled and he felt the world drop out from under him.

"Noah? What is it? What's wrong?" Lily asked, panic tinging the edge of her voice.

His mouth had gone dry. He had to swallow just to get a few words out. "It was cut."

"What?!" Lily grabbed the rope from his hand. "But how—? Who—? Are you sure?"

"Ayuh, I'm sure." He held it up and showed her the backside of the rope where a clean slice was visible.

They both stood, speechless. Lily was the first to get her brain working again. "Who could have even done that?"

Noah's face said he was as baffled as she was. "This is a lot more than a couple of popped tires."

"You think they're connected?"

"Maybe. I don't know." He plowed his hands through his hair and grabbed the back of his neck.

"Oh, no..." Lily breathed.

"What is it?"

"Carmen was holding this rope while we were talking this morning. You don't think...?"

"What I think is that we need to take this to Chief Briggs." He took the rope back from her and tossed it in the Jeep. Lily climbed in and they took off. Traffic crawled through the park, and Noah's agitation grew with each barrier. They emerged onto the main road and he picked up speed, anxious to get to the police station.

Lily rubbed her eyes with the heels of her hands. They had stopped to speak with the police chief, but he had been on the mainland for the rest of the day. She had returned to the inn and hauled Herbert's briefcase out again. She knew she was stalling. She had to deal with it. An hour later she had about enough of the investment reports, bank statements, and earnings projections to last a good long time. None of it needed immediate attention and she needed a break. Was this the life she had waiting for her back in Boston? She shuddered. Noah had planted a seed in her head earlier, and now doubt had taken root. Could she go back?

She had spent the better part of five years doing what she was told by her uncle. Go here. She went. Take care of that. She did. Oversee this. She was on it. She had never taken time to dwell on the reality of running a seventy-two hotel empire. Now she imagined days spent pouring over uninteresting paperwork, always concerned with the bottom line. It wasn't what she had imagined. Maybe running an inn was no different. There must be endless paperwork, and permits, and the bottom line would be more important than ever.

What Lily needed was perspective. She picked up the phone from the desk.

"The Sandpiper, Stella speaking."

"Hi, Ms. Tucker, this is Lily Emerson."

"Hi, Lily," Stella answered, her voice warming, tinged with a smile. "How are you doing?"

Lily hoped she could be a balm for the wounds her uncle had

left. "I'm... well, let's just say I've had an interesting day."

"Oooh, that doesn't sound good."

"I'm just going cross-eyed over business paperwork for EHI. Do you have a minute? I need to pick someone's brain."

"Happy to. I'm not sure I'll be any help, though."

"What's it like? Running a small inn?"

"Well, that's a broad question," Stella paused as if collecting her thoughts. "In general terms, I would say busy but enjoyable. There are days where I do not stop, especially in the summer, but even those tend to be good days. Of course, there's still a lot of parts of running this place that I am still learning. It's good to have people to lean on for advice, for sure. Are you still thinking of buying the inn? Turning it into another Emerson?"

Another Emerson. Herbert had used that exact phrase and it made Lily shudder. "No, I'm thinking it wouldn't make a good Emerson. I just... this place gets into your soul. Do you know what I mean?"

Stella chucked. "Oh, do I ever."

"The more I see of the town and the island the more I fall in love."

"I knew the first day I was here that I didn't want to leave. It isn't my father's hotel, but in the end, I think it is much more 'me'."

Much more 'me'. Is that what Lily craved? A place that reflected who she was? She had loved Emerson Hotels International as long as she could remember. It had been her father's first love and he had passed that love onto her. Over the years since his death, the chain had changed. Gone was the uniqueness of each property, the loyal staff that put the guest first, and the returning customers year after year. In its place, Herbert had created a homogenized collection of impersonal lodgings. They catered to those away from home on business. Luxury on the company's dime. Could she continue that? Did she even want to? A place that was 'much more Lily' and much less Emerson struck a chord in her heart.

"That sounds... splendid."

"I also can't imagine living anywhere else, at least not full time. Summer Harbor is home."

"I don't think I could ever tire of the island," Lily admitted.

"You could live here your whole life and not experience it all."

"I've tried to see— Scratch that. I've avoided dealing by doing things like jogging on the beach and rock climbing."

"I think my absolute favorite things here on the island are wandering in the botanical gardens and stargazing at the over-look above Sandy Bay Beach."

"Oh, those sound beautiful," Lily sighed.

"Do you know what you're going to do yet?"

"I need to go back to Boston." Saying it out loud made it real. She swallowed a lump in the back of her throat. "I have respon-sibilities."

"Mmmhmm," Stella murmured. Lily wasn't sure if it was dis-interest or disagreement that flattened the older woman's tone.

"I need to..." Lily trailed off, feeling the crushing weight of what awaited her in Boston. "I have to take over for Uncle, fill his role."

"If that's what you want."

"It doesn't matter what I want." Her tone sounded bleak, even to her own ears.

"It does matter, Lily. You need to decide if you want the same things that Herbert wanted. If you want to fill his shoes."

The thought of becoming Herbert Emerson sickened Lily. Is that what she was doing? Going home to Boston to become her Uncle? It was a far cry from her dream. Her dream that had been within her grasp a few days ago. Was she ready to give that up? Could she?

"Lily, even if you do choose to return to Boston, be sure to make amazing memories here before you go. They will soothe you in the rough times."

"I will," she promised before disconnecting.

She sat staring at the open briefcase. She could see the blue and white envelopes tucked where she'd left them. If she opened her uncle's last letter, what would she find? The first two had been eye-opening, but a feeling had come over her each time she handled the third one. As if opening it would mean no turning back. She knew she was being dramatic. It was no doubt a summons he hadn't sent yet and meant nothing. Yet she still struggled to reach for the envelope. Instead, she had retrieved the letter opener from the desk and now sat staring at the briefcase.

Enough was enough. With trembling fingers, she slid the letter from its hiding place and with the utmost care slit the top of the envelope.

Oh, God, help me. Give me the strength to handle whatever this is.

She withdrew four sheets of her uncle's blue stationary. The top one was a letter dated four years ago and addressed to her mother.

My dearest Margo,

It doesn't seem possible that you have been gone for over sixteen years. I wish it had been me that day. Or that you had stayed home. I wasn't worth your life. Just as I feared, your absence has left me without any hope of becoming the man you thought I was, once upon a time. I regret that. I often wonder if I would have turned out differently had you stayed. Or was I destined to be the man I am? There are days I want to be different, but it's as if I am beyond my own control. I'm almost glad you aren't around to see what I've become. If you were here I would beg your forgiveness for my foolishness, but as it stands now I do not see the point. After all, Prescott's gone, too, so who is left to care what we did? He kept my feet on the ground and you gave me hope. Now I know it is only a matter of time before the rage wins. I dearly wish I could hear your voice just one more time. I wish I could remember what it sounded like. Every once in a while Lilianna will say something and I hear it for the briefest instant. It kills me. It reminds me of all I have lost. Oh, to have someone love me and believe I still had good in me somewhere. But no one would love who I have become. Not even you.

I will always be your Bub, even if only in my memories.

Lily felt the dampness on her cheeks and swiped the tears away. If only she could have known this Uncle. Why had he kept this part of himself from her? She had loved him, but he hadn't known it. In hindsight, she wondered if she'd ever shown it. Had she shrunk away from him like every other employee? She covered her eyes with a shaking hand and sobbed.

Once her tears were spent she read the letter again. Her mind raced with questions. Uncle had referred again to his foolishness and she wondered what he'd done that required her mother's forgiveness. And what did he mean by 'what we did'? Her heart dropped to her stomach as it occurred to her what it could mean. Had her mother and uncle...? No, she didn't believe it. Her mother had loved her father. She was sure of it. Her mother's death had killed her father, too. No. No! She couldn't do this. She crammed the sheets of paper back into the envelope and shoved them into the briefcase, slamming it closed. She stood and it felt like the world was tipping.

She had to escape. Work. Work would be her escape. She dragged a pile of reports, financial statements, and memos from the table and fled her room.

"Miss Lily?"

She looked up from the papers she had spread across a table in the dining room to find Walter standing in the doorway, twisting his cap in his hands. She smiled at him and wondered, not for the first time, if he could stay on if she bought the inn. And, if he did, how long it would take before he wasn't shy around her anymore.

"Good evening, Walter."

"I just wanted to let you know I've got your tires back on your car."

"Oh, thank you. I appreciate you handling that for me."

"No worries, Miss Lily. No worries. I'm always happy to help a guest." He took a few nervous, stiff steps toward her and handed her keys over. "I put your jack away in your trunk and made sure everything was cleaned up right nice."

"You are a dear."

Walter blushed scarlet at the praise. He began to back away, still smiling. "Oh, I plum forgot. You got a call earlier." He returned to the table and handed her a sheet of Butterfly Cove Inn stationary with a note scrawled across it.

"Thank you," she replied to Walter's retreating form. She turned her attention back to the note.

From Stella Tucker:
Lily, the evening looks perfect for seeing the stars from that place I told you about. Here are the directions. Enjoy!

Lily read through the directions. They seemed easy enough, but the gathering twilight made her pause. God had created a perfect combination for stargazing that night. Crystal clear sky, no moon, cool temperatures, and no fog. However, it would also mean venturing out alone... in the dark. If she didn't get out of the car she'd be fine. Right? It would be spectacular to see the Milky Way stretched above the rugged coast. She wanted to be adventurous, didn't she? She could do this. Almost giddy with anticipation she grabbed up the keys that Walter had just handed her, scooped the papers up, and headed back to her room. She'd stared at the papers a lot longer than she'd intended anyway.

She should invite Noah to go with her. She wouldn't be afraid if he was there. Maybe he was right, maybe she did need him around to keep the boogeyman at bay. She smiled as she dialed the number at the shop. There was no answer. He must still be out with a tour. No matter. Now that she'd made up her mind to be brave she wanted to get on with it.

A few minutes later, after pulling on her tennis shoes and slipping on her cashmere sweater against the cool ocean breeze, Lily headed east down Main Street toward the National Park entrance. The directions lay on the empty passenger seat, but

Lily was confident that she'd remember them. It was a couple of left turns and a right into the parking area for the overlook. Not hard.

The first left was more of a bearing left at a fork in the road. She took it and marveled at how dark it became away from town. Away from streetlights and residences, the only light was that of her headlights. How unlike Boston, where there was never a dark moment. Light poured from buildings, streetlights, traffic signals, cars, stadiums, and docks in the harbor. In the dead of night, you could see just fine.

The pitch blackness was new and eerie. Maybe she'd made a mistake. Maybe she couldn't do this. Slowing the car she tried to decide what to do. No. She would not be afraid. She would drive to the Park, go to the overlook, park, watch the stars, and drive back to the inn. She could do this. She wanted to do this.

Picking up speed again, Lily focused on the small swath of road she could see in the beam of her headlights and the odometer. A few miles out of town she began keeping an eye out for the second turn. It came along quicker than she expected. She braked hard and made an abrupt left onto a much lesser used road. A thick canopy of leafy oaks and maples enveloped the car and darkened the road even more. It was littered with pine needles and dried leaves. The crunch of gravel and old acorns echoed through the car as she drove along.

The total darkness made her nerves hum. The park should put in streetlights. Not a ton, but enough. It didn't seem possible, but the undergrowth appeared to eat the light from her headlights. She started to freak out again. This was a bad idea. She should have stayed at the inn. Or waited for Noah. She'd wanted to be brave and go alone. Not anymore. As soon as she got to the parking lot she would turn around and hightail it back to Summer Harbor. Forget this. She'd see the stars another night. And not alone.

Adrenaline pushed Lily to pick up speed, desperate to reach the parking area and turn around. She peeked at the odometer. She had to be getting close to the last turn. She brought her eyes back to the road and screamed.

The road had vanished. Well, not vanished, but it was no longer ahead of her where it should be. She slammed on the brakes as the front tire careened into the underbrush. Her door struck a tree as the car continued forward carried by momentum toward utter blackness ahead. Why couldn't she see anything?

The reality hit Lily like a heavy chain looping around her chest. In terror, she tried to turn the wheel and struck another tree with the passenger door. She couldn't see ahead of her because there was nothing to see. The blackness of night and sea was all that lay before her. In sickening seconds that felt like an eternity, Lily stood on the brake. She gripped the wheel until her knuckles turned white and ached.

Oh, Jesus, help me!

CHAPTER ELEVEN

The car must have struck a rock or a stump. It came to an abrupt halt and Lily's head smacked the steering wheel. Breathing hard, she rested her forehead on her hands and succumbed to shaking and tears.

Thank you, Lord. Oh, thank you!

As she came back to herself she pried her fingers from the steering wheel and fumbled on the passenger seat for her cell phone. It wasn't there. Don't panic. It was here a minute ago, it's still here… somewhere. With shaking fingers she turned on the overhead light and located the phone on the floor. Why had she brought it? After a week of no cell service, she'd stopped thinking of it when she left the inn. Not caring why she'd brought it, she put the car in park and leaned over, feeling around for it on the floor. Relief washed over her as her fingers closed around it. Using the flashlight on the phone she peered out her window and screamed again.

The front tire had come to rest against a bent cedar tree growing up from the edge of a cliff. Mere inches from disaster. Trying not to let terror push her over the edge into hysteria she pulled the emergency brake as tight as she could. Another peek out the window confirmed that there wasn't even enough room to slip out the door. Panic had her breaths coming in tight puffs. She squeezed her eyes shut and concentrated on not hyperventilating. This could not be happening!

After a few ragged breaths, she felt calm enough to avoid a full-on panic attack and forced herself to open her eyes. A flash of her light on the passenger door revealed a thick tree trunk blocking her exit. She swallowed the hysteria bubbling up her throat. Why hadn't she waited until Noah could join her? Why had she gone alone? Or at all?

Pressing the brake to the floor she eased the car into reverse and disengaged the emergency brake. If she could just get back to the road, such as it was, she could nurse the car back to the inn. She pressed on the gas and felt the front wheel slide sideways, so close to the edge of the cliff she thought she might be sick. She slammed the brake again. Her heart pounded in her ears. She turned the wheel a hair and tried again. With a stomach-turning thump, the tire slipped past the tree and the whole car was jolted by the thwack of the frame hitting the ground.

The shaking in her hand didn't help, but she managed to put the car in park and pull the emergency brake again. The car was not returning to the road under its own power. She clicked her phone on and checked for a signal. Nothing.

God, I need help!

Be strong and courageous, don't be afraid, I am with you. I will never leave you.

Lily took a deep breath. When had the Lord ever let her down? Never. OK, time to stop letting fear take over. God had her back. Instead, it was time to take stock.

No cell service.

No way to get the car off the cliff.

No one knew where she was.

She tried opening the convertible top, but it must have been damaged in the crash because it wasn't budging. The motor whined and screeched, but nothing moved. Next, she tried the automatic trunk release. If she could get the trunk open she could climb through the back seat and out the trunk. Nothing. She jammed the button down again and again in frustration.

If she waited until morning she might have more luck finding a way out of the car in the daylight. Then she could walk back to town. It was only four miles. While that was the smartest option, the thought of spending the night hanging onto the lip of the cliff wasn't an option at all. She needed out of the dark. Now.

With slow, measured movements she unlocked the door and slipped it open. The weight of it yanked the handle from her fingers and the entire car shuddered when the door banged open in midair. Holding her breath Lily used the light from her phone to illuminate the edge of the cliff. The fact that the car hadn't hurtled into the ocean was a miracle. There wasn't even room for a decent foothold along the driver's side of the car.

Wisdom Lord, please. I trust You to get me out of this. Please help me.

Even when you are in the darkest of places I am with you. Do not fear. I will protect you. I will provide for you.

I don't know what to do, Lord.

Just do the next thing.

The next thing? OK, what had God provided for her? She took stock. The light on her phone and the light in the car. Her seatbelt. The tree blocking the passenger door... All of a sudden, a thought struck her. Noah had put her climbing gear in the trunk. If she could get to it she could use it to get out of the car.

Wary of the now open door Lily unbuckled her seatbelt and scrambled into the scant back seat of the convertible. Pulling the release on the back seat, she pulled it down opening a small access space to the trunk. Lying on her stomach she dragged herself into the cramped space. It was devoid of light and she had to grope around for her climbing bag. Before backing out she gave a good tug on the emergency release in the trunk. Still nothing. Why wouldn't the trunk open? Tears of fear and frustration blurred her vision. Dragging the heavy bag of gear behind her, she shimmied out of the trunk.

In the back seat, protected from the open driver's side door, she unpacked her bag. She slipped the harness on and triple-checked each juncture to make sure it was secured. What was she doing? Did she really believe she could rappel from the car, in the dark? She sat back on the seat, pressed against the passenger's side. She was more terrified to stay in the car than she was to climb out of it. She had to do this. She pulled out her belay device, a couple of quickdraws, and two extra carabiners. All she needed now was a rope. Her hand trembled as she pulled the rope out of the bag. It wasn't the frayed one, but the memory of holding that rope coupled with the memory of her fall made her shudder. Don't panic, don't panic, don't panic. She pulled the rope out and slid it through her fingers inch by inch. In the dim glow of the overhead light, she inspected it from end to end. Satisfied that it hadn't been tampered with, she climbed into the front passenger seat and forced the window down enough to loop the rope around the tree. She tied it off with a classic climber's knot. Then added two redundant knots for safety sake. And for her own sanity.

Once the rope was secured in her belay device, attached to her harness, and littered with numerous slipknots for safety, she was ready to get out of the car. Maybe. She peered out the door again with her phone's light. She could do this. She loved rock climbing. Not that she'd ever climbed in the dark, or to save herself. But she could do this. She took a couple of steadying breaths and tried to slow her heartbeat. She didn't need to pass out while hanging from a rope over the ocean! In through the nose, out through the mouth. Slow breaths. Confident she wouldn't blackout, she found a tiny foothold along the top of the cliff under the edge of the car. As comfortable with the purchase she'd found with her toes as she could be under the circumstances, she leaned back out of the car.

Climbing down was painful. Slow, tedious, terrifying. The dark was suffocating. Lily's eyes had adjusted enough that she could make out the edge of the cliff, the hulking shape of the dark trees against the sky, and the inky black of the rolling ocean. Handholds and footholds weren't visible in the smothering darkness. After what seemed like an eternity, Lily was free of the car and began moving to her right. As soon as she was sure she could get behind the car she would climb back up. It was even slower moving sideways. Her shoulders burned and her fingertips were raw from trying to hold onto jagged outcroppings.

"I can do this," she said to the cold night air. "I can do this!"

Just a little farther. She reached out with her right hand and felt along the rock for a ridge or seam to latch onto. Finding a decent lip in the rock, she clamped her hand to it and began pulling herself along and searching for a foothold. She felt the rock begin to crumble a split second before it fell away and pitched her into the black, empty space below. She shrieked, but the sound was swallowed by the crashing surf below her.

Her care with the rope, the harness, and the knots held and she snapped to a halt. Her shoulder slammed into the rock face and her hip caught on a jagged outcropping, ripping her jeans and, by the feel of it, flesh. She sobbed. Every inch of her body hurt from the sudden stop on the rope. She hung suspended over the water for a few minutes and let tears come. Frustration and pain fueled a ragged howl.

"Why? Why did you let me fall, God?" she wailed.

You can do anything I ask you to do, but only in My strength.

God's strength. Not hers. She wiped her face with her sweater sleeve. He was right. She couldn't do this. Climbing a cliff face, in the dark, terrified, was beyond her. But it wasn't beyond God.

"Let's do this!" she yelled. The wind carried her words heavenward. As she began to climb again, Psalm 17:5 came to mind. She all but sang it as she felt for purchase with her hands and feet. "Uphold my steps in Your paths, that my footsteps may not slip."

She climbed upward and to the right for a while, making a small amount of progress. While holding still for a moment to catch her breath and let the screaming muscles in her arms rest, she breathed a prayer for a listening heart.

Climb down.

Down? No, I want to go up!

No, climb down.

I don't understand! Why should I go down?

A man's steps are of the Lord, How can he understand his own way?

OK.

She readjusted her footing and found a handhold that would allow her to move straight down the cliff face. In a matter of a few minutes, she came to an outcropping that was wide enough to stand on. She got her footing and relaxed her arms. Once she had rested, she slid her foot sideways and discovered a step in the ledge. Moving along the cliff on the tiny ledge she climbed up and found another step. Careful not to move too fast and to always find a good handhold, Lily found step after step ascending to the top. At last, she dragged herself onto the soft moss and leaf litter behind her car and flopped onto her back. She was hurt and breathing hard, but she was alive!

"Thank you, God!"

She sat up and undid the rope and her harness. She fished her cell phone out of her pocket and used the light to inspect the laceration on her hip. It had bled and her jeans were ruined, but she didn't need stitches. It would hurt tomorrow, but adrenaline was keeping the pain at bay for now. She turned the light on the car and discovered that the trunk had slid under a branch of a tree and was pinned shut. No wonder she couldn't open it.

Using her phone's light she followed her car's tracks back to the road. Where was it? She swung the light back and forth. Once she was on the gravel she found that the road took a sharp right-hand turn and wound off into the woods. On closer inspection, it was little more than a trail, almost like an afterthought. Was this where Stella came to watch the stars? Lily couldn't picture it.

An hour later found her at the junction with the paved road. Her phone battery had begun blinking and she knew she'd only have light for a few more minutes. She used it to take a closer look at the road she'd taken. A sign was sticking out of the leaves to the side of the road. She pulled it free.

Danger. Road closed. Do not enter.

"Well, that would have been nice to see a couple of hours

ago!" Why would Stella have sent her down this road? A sick feeling seeped into her stomach. What if Stella had meant for her to go down that road, but not for stargazing? Could her hatred of Herbert have spilled over to Lily? Lily's hand clamped over her mouth. Could Stella have intended for her to be hurt? Or worse? For what purpose? A violent shiver rolled over Lily. First the tires, then the climbing rope, now this.

She flung the sign back into the ditch and turned toward town. Her phone buzzed and shut down. Great. She tucked it in her back pocket, and, squaring her shoulders, crept along the edge of the road. Her heartbeat picked up speed as the darkness closed in. Little sounds in the woods made her jump. She half hoped a car would come along, but the city girl in her won out and she prayed no one would come along. The going was slow in the all-encompassing darkness. Lily almost wept for joy when the first street lights appeared in the distance.

It was after 2AM by the time she reached the porch of the inn. The windows were all dark save for one glowing light in the foyer. Every guest was fast asleep. Had anyone even noticed she was gone? If she'd gone over the cliff, how long would it have been before anyone noticed? Before anyone came looking? Would anyone have come looking? A deep sadness settled over her as she realized that she had no one. No one who would miss her. No one who would worry. Yes, at some point, Olivia would start to be concerned. But she could be gone days, or even weeks before her sister would think there was a problem. She was utterly alone.

Lily stood in the warm glow of the chandelier and welcomed the light. With it, clarity dawned. No. She wasn't alone. She had Someone who had promised that she would never, ever be alone.

Thank you, Lord, for never deserting me.

She dragged herself up the stairs to her room, careful not to wake anyone. She was still shaking, whether from fear or the cold she couldn't tell. With the door locked behind her and completely wrung out, she collapsed on the bed. Her body screamed, her clothes were covered in dirt and sweat, her hip was bloody and tender, and she didn't care. She pulled the thick quilt over herself and drifted into fitful sleep.

Noah tapped the toe of his shoe against the back door jam at the shop. He'd called Lily multiple times the night before, but hadn't reached her. At the time he assumed she was out to dinner. However, he'd been letting the phone in her room ring far longer than was reasonable. Where was she? He was about to hang up when he heard the click of the receiver being picked up.

"Hello?" He could hear the wince in her voice. It sounded like she was speaking through gravel.

"Lily? Is that you?"

"Yes," she whimpered.

"What's wrong?" He could hear the panic in his voice. He'd waited to call, not wanting to wake her. Why hadn't he'd gone straight to the inn from his sunrise tour?

"I'm fine. Honest." Her voice said she didn't even believe herself.

"I'm coming over. Stay put."

Noah's hand shook as he hung up the phone. Something was wrong. He yelled to Harley that he was going out and took off down Carriage Street at a dead run. His overactive imagination played out crazy scenarios as his long legs gobbled up the sidewalk. He was breathing hard by the time he took the porch steps of the Butterfly Cove Inn two at a time. He startled Ava when he burst into the foyer.

"Which is Lily's room?"

Her eyes wide, Ava pointed up the staircase. "Left at the top of the stairs, second on the right."

He took the interior stairs two at a time as well and had to come to a full stop and take a steadying breath before knocking on her door. He could have taken it clean off its hinges the way he was feeling.

"Lily?"

He could hear her moving around, but the time it took her to open the door was agonizing. She flinched at the sharp breath he sucked in when he saw her.

"Is it that bad?"

"What..." he swallowed, trying not to lose it. "What happened?" Her face was streaked with dirt and what he feared might be blood. An angry red mark on her cheek would fade to an ugly bruise if she didn't get ice on it soon. The ragged rip in her jeans revealed an ugly gash high on her hip. Both her jeans and sweater were ruined, filthy and ripped. Dark circles marred her cheeks and her beautiful gray eyes were rimmed red from crying.

"It's a long story," she mumbled, leaning on the door frame.

"I've got time," he said in a tone that left little doubt that he was staying put until she told him the whole thing. He touched her chin, bringing her eyes up to meet his.

She stepped back and motioned for him to enter. Wincing, she perched on the edge of a chair. He wanted to hold her, but she looked too fragile, as though a mere touch would shatter her. He scooted the other chair over to hers and, leaning forward with his elbows on his knees, took her hands.

She pulled in a deep breath and let the story spill out in disjointed pieces. Stella suggesting she go see the stars from the overlook in the park. The lousy directions and going off the road. Wrecking her car. Rappelling down a cliff and climbing back up. Walking back to the inn in the middle of the night.

He tried to hold it together, but when she got to the part where she fell while climbing, his face blanched and he sucked a breath between his teeth. Visions of her plummeting into the ocean in the middle of the night scared him unlike anything he'd ever experienced.

"But God had my back. I didn't get back here until after 2AM." She tried to run a hand through her hair and found it tangled beyond belief. "Oh, I must look a sight!" She cringed in embarrassment.

"You are the most beautiful sight I've ever seen," he whispered.

Her eyes had gone huge and they held his. She looked tiny and fragile. Without a thought, he reached for her and gathered her against his hard chest. He felt her stiffen and he loosened his hold. Instead of pulling away as he expected, she sank into his arms. Small sobs shook her shoulders. He brushed his hand over her hair in comfort.

"I was so scared," she hiccuped.

"Shhh," he cooed.

Fighting for composure she pushed off his chest and wiped her face with the grimy sleeve of her sweater. It left more dirt smudges than it helped. The face she turned toward him had a street urchin look and he couldn't help but smile.

"Oh, I was right. I look awful." She blushed crimson.

"And I was right." He hunched down so they were eye to eye. "You are beautiful. That being said, I think you might *feel* better after a shower."

"Everything hurts," she groaned.

"Make that a very hot shower, Advil, and a couple of ice packs."

"That... sounds glorious."

"You work on the shower and I'll go hunt up the drugs and the ice," he winked.

Lily limped toward the bathroom with an armload of clean clothes. Noah waited until the door clicked closed before he allowed himself to react. Sweat sprouted along his brow. Bile rose up the back of his throat. Gulping in air, he doubled over and rested his hands on his knees trying to pull it together. He feared he would start to cry. He tried to tell himself he'd feel the same way no matter who it was, but he knew that was a lie. He was sick thinking that Lily had been hurt. Lily. Feelings he didn't recognize burned through him and he ground the heel of his hand into his chest, gasping.

Unwilling to put a name to the emotions, he pulled it together. She was a friend and she was hurting and he could help. He could do that. He did that. That's who he was. Fix the hurting. This was no different than bandaids on blisters after tours. He shook his head. He was in so much trouble. Because he knew, in his deepest places, that she was different from any other friend he'd ever had and he would move heaven and earth to make things OK for her. However, he didn't need to move heaven and earth to find her Advil and ice, he just needed to find Miss Ava. He came across her in the kitchen making tea.

"Is everything alright, Noah?" she asked.

"I think so. Lily just… had an accident last night."

"Oh, dear." Ava touched her withered fingertips to her lips. "I didn't know. Is she alright?"

"She will be," he said. "Do you have an ice pack, Advil, and a handful of large bandaids?"

"Yes, yes, yes, of course." She shuffled to a cabinet on the other side of the kitchen and produced two old-fashioned cloth packs for ice and a first aid kit. "Will these do the trick?"

"Perfect, Miss Ava. Thank you." He filled the two ice packs from the freezer and fished around in the first aid kit. Holding up the ice, medicine, bandages, and first aid ointment as way of thanks, he headed for the stairs.

By the time he was back at her room, Lily had showered and changed. She was trying to comb the snarls from her hair when he tapped on the door and poked his head in. He'd been wrong. This was the most beautiful she'd ever been. She wore a soft sweater and a pair of leggings. Her legs were drawn up under her in the chair. Her glossy blonde hair, darker because it was wet, cascaded over her shoulders. She looked young and tired and perfect. He crouched in front of her and spread his armload on the floor between them. He handed her an ice pack.

"You're going to want that on your cheek. I'm not sure it will save you from a shiner, but it will help."

"Seriously?" She winced and took the ice pack.

He chuckled. "It won't be that bad, I promise. Now, your hip. Will you let me look at it?"

She blushed but nodded. Judging by the grimace on her face,

rolling down the top edge of her leggings was painful. A nasty cut ran along the ridge of her hip bone. It was no longer bleeding, but it was pink and raw. Noah winced when he saw it, knowing how much it must have hurt. He willed his hands to steady as he applied ointment and bandages. It was all he could do to keep his emotions out of his voice.

"There you go, good as new. Or at least it will be soon," he said as he repositioned the waistband of her leggings. She took the tablets he offered and downed them in one gulp of water.

He sat back on his heels and watched her. She peeked at him above the ice pack she held to her cheek and smiled.

"Thank you, Noah."

"Aww, Sweetheart." He rocked forward onto his knees and closed the short distance between them. He took her face in his hands, careful to avoid the abrasion on her cheek. He searched her eyes for a long breath before he leaned in and brushed her lips with his. It was tender and gentle and he wanted it to be much, much more. Too soon he forced himself to pull back, to look her in the eyes again. There was a stormy quality in their depths that he couldn't put his finger on.

She didn't pull away, but instead, reached out and touched his cheek. He caught her hand and pressed a kiss onto her palm. When she winced, he pulled her hand away and saw how raw her palms and fingertips were for the first time.

"Oh, Lily." His voice choked on emotion and he fought to maintain control. He would not break down. In that moment he wanted nothing more than to protect her for the rest of his life.

"It's not that bad," she said, pulling her hand away from his and fisting it in her lap.

He knew he wore his emotions on his sleeve, right out there for the world to see. He didn't care.

"Do you believe Stella gave you bad directions on purpose?"

"I don't know. I mean, why would she? Revenge on Herbert? It seems far-fetched. But there's also no way the place I ended up was a good place for stargazing. Maybe it was just an accident."

"I think we should speak to Chief Briggs again."

Lily shrugged. "Maybe. I think the man is getting tired of see-ing me coming."

"Do you feel up to walking into town?"

She shuddered but nodded her head. "I think it would be a good idea to get moving and not stiffen up."

He loved her *chutzpah*. She must hurt like crazy, but she pulled on a pair of TOMS and only grimaced a little as she descended the stairs. He wished he'd driven over so she didn't have to walk to the station. In the moment though, he hadn't thought of anything other than getting to her. All logical thought had left him when she'd answered the phone with a whimper.

He took her hand and forced his steps to slow, letting her set the pace. He couldn't believe he'd kissed her. It was like a dream. He could still taste her, could still feel her lips give under his. He hadn't planned on kissing her. He had tried hard to follow Par-ker's advice. To respect her, to care enough about her to not ask of her what he knew she would regret. But she'd been so beau-tiful sitting there. Beautiful, and vulnerable, and... perfect. He had just reacted. He stole a sidelong glance at her. Did she regret it? He hoped not. He didn't. Not by a long shot. It took all of his willpower not to pull her into his arms, right then and there, and kiss her again.

Chief Briggs rose when they entered his office and Noah thought he saw annoyance in the policeman's eyes a split sec-ond before concern for Lily slid into place.

"Are you alright, Ms. Emerson?"

"Yes, just had an... accident last night."

"I'm very sorry to hear that. What can I do for you today?" The policeman asked, directing his question at Noah. Yup, an-noyance.

"Lily's had a string of... unfortunate circumstances the last couple of days."

The cop's gaze flicked over Lily's battered cheek. "Other than the tires, you mean?"

"Ayuh. Yesterday afternoon we went rock climbing and discovered that her rope had been sabotaged. Then last night she was given awful directions to the park that sent her down Cliffs Trail Road."

Chief Briggs whistled. "That road's not safe."

"I know. Something's going on. I can feel it. First her uncle, now her."

"Now, I don't know if I'd jump right to foul play."

"After we found that the rope had been cut, we remembered that a gentleman by the name of Carmen Franco had been holding it and we think he may have tampered with it."

"Well, those are wicked big accusations." Chief Briggs. "Do you have the rope?"

Noah looked at Lily. "No, it's still in the trunk of my car," she admitted.

"The simple facts of the matter, Miss Emerson, are that things happen. Unpleasant things. Tires go flat, ropes wear out, directions aren't followed. I agree that it is unfortunate that all those things have happened to you on this one little trip, but I hardly see anything that points to foul play."

"Jim..." Noah couldn't believe the man wasn't taking them seriously.

"No, Noah, it's fine," Lily said.

The chief raised his hand. "That being said, if you can get that rope for me and I agree that it was cut I would be willing to go speak to Mr. Franco and get his take on this. Where did you say he's staying?"

"The Bellamy."

"Thank you, Chief Briggs," Lily added as they rose.

"Good day, ma'am," the policeman gave her a polite smile.

"Good day," she returned and managed to usher a ticked off Noah out the door.

"I can't believe he all but blew us off!"

"I can," she said, trying to soothe him. "He's right. There's nothing sinister about blown tires, or frayed rope, or bad directions."

"I'd still like to know why Stella sent you down Cliffs Trail

Road last night," he growled.

"Now that I agree with. Let's go find out." She took his hand and led him toward the water and the bed and breakfast. "Come on Watson!"

The bell above the door chimed as they stepped through. Stella appeared behind the front desk in a pair of jeans and a flamboyant orange shirt that should have clashed with her radiant red hair but, instead, made her look young and vibrant.

"Lily," she began with a smile. Then she took in the chafed cheek and her face paled. "Oh, my dear! What happened? Are you alright?" She rushed around the desk to take Lily in her arms. Her concern appeared genuine.

"I had a bit of an accident last night on my way to watch the stars like you suggested."

"No! Oh, how awful. What happened?"

"I followed your directions, but I crashed at the end of the road."

"She went down the Cliffs Trail Road," Noah added.

Stella's face went white. "No. No. I did not tell her to go down that road. Isn't that road closed?"

"The sign's down," said Lily. "The directions said to take a left onto Park Road, go two miles, turn left, go one mile, parking lot on the right."

"Those are close to the directions, except it was six miles on Park Road, not two. Are you sure it said two?"

Could she have misread a six for a two? Lily bit her lip. She wasn't sure.

"You don't think..." Stella's horrified voice rose. "You don't think that I... that I... sent you down there on purpose?"

Lily couldn't make her brain work. That was what she'd thought at the time. Noah came to her rescue. "She was pretty shaken up. We're just trying to figure out what happened."

"Is everything alright?"

All three turned at the unexpected voice behind Stella.

"Alistair?" Lily asked in complete disbelief. "When did you get here?"

Alistair answered, never taking his eyes off Stella. "I've been here awhile now."

"I don't understand. What are you doing here?"

He turned his eyes from Stella to Lily and gave her a sheepish smile that didn't fit at all with the distinguished, silvered-haired man in designer jeans and an expensive white dress shirt with the sleeves rolled up to the elbow. And yet he looked like he belonged there behind the desk.

"I'm here helping Stella," he said. "She's had a little trouble getting things on track here, online bookings and record-keeping and whatnot. I offered to give her a hand." His focus had returned to Stella and she blushed at his adoring look.

"But I spoke to you. At your office. Twice."

"Call forwarding," he said. "You must have had Deidra forward your calls."

"I tried. No cell signal."

"Ah," he nodded. "I have a line here."

"Were you... were you here, when Uncle...?"

He watched the waves crash on the beach for a moment, collecting his thoughts. "Yes, I was already here when Herbert arrived in town. I didn't see him while he was here, but I have a feeling I was on his list. The conversation you and I had the other day confirmed that."

"The Sandpiper, Stella... That's the 'competition', isn't it?"

Stella had moved next to him and he slipped his arm around her shoulders. "It is. As I said when we spoke, I haven't done anything to compromise EHI. Stella and I met at the hospitality expo in Baltimore two years ago. We didn't even know the other knew Herbert for the longest time. Then... Well, helping Stella stay on her feet won't hurt EHI at all, but I doubted Herbert would have seen it that way. Hence the secrecy."

Lily was at a loss for words.

Stella whispered, "Lily, you don't think that Alistair had

anything to do with... anything... do you?"

Lily wrung her hands. Each piece of her world had slipped off its axis in the last few days. She couldn't tell who anyone was anymore. She opened her mouth to answer, but no sound came out. She snapped it closed, looking from one to the other. Noah placed a steadying hand on her shoulder.

"Maybe we should pick up this conversation later," he suggested.

"It's just that I know Carmen Franco was here in town," Stella rushed to add. "There's been bad blood between them for a long time. Even when Herbie and I were seeing each other years ago it had begun. Herbie had wronged Carmen and the man wouldn't let it go. I never did gather what it was, but Carmen was relentless. Calling, showing up at Herbie's office, even confronting us outside the theater one night. I couldn't believe it when I saw him in town."

"If you believe there was any sort of criminal act around Herbert's accident," Alistair added, "Franco isn't the only one here in town who had a problem with your uncle. Before Herbert arrived, I received several irate phone calls from a gentleman by the name of Edwin Hurst. Herbert had promised him a lot of money to make a deal happen and the man wasn't getting paid like he thought he ought to."

Lily and Noah exchanged a look.

"I see that news doesn't surprise you," Alistair added.

"We've already spoken with Hurst," Noah said.

"During a couple of those phone calls, I would have said he was mad enough to kill Herbert. I'm not saying he did, I'm just saying I'm not the only one in town Herbert had a problem with and neither is Carmen Franco."

Memories of all the times she and Alistair had worked together flooded Lily's mind. Long hours spent pouring over reports and plans. Working lunches and business trips. Even the occasional Christmas party or gala. He'd never been anything but kind, filling the father role she craved. She couldn't find a single incident that would lead her to believe him capable of hurting anyone.

"Alistair, I can't imagine you ever doing anything to hurt anyone, even Uncle." Her voice held a sharp note of empathy. "He was a hard man, but you weathered each storm that came along with grace. I never suspected that you had anything to do with Uncle's accident."

Stella breathed a sigh of relief and sagged against Alistair. He leaned down and placed a tender kiss on the temple. The smile she turned on him melted Lily's heart.

The tension in the air dissipated and Alistair took the opportunity to change the subject. "Stella tells me you're seeing the sights before you head back to Boston."

"I'm showing her around the island," Noah added.

She couldn't quite read his expression. Protective? Maybe. Whatever it was felt comforting. Like a warm blanket on a cold day. Or like when he wrapped his arm around her shoulders when she needed it.

"There's no place in the world like Summer Harbor," Alistair added.

"I'm finding that to be the case," said Lily.

"Of course my favorite spot is right here," Alistair said, smiling down at Stella. He nodded out the window toward the sand bar. "And my second favorite is right out there. Bar Island. Don't go back to Boston without seeing it."

"I've had it on my to-do list since I got here," Lily admitted. "Maybe tomorrow."

"Are you returning to Boston soon?" Alistair asked.

Lily felt Noah stiffen next to her. She couldn't look at him. Couldn't stand to see the disappointment on his face. "I haven't figured that out yet."

"I'll be headed back soon. I plan to split my time between the office there and here. If that will work. I don't know what my role will be moving forward," he added with a questioning look at Lily. It occurred to her that she held this man's future in her hands. It was a staggering thought. She couldn't imagine trying to run EHI without him. How could she? She made a split decision.

"I'll be back soon, as well," she assured him. She felt Noah droop next to her and her heart gave a painful squeeze. It hurt that she was hurting him. But what choice did she have? She was now the managing partner in a massive hotel chain. She couldn't just turn her back on it.

They left the bed and breakfast, but Lily felt restless and edgy. The decision she'd made to return to Boston had eluded her for days. The fact of the matter was, she had responsibilities. Others depended on her. She had to go. She hugged her arms around herself as they walked. Noah was quiet and she was afraid to look at him. She knew what she'd see. Disappointment, annoyance, hurt, maybe even anger. *Oh, Noah, I warned you not to fall for me!*

CHAPTER TWELVE

I think a major cheering up is in order." Noah reached out and wrapped his arm around her shoulders, pulling her against his side. He was tired of watching her try to comfort herself. She didn't need to do that while she had him around. His heart made a compelling argument for kissing the top of her head, but his brain told him to hold off.

"More ice cream?" The smile she turned toward him seemed forced. It made him want to try even harder to bring it back to her eyes.

"Better."

"Better than Zoe's concoctions? I doubt it."

He laughed. "We'll see."

They strolled along Shore Drive and stopped at a food truck parked along the curb. Noah ordered two daily special subs, two bottles of water, and a bag of chips.

"Better than ice cream?" Lily asked, eyebrows raised, skepticism written all over her face.

"Nah, these are good, but they're nothing compared to double chocolate salted caramel swirl."

"I didn't think so."

"Oh, these aren't the cheering up," he winked.

They walked out along a wooden walkway suspended over the water. At the end was a magnificent two-masted ship. It took her breath away. Lily slowed, mesmerized. Shiny black paint on the sides was topped by glossy, gold-lettered wood. *Douglas Blye*. It was a nod to a time long past.

Noah didn't even hesitate, but jogged up the steps and swung himself onto the boat. "Harrison?" he called as he reached back to help Lily down onto the smooth wooden deck.

The young man who emerged from the main cabin wore a lazy grin. His hair was bleached nearly white by the sun and hung long over his ears. He was slim and his jeans sagged from his hips above bare feet.

"Noah, man, how's it goin'?" He finished cleaning his hands on a rag that he stuffed into his back pocket as he strode forward. Noah took the man's outstretched hand and clapped him on the shoulder.

"Great to see you, Harrison. How's the old girl?"

"She's holding up just fine," Harrison replied, running his hand over the brightwork along the rail. "Just polishing the brass today. Gotta be ready for the cruise on Thursday."

"You get a good crew this year?"

"Not quite as good as the summer you were here, but they'll mesh before long."

"Harrison, this is Lily Emerson." He saw her reaching out to shake Harrison's outstretched hand and caught her arm in the knick of time. He turned her palm up revealing the abraded skin. "You should skip Harrison's bruising handshake."

The man winced. "That doesn't look comfortable at all." He touched her arm with a gentle hand instead, compassion in his eyes. "Nice to meet you, Lily."

"Lovely to meet you, as well."

"Hey man, mind if we cop a squat on deck for lunch?" Noah asked, hoisting the bag containing their subs.

"By all means, help yourself." Harrison's gesture encompassed the whole deck.

"Thanks, man." Noah took Lily's elbow and steered her to the middle of the windjammer.

"This is... amazing."

"That she is."

"She?"

"Windjammers are all women, even the ones with male names."

"Interesting."

"She's the last of her kind. Of the thousands built in Maine during the eighteen-hundreds, only the Douglas Blye remains."

They'd reached a bench that afforded them a view of the harbor and unwrapped their sandwiches. She pulled one foot up under her. He saw her wince and knew it was a vain attempt to ignore her burning hip. Noah propped himself against the other end of the bench. One foot on the seat, the other on the deck, and dove into his sub.

"And Harrison?" Lily asked.

"He worked on the crew for years, then bought her a couple of years ago when the previous captain retired. He works hard to keep her on the water. Tuesdays are quiet. The crew's off and Harrison is almost always here making repairs, maintaining, cleaning. The man lives and breathes this boat. He summers here and winters out of a port in the Virgin Islands."

Lily raised her eyebrows. "Wow."

"When you live off the water, you have to follow the sun."

"But not you."

"I did a couple of winters, but it isn't for me. Too much time away from home. I'm content to fill my winter days as a handyman here in town."

Her eyes turned wistful as she looked out across the sparkling water. All of a sudden, Lily grinned and tried to cover it by taking a drink of water.

"What?"

"Better than Zoe's ice cream. Just barely, but better. And if you ever tell her I said that I will call you a liar."

Noah chuckled and took another bite of his sub. She was easy to please. Ice cream and impromptu picnics on the deck of a windjammer he could handle. If he was truthful with himself though, she made him feel like he could handle lassoing the moon. If he wasn't careful, there would be a permanent scar when she left. Unwilling to dampen the mood he flashed her a playful smile. "Sufficiently cheered up?"

"After yesterday I doubted it was possible, but yes, sufficiently cheered up."

"I'm sorry yesterday was rough."

"Did I tell you that between rock climbing and my disastrous attempt at stargazing I opened Uncle's third letter?" She stared into the distance, thinking, and he waited for her to continue. "There were four letters in the envelope. I could only get through one. It was written to my mother about six years ago. It was full of regret and sorrow."

"He must have cared for her very much."

"I'm not sure, but it might have been more than caring. Piecing together all three letters I think they might have…" She turned away and pulled her knees up to her chest. "I don't want to think of my mother having been unfaithful to my father."

Noah reached out and pulled her against his chest. They sat in silence for a long time. Seals played in the water off the stern and seagulls swooped and screeched hoping for tidbits from their lunch.

After a while, Lily pulled away from him and smiled. "This was… perfect. Thank you." She stood and leaned on the rail, letting the breeze push her hair away from her face.

Noah leaned back on the seat and propped his feet on the railing, ankles crossed. He'd needed the cheering up, too. The bank had called the day before to make an appointment for Thursday. A chance to save his business. If his guess was right, his last chance. It didn't seem fair that his dream should hinge on a meeting with a loan officer. Like a storm hovering just out of sight on the horizon, ready to roll in and wipe out all his hard work.

It wasn't that he hadn't tried. Maybe he should have gone to college and gotten a degree in business management after all. He had the dream, but the skills were a bit lacking. Parker had a minor in restaurant management and he'd asked his friend to help him with his business plan the last time he'd gone to the bank for a loan. It had been better than anything he could have put together himself, but he knew it was still far from professional.

After the bank had denied his last loan application, he'd

tried finding an investor outside of the bank, but that hadn't panned out, either. He'd discovered that you needed to know people with money to invest. After several failed attempts, he'd given up on the investor idea and was back to a bank loan. He wasn't sure why the business wasn't in the black. Numbers were not his strong suit, but it seemed like Acadian Adventures should be able to hold its own. Maybe he'd ask Harley or Parker to take a look at the numbers for him. Could it be as simple as an obvious oversight?

He ran a tired hand down his face and tried not to let the frustration and worry rob the moment of its serenity. He forced a smile and turned back to Lily. She was studying him with an enigmatic expression. Had she spoken to him?

"Hmmm?"

"You just seemed to be elsewhere for a minute," she replied.

"Sorry."

"Anything wrong?"

He studied her for a long moment. Asking her for help was out of the question. To begin with, she'd flipped out when she thought he wanted her to invest in his business. But beyond that, he didn't want to burden her with his troubles on top of her own. Besides, he didn't have much experience asking for help. Helping? He was your guy. Finding himself on the begging end rankled. It was all pride and ego. Could he set them aside long enough to seek help? Going over his business plan and making suggestions wasn't that big a deal, right? That's what friends did for each other.

He continued mulling it over as he moved to gather up the remains of their picnic. "Thanks, Harrison!" he called as they headed back up the wooden walk away from the boat. The man waved from where he stood in the bow tinkering on the rigging.

Lily was still studying him as they turned onto Main Street and walked away from the water. She'd been quiet, as if she knew he needed to gather his jumbled thoughts. He stuffed his hands in his pockets and hunched his shoulders. Whether he was embarrassed for needing help in the first place, or afraid she'd refuse, he wasn't sure, but his lunch had turned to a lump in his stomach.

"The thing is," he began. "The thing is, I need to go to the bank on Thursday. I applied for a loan and they called yesterday to set up an appointment. I have a business plan, but…"

He couldn't look at her just then. He felt so edgy that he might just bolt back to the shop. No. He needed her. He didn't want to sound as desperate as he felt. He swallowed back the uneasy tremor in his voice and barreled ahead before he talked himself out of it.

"Could you check it out and, I don't know, make a few suggestions?" There. He'd asked. He hoped to see her charming smile lighting her face and hope twinkling in her eyes when he turned toward her. Instead, her face was blank.

"Yes, of course," she said without emotion.

He flashed her a thankful grin and she smiled back, but it failed to light her face the way he loved. Maybe the cheering-up picnic hadn't worked as well as he'd hoped.

They'd reached the shop and he loped to the back to grab the business plan off his desk. More of a table in the corner than an actual desk, it took a minute to find. The jumble of tide charts, tour schedules, employment applications, brochures, photos, junk mail, and bills made him realize, not for the first time, that he needed a filing cabinet. Or a trash can. Or organizational skills of any kind. Maybe he could task Harley with tackling the mess. He snatched the manilla envelope containing the business plan out of the debris and hurried back to Lily.

She waited right where he'd left her by the front entrance. He slowed as he approached and drank in the sight of her. His 'no summer girls' rule had crashed and burned along the way and he had zero desire to dredge it back up.

Lily watched Noah saunter back down the alley toward her with a sick feeling in the pit of her stomach. She was a complete fool. What was it King Solomon had said? Like a dog that returns to his vomit is a fool who repeats his folly. Yup, that was her. Fool. When would she ever learn? She would never be seen as anything other than her position, her status.

If that was the case, why had she said yes to looking at his business plan? She sighed. Because even though he only cared about what she could do for him, she had become quite fond of the man. Whatever his motivation, he had been a friend when she needed one, a confidant, and a source of strength that she craved. She'd be a fool and go over his business plan. At least he hadn't asked her to invest hundreds of thousands of dollars... yet.

"Here you go," he said, handing her the envelope. "It should all be in there, but if you need anything else just let me know. And Lily?" He waited until she looked up. "Thank you. You have no idea how much this means to me."

Oh, she had a feeling she did. She flashed him a too-bright smile and took the envelope.

"I hate to do this, but I've got a tour coming up in a few minutes. You OK to make it back to the inn?"

"Yes, of course."

"Not too sore? I mean I could have one of the guys drive you."

"No, I'm fine. Walking will help, right?"

He leaned in as though he meant to kiss her, but she pretended not to notice and said a cheery goodbye before heading up the street as fast as her aching hip could handle. She should have taken him up on the offer of a ride, but all she could think of in the moment was escaping before she couldn't hold her disappointment in any longer.

The long walk back to the inn took an eternity and by the time she arrived in her room, she was exhausted. She tossed the envelope onto the writing desk in the corner and sank onto the edge of the bed with a moan. First pain meds, then work. Or not. Maybe she wouldn't even bother looking at the business plan. It's not like she'd promised to do anything with it anyway. A simple 'looks good!' would suffice and then she could just walk away. Go back to Boston. Back to— she almost said normal, but there was no normal anymore.

She had to find something to counter the throbbing in her hip. The phone rang as she rummaged in her overnight bag for a bottle of ibuprofen, startling her.

"Hello, Lily Emerson speaking."

"Girl! It's been DAYS since you called and told me you had a hot date and then NOTHING. You're killing me!"

"Hey, Liv."

"No, seriously, I am dying here."

Lily had to smirk at her sister's typical drama. "Well, as I told you on Saturday, it wasn't a date, so..."

"There was a handsome man, there was dinner, and you cared what you looked like. It was a date."

"OK, fine, it was a date... sort of."

"Mmm-hmm."

Lily started to say there wasn't anything worth mentioning, but the words died on her tongue. Nothing worth mentioning? Like the fact that, fool that she was, she'd fallen in love with the man? Or that he'd taken her home to meet his parents and she'd fallen equally hard for them? Or that he'd kissed her? Or that she'd kissed him back?

"It doesn't matter whether it was or wasn't a date."

"How come?" Olivia's voice had turned softer and she sounded...like mom.

"Because I was right, he didn't see me for me, just for what I could contribute to his business."

"Aww, Sis. I'm sorry."

"I feel ridiculous. I mean I have rules against dating for a reason. And I didn't follow them. I can't blame him. I just wish I hadn't fallen so hard before I came to my senses."

"That bad?"

"Oh, Liv, I fell hard. He was helpful and fun and when he kissed—"

"Wait, he kissed you?"

Lily blushed at the memory. "Yesterday morning. I got hurt

on Sunday night and when he found out he came here to the inn and took care of my bumps and bruises. And then... he kissed me."

"OK, back up. You got hurt?"

"Um, yes, just a little banged up from going off the road Sunday night. No biggie." She cringed. She hadn't meant to tell her sister about crashing her car. Or about the climbing rope, or the flat tires. She never told Olivia anything to make her worry. "Anyway, this afternoon he asked me to look over his business plan, so I know it was all just to sweeten me up."

"Seriously?"

"I know, right? I shouldn't have gotten involved with him in the first place." What rankled the most was how easily she'd slipped right back to trusting him. Call her Sweetheart, butter her up with a pretty picnic. She bit down hard on her lip to keep it from trembling. There was no way, no way at all, that she was crying on the phone to her sister.

"No. I mean 'Seriously? You're going to fault the guy for asking for help?'"

Lily was stunned. Couldn't Olivia see that he'd used her to get what he wanted? It was Carmen all over again.

"Lil, guys don't ask girls for help. That must have taken crazy, crazy guts to suck it up and admit that he needed a hand. I mean it's not like he asked you for a million dollars."

No, he hadn't. And she'd already flipped out over thinking that he wanted money, but he hadn't. Was she overreacting to this, too?

"Besides, you just, maybe two seconds ago, said you liked how helpful he was. Let me get this straight, he can help you, but you can't help him?"

Lily opened her mouth to speak, but no words came to mind. Was she so distrustful that a friend couldn't even ask for assistance without her assuming the worst? Tears flooded her eyes. "Oh, Liv, you're right."

"Of course I'm right. You know, most of the time I rely on you for advice. It's nice to be the wiser one for once."

"Don't let it go to your head."

"Never," Olivia said, then continued talking, but it sounded like she had covered the phone.

"What?"

"Oh, sorry. I was talking to Deidra. I hope you don't mind that I borrowed her. Come to find out I don't have an assistant. Weird, right?"

"Liv? Are you... at the office?"

"Yeah, the lawyer sent over this ridiculous stack of papers and I've been trying to get through them for you. Deidra has been a godsend!"

"You're in the office?"

"Yes, silly. How am I supposed to help you out if I'm not here? I mean Alistair's not in either. One of us has to be!"

Lily was speechless.

"Sis, the real reason I called is this morning I talked to the lawyer and... This is weird. Like... crazy weird."

"What is?"

"Uncle Herbert left us both his shares in EHI."

"Yes, I knew that."

"But..."

"What is it, Liv?"

"Well, he... Lil, he left me everything else."

OK, back to being speechless. Uncle had left Olivia everything he owned? Lily held her forehead in her free hand and tried to wrap her mind around that. Herbert had never been close to either of them. She had assumed his estate would go to charities, organizations, his alma mater even. But Olivia? She never would have dreamed that possible.

"Lil?"

"I'm here. That's... great."

"I don't even know what to do with it. I mean the condo I'll sell, but do I have to do anything with the rest of it right now?"

"Of course not. You're smart, you'll figure it out."

"You're not mad?"

Lily was dumbfounded. "Mad? Why on earth would I be

mad?"

"Because he didn't leave you anything except the shares?"

"Oh, Liv, I don't care about that."

"OK, good. I was so worried you'd be furious." Relief infused Olivia's voice. "Now, tell me more about driving your car off the road?"

CHAPTER THIRTEEN

The sun rose the next morning in no particular hurry. Lily felt its lethargy in her core. She'd stayed up until the wee hours of the morning finishing Noah's business plan. He had a great start, but it had none of the business lingo and polish she knew it needed. She'd worked and reworked it until she was satisfied that the bank would take it seriously.

It was an excellent idea. Expanding offerings of tours to include rock climbing, sailing, paddle boarding, biking, and hiking. Minimal expenses after equipment purchases. Good return on investment meant the bank shouldn't see it as a risk. His current financial situation was a bit of a concern. He was a bit in the red. But it was the beginning of the season. To compensate she'd included the addition of an accountant and a bookkeeper in the new plan. When, exhausted, she had finally switched off her lamp and crawled under her covers, she had been happy with what she'd put together. Under different circumstances, she would have been tempted to invest in Acadian Adventures herself.

"Lily, Dea-ah, you had mail dropped off this morning," Ava called to her as she came downstairs for breakfast.

"Oh, thank you, Ava. I've been here long enough that I ended up having my secretary forward paperwork to me." She took the small stack of envelopes and noticed that the top one had no address, only *Lilianna* in chunky, bold print.

"That top one there was dropped off by a rather distinguished gentleman with silver hair. I can't remember the name he gave. It was odd I think. But I do remember he had the most delicious smell. Sandalwood." Ava's face took on a flush that gave a girlish quality to her crepey cheeks. "Just like my late husband."

"Alistair."

"Yes, yes, yes, that was his name."

"Thank you, Ava."

Lily opened the note from Alistair while she ate her breakfast.

Lily,

I want you to know that I will handle the office while you wrap things up in Summer Harbor. Take all the time you need. I am returning this morning and will do whatever is needed on that end. Please rest, focus, grieve, regroup. EHI will still be here when you return.

I know that you want to see as much of this beautiful place as you can, including the sand bar and Bar Island. I saw this morning that the weather report is absolute perfection and I highly recommend taking the day to explore.

Take care,
Alistair

Lily took her coffee back to her room, not wanting to miss a moment of the perfect day. A few hours of sleep must have been all that was needed to soothe her aches and pains, because she only felt a slight sting in her hip. She pulled on a pair of capris, her favorite washed-soft RedSox t-shirt, and her running shoes. The tide chart in her room showed that low tide was about three hours away. The sandbar that connected Summer Harbor to Bar Island appeared a couple of hours before low tide and she didn't want to waste the chance to hike the wooded trails that crisscrossed from the rocky waterfront to the windblown cliffs on the far side of Bar Island.

Within minutes she was headed down Main Street toward the water. The breeze was cooler than she'd anticipated. She should have brought her sweater. The thought had no sooner come to mind and she cringed, picturing the ruined mess she'd thrown in the trash. What she needed was a sweatshirt. She turned down Carriage Street and popped into the store at Acadian Adventures. She'd seen just the one she wanted the first day when she'd stopped with Princess. It was a dreamy shade of yellow and was so thick and luxurious she knew it would feel glorious to burrow into. She had grabbed one the right size and was heading to the register when she heard a familiar voice behind her.

"Where are you off to this morning?" Noah asked.

She turned and smiled at him. She couldn't help it, she was delighted to see him. She felt she owed him an apology. A serious one. However, as he walked toward her his smile said that he was just as delighted to see her. Maybe she'd just keep her overreaction to herself. "Bar Island."

"Want company? The water's a little choppy and my next tour has been postponed until tomorrow."

"That would be... perfect," she said as she paid for her new sweatshirt. As they walked out of the shop she took his offered hand. He turned hers, palm up, and inspected the abrasions on her fingertips.

"These look better."

"Yes, much." How could she have thought he was anything but sincere? Olivia had been right to scold her. She needed to stop assuming the worst in people. She'd become pessimistic. Just like Uncle. That thought sobered her. Was that how it had started with him? Pessimism that turned to rage over the years?

Oh, please God, no.

"What prompted this particular excursion?" Noah asked, interrupting her thoughts. She shook herself free of the gloomy observation.

"Alistair." At Noah's raised eyebrow she continued. "He left for Boston this morning. On his way out of town, he dropped a note off at the inn to tell me not to worry about EHI and to do what I needed to rest and regroup. I realized that I hadn't given myself permission to do that. I kept doing these things that made me feel better, but then I'd beat myself up over the fact that I'd chosen that instead of dealing with my responsibilities and undo any good that the jogging, kayaking, rock climbing, ice cream eating, deck picnicking had done." It was not lost on her that almost all of those activities had included him. "Today I intend to do what I need to do for me, with no guilt."

"Good."

They reached the beach and the sandbar had started to reveal itself. A long ribbon of wet pebbles, seaweed-covered rocks, and gray sand stretched out in front of them.

"Looks like you nailed the timing. We should have about four hours before high tide cuts off the island again."

They reached the shore of Bar Island and wove their way up the path away from the water. The rich aromas of pine and fir mingled with the pungent smell of forest floor and tang of salt air. The path curved past a grove of towering oak trees and began to climb higher onto the island.

"I haven't been here in ages," Noah commented as they clambered up a ragged part of trail littered with rocks. "My dad used to bring me out here on his rare days off, usually in the fall when it was quieter."

"Tell me more about them," she coaxed.

"My Dad's... all the things I want to be. He's strong and kind, smart and brave. He's a lobsterman, which means long hours, few days off, and uncertain pay. But he can weather it all as it comes. He met Mom when she came to Summer Harbor, fresh out of culinary school, to work as a sous-chef at a fancy hotel near the pier. They have been head over heels in love ever since. It gives me hope, ya know?"

"That sounds... wonderful." Hope. In his letter, Herbert had said that without her mother he'd had no hope. But that's not where hope comes from. If only he had known where true hope could be found. She wondered if Noah would ever find that kind of hope.

"My mom, she's a spitfire. She was only a sous-chef for that one summer. She couldn't stand not running the kitchen. Until they moved a few years ago, she was the head chef at a swanky hotel from May to October. The rest of the year she was mom to me and whoever I dragged home. I've never met another person who loves on people the way Mom can. Now she's the head chef at a place on the mainland. I think she's happy there, but I know she misses the island."

They had crested the hill and got a brief glimpse of the turquoise water beyond. The trail they had chosen cut back into the trees and the cool, dew-sodden air before it descended toward the center of the island.

"I never got a chance to thank you for taking me to meet them on Sunday. They were terrific. I hadn't sat at a dining room table for a family dinner since I was eight. It was exquisite."

"Eight?" Disbelief made his voice crack.

"After my mom... You should be thankful for what you have."

"I am." He squeezed her hand.

The trail opened into a field and Lily's breath caught. A rippling blanket of purple, pink, and blue flowers perfumed the air. It was a fairytale in the midst of the forest.

"Oh..." she breathed.

"They're lupines," Noah said on a breath close to her ear. "They're always a little early right here. The ones in town haven't started flowering yet."

"I didn't know lupines smelled like this," she whispered as she closed her eyes and inhaled the delicate aroma.

"They don't by themselves. It's because there are so many." He grabbed her hand and tugged her into the field. "Come on."

They wandered through the flowers, careful not to disturb them. A few times Lily reached out to run her fingers along a unique blossom. Reaching a clearing in the flowers, Lily threw herself onto the sun-warmed grass.

"Come watch the clouds with me," she invited.

Noah joined her, laying on his back with his ankles crossed and his head resting on one bent arm. His strong thigh rested against hers. The wind swayed the lupine blossoms above their heads and skittered the clouds across the sky. Alistair had been right. Perfection.

"What was life like for little Lily Emerson?" Noah asked.

"The fragments I remember of my mom are happy ones, but I was only eight when she passed away. It gets a little dimmer as time goes on."

"Aww, Sweetheart." He took her hand where it rested next to his in the grass. "I shouldn't have pried."

"No, no. It's good to remember. She loved people. I remember these big dinner parties she and Daddy would throw. Lots of laughing and music. She loved music. I wasn't a bit surprised when Stella said my mom had made her feel included."

"Do you remember Stella at all?"

"Not really. A vague image of Uncle with his arm around her, smiling, while she waved at us from the door. But it's fuzzy. After my mom died, those parties stopped. Daddy dove into work and I grew up in boarding schools."

"That must have been so hard."

"In ways, but God turns hard things into good for those who love Him." She paused, deep in thought. "My sister was pretty young when Mom died. She had nannies until Dad passed away, and then I had to decide what was best for her. I was in my senior year of high school when he died and I sent her to the same boarding school that next fall."

"How much younger is she?"

"Five years," Lily murmured as she let her mind drift after memories. It wasn't long before the warm sun and quiet lulled her, and she drifted off.

Lily woke with a start. The light had changed. When she had fallen asleep laying in the grass, long shadows lapped the edges of the meadow. Now the sun bore down on them from high above. She sat up, disoriented. She tried to rub the sleep from her eyes and get her bearings. Hiking, Bar Island. Lupines. Noah. Noah! She turned and found him sound asleep as well, one arm under his head, the other drooped over his eyes. His breathing was steady.

Watching him sleep felt like intruding. She blushed. He was so handsome. All long arms and legs and muscles. She chided herself and looked away, glancing at her watch instead. Her heart hammered in her chest as her mind wrapped around the time. They'd missed the low tide window!

"Noah," she called, shaking his shoulder. He sprang awake at her panicked voice. "The tide!"

He looked around, trying to get his bearings the same as she had.

"OK, let's go see if we can get back across. But don't worry, alright?"

"Alright." She wasn't convinced. They were ten minutes late already.

They took the trail back at a much quicker pace than they had kept earlier. Noah reached out here and there to balance her or catch her from a slip. They burst from the forest onto the shore and were met with an expanse of water. Not a bit of the sand bar still remained. Lily's shoulders slumped.

"Hey, no worries," Noah said as he lifted her chin and met her eyes. His twinkled. "We can hike and explore and be back here in seven hours to go back across. Not the worst way to spend a day. I mean, I'll be hungry enough to eat a moose when we get back but other than that..."

"Not a bad day," she consented.

They turned back up the trail but took a different branch at their first opportunity. The new trail wound around the westward edge of the island, a gradual climb to the summit that took them well over an hour.

As they hiked Noah took Lily's hand in his. He rubbed his thumb along the back of her knuckles making her fingers tingle.

"I had a thought," he began. "What if I came to Boston?"

"Came to Boston?"

"I mean summers are crazy busy, but I could drive down in the fall. Maybe we could... go out."

Oh, Lord, give me the words! Lily silently begged.

"Noah, I have enjoyed our time together here in Summer Harbor. Your friendship has saved my sanity this past week."

The look in his eyes told her he knew a 'but' was coming. She pulled her hand away.

"I tried to tell you, I can't date anyone right now. I just... can't." Her heart ached as she said it. She wanted to just say 'yes' and see where it went. But her resolve held firm. It had to.

"I know, I know." He pushed his hands through his hair, linked his fingers behind his neck, and turned away. "I know I said I understood and that I was cool with it. But honestly? I don't. And I'm not. The more time I spend with you, the more time I want to spend with you. I hate that you're leaving to go back to Boston. I hate that you won't be here every day so I can cheer you up with ice cream, or hold your hand, or catch you when you fall."

His expression had turned dismal as he talked and it killed Lily to see him hurting. But what could she say?

"And then I kissed you yesterday, and I know I shouldn't have, but I did and it was epic. I just want to keep kissing you."

"Oh, Noah." Tears blurred her vision. She tried blinking them away, but they overflowed anyway. "You have no idea how much I want to be able to say yes. I just..."

"Can't. I know." His voice had turned gruff. They reached the summit of the island and Noah stopped with his back to Lily. "I think I need a few minutes," he said, not turning to look at her. Without another word he stalked away and into the woods.

She watched him go. Her shoulders slumped. He was angry. She'd wanted to reach out and touch his shoulder, but indecision had made the choice for her and she hadn't had the chance. As Noah left her heart had broken a little.

That heartbreak woke her up. She was well on her way to falling in love with Noah and if she didn't put an end to things right now she risked permanent damage to her fragile heart. Tears streamed down her cheeks. Maybe it was already too late to avoid the pain. She needed to leave. She needed distance. Feet dragging, she headed back to the sand bar to wait for low tide.

She trudged along. The day hadn't gone as planned and she was desperate to go back to the inn. She almost added 'and pack her bag', but that wasn't the truth. She didn't want to pack her bag or go back to Boston.

God, You knew I needed someone this week and You sent Noah. I thank You for that. But I don't understand why You would send him? Why does he have to be so wonderful? Why does it have to hurt so much?

For as the heavens are higher than the earth, so are my ways higher than your ways, and my thoughts than your thoughts.

He let his long legs carry him away from her, putting distance between them. He didn't turn around. He couldn't. He would not beg. He wanted her to want him, too. He should be enough. It burned his ego that she didn't think so.

Irritation ate at him as he stormed down the trail. He'd spent his whole life being the good guy. He couldn't do much more. What did she expect from him? He followed the rules. He was kind. He was a friend to all. He helped people. He worked hard. He was enough. She was the one who couldn't see that.

"What more do You want from me?" he bellowed into the wind. *If You're real, what more can I possibly do? I am a good person! I don't hurt people. I don't steal or do drugs. I love my family and my friends. I am good! And it should be enough!*

Silence.

What did he expect? He wasn't even sure he believed there was a God, much less One who would listen to him. One who would listen to the cry of his heart. He pressed the heel of his hand against the aching place in his chest. *I've had this ache in my heart for as long as I can remember. I'm so tired of it! I want it to go away! Why can't I make it go away?*

Silence again.

His angry thoughts had clouded his mind to the point that he had no idea how far he'd gone or where he was. The trail he was on had turned downward toward the shore. He lengthened his stride and emerged a few moments later on a rocky strip of shore littered with boulders and chunks of driftwood.

He picked up a rock and heaved it toward the waves in frustration as a bitter cry erupted from his lips. His eyes traced the path of the rock until it plunged into the frothy water. Hot, angry tears coursed down his cheeks and he dropped to his knees.

There is no one who is good, but Me. Come to Me, bring me your burdens, and I will give you rest.

Noah stilled. He didn't so much hear a voice as he did feel it. In his core, he felt it. In the hard, painful, hollow places he felt it. He stayed rooted to the ground. His tears had stopped, but he didn't dare look up. He strained his ears hoping for more. He heard the whip of the wind and the calls of the gulls, but his soul longed for a Voice he didn't hear. He waited. A peace began to settle over him as he knelt there. *Please God...*

"Please!" he cried, dropping his face into his hands on a sob. "Please, help me."

My grace is enough. Not you. Me. My grace is enough and My power is made perfect in your weakness, not your strength.

Grace. All his striving to be enough and in the end, it was God's grace that was enough? Could it be that simple?

A low rumble caught Noah's attention and he lifted his face from his hands. The rumble grew louder and his heart slammed against his chest as he saw the thunderhead moving toward him. Enormous black clouds rolled heavenward. Lightning lit the clouds from the inside. Rain poured from the base of the clouds so thick he couldn't see through it. It was miles away, but moving fast. The water was already slashing at the shore in a raging swell that grabbed at rocks, clawing its way to the island.

Lily! Noah sprang to his feet and bolted for the trail he'd come down. He scraped and tore at rocks and trees trying to gain ground faster. It felt like he would never reach the summit of the hill. He tried to swallow down panic, but he knew what storms like this were capable of. This one would wreak havoc with the island. The thought of the lightning alone spurred him on to reach Lily and protect her.

The clearing at the summit of the island was deserted. Noah turned in circles trying to catch a glimpse of her. He laced his fingers behind his neck and tried not to panic.

"Lily!"

The only answer was the wind, now howling and bending the trees. That roaring of the wind drowned out his repeated attempts to call her name. While the sky above was still a dazzling blue, the storm had darkened the sky on the northeast side of the island and cast the clearing in an eerie yellow light.

Dread had a hold of Noah's throat making it hard to breathe. He'd spent enough time outdoors to know you don't mess with a storm like this one. The wind and rain would be enough to drive a grown man to the ground. Lightning was indiscriminate in its quest for a path to the earth. It could also produce hail large enough to cause serious injury if you were out in the open. He had to find Lily. Now.

He tried to silence the fear that burned through him. Fear that made it hard to think straight. A cry of anguish tore from his clenched teeth.

"God! Please, help me! Lily loves You. Please help me find her!"

A strange peace swept through him. The storm still raged, but his heart stopped slamming against his chest. His mind cleared of panic and he focused on the trail ahead of him. It was the one that led to the sand bar. Would Lily have gone back? He leaped to his feet and bolted for the trailhead. The trees blurred in his peripheral vision as he flew down the trail. Rocks and downed logs blocked his path, but he cleared them with skill that would have made his high school track coach proud. His mind was focused on one thing. Finding Lily.

Her first inkling of the storm was a darkening of the light

streaming through the trees. At first, she thought a cloud had blocked the sunlight, but her unease increased with each new indication that a storm was coming. Her hair had long since been pulled free of its elastic by the wind. The air had turned cold and Lily stopped to pull her sweatshirt back on.

The rumble of distant thunder had gotten louder until the ground shook with the concussive force of each new clap. Adrenaline surged through her increasing her heart rate and her pace. She wasn't sure where she was even heading, but her flight instinct was in high gear, pushing her down the path. Was she even headed toward the shore?

She slipped on the rain-soaked leaves and went down, jostling her already injured hip hard against a wet rock. She yelped. Tears of pain, frustration, and a broken heart coursed down her cheeks. She wiped at them, furious.

Oh, God, I need You!

The words to a favorite hymn drifted into her mind, bringing peace to her soul.

> *I need Thee every hour*
> *Most gracious Lord*
> *No tender voice like Thine*
> *Can peace afford.*
> *I need Thee, O I need Thee*
> *Every hour I need Thee!*
> *O bless me now, my Savior*
> *I come to Thee.*

Yes! I come to You!

She sat where she'd fallen, trying to collect herself. The first fat raindrops splashed onto her shoulders and mingled with her tears.

"Every hour I need Thee!" She laughed at the ridiculousness of the situation. There she sat, in the middle of a thunderstorm, singing. The laughter turned to a groan as the rain picked up and drenched her sweatshirt.

"Lily!"

She thought she heard her name through the torrent and she turned to search the trail. Noah emerged from the deluge and raced toward her, concern etched hard lines in his face.

"Lily," he gasped, dropping to his knees beside her. "Are you OK?" He held her face in his hands, searching her eyes.

She nodded, overwhelmed by relief. "Yes, I just slipped."

"I was so scared," he breathed as he crushed her against his chest. "I'm sorry I left you. I'm so sorry."

Rain pelted their faces. The wind howled and thunder shook the ground. Visibility was nil. Noah helped her to her feet and she tried putting weight on her injured hip. It throbbed but didn't appear to have suffered any additional damage. He pulled her back the way they had come, and they scrambled up the trail away from the rising surf.

"We need to get out of this weather!" Noah yelled.

Lily nodded. She was already soaked to the skin and starting to shiver. How was it that he seemed to appear every time she found herself in need of a knight... in flip-flops? She had gone quite a while not needing anyone. Years in fact. And yet in the span of one week, she had come to depend on him. It was equal parts scary and comforting.

"C'mon!" he yelled over the roaring of the storm.

Noah's long legs were hard to keep up with, but Lily managed. Her feet slipped, but she found a way to stay upright as they tore up the path.

"Where are we going?" she yelled.

"An older fire warden's cabin!" he yelled back.

Conversation was impossible. Noah left the trail and they dashed through trees and underbrush. Lily hoped he knew where he was going. He'd said he knew the island. She hoped he knew it well. Despite the canopy of oak, maple, and ash, they were still getting drenched. The wind whipped the towering trees back and forth. Images of the wind ripping the colossal pines out of the ground and sending them crashing down on them as they ran spurred her to move faster. She slipped and went down hard on her backside. Lightning struck a tree on the far side of the island and the thunder that followed a split second later was deafening. She yelped and scrambled back to her feet.

They'd reached a level area near the westward edge of the island, far above the dangerous waves battering the rocks. Lily could just make out the silhouette of a small cabin through the trees. She was out of breath and felt like her legs would give out if they didn't stop running soon. Her clothes were dripping and plastered to her body.

"Almost there!" Noah yelled over his shoulder.

The cabin began to emerge from the haze of driving rain and fog. It was tiny but solid. Lily wondered for a fleeting second if the warden was home, but when Noah threw his shoulder into the door to break it open she figured the answer was no. The door crashed inward and banged against the wall behind it. Noah grabbed Lily's arm and pulled her through the opening just as lightning struck a tree several hundred yards away.

Lily stood in the middle of the room shaking while Noah propped the door closed with a chunk of firewood. She rubbed her drenched arms and willed her teeth to stop chattering.

"Where—" Her teeth clenched so hard it hurt trying to still the tremors in her arms and legs. "Where— did that— come— from—?"

"Nor'easter. We get doozies. This one blew in fast, though," he answered as he pulled his dripping t-shirt off and started wringing it out. Lily averted her eyes, but not before she'd seen the sculpted planes of his toned chest.

"What's a— 'nor'easter?'" she asked as she took in the small cabin. It was one room with a window on either side, one by the door and one opposite the door facing what Lily assumed would be the mainland if you could see that far. The cabin was devoid of any signs that it was lived in. There was a built-in table under the window by the door, a built-in bunk at one end, and a small fieldstone fireplace at the other. It didn't look like anyone had entered the cabin in years. No bedding, chairs, dishes, or homey touches existed anywhere, and a thin layer of dust covered every surface.

"It's a storm with winds blowing from the northeast. They tend to be a bit more brutal than the average storm."

Lily made a sound a bit like a harrumph. She tried to see out the window. Another close lightning strike made her duck and she stole a peek at Noah out of the corner of her eye. He'd put his shirt back on and was bent over inspecting the fireplace.

"How'd you know about this place?"

"When I was a kid and my dad would bring me to the island we'd stop here and visit George, the fire warden. He was the last of his kind. The national park has a lot more sophisticated ways of spotting fire now than an old guy in a cabin keeping an eye out. Lucky for us, they haven't gotten around to tearing it down," he added with a wink. He headed for the door. "Be right back."

"What?" Lily hated the panic in her voice, but… he was leaving? Was he serious?

"Just stepping out on the porch, no worries." He was only gone a few seconds. When he returned his arms were full of wood. He placed it on the floor beside the fireplace and began building a careful pile of small twigs, bits of bark, and pine cones. He fished a keychain out of his pocket and held a small, dark gray rectangle near the pile. He struck it with something in his other hand and a shower of sparks rained down on the kindling. He did it a couple more times and a small flame started to eat up one of the pine cones. It caught and in seconds had moved to larger sticks.

"Did you just start a fire… with your keys?" she asked in disbelief.

"Flint," he chuckled. "It's my key chain. Seems more practical than a plastic lobster."

The storm raged outside, but inside the little cabin felt dry and safe. The fire soon started to crackle, sending a bit of heat into the room. Lily moved closer trying to warm her hands. Noah disappeared to the porch again and returned with two big, round chunks of firewood. He set them on the floor in front of the fire and sat on one. Lily perched on the other.

"Lily, I—"

"Noah, we—"

Noah gestured for Lily to continue.

"We need to talk."

"Ayuh… we do," he agreed. "May I go first?"

Lily nodded. She didn't want to say what she knew needed to be said anyway.

Noah's gaze appeared to be on the fire, but he was focused elsewhere. "For a long time, I've thought that I had to be enough. I had to be the guy people counted on, the guy who did the right thing. When you told me the other day what the chaplain said about the hole not being from other people? I got that. I know what hole you were talking about because I have it, too. For a long time, I've thought that being 'that guy' was the remedy to the aching hole. But today I think I finally got that *I'm* not enough, but God is."

Joy began to bubble up inside Lily. "What are you saying?"

"I'm saying, I'm not enough, but God is. I believe God exists. I prayed. *I*. Prayed." He shook his head as if he still couldn't quite believe it. "Maybe for the first time ever. And He answered. I was so scared when I saw the storm coming, and then when I couldn't find you… God held me together while I searched. I think He's real."

Lily could feel the hope that bloomed on her face. Emotions clogged her lungs making it difficult to talk. She clutched his hand and studied his face. "Yes, Noah, He is real." She continued holding his hand and rested her head on his arm. Even with a damp t-shirt, he radiated warmth. She closed her eyes and lifted silent prayers heavenward.

Thank You, God! Thank You for drawing Noah to Yourself! Please continue to pull him until he surrenders to You. Is this why You sent him? Did You put him in my path for this reason? For me to help him seek You? Help me to know the words to guide him into a relationship with You. And if that is the only reason You have brought Noah into my life, please guard my heart so I don't fall any more in love with him than I am already!

CHAPTER FOURTEEN

An odd pinging sound on the roof and sides of the cabin startled Lily. The sound got louder and louder until it reverberated off the walls like a train rushing past. Her eyes darted around the room trying to identify the source of the deafening sound.

Noah grabbed her shaking shoulders and forced her to look at him. "Hail!" he shouted over the din. He took her hands and placed them over her ears and then gathered her to himself. The warm cocoon of his arms and the muffling of the sound of the hail soothed Lily's frayed nerves. She leaned into his shirt and thanked God that they were inside.

He held her until the hail stopped pelting the roof and Lily had stopped shaking. She sat on her log stool letting the fire dry her clothes, a little sorry that Noah had gotten up to put more wood on the fire. Her mind wandered.

"I don't get it," she said.

"What?"

"Alistair's note said that the weather report for today was perfect, but this storm had to have been predicted."

Noah poked at the fire with a stick and added another log. "Seems like there's been a lot of that since you first questioned the cause of your uncle's... accident."

"If I believed in luck I'd think mine had turned quite bad."

"OK, what do we know?" he asked. He'd braced himself against the mantle with one elbow and crossed his ankles, looking solid and relaxed.

"We know that Alistair dropped off a note this morning telling me that the weather was perfect for a hike, when obviously," she gestured toward the window, "it isn't. Do you think he meant for me to get stuck here... alone?"

A chill ran down Lily's back that had nothing to do with her still damp shirt.

"Let's concentrate on what we know and worry about the rest later. What else do we know about Alistair? He's been in town since before your uncle arrived, right?"

"Yes. He's been here helping Stella get her business back on track."

"What else?"

"I know he wasn't happy being sidelined at EHI."

"Unhappy enough to take matters into his own hands?"

"I can't imagine it."

"What would he gain from your uncle's death?"

"More control in EHI."

"Good motive."

"But this weather isn't the only thing that's... suspicious."

"True."

"Yesterday I came within inches of driving off a cliff following directions that Stella Tucker gave me."

"Stella, who is seeing Alistair."

"I can see a person who was hurt as much as Uncle hurt Stella pushing him off the pier, but what on earth could she hope to gain by hurting me?"

"Again, if Stella and Alistair are together... What would Stella gain from Herbert's death?"

"Revenge?"

"Always a motive."

Lily sighed. She didn't want it to be Stella. "She did know that he was in town."

"She was also pretty adamant that Carmen Franco had more motive than either her or Alistair."

"That I could imagine."

"And you saw him handling your climbing rope."

"And he was here when Uncle drowned," she added. "But he couldn't have had anything to do with the bad directions or the note from Alistair."

"Could he have popped the tires on your car?"

"It just seems far-fetched. Back to motive. Herbert I can see. Carmen hated Uncle. But me? What possible motive could he have for hurting me?"

"Hatred is a monster that grows out of control. Maybe it just spilled over to you. Maybe Carmen couldn't see the difference between you and your uncle."

Lily shivered. "Or... he let his anger at me build. When I told him we were through, he was furious. He lost out on joining EHI and he thought he was losing out on money and position. Maybe he's carried that anger around for years and finally snapped when he saw me again."

"Or that."

"What about Edwin?" Lily asked. "I'd almost forgotten we'd talked to him until Alistair mentioned him."

"What does he gain by getting rid of your uncle?"

"Maybe it isn't gain. He could have been angry enough about not getting paid that he pushed Uncle off the pier."

"And you? What motive does he have for hurting you?"

"I was asking questions. He could have done it to try and keep me quiet."

"He's pretty smarmy, but I have a hard time picturing him going after you."

"Money and greed can turn a person into someone they didn't intend to be," Lily added. The look Noah cast her way showed he knew she wasn't talking about Hurst anymore.

"Edwin was owed money. A lot of money. He could have pushed your uncle off the pier out of anger over not getting paid. He was also at the inn when you discovered that your tires had been punctured. Then we have Stella Tucker, the jilted ex-lover, who could have pushed Herbert off the pier out of revenge."

"And she almost got me killed with her directions," Lily added.

"Right." Noah shuddered at the thought.

"Carmen is a rival of Uncle's. He could have pushed him off the pier out of pure hatred. He also had access to my rope and could have cut it while we weren't paying attention."

"You know him. Could he have done that? Would he have?"

Lily pondered that. Carmen had been livid when she had broken things off. But carrying a grudge this long before acting on it seemed doubtful. Unless he had let it fester. "I don't know. Maybe. I'd like to say no, but the rope…"

Noah made a face that said he had no trouble believing Carmen was capable of hurting her, but he let it go. "Last, your uncle's business partner. Herbert planned to cut him out of the business. He could have pushed Herbert off the pier for the sake of self-preservation. He is also responsible for you getting caught in this storm."

"If we'd made it back across the sandbar at low tide, we wouldn't have been here when the storm came up," she reminded him.

"True. Maybe we can't pin getting trapped here on Alistair. But he did lie to you about the weather, which seems odd."

"It does at that."

"It feels like we're missing an elusive clue. A vital piece of information that would make this all click."

"We could go talk to Edwin and Stella again tomorrow," Lily volunteered.

"I thought you were headed back to Boston?"

"I am, but… maybe not tomorrow."

The light had changed from the darkness of thick clouds to the cloying yellow of a spent thunderstorm. Rain no longer buffeted the cabin. Noah opened the door and stepped out on the porch.

"Is it over?" Lily asked from her perch by the fire.

"Looks like it."

She joined him outside the door. Branches and fallen leaves littered the ground. Hailstones as wide as her thumb had accumulated at the base of trees, against rocks, and in piles where they'd tumbled off the roof. Sunshine was just beginning to filter back through the soaked trees and had yet to warm the air. Noah stepped off the porch and started gathering up a handful of hailstones.

"What are you doing?" Lily asked.

"I need to put out the fire before we head back to the sandbar. Wicked dangerous to leave it burning."

"Is there anything you don't know, Boy Scout?"

"I thought I was Hardy Boy?"

Lily laughed. "I'm guessing the Hardy Boys knew to put a fire out when they were done, too."

He winked at her before dousing the coals.

By the time they reached the sandbar, low tide had cleared them a path back to the beach. Lily had a fleeting thought to drop to her knees and kiss the pebbled sand.

Fed, showered, and wearing a pair of thick sweatpants and a thermal shirt, Noah almost felt human again. He was glad that all that day's tours had been postponed because he doubted he had the energy left to lift a paddle. He padded barefoot down the back steps of the shop and around to the open back door of The Hungry Whale in search of Parker. He wasn't surprised to find him in the kitchen.

"Hey man," Parker greeted him as he appeared in the doorway. "You look beat."

"Long day. Long story." Noah propped his hip against the doorframe and crossed his arms. "I'd like to talk to you about part of it when you've got a minute."

In true Parker fashion, work was set aside and Noah had his full attention. The man would never give up his kitchen, it was too much a part of who he was. That being said, he had a phenomenal staff who could step in as needed. He signaled another chef to take his place and, drying his hands on his apron, followed Noah outside. "What's up?"

"I prayed today."

"You? Prayed? Like... to God?"

"I know, right? It shocked me, too." He leaned against the back wall. "But I think I get it now. I believe God exists."

"Aww, man," Parker said with a grin. He clapped Noah on the bicep then, unable to contain his excitement, he thumped the door with his fist. "Praise the Lord! I've prayed for your eyes to be opened since... well... a long time."

"Really? You... pray for me?"

"Of course, man. You're my best friend and when I get to Heaven I'd kind of like my best friend to be there, too."

Noah couldn't help but smile at that thought. "I had this moment on the beach today where it just got real and for the first time ever, I just kind of knew that God was out there."

Parker studied him for a moment before continuing, his tone turning serious. "I want to ask you a question."

"Shoot."

"Do you remember that singer that was in town last summer? Phoebe..."

"Phoebe Jennings?"

"Yeah, that's the one. You couldn't wait to go to her concert on The Green, right?"

"Yeah..." Noah had a perplexed look on his face.

"Hear me out." Parker put one hand up. "You can tell me a bunch of facts about Ms. Jennings, right? You know what albums she's made. Can sing along to her songs. Can describe what she looks like. Am I right so far?"

"I guess. What are you getting at?"

"Here's my point. Does she know you?"

"Of course not," Noah laughed.

"Now, let's say Ms. Jennings had a party after the concert, and all her friends were invited to come and you showed up."

"One of those linebackers that follow her around would bounce me right off the front walk."

"Exactly."

"So what?"

"It's the same with God."

"Say what?"

"There are these verses in the book of Matthew that are pretty sobering. They say that there will be people who will say 'Lord, Lord' but God will say 'I never knew you'. See, God demands more than belief in His existence. He demands that we surrender our lives to Him and believe solely on Jesus Christ for our salvation. I'm hearing you say that you believe He exists, but have you introduced yourself? Have you given Him your life? Have you trusted the grace of Jesus Christ to save you?"

"Whoa. Hold up. Surrender?"

"Yeah. When I was saved I handed over everything I was to Him," Parker continued. His tone was at the same time gentle and serious. "Do you believe He exists? Or are you ready to give yourself to Him?"

Noah puffed out a ragged breath. "Look, going from 'how could anyone know for sure if there's a god?' to 'I believe God exists' is a pretty significant step. I don't think I can do that whole giving myself to Him thing."

"You're right, man, it is a huge step. And I am happy for you! Just... think about what I said. There's a big difference between knowing and being known."

Noah pushed off the wall and gave Parker a thump on the shoulder. He wasn't sure what he'd expected. Cartwheels? Parker was the real deal and always shot straight with him. If Parker said there was more, there was more. But handing over control of his life to a God he didn't even know seemed a bit extreme. He'd worked too hard and too long to carve out this exact life and the thought of handing that over to anyone else, even God, coiled a knot of dread in his stomach. No one could care for his dream as well as he could.

Handing over one's life was fine for guys like Parker. He'd built his entire life after finding God at the ripe old age of six. Noah didn't need to start over. He didn't need a new life. He just needed to not feel hollow anymore. To not feel like what he did and who he was didn't matter.

❧

Fed, showered, and wearing a pair of warm leggings and soft sweater, Lily felt almost human again. She burrowed into a chair by the darkened window in her room and sat drying her hair.

The last two days had been appalling. Yet she couldn't help smiling when she recalled how God had placed Noah there when she needed him. Ice cream and deck picnics, Hardy Boy to her Nancy Drew, dinner with his folks. His easy smile and strong hand holding hers. His soft kiss. Her cheeks pinked as she remembered him taking her face in his hands the morning before. Tender and gentle.

Despite all that, while alone earlier in the day she'd made up her mind to return to Boston. She'd planned to talk to him about it when he got back. Then Noah had told her that he's come to an understanding that God was real and she couldn't bring herself to end it after all. She couldn't risk smothering the tiny flame of belief that had sprung to life in him.

She dropped her wet towel on the floor and pulled her legs up to her chest. With her arms crossed over her knees and her chin resting on her forearms she surveyed her room. This little yellow suite felt more like home after a week than her apartment in Boston ever had. Lily's heart hurt thinking of packing her things and heading back to the daily grind of business in the city.

Sick of the funk that thinking of her return to Boston produced, Lily stomped to the closet and threw it open. Like ripping off a bandaid, she just needed to pack her suitcase and get it over with. The insurance company had dealt with her car and had promised her a rental by morning. She could be back in Boston by dinner. Tears burned her eyes and scalded the back of her throat as she groped in the closet for her suitcase. Her hand closed around the handle of her uncle's briefcase instead. She hauled it out and realized that she had never finished going through his papers.

An hour later Lily was through sorting the bank statements, productivity reports, and construction proposals. She tossed the last one on the table and reached for one of the two remaining items. It appeared to be from the bank and Lily sighed. Another bank statement. She rolled her shoulders and squeezed her eyes shut as she ripped it open.

"OK, not a bank statement," she whispered as she pulled a cashier's check from the envelope. It was dated the day before her uncle had drowned. A ridiculous dollar figure and Edwin Hurst's name were neatly typed. The memo line read *Real estate services*.

The mattress creaked under her as she sank down. If Herbert had the money in hand to pay Hurst, what motive could the man have had? Maybe he hadn't pushed Herbert off the pier. That didn't mean he was innocent of popping her tires, but to what end? Anger over not getting paid? He was the only one she'd seen at the inn that morning, but she hadn't seen him sabotage her car.

Lily tossed the check on the table and frowned at the blue envelope sitting on the bottom of the now-empty briefcase. She had to read the rest. She reached for it and slipped the sheets of paper free. The top one she'd read and while she wanted to read it again, she set it aside and braced herself for the second letter. It was addressed to her father.

Brother,

It pains me to write this, even though I know you will never read it. There was a time when I would have done anything humanly possible to make you proud of me. But then, in one moment I betrayed you in the worst of all possible ways. I tried to go on living as though I hadn't, pretending, playing the role of my former self. But the guilt ate me alive. You and I fell in love with the same woman, on the same night. She chose you because you have always been the better man. I couldn't stop loving her though. And then one night I convinced her to see me in that light, just once. I have never regretted anything more. If I lived a thousand lifetimes I would not have lived long enough to rid myself of what I did. And then something even worse. Margo was coming to see me when she died. Me. How can you ever forgive me for that? How can I ever forgive myself? I can't! You don't know how I wish it had been me. I would have taken her place in a heartbeat if it were possible. Once she was gone everything good about me vanished as though she had been the one holding it in place. Did you feel it, too? If there was a way to undo the past I would. I wish you could forgive me. I wish it with all my heart.

Your foolish Bub

Lily was numb. Her suspicion that Herbert and her mother had had an affair, albeit brief, had been confirmed. It soured her stomach to think of either of them betraying her father in such a way. Had he known? Had he figured it out along the way? Or had he gone to his grave thinking her mother as perfect as Lily remembered her being? She hoped he never knew.

Her fingers trembled as she set the letter on top of the one written to her mother and saw her own name at the top of the third letter. A peek at the fourth confirmed that it was written to Olivia. She pinched her eyes shut and breathed in a deep breath. What in the world could Uncle have to say to her? What horrible sin was he going to confess? She opened her eyes and began reading.

My Dearest Lilianna,

You are a treasure. You have so much of your mother in you that it causes me physical pain to be near you. But you are also so much like your father. It's as if you got the best of each. You think I push you too hard. And I probably do. When I look at you all I see is potential and I get carried away. Over the years I have arranged for you to learn every aspect of our business from the best. I don't think you always appreciate it, but it has all been for your good, I promise.

I regret that I did not remain the Uncle Bub you used to love. I made choices that pushed me away from you and your parents. Choices I would give anything to change. But one cannot change the past no matter how hard one tries. Then, once your mother was gone I stopped trying. I let all that was bad inside me fester and grow. And now all I am left with is regret. I hope that somewhere in your memories you'll be able to remember who I was, once upon a time.

I am so proud of you.
Forever,
your Uncle Bub

The last lines blurred in tears. How could she have not known? She let the letters fall to the floor and covered her face with her hands. Oh, why had he kept it all to himself? If she had only known... Sobs shook her. It was too much. She snatched the letters up and crammed them back into the briefcase, slamming the lid closed.

CHAPTER FIFTEEN

Despite complete exhaustion the night before, Noah hadn't slept more than a few fitful hours. Every rotten deed he'd ever done had haunted both waking and sleep. He woke in the wee hours of the morning with remorse strangling him. He took the back steps two at a time and wrenched a one-man kayak and a paddle out of the shed. On the water was the one place he could think. The one place he felt whole. Hoisting the kayak on his shoulder and carrying the paddle and life jacket he headed for the beach.

The town was silent in the predawn hours. Harley would be organizing the sunrise tour soon, but his backup this morning was Jeremiah.

Thank you, God, he thought as he neared the beach. His head wouldn't have been in the right place to conduct a tour. He reached the water and heaved the kayak off his shoulder and onto the sand. He'd kayaked at night many times. It was cold and still. As he pushed out into the water he waited for the peace he always felt to wash over him. It never came.

Frustration had him stabbing the water. Grueling blows that burned his shoulders. He wanted to scream with each brutal stroke of the paddle. He clenched his teeth against the agony, in his arms and in his heart. He pushed himself, stroke after stroke. On and on until the lights of the town faded away and he was good and truly alone. Unable to hold it in any longer, an aggravated howl ripped from him. He slammed the paddle down in front of him, almost relishing the sting of the metal snapping across the fiberglass gunwales of the kayak.

"OK, You win!" he yelled. The wind carried the words away

as soon as they left his lips. Tears scalded his cheeks and clogged his throat. He sobbed into his hands until it felt as though he couldn't have any more to cry.

"I can't go on like this. I can't live with this gaping void! Please God..." Despite the fact that he had cried himself dry, more tears choked out his words.

Give me your burdens and I will give you rest.

Noah turned his tearstained face Heavenward and let the wind dry it. "I am so tired, God. I'm tired of trying to be enough. I'm tired of striving for more. I need you to take it all. I can't carry it anymore!"

Confess your sins and I will forgive you.

"But God, I'm unworthy of forgiveness."

I have already shown you how much I love you. Even though you are a sinner, My Son died for you. My grace and My mercy are enough for you.

"Oh, God," Noah wept. "Please forgive my pride. You are enough. I am not. Please forgive my unbelief. Show me who You are! Please show me You. Forgive my years of living only for myself. I have been so selfish and absorbed in my own plans that I had no room for Yours." He took a deep breath of sea air and, on a sob, added, "I surrender everything I am to You."

In Me, you are a new man. Your past is gone. You are My handiwork.

The sky had lightened to a dull gray on the thin edge of the eastern horizon, but above him still stretched with stars. Peace unlike anything Noah had ever felt washed over him. It seeped into all the empty places and filled every void. Joy bubbled up from his core. More tears streamed down his cheeks, but these tears cleansed as they washed away the pain and frustration.

"Thank you, God. I am so humbled. Thank You for forgiving me. Please help me live for You from here on."

My mercies are new every morning.

The sun crested the eastern horizon with a dazzling display of oranges, purples, and blues. Intense yellow rays dappled the waves. The enormity of God's mercy and grace hit Noah like a wave. Like the frigid North Atlantic water, it stole his breath from his lungs. The realization that God would extend that mercy to him with every sunrise drew his hands heavenward in praise. Noah wanted to sing. What do you sing to a God that just saved your soul? The tune to Amazing Grace filtered through his mind and Noah sang the first couple of lines at the top of his lungs.

"Amazing grace, how sweet the sound that saved a wretch like me!" Tears continued to stream down his cheeks and he hummed the rest as best as he could remember the tune. He had to find some songs to sing to his Savior. Lily would know a bunch!

Lily.

A new joy exploded within him. He had to tell Lily. He scooped up the paddle and spun the kayak back toward shore. He'd pushed himself much farther out than he thought, but he didn't care. Nothing could dampen his spirits. The burning shoulders that accompanied his return trip meant he was alive. The earlier agony was gone and he drew in great gulping breaths of cool air and pushed harder.

Lily rolled over and checked the time on her phone for the umpteenth time. If only sleep would come, even for a few blissful minutes. It was too late to take a sleeping pill and too early to get up. The letters she had read the night before had left her restless. Parts of her world that had seemed sure and solid had crumbled in the space of a few lines scribbled on blue stationery.

Grappling with what her mother and uncle had done, how her uncle had seen her, and who he'd become had left her drained. Tears had come, but so had anger, disappointment, and resignation. She had cried out to God in the long parade of dark hours and had come to a peaceful decision. She had responsibilities and she had to step up to them. The history of EHI was fraught with wrongs. It would not continue to be. Not under her leadership. Never again.

In the dull gray light of pre-dawn, she crawled out of bed and packed her suitcase. All of the papers and letters were returned to her uncle's briefcase. The letter to Olivia rested, unread, in its envelope and tucked into her own briefcase. That was not hers to read. She wasn't sure what revelations it would bring to Olivia, and she struggled with how much to share with her sister. Could she handle knowing what their mother and uncle had done? One day she would share the other letters. One, far away, day.

Only the check to Edwin Hurst remained on the table. A part of her wanted to rip it up. The man had done nothing but cause problems. Best she could tell he'd done nothing to help her uncle obtain the inn. It was, however, a cashier's check. Ripping it up would be akin to ripping cash to shreds. In the end, she'd decided to drop it off on her way out of town and be done with Edwin Hurst for good.

By the time the sun broke free of the eastern horizon, she was dressed in her navy blue dress pants and pinstripe blazer. The familiar clothes made her feel like her old self, yet not the same woman who'd driven into Summer Harbor the week before. Not by a long shot.

The bruise on her cheek had faded to a pale chartreuse that she was able to hide with a layer of makeup. After sliding her feet into her bright yellow heels, she checked her reflection in the mirror and smoothed her slacks. She had a mental list of things she needed to wrap up before leaving town. First on the list was to make sure Noah had the business plan for his meeting that morning. Her heart ached to near breaking at the thought of leaving him. Of the hurt she was about to inflict. She'd begged God during the night to mend any damage she caused.

No one was up as she slipped out the front door into the crisp air that had settled overnight. It fit her mood. Still and damp with dew. Since she still didn't have a car she was hoofing it into town, heels and all. The insurance company had promised her a rental bright and early, but it was still a long way from business hours. Her heels clicked a rhythm on the sidewalk as she headed down Main Street. Most of the shops were still closed. Only a few eateries offering breakfast had opened their doors. She hoped the coffee shop on the corner was open on her way back to the inn. One last latte before she hit the road.

The kayak shop was empty when Lily slipped in the back door. She set the manila envelope on top of the disarray that was Noah's desk. She almost laughed at the chaos. It would drive her crazy, but it was indicative of his personality. Carefree, easygoing, laid back. Why wouldn't his workspace be the same? She pressed her hand to the envelope and breathed a prayer for Noah to find favor with the person looking at the plan. She'd done her best, the outcome was up to God.

She slipped out the back door and down the alley, glad he hadn't returned with his tour yet. She couldn't look him in the eye and tell him she had decided to leave. She was a coward. She knew it, and yet she still couldn't muster up the courage.

Her next stop was Herbert's hotel to settle his bill. Then onto the kennel to pay for Princess' stay. A few of the town's early risers had started to emerge by the time she neared the Creature Comforts. Pastor James, coffee in hand and paper under his arm, waved as she passed the church and an elderly woman wearing a pair of gardening gloves and a floppy hat watered the flowers in front of the historical society. They seemed happy and content and Lily wanted to scream with the unfairness of it.

Micah came to the desk looking like she may have woken him. A stab of remorse hit her, but she couldn't wait any longer. She needed to get out of town before something... or someone... changed her mind and convinced her to stay.

"Good morning, Ms. Emerson," Micah greeted her as he stifled a yawn.

"Good morning, Micah. I'm sorry to stop in this early."

"Not at all. I've been up for a few hours with a pregnant beagle. Not ready to call the vet yet, but she was miserable and didn't want to be alone."

Lily liked him. If she was staying, she could see them being friends. But she wasn't. Couldn't. She tamped down the tears that threatened. "I need to take care of my bill for Princess. I can't take her with me to the inn, but I'll pick her up in about an hour."

"No problem."

"Thank you. I want to get on the road as soon as my rental car arrives."

"Heading home?"

"Yes."

"Not for good I hope." He'd printed her bill and smiled as he took her credit card.

The tears threatened again and she avoided his eyes as she signed her slip and took the bill. She didn't want to think about leaving, she just needed to get it over with.

The coffee shop had just set their sandwich board on the corner when she walked back and she ducked in. A scrumptious latte for the road? Yes, please. Anything to ease the gloom that had settled around her. Coffee in hand she made a straight line for the inn. Time to pay the piper.

By the time he pulled himself back into the harbor, Noah could see Harley bringing the sunrise tour into the beach. He pushed hard and pulled in behind them.

"Hey, man!" Harley greeted him.

"Hey," he replied, lifting his hand. "Can you get my kayak back to the shop for me?"

"Sure thing, Boss."

"I have to talk to Lily!" Noah called and flashed Harley a grin as he tossed his lifejacket onto the seat before jogging backward toward the inn. Harley lifted his hand in response and turned back to the tour.

Noah whirled around and took off down the beach. He should have been exhausted, but exhilaration and adrenaline coursed through him. His feet felt like they were running on air, his fingers tingled, and his heart felt full to overflowing. The beach and path up the cliffs passed in a blur. Before he knew it he was at the inn and climbing the porch stairs two at a time.

Breakfast was in full swing so he made a beeline for the dining room. Ava spotted him and raised a withered hand.

"Have you seen Lily this morning?" he asked, out of breath and grinning like a fool.

Ava shook her head. Noah retraced his steps to the lobby and thundered up the stairs to her room. Outside her door, he stopped and drew in a calming breath. Deja vu made him laugh. Was it just two days ago he'd run up the same stairs? The fear he'd felt that morning had crippled him. His joy this morning gave him wings. He shook his head, still overwhelmed by what God had done.

A gentle tap on the door went unanswered. He waited, debating on waking Lily up. He was too excited, he had to talk to her. She'd forgive him for waking her up. He rapped louder and waited. Still no response.

"Lily?" he called, banging on the door with his knuckles. Only silence greeted him. He shifted from one foot to the other in impatience. Why wasn't she answering him? He jogged back to the dining room.

"Ava, is it possible that Lily went out? She isn't answering her door."

"Let me just try calling up to her room," Ava offered, hobbling toward the front desk. Her call to Lily's room went unanswered, too. "Maybe she left? She talked yesterday about leaving for Boston today and I told her she could just leave her keys in her room."

A sick feeling started in the pit of Noah's stomach. Had she left? Would she have left without saying goodbye? A melancholy trickled in to replace the giddiness of a few minutes before. He'd known she would leave sooner or later, but why did it have to be that morning? When he had so much to tell her, so much he wanted to share. She would be overjoyed. It wasn't like he couldn't contact her, but could he contact her and hold onto any part of his heart? Doubtful.

"Do you want me to check and see if she left the keys?"

"No, Miss Ava. It's fine. I'm sure you're right."

The older woman smiled and patted his hand before returning to her guests in the dining room. He ambled back down the front steps and found Walter hunkered down in the flowers at the edge of the path. As Noah approached the man sat back on his heels and tipped his hat.

"Walter, have you seen Lily Emerson this morning?"

"No sir. She ain't in her room?"

"No. Ava said she might have headed back to Boston."

"She said she expected her rental car this morning. Must have come before I was even up."

Noah nodded. "Thanks, Walter." He trudged down the drive toward town. It wasn't that the joy and peace he'd been given that morning had dissipated, it was the disappointment of not sharing them with Lily that was eating him up. He walked back to the shop feeling dazed.

Behind the counter, Gemma flashed him a grin full of braces. "Hey, Noah."

"Hey, Kid," he replied, thrusting the gloom aside.

"I grabbed the shipments when I got here. There was another box of shirts, the new brochures you ordered, and this." She handed him a stiff cardboard mailer.

He pulled the tab on the back to open the pouch and slid the contents out onto the counter. A grin lit his face. Photos of the Kessler family from the tour the week before. He'd captured it all. Norm trying to convince his daughter that he could do magic, her obvious disbelief, his ridiculous moves as he 'conjured' the seal from the water, and the astonishment on his daughter's face as the seal broke the surface. His heart swelled. That had been the highlight of the kayaking season to this point.

He selected a picture of Norm and his daughter wearing matching looks of bewilderment at the appearance of the seal and pinned it to the bulletin board behind the register. A couple of clicks on the computer pulled up the man's contact information. Noah jotted it down and grabbed the photos off the counter.

"Can you mail these to this address for me on your way to school?"

"Sure thing," Gemma said, her happy-go-lucky grin mirroring his own. Norm was going to love these and she knew it, too. She grabbed her backpack off the floor and slung it over her shoulder. "I'm glad you didn't take any tours out yesterday. That storm was crazy!"

Memories from the day before raced through his mind and with them came the ache in his heart over Lily leaving. He needed air. And to be alone. "Hey, make sure Harley's here to watch the shop before you leave, OK? He should be in the back."

He didn't wait for her answer before he fled. Mindless, he wandered away from Main Street. Turning here and there he soon found himself in front of the church. An odd sense of comfort washed over him at the thought of attending that coming Sunday. He stopped and regarded the building. He'd sat on its pews as a child, but had never taken it seriously. Now, as a man, he couldn't wait for the opportunity to learn more.

As he turned away from the churchyard he caught sight of Micah walking toward him from the direction of Main Street. His friend wore a troubled expression.

"Hey man, you OK?" Before Micah could answer Noah focused on the fluff ball on the end of the leash he was carrying. "Wait. Isn't that Lily's dog?"

"Yeah. It's weird. She stopped by this morning, paid her bill, and said she'd pick Princess up in an hour. That was three hours ago. Princess needed to be walked anyway, so I decided to just take her up to the inn. I get there. No Lily. Ava said she must have left for Boston, but... without Princess? It doesn't make sense."

Noah didn't even wait for Micah to finish before he took off toward The Butterfly Cove Inn.

God, please keep me level-headed.
I don't give fear.

As he breathed in that promise he dashed back up to Lily's room. Unsure what else to do he tried her knob. It clicked open. Noah peeked through the crack. Under any other circumstances, he would have felt like an intruder, but a whisper of trepidation had settled around him. Not fear, just the feeling that he needed to find out what was… off. Her room was empty. No suitcase, no high heels kicked in the corner, no indication she would be back.

"Lily?" he called again. No answer and the bathroom stood dark and silent as well.

A single piece of paper on the floor by the window caught his eye and he scooped it up. A cashier's check made out to Edwin Hurst? Could Lily have gone to confront Hurst without him? They had planned to go together this morning, but maybe she'd gone alone.

With her door closed behind him, Noah made a straight line for the front door and down the drive toward town.

God, help me find her. Keep her safe until I can get to her. Help me!

Hurst's office was dark. The door was locked and the thunderous banging of Noah's fist on the wood brought no one from inside.

"Edwin!" he yelled, pounding again on the door.

"He's gone down to Portland," said a deep male voice.

Noah swung around to find Hurst's neighbor standing on the sidewalk with a Summer Harbor Gazette tucked under his arm and a coffee from the corner shop in his hand. The guy was a lawyer Noah thought, or maybe an accountant. He couldn't remember. "How long has he been gone?"

"Left around lunchtime yesterday. Asked me to keep an eye on the front step so these didn't pile up," he added, tapping the paper.

"Have you seen a lady here today?"

"Here at Hurst's?"

"Ayuh."

"No. I just went to grab a coffee," the man gestured with his cup, "but I haven't seen anyone."

"OK, thanks." Noah ran both hands through his hair and laced his fingers together at the back of his neck.

"Sir, are you alright?"

Noah forced himself to relax. "Ayuh, sorry, just trying to find a friend."

"You're sure?"

"Totally." Noah needed to think. Where could she be? He walked back to Main Street and stood, hands in his pockets, watching the crowd. Had she gone for a jog? No, he would have seen her on the beach. After the last few days, he couldn't picture her going anywhere. Something wasn't right. He could feel it, like a shadow.

He walked toward the shop on autopilot. As he neared the alley he detoured into The Hungry Whale and tracked down Parker in the kitchen. His friend flicked his eyes up from where he had just turned a perfect omelet out onto a plate.

"Hey man, want breakfast?" Noah didn't answer right away and Parker flashed a glance in his direction. "Ouch. By the look on your face, I think you need comfort food."

"No, that's not—" Noah laced his fingers behind his neck again and groaned.

Parker whipped up another batch of eggs with methodical strokes and slipped them into a pan. He kept an eye on Noah as he worked, but let him collect his thoughts without interruption.

"Lily wasn't at the inn."

"OK..." Parker prompted after a long pause.

"What you said last night, about surrender. Man, I couldn't even sleep last night."

"MmmHmm," Parker murmured.

"After tossing and turning for a while I just got up and went out on the water. I had all these empty places and I couldn't shake this feeling like I'd screwed up."

"Mmm, sounds familiar."

"I took a kayak out and I just paddled, like I could outrun those feelings. But I figured something out."

"What's that?"

"I couldn't outrun God."

A slow smile spread across Parker's face. He slid the eggs out onto a plate and pushed them toward Noah. His eyes sparkled like he was in on a delicious secret. "Go on."

"Man, He saved my soul."

Parker let out a whoop that startled Noah.

"Aww, man, you have no idea how much I've wanted to hear you say that!" He moved across the room and clasped Noah in a tight hug.

"I have so much I want to tell you and ask you," Noah said as Parker stepped back and clapped him on the shoulder.

"I'm sure you do." Parker shook his head in wonder again, then gave him a long, considering look. "So what was with the long face when you came in here?"

"Oh, man, where do I start?" He paused. "OK, you know that guy who drowned last week? Herbert Emerson? Lily's uncle?"

"Sure."

"Well, Lily thinks that something's... not quite right about his accident."

"Like...?"

"Like maybe he had help."

"Woah."

"Yeah. We asked around and found a couple of people who might have had reason to... help... him off the pier."

"I'm going out on a limb here, but isn't that a job for Chief Briggs?"

"We've visited him enough that he rolls his eyes when he sees us coming. Doesn't want to hear about it."

"Hmm," Parker frowned.

"Anyway, Sunday afternoon we went to talk to the first guy on the list. Edwin Hurst."

"That guy with the real estate office?"

"That's the one. We went and talked to him. Then Lily found this memo in Emerson's briefcase about Stella Tucker."

"Stella? Who owns the Sandpiper?"

"Ayuh, we went over there and talked to her. Turns out she and Emerson had a fling years ago and then he weaseled a hotel right out from under her."

"He sounds like a gem."

"You have no idea." Noah, done with the eggs Parker had made him, started to pace as he talked. "The next day Lily found that two of her tires had been knifed."

"Seriously?"

"Oh, it gets worse," Noah continued. "Lily and I tried to track down this guy who she saw in town. Turns out he was a rival of Emerson, and… her ex."

Parker let out a long whistle.

"We talked to him while we loaded up gear to go rock climbing over at The Cliff. While we were getting ready to climb later that morning, Lily discovered that her climbing rope had been cut." Noah stopped pacing and turned to Parker. His friend's face, usually a deep olive and tinged pink from the heat in the kitchen, had drained of color.

"This guy we'd talked to had picked the rope up earlier. Not saying it was him, just… well, he'd had the rope."

"Did you guys go to talk to Jim?"

"Ayuh. He wasn't concerned. Said accidents happen."

Parker whistled again.

"There's more. Monday night Lily got a call from Stella down at The Sandpiper telling her about a great place to go watch the stars."

"Lookout Point?"

"You would think, but the directions took Lily down Cliff Trail Road."

"Oh, man."

"She crashed her car and got pretty banged up."

Parker made an upset sound under his breath.

"When we went to talk to Stella about the directions we

discovered that Emerson's business partner, who he was on the outs with, is dating Stella and was here in Summer Harbor when Emerson drowned."

"Whoa."

"Lily didn't think he had anything to do with Emerson, but then yesterday he sent her a note telling her that the weather forecast was perfect for hiking Bar Island."

"Yesterday? The weather forecast yesterday said severe thunderstorm warning, stay inside."

"So we discovered."

Parker flinched.

"That's a lot of bad stuff in a short amount of time."

"Tell me about it." Noah dragged his hand across his face and stopped pacing, turning to face Parker. "This morning we had planned to go speak to Hurst again, but I can't find Lily any-where."

Parker stood up from where he'd been perched on a stool. Concern was written on his face. "Should we go talk to Hurst?"

"Already been. He's been out of town."

"Stella and this other guy? The partner?"

Noah pointed at his friend. "Good idea."

"I'm coming, too," Parker yelled after Noah's retreating form.

Noah slowed and waited while Parker whipped off his apron and hurried to catch up. "Thanks, man."

The walk to The Sandpiper was quiet. Noah wracked his brain trying to sort out where Lily could be and he hoped Parker was praying. And that God was listening.

"I'd like to speak to Stella Tucker, please," Noah asked the woman who greeted them at the front desk.

"I'm sorry, sir, she's out of town."

"Out of town? I just spoke with her the day before yester-day."

"She went to Boston yesterday morning with Mr. Amias. They are just the sweetest things!"

"She's in Boston? With Alistair?"

"Yes sir. I wouldn't be surprised if one of these times she comes back Mrs. Amias," the woman said in a loud, conspiratorial whisper.

"Thanks," Noah mumbled. Hurst, Stella, and Alistair were all out of town? He tried to calm his nerves. Where was Lily? They left the bed and breakfast and Parker urged him back up the hill. His pace quickened, but he had no direction.

After a few minutes of aimless walking, Parker spoke up. "How about this other guy? The one who could have cut Lily's rope. Could she have gone to see him?"

"Maybe. He's staying at The Bellamy."

They picked up the pace. Noah was thankful for the solid support of his friend. He also got the distinct impression that a great deal of serious praying was going on. In awe, he realized what a comfort it was to know that his friend was praying for him. And had been, for years. He clamped his hand on Parker's shoulder in silent thanks.

Hope Bellamy greeted them with a brilliant smile. "Parker. Always great to see you. And Noah! Twice in one week, must be a record."

He forced a smile and tried to mask his frayed nerves. "Hi, Hope. I need to speak with Carmen Franco. Could you call his room, please?"

"Oh, sorry Noah. He checked out two days ago."

"Two days? As in Tuesday?"

"Yes, right after you stopped by. It was odd. When he came the week before he said he needed the room for a couple of weeks. Then you guys stopped in and within an hour he'd checked out. Said his business had wrapped up quicker than he expected."

Noah thumped his fist on the counter, trying not to freak out.

"Thanks," Parker muttered as he steered Noah out the door. "What now?" he asked once they were back out on the sidewalk.

Noah laced his fingers behind his neck, pulling his gaze to the ground, and started to pace. "I don't know. Where could she be?"

Panic had started edging in on his voice, despite willing himself to stay calm. "The people we thought might be involved aren't even in town. I have to find her, Parker. I... I love her."

"Whoa, man," Parker grabbed his arm. "Have you prayed about finding her?"

"Ayuh. Sort of. When I first realized she wasn't at the inn."

"Alright, time to get real with God. Let's go to The Green."

They jogged across the street and found a quiet corner of the park. Parker dropped down on the soft cushion of grass and leaned back against a tree trunk. Noah wasn't sure he'd be able to sit still. He was already wearing a path in the grass in front of Parker.

"Man, sit down."

Noah collapsed on the grass. With his arms wrapped around his bent knees, he hung his head between them and tried to concentrate on Parker's words.

Parker clapped a firm hand on Noah's shoulder and in his customary deep, soft voice began to pray. "Heavenly Father, we come before You, humble, meek, and patient. We know that You are sovereign and in ultimate control. We also know that we are weak sinners who can do nothing in our own power. We are worried about our friend Lily and ask that You show us where she is, and give us wisdom for the situation. We know that Lily is Your child and that You love her. You are a Good Father who cares for His children. Please keep her safe. In the name of our Lord Jesus Christ. Amen."

Noah couldn't raise his head and Parker kept his hand heavy on his shoulder. Drawing in a ragged breath Noah added his own hoarse words to Parker's plea. "God, I've only been Your child for a few hours and I don't think I have any right to be asking for anything after all You've done for me today. Forgiving me and all. But, man, I'd really like to find Lily and have her be OK. Please. Amen."

Parker squeezed his shoulder hard before letting go. "There's this verse in Hebrews that says 'Faith is the substance of things hoped for, the evidence of things not seen.' We have to have hope. Not hope like 'I hope it's sunny tomorrow', but hope like a kid jumping into his dad's arms. The kid 'hopes' his dad will catch him, but it's a knowing hope. Faith is what we have when we have that hope. We may not be able to see Lily or know where she is right this second, but we have hope that God is taking care of her and faith that He will help us find her."

"Thanks, Reverend Donovan," Noah teased.

Parker laughed. A rich, hearty sound that rumbled from deep inside. "Nah, not even close. I just read my Bible and try to pay attention when Pastor James is preaching."

"May I come to church with you on Sunday?" Noah asked, his voice tentative.

"Man, of course! You'll know a lot of people there. There's a good chance Walter will insist you sit with him."

Noah's face paled and he gaped at Parker.

"Hey, relax! You don't have to sit with him, OK?"

"No. Walter."

"What about Walter?"

"What would have happened to Walter if Herbert Emerson bought the inn?"

"He'd be out of a job."

"What happens to Walter if Lily buys the inn?"

"I don't know. Maybe she'd keep him on. Why?"

"Or?"

"Or he's out of a job."

"Either way Walter would think he's out of a job. He could have overpowered Herbert at the pier. Later he had access to Lily's car and her climbing gear. He could have altered the directions Stella left and the note Alistair sent. It's Walter Ashe."

CHAPTER SIXTEEN

Alright. I'm going to get Chief Briggs," Parker said as he sprang back to his feet. "You go back to the inn and find Walter. I'll meet you there. And Noah... be careful."

By the time Parker and Chief Briggs arrived at The Butterfly Cove Inn, Noah had destroyed the grass at the edge of the parking area. He'd traipsed back and forth so many times he'd lost count. The new spring shoots were no match and had succumbed. Parker and the policeman pulled up the drive and Noah met them at the cruiser. Chief Briggs wore an irked expression and sighed as he climbed from the cruiser.

"Alright Noah, what's this all about? Parker was... shall we say, persuasive, so I'm here. You have to know I still think this is nothing."

"I know, I know. I just... I can't find Lily and I'm worried. I think Walter Ashe might have had a hand in it."

"Walter?" The incredulous tone in Chief Briggs' voice was blatant.

"When Miss Ava sells the inn, Walter will be out of a job. He'll lose his home, his family. I think he's been trying to stop the sale. First Herbert, then Lily. He was either present or could have manipulated situations to cause all the problems Lily's had."

The first glimmer of uncertainty flickered across the cop's face. "Let's ask him a few questions. Mind you, I'm not saying I agree with you, just... let's ask him a few questions."

The three men made their way around the side of the inn to Walter's garden shed. He was outside the front door winding a garden hose onto a reel.

"Walter," Chief Briggs began.

"Jim," Walter grinned. He pulled his ever-present cap off and offered his hand. "What can I do for ya?"

Chief Briggs shook the offered hand, but his serious expression must have tipped Walter off to the fact that this wasn't a social call. His smile dimmed as his eyes flicked from one man to the next.

"Walter, do you know where Lily Emerson is?"

"No, no. I told Noah earlier. I ain't seen 'er this morning."

"Walter, do you know about the bad things that have been happening to Lily?" Parker asked.

"You mean her tires bein' flat?"

"Well, yes, that was one incident. She also had an accident the other night," the policeman replied.

"Miss Ava said she took the wrong road. That was terrible unlucky."

"We're thinking it might have been a little more than bad luck," Noah added under his breath. Misfortune was one thing. Multiple scrapes with death was quite another.

"I don't understand," Walter said as he worried the edge of his cap.

"We're just trying to sort things out," the Chief said. His tone was calm and patient. Noah was a bit in awe. He was ready to come apart at the seams.

"I don't see how I can help none. Like I done said, I ain't seen Miss Lily since the day before yesterday."

"Let's just go down to the station Walter. We'll talk there."

"No! I didn't do nothin'!"

"C'mon Walter. I'm not arresting you..." He let the 'yet' hang in the air unsaid.

"No, please. I just want to stay here. I don't want to go." The older man was near hysterics. Tears coursed down his weathered cheeks. Noah couldn't look at him. He'd known the man his whole life. How could kind, gentle Walter have done this?

"Please, Walter, just tell me where Lily is," Noah demanded.

His tone was sharper than he'd intended, but he didn't care. Fear clawed at his throat and he hated the taste of it. "Tell me!"

"I didn't do nothin' to Miss Lily! Please, Chief, you have to believe me."

Chief Briggs had unsnapped the pouch on his belt containing his handcuffs. "I don't want to cuff you Walter, but if you won't come with me I'll have to."

Walter began to wail.

"What is the meaning of this?" came a sharp voice from the porch.

"Oh, Miss Ava, they think I done somethin' to Miss Lily! But I didn't! I swear!"

Ava Allen came down the porch steps one at a time, leaning on her cane. She scuffled across the lawn to Walter and laid a calming hand on his arm.

"Jimmy Briggs, how could you suspect Walter?" She turned a motherly smile on Walter. "He couldn't hurt anyone. He wouldn't even think of such a thing."

"Miss Ava, we just want to ask him a few questions, that's all."

Ava's voice became more agitated as she tried to explain. "Walter is... slow. He doesn't comprehend things the same as we do. I'm telling you, he couldn't have done anything to Lily!" she shrilled. She had maneuvered herself between Walter and the three men while she spoke.

"This isn't helping us find Lily," Noah muttered.

Parker put his hand on Noah's shoulder, whether to reassure him or restrain him Noah wasn't sure.

"You cannot have any proof that Walter has done anything," Ava added.

"No, ma'am, we don't. That's why I'm not arresting him. I just want to ask him to clarify a few things."

"Well, ask him here, then let him be!"

This was getting them nowhere and Noah still had no idea where to find Lily. He ran his hands through his hair and grabbed the back of his neck as he turned away from the drama playing out before him. Parker let him go.

Oh, God, give me something! She has to be... somewhere.

He turned back and studied the little tableau. None of the people in front of him appeared to be who they really were. Chief Briggs appeared to be a tough and seasoned man of the law. The truth was he would downplay anything that came along to keep the town of Summer Harbor looking good in the public eye. Even murder. Next to him stood Parker. In his dress shirt and slacks, he appeared to be a capable businessman, but that was only a tiny piece of who he was. He was a superb chef whose unique and delicious creations kept his restaurant packed. Standing before Parker was Ava. A frail woman clutching her cane as though she would crumple without it. However, Noah had seen her climb ladders to wash windows and haul furniture around the inn. She might be small, but the feeble-old-woman was an act. Behind her stood Walter. To the ordinary eye, he was a pleasant gentleman in his fifties holding down a decent job as a landscaper. The truth was, his mind had never developed past about ten years old. His life at The Butterfly Cove Inn was the result of loving care from a woman who was not his mother, but who had stepped into the role.

"I know, beyond a shadow of a doubt that Walter is innocent!"

Ava's piercing voice cut through Noah's thoughts. He stepped back into the group, his gaze unwavering. "Ava?"

She snapped her mouth shut and turned to him, her rheumy eyes not quite meeting his.

"Ava," he said in a calm, unhurried tone. "Where's Lily?"

CHAPTER SEVENTEEN

Lily woke to the feeling of damp, sandy earth beneath her cheek. Her head throbbed. It was so dark that she wondered if the same bump causing the screaming pain in her temple could also have caused blindness. She reached up and brushed her fingertips across the lump above her right ear and winced. Blood had congealed in her hair making it stiff and sticky. She tried sitting up, but waves of nausea washed over her and she slumped back down with a whimper. The cold fingers of unconsciousness clawed at her. She wanted to succumb. The murky shadows in her mind promised painless oblivion.

Even though you walk through darkness, I am with you.

She tried to focus her thoughts, but her head throbbed with each beat of her heart. What had happened? She remembered coming down for breakfast, walking to Noah's shop. Had she walked back to the inn? Her thoughts were muddled. A moan escaped her lips and tears soaked the bare ground beneath her cheek. She had to have a concussion. Had she fallen? Her left arm was twisted under her and ached like she'd bashed it against something, wrenching her shoulder in the process. She flexed it. It didn't appear to be broken, but she couldn't be sure without moving off it.

Willing herself not to pass out, she pushed herself up again. She tried to feel her surroundings. With her uninjured arm, she slid her hand across the packed dirt. Nothing in any direction. Panic rushed over her like an icy wind, stealing her breath. The darkness strangled her until she was delirious with fear. She willed herself not to faint, but she couldn't seem to get enough air and was light-headed to the point of dizziness. No, she couldn't pass out. She wouldn't. She had to find the strength to find a way out… of wherever she was.

She rolled up onto her knees, protecting her head with her arm. The reality of being trapped in the dark sank past the pain and made her hands tremble. Frantic now she waved her hand in front of her as she inched forward on her knees. The occasional rustle from the shadows made her skin crawl. Mice? Snakes? Her imagination began to run wild. There was an eerie, rhythmic swishing sound that added to her unease.

Don't be afraid, I am with you. I am your God and I will strengthen you, I will help you, I will hold you with My righteous right hand.

Deep breaths of dank air calmed the terror Lily slipped toward.

Oh, God, help me.

She started moving again. Inching toward the unknown. Feeling the floor and then the air in front of herself she crept forward bit by bit. The time it took to check for dangers made it feel as though she made no progress. She yelped when pain ran up her arm from where her wrist connected with stone. She held it to her chest and swallowed back the pain and panic. Again she reached out and felt the wall. Not man-made, she thought as her fingers ran over rough stone.

Resting with her back against the stone she tried to formulate a plan. There had to be a way to escape. If she kept the stone wall on her left and worked her way along it in a deliberate manner she just might find a way out. A door? Stairs? Something? If she'd gotten in, she could get out. How had she gotten in? She couldn't remember anything from the morning and thinking made her head hurt. Taking a bolstering breath, she squeezed her eyes tight against the pain and rolled back to her knees.

Words from a favorite hymn wafted into her mind like a sweet-smelling flower on the breeze. She began to sing. Over and over her clear, quiet alto pushed back the panic.

O soul are you weary and troubled?

No light in the darkness you see?
There's light for a look at the Savior
And life more abundant and free
Turn your eyes upon Jesus
Look full in His wonderful face
And the things of earth will grow strangely dim
In the light of His glory and grace

Noah stood, arms folded, watching Ava. The only indication of emotion was the occasional twitch of a muscle along his jaw.

"Noah..." Chief Briggs put a hand on his shoulder. Noah shrugged it off. The policeman cleared his throat. "I think you need to..."

Noah put his hand up to silence the man, but never took his eyes off of Ava's face.

Silence.

Then, in a fractured voice, Ava hissed "In the cave."

Noah bolted around the house. As he ran he heard a keening wail burble up, deplorable and heartbreaking. Ava's legs had weakened and she had slumped toward the ground. Walter knelt on the ground holding her in his arms while she sobbed.

He charged around the corner of the house and was in a full-out run by the time he reached the backyard. If childhood memories were correct there was a small cave in the cliffs overlooking the beach. He stumbled down the path to the pebbled shore but found it already immersed in frigid water. The cave entrance submerged under the freezing surf. Back at the top of the cliff, Parker joined him. Noah had a vague memory of a second opening near the gazebo. They scrambled across the lawn, his heart hammering so hard he couldn't hear above the beat, let alone think.

God, please make her OK!

As they neared the structure he began a wild search for the topside entrance.

"There!" Parker was pointing toward the edge of the grass.

Noah's eyes landed on the wooden cover protecting the opening. He leaped on it and clawed at the latch. As he lifted the heavy wood he thought he heard singing. It brought him up short. *Turn your eyes upon Jesus, Look full in His wonderful face.*

"Lily!"

The door banged back onto the grass. The singing stopped on an agonizing moan. Noah's heart couldn't make up its mind whether to stop or race out of control as he peered into the shadows.

She sat in a crumpled heap against the wall of granite. Dirt covered her hands, her knees, and the side of her face. Her hair was matted with blood and stuck to her face and neck. She clutched one arm to her chest, while the other hand was braced on the stone as though she was trying to keep it, or herself, up-right.

He had to hold her, had to look into her eyes and prove to himself that she was OK. Beyond where she was huddled, he could see the water creeping closer. The tide was still rising. He had to get her out, now.

"Lily!"

"Noah?"

"I'm going to get you out, Sweetheart!" He lunged toward the opening but came up short when Parker grabbed his arm. He tried to shake him off, but his friend held tight.

"Dude, you can't just leap into the cave, then you'll both be stuck in there."

"Parker, I have to get to her."

"I know, just… let's be smart about it. What about your rock climbing gear?"

"It will take too long to go get it. That tide's coming in fast." He spun toward the hole again. "Lily, I need your climbing gear. Where is it?"

"In my room." Her voice was weak and even from where he stood far above her he could see her shivering."

"I'll be right back. I promise!" Then to Parker, "You keep her talking. And calm."

"Got it."

Noah tore across the yard and up the back steps to the kitchen door. Frantic, he threw open the door to her room and searched for her things. There weren't many hiding places and he found them under the bed. He snatched her pack of gear and a blanket off the back of a chair as he ran back out.

At the gazebo, Noah dumped out the gear and started searching for what he needed.

God, help me focus. I can't miss anything here.

He tied off two ropes and stepped into a harness. Satisfied that he had what he needed and that there was a rope arranged for Parker to pull Lily out of the cave, he began lowering himself into the hole. The icy water was edging closer and closer to Lily with every wave. He tried to stay calm as he rappelled down the sheer face of the rock, but he was sick to his stomach by the time he reached the floor. Unclipping his rope from his harness was difficult with his fingers shaking.

Once free, he squatted down level with her and searched her face. The blood smeared down her neck and cheek concerned him, but she was alive. That's what mattered.

Thank You, God!

He took her face in his wide, calloused hands and brought his lips to hers. The kiss was gentle but hungry. She melted against him. Tears of relief overflowed down her dirty cheeks.

"Sweetheart," he murmured. He rested his forehead against hers, careful not to cause her pain.

"Where...?" She tried looking around now that light chased the shadows back to the corners of the cave.

"We're in a cave at the base of the cliffs behind the inn. Do you remember how you got down here?"

"No."

"The tide's coming in fast. We need to get out of here." He scooped her into his arms and pushed to his feet as if she weighed nothing at all.

"Noah?" Parker called from above. "You got her?"

"Sure do!" Noah called out as he hooked her into a second harness and clipped her to the rope with a pulley. "Can you climb?"

"I... I don't think so."

He kissed her again and then yelled up to Parker. "Pull her up!"

The rope tightened and she began ascending. He worked on reattaching his self-belay device to the second rope when the first wave washed over his ankles. The biting water of the Atlantic stung and drained his feet of feeling as wave after wave washed over them. It inched up his legs as he tried to tie a three wrap prusik knot to attach a leg loop. They say a human being can survive for about forty-five minutes in water that cold. How? His leg muscles were already cramping as he finished tying the knot with shaking fingers.

Parker had managed to pull Lily halfway up by the time Noah was able to slide the climbing heist up and step on the leg loop.

They toppled, one right after the other, out of the mouth of the cave into the warm sunshine. Lily caught her eyes in the crook of her elbow and whimpered at the stab of light. Noah's body screamed for him to rest, breathe, but he had to know that Lily was alright. He grabbed the blanket and wrapped it around her, holding her to his chest.

"She's a little banged up. I'm worried about her head. It needs to be looked at," Noah said, pitching his voice low and quiet.

"What happened?" she asked.

"I'm not sure."

Noah scooped Lily up and the two men retraced their steps to the front yard. Ava sat in the back of the police cruiser. Her glazed eyes staring straight ahead. Chief Briggs stood, arms crossed, next to the cruiser. His radio crackled and he threw an uncomfortable look Lily's direction as he asked Thelma to contact Ava's son up in Bangor. Walter stood near the open door of the car twisting his hat in his hands until it was ready to rip. Tears slipped down his cheeks and dripped onto his shirt. His eyes darted around, dismay etching deep lines into his leathery face.

"Ava... hit me," Lily whispered.

Noah's arm had tightened of its own volition and he hoped he wasn't hurting her. A million what-ifs flashed through his head. What if he hadn't figured out it was Ava? What if he hadn't thought something was wrong in the first place? What if, what if, what if!

Her cool hand tightened on his. "I'm OK, Noah."

"I was terrified when I couldn't find you," he ground out. He loosened his hold on her, but couldn't bring himself to set her down. Not yet.

"I know."

"What if I hadn't—?"

"Shhh. God had me. His promise is to never leave me."

"I liked that song you were singing," he whispered as he nuzzled her ear.

The blush that kissed her cheeks was endearing, even through the smears of blood and dirt. "There's a verse in Psalms I love that says 'God has put a new song in my mouth, even praise to our God'. I was scared, but He gave me a song."

"Lily, I need to tell you—"

"I've called for an ambulance," Chief Briggs interrupted as he sauntered up to them. He swiped his hat off his head and looked chagrined as he continued. "I'm sorry I didn't take you more seriously. I just couldn't imagine murder happening in our little slice of heaven."

Lily's eyes turned to saucers. "Murder? It's true? Uncle?" Her already pale skin tinged green.

"It would appear so."

"Ava? But... How?"

"She told him that if he would meet her down at the pier she would make a deal with him. She says she hit him with her cane."

"Why did she confess now?" asked Lily. "No one would have ever guessed it was her."

"She couldn't watch Walter arrested for her crime," Noah said with respect edging his voice.

"Ayuh," Chief Briggs agreed. "That man's like a son, maybe even more than her own boy these days."

"Any idea why she did it?" Noah asked.

"Didn't want to lose this place," Chief Briggs said. He waved a hand to encompass the inn and grounds. "She was afraid that once the place sold, Walter wouldn't have a place to live."

"Then why list it in the first place?"

"Her son insisted."

Sirens whined from the road and an ambulance sailed into the yard. Lily winced away from the sound and Noah pulled her into his chest. He used his embrace to muffle the shrieking blast and throbbing lights. With his hand against her hair, Lily sagged into him, spent.

"I've got to get back to the restaurant," Parker murmured to Noah. He clapped his friend on the shoulder. "I'm glad you're OK, Lily."

"Thanks, man," Noah nodded. "For everything."

"Over here." Chief Briggs motioned the two paramedics to where Lily slumped in Noah's arms. As they hurried forward, he turned to Noah. "I'm going to take Ava down to the station until her son gets here and we can figure out what to do."

Lily clung to Noah. She looked as though the pain and nausea were still pulling her toward oblivion and he feared if she let go of him she would succumb. The paramedics, who she wasn't surprised to find he knew, were kind enough to let her stay in the shelter of his arms. They were thorough and, in the end, they said she didn't have to go to the hospital if she didn't want to.

"You need ice on that bump," the male EMT said, handing her an instant ice pack. "If anything at all changes you come down to the ER immediately."

She tried to nod her head, but it hurt too much. "Of course," she whispered.

The two packed up their things and loaded them into the ambulance before crunching their way back down the driveway.

"Riley and Tim are fantastic," Noah said, watching their tail lights turn onto Main Street.

Lily didn't answer.

"Are you OK?" he asked. "I mean, other than the obvious."

She tried to muster up a smile, but it fell flat. "I want to go wash this out of my hair." She lifted a dark mat of grimy hair.

Noah turned her toward the inn and helped her up the stairs. Once in her room, he pulled the rest of her things from beneath the bed. She watched him, bewildered.

"I take it you didn't put them there?"

"No."

"I'm guessing Ava hid them. She told me you'd left for Boston already."

She didn't meet his eyes. Instead, she grabbed clean clothes and disappeared into the bathroom, trudging through the door and closing it with a quiet click.

Noah tried not to pace and tried not to worry about her falling or passing out. Failing at both he searched for a distraction. Seeing her Bible in the top of her open suitcase, he scooped it up and took it to the hall. He lowered himself to the top step and began thumbing through the thin pages. Verse after verse had notes written in the margins. In no time he had lost himself in reading. First a verse and then her thoughts, recorded in her distinctive neat script along the edges of the page.

Her understanding of God and scripture was staggering. It occurred to him that he knew nothing. Feelings and limited experience couldn't compare to the relationship Lily had with her Savior and His Word.

God, please give me this level of understanding someday. I want to know You like she does.

Parker's words came back to him as he read. *As a Christian, Lily needs a partner who will draw her closer to God.* How could he ever hope to lead Lily toward Christ? He would play catch up the rest of their lives. Parker was right. He'd get what he wanted, but Lily would end up resenting him. He cared too much for her to offer less than the ideal. She deserved much more than he would struggle to be. He returned her Bible to her suitcase and perched himself back on the top step to wait.

He rubbed the heel of his hand on his chest. A different kind of ache had settled into the area of his heart. No longer an empty pit in his soul, but the sting of knowing the right, yet painful, choice he was about to make.

Lily's bedroom door opened with a soft whoosh and she stepped out. Dressed in an old pair of jeans and her thick Acadian Adventures sweatshirt he was surprised how young and lost she seemed. Pain lodged in his chest as his heart tightened. Why did he have to fall in love with her before realizing that she was right all along? She couldn't date him.

He forced a smile. "Feeling better?"

Her half-hearted attempt at a smile didn't reach her eyes.

"You want to take a walk? Maybe on the beach?"

"Could we just sit outside?"

They strolled along the wraparound porch in silence. Lily tugged the sleeves of her sweatshirt down over her hands. Noah tucked his hands in his pockets and hunched his shoulders. They stopped at the end of the porch. Lily sat in the corner of the creaky swing and tucked both feet under herself.

Unable to restrain himself he pushed off the porch rail, slipped onto the swing next to her, and gathered her into his arms. He breathed in the now familiar smell of lilacs and nestled her against his chest.

"I refuse to soak your shirt... again," she mumbled against the soft fabric.

He chuckled and kissed the top of her head. "You can soak my shirt anytime."

She let out a breathy laugh as she pulled away and sat up straight.

He held her arms and looked into her eyes. He wanted to remember each shimmering violet fleck and silver streak. Finally, he pushed off the swing and returned to the railing, hands in his pockets, ankles crossed, the afternoon breeze ruffling his hair. "I need to tell you about last night," he said at last.

"Alright."

"When we got back, I couldn't wait to tell Parker about my realization. Did you know he's a Christian? Anyway, I wanted to tell him that I got it. That I believe God exists. I found him at the restaurant. I don't know what I expected, but it sure wasn't him telling me I didn't, in fact, get it." He turned toward the yard and braced his hands on the railing. "I thought he'd be excited, you know?" He paused. "Well... I was mad and confused. I mean I thought I'd figured out what it was that you and Parker had. Then he told me all this stuff about my relationship with God and surrendering. Not what I wanted to hear. I tried to go to bed, but I couldn't sleep. I had to find peace. I was desperate, so I took a kayak out."

"In the middle of the night?"

The awe in her voice made him chuckle. "It's beautiful on the water at night. But last night I just couldn't find the tranquility I longed for. In the end, I just begged God to take all my bad stuff and you know what?"

"He did."

"Yeah! He did! He took it all and gave me this... this... amazing peace. He took my sin and I gave Him my life."

A tearful smile spread across her face. "Oh, Noah..." She got off the swing and came to him at the railing. He turned toward her and she flung her arms around his neck. He returned her exuberant hug with one that was fierce and lifted her toes clear off the porch floor.

"I'm happy for you, Noah," she managed through tears as she clung to his neck. He swung her around and her laughter was warm against his neck. For an instant he let himself think that he could have this. He pretended that he could have Lily in his arms, that he could have this kind of joy. That this could be his life. Yet he knew the truth and it sliced through him. He tightened his arms around her, unable to let her go just yet.

"The Bible says that the angels in Heaven rejoice when a sinner repents and comes to Christ. I understand that feeling," she said as she pulled back and looked him in the eye. He didn't respond, but instead, set her back on her feet. "Noah?"

He turned away from her and rested his forearms on the porch railing. What he had to say needed to be done quickly and not while he looked into those beautiful silvery gray eyes of hers.

"I surrendered to God because that was what I needed to do. I needed Him to save me. I needed His grace and mercy. I also did it because it's what He demands of me. You and Parker pointed me in the right direction, but this was all between me and God. This morning, on the water, I had this crazy idea that this would change our relationship. After all, you wouldn't date me because I wasn't a Christian and now I am. But, while you were in the shower I realized that it can't."

Her silence beckoned him to turn, but he knew the disappointment in her eyes would unravel him so he stood, stoic, eyes intent and unseeing on the yard. "You would always wonder if I did this just to win you. I couldn't live with myself if you thought that. You were right all along, Lily. You can't date me."

"Noah..." Her voice hitched on a sob that undid him.

He dropped his face to his hands "You need a partner who can understand, and even add to, the notes in your Bible. I'm not that person." It took long, aching moments before he could look at her. The happy tears that had glistened in her eyes only moments before now turned bitter.

"What are you saying, Noah?" Her face told him she knew this sounded a great deal like goodbye.

"I'm saying..." Oh, why did it have to hurt this much? "I'm saying, I care too much about you to make you regret being with me." She couldn't have looked more stricken if he'd slapped her. She backed away, unable to meet his eyes. He had to escape before he took it all back. He caught her hand and pressed a hard kiss to the top of her head. Tears hitched his voice. "Lily, I wish you all the best. You are amazing. Don't forget that."

❦

Lily choked back a sob as she watched him lope across the lawn. Her heart screamed for her to follow him. To chase him down, tell him he was wrong, convince him that they could make it work. But ultimately, he wasn't wrong. Even if she could believe that he had come to God for himself, if he thought she believed he'd done it to win her, it would fester.

Knowing he was right didn't ease the pain one bit. As much as she had tried to guard her heart, in the end, she had fallen in love with Noah Kingsley. She watched him until he rounded the corner onto the road and then let her heart shatter into a million pieces.

The crunch of gravel on the drive drew her attention. The police cruiser pulled in and Chief Briggs got out. "I hope I'm not interrupting. I need to get your statement," he said as he climbed the porch steps.

"Yes, of course." She made a valiant effort to pull herself together. She could fall apart on her own time. "While I was in the shower, I remembered most of what happened this morning."

"What do you remember?"

"I walked into town early, before breakfast. When I came back to the inn Ava asked me when I planned to return to Boston. Last night I'd decided to go back today, but this morning I just couldn't bring myself to say it out loud. To throw away the dream.

"She offered to show me around the grounds. She's sweet and I can't say no to her. I was just humoring her, but... Well, anyway, we went out and walked around. When we got to the cave entrance at the top of the cliff she tried to open the cover to show it to me. She couldn't lift it, so I did. That's the last I remember. Looking into the dark and then blinding pain and falling." Her voice caught and she looked away.

"Ava's son arrived a few minutes ago. She confessed to the

whole lot of it."

"Everything?" Lily asked in a voice rich with disbelief.

"According to Ava, she thought getting rid of Herbert Emerson would allow her to keep the inn. When she realized that you were still interested she, and I quote, 'tried to scare her'."

"How on earth did she...?" Lily swallowed. "How did she... overpower Uncle?"

"In her statement, she said that she called him at the hotel and told him if he met her on the pier she'd make a deal with him for the inn. Then she walked from the inn to the pier, alone, and waited for him. I don't know how she did that. Anyway, when he arrived she hit him with her cane."

"Oh, my..." Lily's fingers were pressed against her lips in shock.

"She punctured your tires with the tip of the cane she uses on ice. Then she cut your rope while Walter had the trunk open using the jack to take the wheels off your car. When that didn't make you leave, she altered the directions from Stella Tucker, sending you down a closed and dangerous road. When a..." He flipped through his notebook, "'good-smelling man' dropped off a note for you, she copied it but changed a bit about bad thunderstorms to perfect weather. This morning she got desperate and hit you with her cane, the same as your uncle."

Lily shivered. "I can't believe Ava was capable of all that. What's going to happen to her?"

"I'm not sure yet. I have a call into the DA." He tucked his notebook into his pocket and adjusted his belt. With a tip of his hat, he started down the stairs, but stopped partway down and turned to Lily again. "I apologize for not taking you seriously before. We get our fair share of silly accidents around here, but nothing like this. It just seemed... impossible."

"I doubt you would have suspected Ava anyway," Lily conceded. She watched him until the cruiser was out of sight.

CHAPTER EIGHTEEN

Noah knew Harley had an eye on him as he put away dry bags the next morning. They were both silent. He'd arrived in the dark, early hours, knowing he wore a tortured expression. He'd been silent as they set up for the tour and hadn't spoken the entire time on the water. Instead, he'd lagged behind, vigilant but distant. It wasn't the first time he'd let Harley run things, but he knew the man could sense that his mood was different this morning.

Harley clapped a hand on Noah's shoulder and squeezed. "If you need to talk…"

"Thanks," Noah murmured, not looking up. He'd missed his appointment at the bank the day before because of his search for Lily. He didn't care, and he'd do it again in a heartbeat, but the bank didn't take too kindly to skipped appointments and had declined his request for another. However, all that paled in comparison to the fact that Lily was no longer a part of his life. He slammed his hand against the wall hoping the pain would take the focus off the agony in his chest. Harley didn't even flinch where he stood at the whiteboard.

"Hey, boss," Gemma poked her head through the door. "Some lady dropped this off this morning while you were out on the water. Asked me to give it to you. And I gotta get to school, soooo… you all set?"

"Ayuh, Gemma, thanks." He took the small package wrapped in brown paper from her without meeting her eyes. Had she seen that little outburst? He hoped not.

There was a note attached to the top of the package. Curious, he opened it.

Jeremiah 33:3
James 1:5
2 Timothy 2:15, 3:16-17
Joshua 1:8
1 Peter 3:15
Numbers 6:24-26
Thank you for everything
All my best, Lily

He ripped the brown paper away and stood, dumbfounded. In his hand rested her well worn Bible. He ran his thumb over the age-softened front cover, emotions choking him.

"I've got the front, man. Take all the time you need," Harley said, moving past him.

Noah read through the list of verses and tried to figure out how to find them. After a few minutes of frustration, he trotted next door to Parker's kitchen. His friend stood prepping vegetables at the wide stainless-steel counter.

"Hey, man," Noah called from the doorway.

"Hey. How's Lily?"

"I think she's fine. She headed back to Boston this morning."

"Aww, Noah. I'm sorry, man. I know how you felt about her."

"Yeah."

"What's up?" Parker asked as he sliced a carrot into perfect ovals.

"Lily… gave me this." Noah held up the Bible. "I don't know how to find stuff in it."

An enormous grin transformed Parker's face. "Man, I dig this new side of you."

Noah gave a self-conscious shrug. "How do I find these?" he asked, handing Parker the note and the open Bible. He was struck again by the handwritten notes in the margins. This had to be a cherished possession and she'd given it to him. He was unworthy of such a gift, and the magnitude of what she'd given him settled into his chest.

Parker, always patient, showed him how to find the books and then chapter and verse. He ran his hand over the page in reverence before handing the Bible back to Noah, open to the first verse Lily had given him.

"When you're ready to read through a whole book I'd start with John," Parker told him in a quiet voice with a firm hand on his shoulder.

Noah thanked his friend and returned to the quiet of the shop's back room before turning his full attention to the first verse.

Jeremiah 33:3 'Call to Me, and I will answer you, and show you great and mighty things, which you do not know.'

God, I know nothing. Please teach me!

He searched for the second verse. It took him a lot longer than he would have liked to find them all, but he managed to find and read each one, his heart beating hard in his chest. As he finished the last verse he closed Lily's Bible and rubbed a gentle hand across the worn cover. He stood in the empty space for long seconds thinking about what he had read.

Overwhelmed by it all, he fell to his knees, right there in the back room of the shop, and called out to God. With his forearms braced on the floor and his face buried in them, he prayed.

God, those verses Lily wrote down for me say You'll teach me and give me wisdom if I ask, so I'm asking. I am painfully aware that I lack it. In everything. Please, help me, God! Give me Your wisdom. You say that You will give it generously and graciously, and I trust You to keep Your word.

The enormity of those words settled over him. Never had he been able to ask for wisdom and the thought that the God of heaven would just give it to him because he asked was exhilarating. He pushed back the rush of emotions to continue.

Please teach me about You. I want to know all there is to know. Help me to be diligent so that I can give myself to You each day, not ashamed of who I am, but confident in who You are making me to be. I know I need to study Your Word. Please show me how to understand it.

A grin spread across his face as he prayed. It was Friday morning. He'd only have to wait two days before he could go to church. Two days until he could learn from Pastor James. He thumped his fist on the floor in excitement and laughed at himself. It felt good. He felt new.

I believe that the Bible is from You and that You have given it to me for my own good so that I can learn and be shaped. God, please make me complete and give me what I need for the good work You want me to do.

The idea that God had things for him to do was humbling and he sobered at the thought. This was a big deal. He took a long breath.

This Bible that Lily has given me is a precious treasure. I want to know Your Word so well that I can mull it over all the time. I want to learn, and do, and live what it says. I want to glorify You in my heart every minute of every day. Like Parker and Lily, I want to be ready to tell everyone who asks why I am now filled to overflowing with hope, humility, and respect for You.

That struck him with wonder. In the space of one week, he had gone from doubting that there was any kind of a god out there, to holding God in the utmost reverence. How had that happened? But more baffling was how he could have ever believed there was no God. It boggled his mind.

Please bless me, keep me, make Your face shine on me, be gracious to me, and give me peace. In Your precious name, Amen.

Noah stayed on the floor and pulled the Bible onto his lap. Parker had recommended John and Noah couldn't wait another minute to dive in.

CHAPTER NINETEEN

The late-summer sun was hot and dry making people long to be on the water. The sunrise tour had been full and Noah had to rush to get life jackets and dry bags back in place before the next tour arrived in a few minutes. The new guys had all worked out great, just as Harley had predicted. He hoped a few of them would return the following summer. Good guys. They needed Jesus, but Noah was working on that. He grinned remembering the day before. Gage had called him Reverend Kingsley, much like he'd done with Parker for years. Had Parker felt as undeserving of the moniker as Noah did? No doubt.

"Excuse me, I was wondering if I could sign up for a tour this afternoon?" came a voice from the open back doors of the shop.

Noah's hands stilled on the dry bag he was wiping down. He swallowed. It couldn't be her. And yet... He turned toward the door and there she stood, silhouetted against the mid-morning sunshine. She wore jeans and a t-shirt and looked carefree and happy and shy. He didn't know whether to weep or whoop for joy. He opted for neither.

"Hey."

"Hey," she said as she stepped into the room. She ran her hand along the row of life jackets and stopped when she got close to where he stood. "I've missed you."

Her timid voice broke him and he closed the distance between them in the blink of an eye. He pulled her against his chest and leaned in, stopping at the last second to search her eyes, seek her permission. Her eyes smiled at him, inviting, and he was lost. The fingers of his left hand tangled in her hair and all the longing of the entire summer poured into his eyes.

He touched his mouth to hers. Feather-light at first and then with deepening passion. Her fingers twisted into his t-shirt and dragged him closer. His right hand held her tight against him as he relished the taste and smell and feel of her. Breathing hard he pulled away enough to rest his forehead against hers.

"I've missed you, too," he chuckled and a smile curved his lips. She hadn't let go of his shirt yet and he loved the way her desire to keep him close felt deep inside. In the midst of kissing her, he'd pushed her back against the shelves of life jackets and he eased off just enough to let her catch her breath.

"I know this is a busy time, but... do you have time to take a walk with me?" A shy smile lit her eyes.

"No point being the boss if I can't call the shots," he winked. Without taking his eyes off hers, he called to Gemma whose head popped through the door to the front of the shop. One look at Lily wrapped in Noah's arms and the girl's face went scarlet.

"Yeah boss?" she squeaked.

"I'm going out. Call the guys and find one to cover the rest of my tours today."

"Sure!" She'd regained her composure and flashed an eye-brow-wiggling smile at Lily before slipping back into the front room. Lily giggled at the comical expression on Gemma's face. Noah laughed too and stole another quick kiss before letting Lily go. They meandered down the alley and onto the street, headed in the general direction of the water. Lily started to raise her arms to wrap them around herself, but instead, looped an arm around his waist and leaned into his embrace. His heart swelled at the change in her. Gone was the woman who had no one and in her place was one who knew she was cherished.

"I didn't expect to see you again," he admitted as he traced circles on her upper arm with his thumb.

Lily was silent for a long time. Her face was an intriguing mix of serenity and determination. Like she had important things to say and was at complete peace with them. He wanted to tell her a million things, but a still, small voice ran on repeat in his brain.

I'll take care of this for you, just hold your peace.

They reached the pier and took the stone steps down to the shore. Noah laced his fingers with hers and raised them to his lips to kiss her knuckles. Low tide had, as usual, littered the pebbles with bits of this and that. They picked their way along the shore toward the sandbar. Noah kissed her hand again and the smile she flashed him was brilliant.

"When did you get back into town?" he asked.

She held up her watch. "About fifteen minutes ago."

He grinned, his heart swelling with the realization that he'd been her first stop. Nothing had changed since he'd left her on the porch of the inn a couple of months before, and yet it felt as though everything had changed. He opened his mouth to tell her but snapped it closed again without speaking.

I'll take care of this for you, just hold your peace.

"I closed on The Butterfly Cove Inn yesterday," she said after a long pause. A smile tugged at the corners of her mouth as she squinted out over the sun-dappled water.

Noah almost stumbled. "What did you say?"

"I said, I closed on The Butterfly Cove Inn yesterday."

"But I thought… Didn't you decide to stay in Boston?"

"I went back thinking that's what I had to do, but I was miserable." They continued walking, his fingers laced with hers. "I realized that if I stayed it would be putting my dreams away and never leaving the shadow that Uncle had cast. A change in circumstances shouldn't have to change my dream."

"The Butterfly Cove Inn is now an Emerson?"

"Not… exactly. The inn is now privately owned and operated by Lily Hayes."

I'll take care of this for you, just hold your peace.

Trying God!

"When I got back into the office, I was a wreck. Everyone could see it. After a couple of weeks, Olivia and Alistair came to see me. They had drawn up a business plan that was… amazing." As an aside, she added, "I never knew Olivia was serious about wanting to be a part of EHI. I'd never seen her as anything other than my baby sister. Turns out she's a talented business-woman."

"She has a good role model."

Lily blushed at the compliment but surged ahead. Now that she'd started she couldn't seem to stop. "In short, their idea was that we three would retain our portions of EHI, but that Olivia and Alistair would run the business from Boston while I pursued my dream of owning my own inn."

"Sounds like a fantastic business plan."

She grinned and then fell silent as she tried to formulate the next part.

"What is it?"

"Olivia's letter. The one from Herbert? It... it said that Liv is his daughter. He and my mother..." She trailed off. It was still hard to say aloud. "Anyway, that's why he left her his entire estate. She was shocked, but she took it in stride. I mean I would have freaked out, but I think because Liv was never close to either our mother or my father, it was easier on her. And now she has Alistair. They work well together, it's quite extraordinary. I think Liv is the daughter Alistair never had. He dotes on her and is so proud. They made it easy to just walk away."

"That's a lot to deal with. I'm glad she had you."

Lily smiled and drank in the sight of him. She'd been picturing seeing him again since the moment she knew she would return. It had been an exercise in patience she'd come quite close to failing. It felt wonderful to be walking with him, hand in hand, on the beach. Maybe even better than she had imagined.

"I contacted Ava's son and made an offer on the inn. He couldn't sell it right then because of legal matters with Ava—You know they put her in a nursing home instead of pressing charges?"

"I did hear. Are you OK with that?"

"Oh, my, yes! Did you hear why they didn't press charges?"

"I guess not."

"You know that nutmeg tea she drank by the bucket load for years? It turns out she was suffering from nutmeg toxicity, the poor thing."

"Nutmeg? For real?"

"Crazy, huh? I guess it's fine in normal amounts, but she'd been drinking it in her tea day in and day out for years. There are a bunch of symptoms, including confusion and delusions. She honestly believed that the only way for Walter to be cared for was if she got rid of anyone trying to buy the inn."

Before she could continue he kissed her again. A quick kiss that left her a little breathless and giddy. She giggled and tried to regain her train of thought.

"Oh, and Stella! She and Alistair got married last weekend. Liv, Alistair, and I decided to give her back the Boston property that Uncle had... taken. She's going to split her time between the one in Summer Harbor and the one in Boston. It felt good to right that wrong."

He was still holding her, gazing at her beautiful upturned face. "I'm proud of you, Lily."

I will teach you what you ought to say.

"Noah, about how we left things before—"

He pressed a finger to her lips to silence her. "My turn."

She nodded, her eyes speaking volumes instead of her lips. Hope, fear, desire, doubt, and faith warred in their silver depths. He had to look away just to get out what he needed to say without stopping every few seconds to brush his lips across hers. He turned her away from the shore and they wandered up tree-lined streets toward the shop.

"First, thank you for the Bible. I know it was not easy to part with. I have cherished it, and read it... a lot. That first day I read the entire gospel of John, at Parker's suggestion. I've read through most of the New Testament, and God has used your notes to help me understand what I've read."

He pulled her hand up to his lips and kissed her fingers. "Of course there's a ton I don't understand at all. I am sure that Parker and Pastor James are getting tired of all the questions." He knew it wasn't true, but many times he felt like the little kid running behind his parents asking 'Why? Why? Why?' until they came apart at the seams. "The Sunday after you left, I went to church with Parker. Pastor James and I talked all afternoon. His wife is a saint, by the way. I'm sure it isn't easy being a pastor's wife. Toward the end of the day, he offered to baptize me. I didn't really understand it, but I knew I wanted to follow Jesus' example. We walked down to the shore and he baptized me right there in the ocean. I wish you could have been there." He glanced down and caught tears in her eyes. Happy tears that mirrored his own.

"I've been going to church whenever the doors are open. I can't wait to learn more. The men's Bible study that Parker goes to is great. I've known most of these guys my whole life, but never stopped to think about whether they were Christians or not. Now that I know, I can see it clearly in their lives! I don't know how I missed it before."

"Noah..." her voice was husky. "I'm so happy for you."

They had reached the shop and he pulled her into the back room again. He leaned back against the work table and pulled her to stand between his legs. He tucked a lock of hair behind her ear, his emotions written all over his face. "I know what I said a few months ago was the truth, but... Lily, I would like the chance to prove to you that this change," he said, thumping his heart. "It wasn't *for* you. It was *because* of you. Because of you being who you are and showing me what it meant to love God."

A tear escaped her lashes and slipped down her cheek. He brushed it away.

"I didn't think there was any way that I could ever be the man you need. Now I see that I can do anything and be anything that God desires me to be. I would like the chance to convince you that I can be the man who doesn't see a hotel heiress but sees you. The man who can understand business and responsibilities and still find time to love you. The man who can seek Christ by your side and lead you when and where He sees fit. I know I'll fail, probably over and over all the time, but I still want that chance... if you'll give it."

"Noah—"

A voice cleared at the doorway. Noah turned expecting Harley. He was surprised to see a gentleman in an expensive suit standing there instead. The man was familiar, but Noah had a hard time placing him. He wasn't a large man, but he carried himself with an air of authority. His bald head was fringed with gray hair and his eyes sparkled when he smiled.

"Can I help you?"

"I'm sorry to interrupt. Not sure if you remember me..."

The voice did it. "Norm?"

"Ah, you do remember." The man grinned.

"Of course." Lily stepped back as Noah stood and crossed the room to take the other man's outstretched hand. "What can I do for you?"

"I came to speak to you about this." Norm slid a manilla envelope from his briefcase and handed it to Noah. Norm's name and address, in a loopy script, was all that was written on the envelope. He opened the flap on the envelope and slid the contents out.

"I don't understand," Noah said as he stared, confused, at the papers in his hand.

"Well, I received those in the same envelope as the delightful pictures you sent of me and my daughter."

"Oh, sir. I'm sorry. I'm guessing I know how that happened." He made a mental note to have a gentle word with Gemma later about checking the contents of envelopes before she used them. "Please accept my apologies. This was not intended for you."

"I gathered that since the cover letter was addressed to a bank. But you misunderstood me. I came to talk to you because I am very interested."

"In this?" Noah asked, holding the papers up. "You're interested... in this?"

Norm laughed. "Yes, Mr. Kingsley. I'm an investment banker and I have been looking for a business to invest in personally. When I received your business plan by accident, I thought maybe God was telling me that this is the one."

Noah was speechless. He looked from Norm to the business plan to Lily and back again. Could this be happening? In the weeks since he'd missed his appointment at the bank, he had prayed for guidance and wisdom in running his business. With God's help, he had managed to move the books back into the black. But only just. Could God have sent Norm to help him fulfill his dream for Acadian Adventures? He rubbed his hand down his face in awe.

"The fact of the matter is, Mr. King—"

"Noah. Please, call me Noah."

"Noah, you were instrumental in turning our daughter back to us. There is no way I can ever thank you enough for that. But if I can help you expand your business, you'll have that many more opportunities to help other families. You're a good man, Noah Kingsley. And you did a good thing for us. Now, let me return the favor."

CHAPTER TWENTY

An hour later, Norm had left to check into his hotel, with a promise of bringing all the necessary paperwork by the next morning. Alone again, at last, Lily stepped into the circle of Noah's arms and wrapped hers around his waist. She grinned up at his bewildered face.

"I do believe you were in the middle of saying something important when Mr. Kessler graciously interrupted us."

"Was I?"

She rolled her eyes and kissed his chin. "Hmmm... love, was it?"

"Oh, right." His eyes glowed as he studied her face. "I love you, Lily, and I would like the chance to show you that the only reason I *can* love you is because God loved me first and showed me what true love is."

She nodded, too emotional to speak.

He kissed her again, long and thorough, oblivious to the rest of the world. In that moment there was only them. She wrapped her arms around his neck in a tight embrace and returned his kiss.

"I love you, too," she whispered when he pulled back to look at her. "I fell in love with you the first time you let me cry on your shirt. Remember? That day we kayaked to the beach and sat on the sand where the sea lavender grows? And every day after that. But never so much as right here, right now."

THE END

DEAR READER

Thank you for reading my debut book. Noah and Lily have lived in the back of my mind for years and I am thrilled to finally tell you their story. I hope to tell other characters stories' as the years go by. Why is Harley in Summer Harbor? What was Edwin up to at the inn? What does Parker struggle with? How did Pastor James and Maggie find their way to town? Can Olivia handle a few weeks away from the hustle and bustle of Boston? Each person in this town has history, flaws, faith, and dreams. I want to tell them all and I hope you'll join me on the journey.

JENNY

ACKNOWLEDGEMENT

*And whatever you do, in word or deed, do everything in the name
of the Lord Jesus, giving thanks to God the Father through him.*

COLOSSIANS 3:17

I would like to begin by thanking God for His direction and wisdom as I wrote this book. I could not have done it without Him. As I began writing, I realized that I needed a constant reminder of my purpose. I wrote it on a blue index card: To glorify God, To edify others, and To bring myself pleasure. I am so thankful that He held me to that throughout the entire writing process.

I never would have written this book without the support of my husband, Ken. He managed to keep me sane, give me time and space (which wasn't easy with twelve people living in our house!), and encourage me to keep going when I wanted to quit. I love you, Sweetheart!

To my children, Caleb, Lincoln, Bethlehem, Ellissa, Lydia, Yosef, and Fiona, thank you for letting me write, for putting up with some long days and distracted moments, and for thinking it's pretty cool that mommy wrote a book. You guys are amazing and I love you more than words can say.

Jared, my "oldest", you have been along for this entire ride. I would not have been able to write much of this book without your input. You sparked the idea and helped every step along the way. I can't wait for a chance to walk along the streets of "Summer Harbor", wander across the sandbar and hike the trails of Bar Island again while I pick your brain about another book. Thank you! Love you!

A huge shout out to my first two readers, my Mommy and Papa. Having you read the book first was good for my ego and gave me the confidence to pass it on to others. I also appreciated your input in the story and your help in making certain sections work.

A great big thank you to Angela for pushing me to start this book, allowing me a quiet week on her front porch swing to outline the story, and encouraging me all along the way. Love you, Cuz!

Karen, Tiffany, Rose, and Brooke, thank you all so much for reading my manuscript and giving me feedback to make the book better. You are dear friends and I thank God for you!

Tim Cotton, thank you for clarifying police procedures for me. (Tim is a fellow Maine author and all-around great guy. If you would like to get a taste of his writing head on over to the Bangor Maine Police Department's Facebook page. If you want a full meal, grab a copy of his book The Detective in the Dooryard. You won't be disappointed.)

ABOUT THE AUTHOR

Jenny Worster

Jenny Worster was born and raised in rural Maine where she and her husband still live with their seven children. She was a teacher before becoming a stay-at-home mom. In addition to writing, Jenny runs a non-profit with her husband which works in Ethiopia. Where the Sea Lavender Grows is her debut novel.

A NOTE ABOUT VERSES

I believe the Holy Spirit speaks to Christians through the Still, Small Voice mentioned by Lily while she and Noah are rock climbing. I believe that whisper to 'step to the side', 'look again before crossing the street', 'go check on the toddler', 'hold on tighter', 'take another route', 'do the next thing', 'get ahead of her', and so on, is that Voice. More often, though, I believe that He speaks to us through scripture, bringing it to mind at the exact moment it is needed. Sometimes it is a verse we know well (Psalm 23, John 3:16, the Lord's Prayer), and sometimes it's a verse we didn't know we knew. With that in mind, I decided to have God speak to Lily, and later to Noah, through scripture. Lily knew the verses from years of studying her Bible, where Noah had only Parker and some Sunday School classes to rely on. Isn't it wonderful that God is not limited by our ability to remember things? Below are the verses I used. I hope they bless you today as you read through them.

Galatians 3:27
Isaiah 26:3
Psalm 37:4, Proverbs 16:3, 9
Psalm 61:2
I Kings 19:11-12
Joshua 1:9, Deuteronomy 31:6
Psalm 23:4
Proverbs 26:11
Philippians 4:13
Psalm 17:5
Proverbs 20:24
Isaiah 55:9
Romans 3:10

Matthew 7:21-23
Matthew 11:28
I John 1:9
II Corinthians 12:9
Romans 5:8
Ephesians 2:10
II Corinthians 5:17
Lamentations 3:22-23
II Timothy 1:7
Psalm 23:4
Isaiah 41:10
Psalm 40:3
Luke 15:10
Jeremiah 33:3
James 1:5
II Timothy 2:15, 3:16-17
Joshua 1:8
I Peter 3:15
Numbers 6:24-26
Exodus 14:14
Luke 12:12

www.ingramcontent.com/pod-product-compliance
Lightning Source LLC
Chambersburg PA
CBHW020300200626
46814CB00006BA/2011